THE
WORLD ANVIL
ANTHOLOGY

THE

WORLD ANVIL

ANTHOLOGY

EDITED BY

B.K. BASS

KYANITE
Publishing

THE WORLD ANVIL ANTHOLOGY
Copyright © 2020 by Kyanite Publishing LLC

All individual works in this publication are Copyright © 2020 by the respective author. All rights belong to and are reserved by the respective author, as listed below:

"Iron Sharpens Iron" by M.K. Beutymhill; "Dead Meat" by Nicklas Erik Larsson; "Looking for Light" by Christopher Dravus; "The Furious Vexes" by Tepherial; "The Rains" by Alan G. Provance; "The Realm of Moments Passed" by Larnce Hicks; "Hunting Misfortune" by J.L. Allred; "Sanctum of Snow and Blood" by C.R. Christiansen; "Fulcrum" by Travakh; "Upwards, or The Great Fall" by Garrett S. Lewis

For permission requests, please contact the publisher, Kyanite Publishing LLC, via e-mail, with subject "Attention: Permissions Coordinator," at the e-mail address below:

info@kyanitepublishing.com

ISBN
Hardcover: 978-1-952152-51-1
Paperback: 978-1-952152-50-4
eBook: 978-1-952152-49-8

Cover design by T.J. Trewin
Interior design by B.K. Bass
Associate Editor: Sam Hendricks

www.kyanitepublishing.com

TABLE OF CONTENTS

FOREWORD

Welcome, Traveler of Worlds.

This book is filled with extraordinary tales and faraway places. You'll read about lost civilizations and magical, urban struggles. Time—and even history—will bend and flex around you as you consume these wondrous stories. But at the core of this anthology, at the very beginning, is another kind of story: A love story.

World Anvil was a love letter from husband to wife; an urgent wish to help her with something she desperately wanted, but struggled with. Janet was fighting with her first novel—more particularly, with the worldbuilding behind it. And so, Dimitris created a worldbuilding platform: A place to keep track of a fictional world in articles, interactive maps, family trees, timelines and more. And, World Anvil was born.

Since then, World Anvil has grown immensely. We—Dimitris and Janet—thought we'd maybe find a hundred crazy people who shared our passion for stories and fictional worlds. By our first month, we'd hit ten thousand. Now, three years later, we have over a million worldbuilders and creatives in the community. The platform now includes a full novel writing software and publishing tool, a Campaign Manager for tabletop RPGs, and people are literally building their creative careers with World Anvil.

And yet, despite all that, World Anvil has remained a close, friendly community with a culture of support and kindness we never thought we'd find online. And so, World Anvil has become a new kind of love story, too: The story of thousands of creative people supporting each other, lifting each other, and helping each other succeed. Whether you're writing worlds of sentient tanks or flying gnomes, cyberpunk vampires or far-future military scifi;

there's a place for you in the World Anvil Community. And that's the kind of love this world needs more of.

Now, read on and enjoy these wonderful stories! Then we hope you'll be inspired to grab your own hammer and go worldbuild!

All our love,

Janet and *Dimitris*
Founders of World Anvil

IRON SHARPENS IRON

by M.K. Beutymhill

PART ONE
In Which a Cookbook Causes an Upset

I could run. From where Caileth perched upon the mantel, the chubby, curly-haired halfling hadn't yet seen her. He toddled about the breakfast cart he'd wheeled in through a door that bolted from the outside of the enclave's locked tower. *Out the compound, beyond imperial borders, to the free nations in the south…*

An exhilarating wave trilled up her spine, and she scratched idly at goosebumps prickling the chattel tattoos webbing her arms. She sat up, hooked her fingers upon the narrow window ledge, and blinked against the early morning light. Bars partially obstructed her view of a shipyard teeming with preparations—the *Bravado's* ceremonial launching. Her resolve faltered. Too many people, more than usual. The magnificent airship gleamed at her from the docks, its masts stretching to the sky and the Baronet's imperial banners flickering as if to tsk *oh, no you don't*.

Caileth returned her attention indoors, to a common room so utilitarian that the sparse furnishing better identified their master than the gnomes residing there. Bophin spotted her upon the ledge, and he paused with a stack of wooden plates pressed against his apron. His gaze shifted from her, to the door, and back again.

"Come down, kid," he said, not unkindly, and nodded to the leather-bound journal in her lap. "Before they see what mischief you're up to."

As if on cue, the familiar steam whistle blew from outside, and the floorboards creaked overhead as her kin stirred from their beds. Bophin was right, of course—the enclave would be remiss to see Caileth hunched over her private collection of schematics and alchemical recipes, especially without Grandmaster around to quell their backbiting. It was best to keep the thing scarce, at least until *someone* had forgiven her.

She dropped it to the floor, then climbed down the hearth with the ease of one accustomed to scaling airship rigs. The gnomish script upon its cover—COOKBOOK—was hardly legible under all the chemical blotches, but she pinned it under her knees until the overstuffed pages compressed enough to latch the brass clamps.

Caileth strapped it onto her work belt just as two dozen gnomes filed down the spiraling staircase amidst unintelligible conversations. All were dressed similar to her, sturdy work pants laced into steel-capped boots, and plain grey tank tops that exposed the blank-inked geometric bands of their chattel tattoos.

Their eyes lit up at the breakfast Bophin laid out in honor of the launching. Bread pudding steamed with aromas of wild mushrooms and sausage, and enough sweet butter—Caileth's favorite—to slather the toast from edge to edge. The gnomes

The *Bravado's* pressure quelled, albeit reluctantly, and Caileth turned as her escort coughed with impatience. She didn't bother explaining her delay, for the empathic connections of Cognizance were dismissed as insufferable egotism. It smacked too much of the haughty elves they shared fae blood with, though it was this very relation that made them natural-born tinkerers.

Caileth passed through the manor's chasmic halls in mechanical detachment, barely noticing the celebratory wall hangings or the excited chatter. She scaled steps and traversed corridors without a word from passerby. When she found herself standing at the entrance to Rivaz's quarters, her stomach churned.

She knocked.

Her long, pointed ears tilted up—was that a grunt from within? It was enough to merit entrance, yet the darkness inside gave her pause. The parlor curtains had been drawn, something Rivaz did when heavy drinking made the sunlight unbearable. She stood by the door until her eyes adjusted.

"Hello? Sir?"

No answer, just countless heads of prize kills—orc chieftains and rocs and ankheg pinchers as large as Caileth herself—snarling back at her from the walls. Hunting packs lay discarded on the floor, and various pistols and muskets were scattered unceremoniously on the table, just eye level from Caileth's vantage.

Rivaz was slumped in an armchair, asleep. He was portly, even for a dwarf, with a long unkempt beard of reddish brown that twitched as he snored.

Not wishing to be within kicking distance when he woke, Caileth retreated and drew the heavy drapes. Sunlight flooded into the room and, vitalized by the warmth, she climbed onto the window bench and switched the latch. The double casement windows swung open to a rush of fresh air and gaiety from the streets below. From here, the city of Artane sprawled before her, massive in reach yet somehow insignificant between the sea to the east and the snowcapped mountains to the west.

Caileth smiled. These rare glimpses outside the compound were a better treat than sweet butter, today especially as confetti rained in the plazas and a parade ambled down the main boulevard. Revelers danced to music with lightheartedness not often seen in her stone tower. In moments like these, the urge to flee gnawed strongest. And yet...she'd never dared to try. Not only was the enclave kept under near constant supervision, but the chattel tattoos were more effective trackers than any ranger. If she was caught...well, less lenient masters were the least of her worries.

She climbed down as Rivaz stirred. He looked miserable and smelled little better as he released a groan that hinted of the ale and strong cheese he was fond of. It made Caileth sick to her stomach.

"Good morning, sir."

"Morning." It wasn't as much a greeting as it was an affirmation, or rather, bitter acceptance. He rubbed at his face as if a hangover could be simply pushed away, but when his bloodshot eyes focused on Caileth, he sat up with more alertness. "I summoned you hours ago."

Her stomach twisted. "I came as soon as I was told—" She stepped back when he hoisted himself from the armchair. The hunter towered a foot taller than her, nearly as wide as he was tall. "I'm at your service, sir."

"Right." Rivaz's calloused hand clamped over the back of her neck and he dragged her towards the firearms. "Service that."

He shoved Caileth hard toward the table, and it was only by luck that she caught herself without cracking her teeth on the edge. She stared down the barrel of a heavily embellished pistol that she knew well: Baradian Model Type 2, single shot .54 caliber.

It was her design, or redesign, from the unreliable Type 1, laced with enhancements to improve its performance and accuracy. The construct had garnered the Baronet newfound favor with Imperial officials, which in turn secured him one contract after another. And not even the resentment of the enclave had eclipsed Caileth's pride when her chattel marks were updated to reflect her gunsmithing proficiency.

On sixty-five pistols, she'd meticulously etched scroll and feather motifs unique to each serial number. She remembered every single one of them, even this one—No.15—that had since been fouled beyond comprehension. Annoyance flickered in her fae blood as she sensed the pistol's sluggish ache like cramps within her own joints. She'd "fixed" other firearms for him before and the only problem was Rivaz's negligence.

"Guaranteed not to misfire, guaranteed shot," Rivaz mockingly recited from the familiar merchant pitch. He leaned close enough that his hot, sour breath curled the loose whips of hair at her neck. *"Under any conditions."*

Caileth's nose pinched involuntarily, and she picked at a spot of rust.

"That's in reference to poor weather conditions, not lazy maintenance habits."

Rivaz was quiet. Too quiet. Just as she turned to gauge his expression, his thick arm made a vicious swipe, knocking Caileth aside. He grabbed the No.15. Its curved handle swung down on her, and though she raised her arms in defense, the pistol cracked against her cheekbone and ignited fireworks below her eye. Her legs faltered, and she scrambled under the table.

"Insolent, cocky bitch!" He caught her ankle and dragged her out shrieking. "I'd see the whole lot of you grease brats hunted down with your own pistols, were it up to me!"

As he lifted her, Caileth wished—not for the first time—for the punishment to stop and for the Lord-Son to simply go back to sleep upon his chair. Fae magic stirred in her veins as her arms flailed.

It occurred to her that her breathless whimpers were the only audible sound, and she dared to peek around her raised elbows. Though Rivaz's arm was wound back for another blow, he was oddly still. His mouth hung open and he stood there, unseeing, before his eyelids fluttered and he fell ankles over ass.

Caileth braced herself, but landed ungracefully with a tumble over fleshy dwarf bits. She was sore from head to toe and blood salted the inside of her mouth, but when she realized what she'd done, she forgot her ailments long enough to skitter away from the unconscious dwarf.

She'd be sent to the Deep Dungeons, surely. No Cookbook, no scenic views from the manor, no more travelers' tales in the shipyard, or dreams of freedom in the southern lands.

Her stomach turned over violently, and she dashed behind a potted plant to retch.

Cheers and music drew her attention towards the open window. The city—freedom—was just there, beyond the walls of the manor. But where would she even go? The southern nations were rumored to be free, but she'd never set foot outside the Baradian compound. What if there weren't any free nations? What if she couldn't compete with their artificers' standards?

Caileth paced. Maybe she could return to the shipyard like nothing happened. After all, Rivaz wasn't supposed to have summoned her, let alone struck her. He might keep his mouth shut. But, no, she'd retaliated with magic, the very thing that made the empire wary of mutinous enclaves. Chattel marks or not, if she was already bound for the Deep Dungeons, she had nothing to lose by running for it.

She hiccupped, but swallowed back her nerves and swiped the No.15 from where it lay just aside of Rivaz's hand. She kicked his arm for good measure, collected the pistol's accoutrements, and shoved everything into her work belt.

An out-stuck tongue was her only farewell as she slipped the unobservant escort in the hall. Her deliberate stride down the staircase caught no notice from the staff, but she hesitated when she reached the front entrance of the manor. The thick, engraved doors were manned by a pair of dwarves requesting credentials from those passing through. No getting through them without a spectacle.

Opposite them was the Great Hall. Servants were in and out—a mixture of humans, dwarves, and halflings—and she followed a pair of the latter in. An exceptionally long dining table crossed the length of the hall, which Caileth ducked under to obscure herself further from view via the wide-backed chairs flanking either side.

At the opposite end, she caught sight of a passageway through which servants in aprons carried smaller parcels. The kitchens! Perhaps the delivery entrance down there wouldn't be as heavily guarded. When the coast was clear, she continued at a brisk pace.

The corridor was narrower than those throughout the manor, with low ceilings and plain stone mortar that reminded her of the enclave's tower in their simplicity. The familiarity was comforting, short-lived though it was. After rounding two corners—or was it three?—Caileth lost her orientation. The shouts of servants calling one another kept her anxious, afraid that at any instant someone would notice how displaced she was.

The corridor finally opened to the humid kitchen air, and a long room bustling with activity. A dozen sweaty halflings worked over sizzling iron plates, unaffected by the sudden bursts of flames and excess smoke disappearing into chimney chutes overhead. Ovens stacked with trays lined the length of the far wall, and farther down a team of prep cooks chopped ingredients with astonishing precision. Traversing the room in a constant sprint were a handful of runners delivering fresh ingredients and removing used pots, the latter of which were abandoned upon a sill leading to the scullery.

Caileth dodged one of the oncoming runners and dipped behind a stack of crates, eyes scanning for a way out. She moved quickly, crossing the throughway past the first pair of ovens. As she sneaked under the counter ledge to avoid a baker, her fingers brushed a discarded, nearly empty potato sack, and it occurred to her to grab provisions. She helped herself to the lower shelves of a nearby cart, swiping rolls, apples, and meat pies wrapped in napkins.

She paused as she felt eyes upon her—truly upon her, not the grazing awareness of a preoccupied servant—and realized she was being watched by one of the bakers near the ovens. Holding her breath, she raised her eyes.

It was Bophin. He stared quizzically from her to the bag, then put a chubby finger to his lips. He appeared to return to his task at first, but once he'd sliced a thick sandwich in half, he cleaned off his knife, turned to her, and slipped the blade into her bag. He motioned for Caileth to follow.

She did, creeping behind as he maneuvered towards a side door she hadn't noticed. At his urgent wave, she kept close to the wall as the door swung inward. Bophin was instantly bathed in sunlight as noise from the street flittered in.

"Allo there!" came a thunderous voice just beyond the threshold. Caileth hiccupped from behind the door. Another guard. "What'ch'you got there?"

"I blundered this one," Bophin said, extending the sandwich. "I was at the end of my dressing mixture, so it hasn't got the proper blend of spices. I can't send it out with the others, but it would be a shame to waste."

The guard stepped inside, his back partially to Caileth. She tucked deeper into the shadows. "All right, if you insist. Was feeling a bit peckish anyway!"

"Should be a grand show," said a stocky man accompanying her. "But security's gonna be tight."

The Laurels exchanged apprehensive glances, and Leora said, "Wait, what? How tight?"

The *Stalwart* gave a jolt then, and she snatched a leather strap bound to the railing. Even with the support, she fell off balance as pressure from the airship's bowels released. Another nasty tremor rattled them, and blasts of hot air spewed from the hull. The landing bay sped closer and closer, a little too quickly for comfort, and Leora looked away, sweat beading her brow. Reja tossed her hands to the sky and whooped. Astælle picked at her nails.

The impact upon the waves knocked more than one passenger off their feet, Leora among them. Once she was upright and the shrieks subsided, she realized the heavy vibration under her feet was the fuel drivers steadily putt-putting the Stalwart to port. Onlookers gaped from the docks, just as shocked the ship remained intact.

"You good to get through?" Reja asked in a low voice, reminding her of the impending customs situation.

"Take my weapons," she replied, unloading knives, brass knuckles, and her thieves' tools in a discreet fashion. "The dwarves like you here, just play along. Astælle?" She gestured with her hand, a simple thieves' cant instruction, and Astælle surrendered what contraband she carried to the sheaths behind iron boning in Leora's bodice. The Laurels had employed their ruse countless times before, relying on her stealth and her iron lined garments to mask magical properties from detection.

Two sets of Artane's guards barred either side of a makeshift checkpoint on the docks, where passengers deposited their bags onto a mechanical inspection tray. It was so crowded that everyone was a mere shove away from cannonballing into the water, and the guards hustled to move them through.

"Where's the best place for a drink around here?" Reja asked them, unfastening her armor as they stared right through Leora to marvel at the statuesque barbarian. It thunked unto the inspection tray, followed thereafter by a large hunting knife and hand axe.

"The Rust Bucket! Best tavern in town."

The muscles of Reja's bare arms flexed as she reached for her belt, and the guards' toothy grins faltered as she tossed blade after blade into the tray.

One looked up from the menacing pile and said, "You a mercenary?"

"I dabble."

Leora waited for the other two guards to hone in on Astælle's fae features. Sure enough, they detained her for a barrage of questions and inspection reserved specifically for elves, who were forever deemed untrustworthy, magic-wielding rascals. Leora grabbed her bag and slipped through the gate just as Reja began to reassemble her gear.

"Whew, this sun's making me thirsty! The Busty Fuckit, you said?"

No one stopped Leora, and she moved through Artane's wide mason streets, trusting her companions would catch up. She jumped across the path of oncoming cable cars to break line of sight. They'd been prone to mechanical problems and delays the last she'd been here, and by the sour-faces upon the crowded platform, Leora suspected the issues persisted.

She waited at a fountain in a minor plaza, their prearranged spot where Leora could keep an eye on the clocktower. Reja was quick to rejoin her, but as usual they dawdled until Astælle finally appeared.

"There's a presentation before the launching," the elf told them. "If we hurry, we can catch it. And the parade."

"Sure," said Leora. "Let's make the drop, and we'll come back."

dancing mascot passed, two figures caught Leora's eye—one from ahead and one aside. She caught the hand gesture just in time—another gang, she realized, and she was their mark.

She swore under her breath, reconsidering the alley. Her companions were still too far back; if she waited for their protection, Dodgy would point Leora out to the guards. She'd have to run for it. Bracing herself, Leora caught Reja's eye with urgency, then sprinted down the alley with every ounce of gusto she had.

A plank swung out and clotheslined her across the midsection. Sharp pain stung her ribs. Her breath left her, and she crumpled.

The plank clattered against the cobblestone, and scuffed boots stepped into her teary vision. Someone reached down and wrenched away the Bag of Holding.

"Thanks kindly," the thug said, as his two partners caught up. He tossed the bag towards them. "Reckon we need this more'n you anyway."

But the live, squirming contents caught the thugs unaware, and they tossed the bag back and forth before dropping it altogether. It inchwormed away as they stumbled over themselves to snatch it, and Leora rolled onto her side with a cough. She could grab it and —

Nope. A hard shove put her back on her ass, and as the leader wound up for a vicious kick, Leora braced herself. In flew Reja, bum rushing him with her shield, and she slammed him against the wall with enough force that he slid into a trash pile for a nap.

The two remaining thugs blinked at Reja, turned, and bolted with the Bag of Holding. Ignoring the sting in her ribs, Leora sprang upright.

"Forget the chump change!" she hissed, as Reja bent to the unconscious thug. "We need that potato sack!"

Leora dashed after the thugs, but the stairs to the Underbelly were just ahead. She had to slow them somehow, or she'd lose line-of-sight. Leora unsheathed her knife and hurled it at the one carrying the bag.

It stuck in his butt cheek, and he faltered with an angry cry. As Leora leapt to tackle him, he tossed the wriggling bag to his partner. Leora swore as she went down in a tangle with him, and recovered her knife with a vindictive twist. She was back on her feet in an instant, trusting Reja to handle him while she pursued the final thug.

He'd caught the bag at the bottom of the Underbelly steps, and for a split second, Leora locked eyes with him. Surefire confidence glared back from that scrawny, hollow-faced punk. With the ghetto's gnarled paths and shady alcoves, he'd break line-of-sight quick. He sprinted towards an underpass.

Leora's jaw tightened. It was now, or bust. Steeling herself, she took a running jump off the arcade. She broke her fall atop him, and a muffled shriek emitted from the bag as they tumbled. It was an instant wrestling match as they jockeyed for control. As they rolled into crates and kicked over flowerpots from a nearby stoop, Leora spider-crawled onto his back, hooked her arm under his chin, and waited for him to pass out. Her eyes were locked on the Bag of Holding lying just out of reach, her incentive to maintain her grip however her muscles ached against his flexing neck.

When he finally went slack, Leora pried her cramped arms from his neck and craned her neck upwards to the applause overhead. Reja sat with her fur-lined boots hanging over the edge of the arcade, her knees visible through the skins skirting her waist. Leora would have flashed her a rude hand gesture if the appropriate fingers weren't jammed.

"You just sat there and watched? You twat!"

Reja's grin settled into something cheekier as she leaned her hands against her knees. "I distracted the Imperial guards for you. They went that way, if you're wondering. Bunch of flirts, really."

"That's Astælle's job. Where'd she go?"

She scratched at her neck and shrugged. "Well ...the parade came through, and you know how she is." Reja hoisted her long legs up and disappeared from view.

The smell of cheap cigarette smoke permeated the air, and a dowdy wet-nurse with a sour expression tsk'd from a nearby stoop. Dried soil and cracked leaves from the broken flowerpots was strewn everywhere, and she shook her head at Leora.

"Filthy drunks."

Leora winced as she dragged herself to her feet, but she managed a half-hearted, "Sorry about the flowers," as she limped towards the Bag of Holding. It lay motionless, but as she picked it up and felt stirring within, Leora suspected the gnome was just a mite stunned.

"There's Astælle," Reja said, nodding towards the mouth of the alley as Leora rejoined her.

The absurd dwarven mascot waddled towards them, its padded head pushed back to reveal Astælle from the shoulders up. The suit was exactly the type of odor-consuming germ factory that she deplored, but she seemed content enough as she nursed a sizable cream cone wrapped in pretty pink paper.

"What did you find, my lady-Laurel?" the elf asked as they reconvened.

Leora was about to suggest they go elsewhere as a handful of guards sprinted past the alleyway entrance, but a few acute kicks from the bag to her midsection silenced her. She fumbled at the knotted ties.

Reja considered the bag. "Oh, it's a live one?"

"Knock it off!" Leora snapped into the darkness. A glimpse of auburn hair shifted inside, along with tarnished metallic. "You're making this wor—"

BANG!

The Laurels jumped back, shrieking, and Leora barely noticed the gunpowder in her lungs for the sheer terror of having stared down the barrel of a pistol. A chunk of stone fell out from the wall behind her—a block of mortar intended to be her face, now shattered at their feet.

No time to panic though. The gunshot drew attention from guards and loiters, and the Laurels quickly made themselves scarce.

"What kind of creature's in there?" Reja hissed. "It's upset. Maybe it needs some air."

"Upset?" Leora echoed, louder than intended. She forced her next words into a hush. "She shot at me!"

"I know, my lady-Laurel," said Astælle. "But some people don't handle deprivation well."

Reja beckoned for the bag. "It's gonna blow our cover. Just let it out."

"No!" Leora swatted them away, and bear-hugged the bag though it reeked of gunpowder. "You didn't see how fast she was. Let's just return t—*oh gods, she's murderous!*"

She sucked in her stomach just in time as a kitchen knife sliced through the bag in a sawing motion. Thick smoke drifted out and the gnome coughed for air. Mortified, Leora extended the bag as far as she could manage, her eyes fixed upon the shine of the blade.

"Someone get that!" she wheezed through tight lips.

Reja was intercepted as Astælle reached forward, emboldened with the mascot suit's protection. With one hand holding her cream cone at a safe distance, she swiped the weapon, but the weight of her glare rivaled the gnome's.

"What did you say was in the bag, my lady-Laurel?"

"I didn't," snapped Leora. She tried to blow the loose hair from her eyes, but it stuck to her damp brow. "Can we get somewhere secure first? And take that damn costume off!"

Astælle didn't remove the suit, and the Laurels retreated to the Broken Pidgeon Foot in tense silence. The elf lagged and slurped her cream cone, amplifying Leora's anxiety, but eventually the paper crinkled as she balled it up for trash. Something bounced off the back of Leora's head, and though she clenched her teeth, she said nothing.

Back at the seedy tavern, the Laurels obtained an hourly room from the barkeep, and finally secure behind a private door, Leora dropped the bag.

Out tumbled the gnome, kicking along assorted items as she sprawled on the floor. She was worse for the wear with a blackening eye and split lower lip, and though she had no conceivable time to recover her bearings, she fixated upon Leora and chucked a potato straight at her eye.

"*Gaahh!!*" Leora slapped her hand to her face as the offending potato thumped to the floor. "Asshole! Goddammit!"

The gnome sprinted for the door, but couldn't reach the top bolt even with a running jump. She darted to the window instead, scrambling onto the sill, yet no matter how she pushed, the frame remained firmly stuck. Whimpering, she dropped and vanished into the storage cabinets along the wall, where a clatter of various housekeeping items broadcasted her shoving through. Sure enough, she emerged on the other end and dove behind the stovepipe. Then it was quiet, save for some determined mewling and the faint squeaking of screws cranking against metal.

The Laurels, idle during this whole escapade, exchanged uncertain looks, mostly directed at Leora. Astælle folded her arms and tapped a fingernail against her elbow.

"I'm certain there's a good reason you captured a fae-kind, my lady-Laurel?"

"She was already captured," Leora said. "We just saved her."

"How considerate. Why didn't we release her outside?"

"For what, so she can get herself caught again? She's obviously lost. If we return her to her masters, they're bound to pay us something handsome, considering their loss otherwise."

Astælle's eyes flashed, and she pointed a seething finger at Leora as if to curse her. "The only thing that'll pay you is a nasty return from the winds of destiny," she said, finally tearing the mascot suit from her shoulders and shimmying out from the padded limbs. "You've got some brass lady-balls, thinking I'd help enslave another fae-kind to those foul dirt-dwelling dwarves!"

"You're certain she's a slave?" Reja asked. The shieldmaiden wasn't well versed with the fae's fate under dwarven empire and certainly wouldn't have understood the significance of the tattoos sleeving the gnome's skinny arms. As Astælle gave a livid account of their misfortunes, Leora turned her attention toward the stovepipe.

Creeping closer, she discovered the gnome hastily releasing a vent she was probably lithe enough to escape through if she got it open. Leora tried to catch her by the collar, but the gnome startled, and abandoned her task to flee under the bed. She scuttled on her belly into the farthest shadows, whimpering.

"Ohh," said Reja, barring Leora with her arm. "She's scared."

"No reason!" Leora called, giving her best effort at an encouraging tone. "I know we got off on some bad footing, but I promise we'll get you home safe."

"So help me, my lady-Laurel, I will curse your ass if you go through with it."

"Cut me some slack—I didn't write the Imperial laws!"

"Forgive our friend." Reja half-bent, peering under the bed. "Do you want to go home?"

"No," came the reply, and the gnome shuffled amid the distinct jingle of coin. "I'll pay you, if you won't turn me in."

Out flew several coin purses, tossed one after the other, different sizes and cuts of cloth that Leora suspected Dodgy pilfered from the streets. Crouching, she emptied them onto the floor, and the Laurels considered the offering with varying degrees of pity. A gold piece or two here, some silver, a pile of coppers… the amount pathetic when weighed against her chattel value.

Astælle was the first to move, pocketing the choice coins with a pleased glimmer in her pale eyes. "Well that looks like just the right amount to buy some cream cones for everyone."

And before anyone else spoke, the elf was out the door.

PART FOUR

In Which Gnomes Are, Indeed, Assholes

Leora peered under the bed skirting. Still prone on her belly, the gnome scooted even farther back on her elbows.

"Leave her alone," said Reja. "She won't cooperate without assurance you won't return her—which you should give, since Astælle just took her money."

Leora pointed deliberately under the bed. "D'you know how much she's worth?"

"Sure, but my people only take thralls bested in battle."

"Well, in the empire, some shady fence will sell her like any other trinket, and who knows where she'll end up? Half the degenerates here don't even know what a gnome is anymore."

Reja gathered up the assorted items scattered across the floor, and set them upon the small table in the corner. "Is this worth losing favor with Astælle?"

"She's not considering the whole situation—"

"Maybe you're not either."

31

Leora couldn't deny that pissing off Astælle came with its own problems. At best, the Laurels lost their connection to valuable contraband from the Fae Wildes. At worst, well...she was fae through and through, and if she left with a grudge, she'd follow Leora like a bad haunting.

Heaviness pressed upon Leora's shoulders. She didn't need another powerful enemy. One vengeful husband was more than enough, and allies weren't found overnight. Survival forged powerful bonds, and the Laurels were strongest together despite their differences. Iron sharpens iron, as her mentor used to say.

"All right," Leora sighed, directing the statement under the bed. "You got a name, Trinket?"

No reply, save for a hiccup.

Leora dropped the bedskirt and got to her feet. Leaning back in her seat with ankles crossed, Reja gnawed on licorice root and shuffled cards for a round of Salt-Lick-Sallie. But Leora was more interested in Trinket's stash.

There wasn't much to identify her by. Aside from the Bag of Holding, there was just a burlap sack with some food, a horn of gunpowder, the pistol and bag of shot, knitted arm warmers, and an overstuffed, leather-bound journal that looked like it had weathered a rough life. Though labeled 'COOKBOOK,' the alchemic stains and tread marks disfiguring the leather didn't suggest culinary.

Trinket's chattel tattoos would reveal her masters. But...wait a tick. Leora frowned at the items on the table. Something was missing. She whirled just as the arm warmers slithered under the bed, and by the time she crouched to look, Trinket had pulled the sleeves over her elbows. Leora frowned. Sure, the gnome was swift, but couldn't have emerged from hiding without either Laurel noticing...could she?

"How'd you pull that off?"

around, the upper half of the body lolling from the rest. Joey groaned and rolled away from it, struggling to get his balance. The dog crept after him on its three remaining limbs, the fourth mangled.

"Fuck! Andrew! Help!"

"Quiet! You're gonna give us away!" Andrew hissed. He grabbed the fence and started to climb, but a movement out of the corner of his eyes made him pause. Several shapes started to emerge from hatches along the fortress-morgue.

Joey kicked the dog again. The head was pitifully twisted to the side and the jaws worked as best they could to grab him. A final kick and the head snapped with a loud crack, then again and again until the head came loose and rolled away on the muddy ground.

"Hah! Take that. You were right, Andrew. This is going to be easy!" Joey gave the corpse another kick before he climbed to his feet.

"Joey, get the fuck back up the fence!" Andrew watched as the other dogs crawled out and silently advanced. Joey blinked and whirled around. There were only a few meters between him and the dogs. Andrew dropped back down and kicked and slapped the fence, but the dogs kept their eyes on Joey.

Joey stood transfixed as they crept closer without sound. When he turned around and scrambled to scale the fence, they were too close. One dog latched onto his left ankle. Another started to chew on his right leg.

"Come on, climb!" Andrew looked around. There were no guards or workers on the other side of the fence, no one there to control the stiffs.

Another dog crawled close enough to close its jaw around Joey's leg. It almost came loose from the stiff's skull when Joey started to thrash and scream. He clung to the fence and flailed his legs at the gathering stiffs, but more bit into him. One hand slipped, then the other, and Joey crashed to the ground.

The dogs swarmed over him and Joey screamed. Andrew stepped away from the fence, heart racing in his chest.

"Andrew! Help!"

Another scream jolted him and he kicked the fence again, but the dogs ignored him. There was no way he was going over the fence. The stiffs bit hard and held on, the flesh tearing loose from Joey's arms and legs as he struggled to get free. When Joey kicked them away, they clawed and nipped until they could find their grip again.

Andrew jammed a finger through the links and into the eye of the closest dog. It popped like a cyst, spilling out over his finger. The dog kept its grip on Joey's shoulder. Andrew hooked his fingers inside its skull until he found a grip, then pulled. The teeth sheared through clothes and meat as the dog followed his grip. Andrew grabbed the fence for leverage and strained until the head of the stiff pressed into the fence, metal cutting into the rotting flesh.

Sharp teeth closed around the fingers of his other hand and pressed hard. Andrew yelped and turned to see another of the stiffs closing its maw around them. It felt like his bones would crack, pressed together like a vice in the zombie's mouth.

He battered it with his other hand, the stiff he had just let go of lunging for Joey's throat, his screams for help becoming choked.

"Get... the fuck... off me!" Andrew beat at the fence and tried to pull, then stumbled back and fell. The two fingers remained in the dog's mouth and it stared at him through the fence. Andrew felt his entire body go numb and the world became quiet. He looked down at his hand, where blood spurted from the severed ends of his middle fingers. They had been cut through at the second and first joint. The moment passed and a burning pain spread from his hand down his arm. He howled and clutched his hand close to his body, blood smearing over his jacket. Andrew looked once at Joey. He had kicked the dogs away from his face and was screaming again.

Andrew forced his legs to obey, crawling up to his feet before turning back around and running as fast as they would carry him away from the morgue. Joey's screams chased him, weakening as he put more and more distance between them. Andrew didn't stop running until he barreled through the door to his apartment and crashed down onto the floor. Bottles spilled out in all directions and liquor mixed with his blood, dripping out between his fingers. He held the stumps as tightly as he could, but they wouldn't stop bleeding.

He dragged across the floor and past the stiff in his apartment still laying where Andrew had left him. The small bedroom was damp and suffocating, with bottles of liquor stacked up near the window gathering dust and mold. Andrew pulled over the drawer near the door and clothes spilled out onto the floor. He found a shirt that didn't look so dirty and wound it tightly around the maimed hand. It soon became heavy and red. He saw how his father was looking at him.

Andrew grabbed a bottle of liquor from the windowsill, the rest crashing down around him. He emptied it over his wrapped hand and winced as it stung; it was a throbbing pain now. He brought the bottle to his lips and drank until there was nothing left in it, then hurled the empty bottle at his father. It bounced off his skull, whipping the head back before it fell down to watch Andrew again.

"This is all your fault!" he screamed. He found another bottle, its contents gushing out onto the floor, and grabbed it.

"No, you fucking listen to me!" Andrew stumbled back to his feet. Pain shot through his hand when he placed it on the bed for support, staining the sheets with red. "If you hadn't been such an asshole, none of this would've happened!"

He found his footing and sat on the bed, drinking again from the bottle. It was soon empty, before he was done. He threw it and missed, the glass shattering against the floor, shards spreading across the grime.

"Don't you dare call me a disappointment." He jabbed an accusing finger towards the corpse, still on the ground. "I always tried to do whatever you wanted me to, and look where that got me!"

All the other bottles were empty or broken, puddles of liquor forming on the floor of the bedroom. Andrew stumbled out of the room, stepping on the back of the stiff. The shards of glass crunched under his shoes. He swept empty bottles out of the way and sent them crashing to the floor, searching for one that still had something in it. He found one and drained the last dregs of alcohol into his mouth. He closed his eyes and saw Joey in front of him, the last look he had seen before fleeing. He could hear the screams.

Andrew flung the bottle into the wall then hunted for another, crashing through the unsteady piles on his sink. He found one, drank it all, and then another.

"Get up... Get up!" He turned his attention to the corpse. The stiff obediently climbed to its feet. Even dead, how did he look so disapproving?

Andrew looked away, then gritted his teeth. He grabbed a bottle from the sink and pounced the stiff, smashing it over his head. He started beating the corpse, punching and kicking. The alcohol was beginning to dull the pain of his mangled hand and without thinking he slammed it into the corpse. Agony exploded down his arms and he stumbled back with a howl. The stiff had been pushed back but never raised its arm, never responded. It watched him with jagged pieces of glass stuck to its head, waiting.

Andrew's temper flared again. He heaved the kitchen chair over his head and swung it down on his father with as much force as he could muster. When the stiff fell, he started to kick it. His shoe cut into the side of the flesh and cut the stitches that kept it together. It spilled open and a foul-smelling mixture of decayed organs and embalming fluids erupted out over the floor and over his shoe. The stiff kept looking at him, its gaze never wavering until Andrew had stomped its head in. Andrew drew hard, ragged breaths and stumbled back. What remained of the stiff was little more than a disfigured heap of flesh. The spine twisted at a sharp angle, broken bones jutting out of the skin. The head had been caved in, its brains leaking out on the floor. It moved, struggling to sit up again. Even here, with all his anger, Andrew had failed in the eyes of his father. He kept kicking and striking the lump of flesh until it stopped moving.

Then he drank, until the floor rushed to meet him and all was black.

*   *   *

Andrew groaned and rolled over. His head was pounding, and his lips were parched. He was covered in blood, interrupted by a streak of vomit splashed down his body. The embalming fluid had spread to where he lay, sticking to his clothes and hair. There was an unrecognizable mass of meat at the end of the room with two legs sticking out of one end. It was all that was left of his father; the entire reason for his debt.

Everything hurt and it was only disgust that compelled Andrew to move. He rolled away from the pile of vomit and gore before pushing himself to his feet. Fresh pain sprung from his hand. The fingers were still gone, severed at the joints. The bone had been broken apart into sharp little splinters.

The only way I'm getting into the morgue is after Kerensky catches me, he thought. "Looks like you were wrong after all." Andrew laughed, without much joy. "You said I would never amount to anything, but it looks like I'm going to be a boxer!"

The laugh made him cough, his throat dry and hurting. Death couldn't be much worse than this. He walked into the bathroom and did his best to clean himself, scrubbing the dried vomit from his torso. There would be no point in trying to scale the fence again, even if he could get past the dogs. Someone would have found Joey—or what was left of him—and it was hard to imagine they wouldn't keep a better eye out. It was a small comfort, but at least that meant he'd be shot instead of eaten alive. He wondered if they would drag his body right into the morgue or if there was paperwork first.

He stared into the mirror. A beaten man looked back at him, bruised and bloodied. He'd make a cheap stiff for someone. But if he looked the part already...

Andrew finished washing himself off and changed. He hurried out of the apartment, leaving the door unlocked. There was little left for anyone to steal and no one could wreck it as thoroughly as he already had. If this didn't work, it didn't matter anyway.

Andrew waited this time. He watched the trucks drive into the maw of Lily's workshop. The drivers would exit; corpses would be loaded into the back of the truck. Others would dump unprocessed bodies down on the concrete and cart them into the factory by wheelbarrow. The trucks were orderly and the timing precise—probably Lily's doing, he wagered. She had never been very pleased when he was late.

He waited for the next truck to arrive and watched. The drivers got out of the truck and exited into the factory without so much as looking into their vehicle. It was a pick-up. Andrew sauntered over to the corpse cart. There were no barbed wires here and no dogs that guarded the truck, no rain to make him miserable. He hurried his step as he came closer to the truck, counting the minutes until he guessed they would come back out again with their cargo. The driver compartment was cramped, two seats with nothing behind them.

Andrew peered into the back, eyes adjusting to the gloom. The bodies were naked and bald, torsos sunken in. Some were a jumble of flesh, new limbs stitched and bolted onto old bodies. He hesitated, but he could hear the creaking wheelbarrow from the factory. Andrew took a deep breath, then vaulted into the truck and sunk in among the corpses. He shoved them aside and burrowed down, pulling another body over his as cover. Moments later, another corpse landed heavily on top of him. He could hear them laugh and talk, but they hadn't seen him. Andrew held his breath and waited.

"What's the matter, Lily?" a woman's voice asked. Another corpse was tossed into the back. "See someone you recognize?"

"I thought so," Lily's voice was muffled as more bodies were stacked into the truck and over him. The weight crushed down on him, cold clammy flesh pressing against his face. "But I'm not that lucky."

The loading stopped and the squeaking wheelbarrow slowly faded out. The truck started again, gasoline and rot mixing in the back, then it moved. So far, so… good.

All he had to do now was get out before they could get a good look at him. Andrew groaned and tried to shove the bodies piled over him to the sides, shifting the weight of dead flesh away from him. He couldn't see anything. The truck drove along the narrow streets, the sky blocked out by towering structures of bleak concrete and brick. He pinched his nose shut and breathed through his mouth in a futile attempt to block the smell from the corpses. It was thick and cloying, sickly sweet even through the heavy coating of preservatives and embalming. His stomach turned as he felt cadavers press against him. Fingers and faces shifted and moved against him with every bump in the road.

Andrew wasn't sure how long they drove for. The world turned black and the truck's engine echoed outside. They were close now. Every muscle in his body tensed when the engine stopped, and he strained to hear the workers move outside. The back of the truck opened.

This is my chance.

He waited, holding his breath. The press of bodies eased, and he could see the corpses get pulled out. He peered between the tangle of arms and legs until he couldn't see any movement, then pushed to get free.

He was stuck.

Andrew pushed again; his legs were jammed in between several bodies. He grabbed a hold of his legs and pulled. One leg came loose, and he placed the foot on the one of the bodies, then pushed. His feet started to sink into the corpse, and he thought it might go through. It gave, followed by the corpses piled over it. Several bodies tumbled out of the truck and onto the floor outside, with Andrew following them. His landing was cushioned by the mess of bodies that fell first. He rolled off the mound with a groan. He couldn't make out where the drivers had gone but he heard footsteps echo. He looked around for some escape but could make out very little against the harsh glare of the daylight that flooded in behind him. A trail of rot led to an open pit, with nothing but gloom beneath. Without looking, Andrew crawled to the edge. The stink from it made his eyes water and he could make out bodies. The steps were getting closer.

He plunged into the darkness, falling a few beats before hitting the surface. A carpet of bodies bobbed on a bed of liquid. It burned his skin and Andrew lifted his head away from the surface, paddling with his feet to stay afloat. The mass of bodies around him shifted and merged as one single thing. They formed an unbroken carpet of bodies, limbs and preservatives that disappeared into the gloom. He half-crawled and half-swam across the bloody pit. He crested a heap of bodies that had clumped together like an island and hung on.

Behind him, something fell through the pit he had just entered, then another. He waited and watched as several more were dumped in through the hole. Something was pulled over the opening and darkness enveloped him.

All he could hear was the sea of preservatives lap against rotting flesh, rippling out from his paddling legs. The stench made his head swim. His weight proved too much for the body he hung onto and it came loose from the rest. It tumbled and Andrew went with it, head plunging down beneath the surface. He'd opened his mouth to scream, the chemical water burning his throat on the way down. He closed his eyes tightly and pushed upwards with all his might. He sputtered and coughed, drifting down the darkness. It felt like hands reached for him from below, fingers snagging a hold as he passed them by.

Light pierced the gloom further down and a hook came to snag one of the bodies, pulling it back into the light. Andrew started to swim towards it, no longer caring whether or not he was caught. He reached up towards the ceiling and towards the light but couldn't reach the edge.

"Wait, help!" The hatch had started to close again. The words spilled out before he could stop them. The pit ahead of him opened wide again, and someone peered down.

"What in the hell? Here! Hold on!" The hook was lowered down again, and Andrew clung to it. It lifted him up from the pit until he could reach the edge. A strong hand grabbed a hold of his wrist and pulled him the rest of the way.

"What the hell were you doing in the tank? Are you okay?" someone spoke.

He could barely hear him. Andrew coughed and sputtered, his eyes and throat seared with boiling heat. He rolled around and crawled away from the pit. Machinery thrummed around him. It wasn't a large room, dominated by a stained and rusting conveyor belt that continued past the wall.

"You wait here, I'll get some help." The man who'd helped him was a large, brawny type with blonde hair. For a moment, Andrew almost thought he looked like Joey. But if he stopped here, what use would any of it be?

Andrew dragged himself to his feet and grasped a heavy wrench from the floor. If he got caught Kerensky would kill him, and Joey would have died for nothing. He clutched the wrench tight, knuckles turning white. His rescuer hadn't seen it, and was moving towards the door when Andrew sprang on him.

The wrench cracked into the back of his skull and sent the man sprawling forward into the ground. Andrew struck again and bone broke. He lost count of how many more times he struck before the bloody wrench fell to the floor. Andrew fell back, heart pounding in his chest and eyes wild. Adrenaline made him forget, but only for a moment.

He had just killed a man.

The realization made him numb. The room was humid, but he felt cold and a shudder ran down his spine. It was different from a stiff. Blood was pumping out from the shattered skull and pooling around the body. No grey ooze or embalming fluid, no stitches that could be reknit. No fuzzy mold, spilling out from some crack that the butchers missed. Nothing like the expression on the man's face, contorted in shock and pain.

Andrew's stomach twisted itself into a knot and strength drained from his limbs. He sat down against the floor and sobbed.

Tears mingled with the liquid from the tank and dripped down onto the floor beneath him. The machines rattled on behind him, drowning out his long, jagged cries.

It was him or me. If I don't get this body, Kerensky will kill me.

The thought rang hollow to him. He heaved, the contents of his stomach threatening to spill out again.

It's their fault that Joey died. Him, controlling those dogs. Those little monsters. They're all murderers. They killed him.

Andrew didn't look at the body and could not muster any real anger in his heart. When the last of the adrenaline ebbed from him, all he felt was cold and numb. It didn't feel real—he almost felt disconnected. As if he was puppeteering his limbs, forcing them to move.

Like a stiff, he thought to himself.

He should take the man's coveralls and use them to blend in, to get to the parts of the facility where they'd keep the rich. Andrew reached for the body but froze before he could touch it. No matter what he told himself, he couldn't reach any further.

Andrew crawled to his feet and grabbed the long, hooked pole that the man had used to fish corpses out of the tank. A few bodies hung from hooks, waiting to be sent further down the line. He snagged the man's foot and pulled, then pushed, until the dead man rolled down into the pit. He disappeared out of sight, consumed by the mass. The last thing Andrew saw of him was the dead eyes, staring up at him.

Andrew forced himself to move. He wanted out of the room and away from the pit. He opened the door and peered outside. Deep inside the morgue, he had little idea where he was or where he needed to go. It was a labyrinth of stone and iron. In a stroke of luck, there was no one in the corridor outside and a short distance down he came across a small room full of lockers. He snagged one of the coveralls hanging from a hook outside. The fabric was stiff as a board, thick with old sweat and dried blood.

But it didn't come off a dead man. Andrew flexed the overall until it softened and then got dressed. The legs dragged on the floor below his shoes and the arms extended past his arms, but it would have to do. He rolled up the sleeves and the legs to make them fit, then tried to figure out where he would go next. With no other plan, he headed down the hallway.

The space opened into a cavernous vault, the air reeking of death. There were flies everywhere. Conveyor belts passed down the hall and deeper into the facility, corpses stacked neatly on the band. Andrew put his hands over his ears to shut out the thundering machinery. Along the belt, workers inspected the dead and one grabbed a hold of a body to pull it off.

He continued down the hall, skirting along the wall to stay out of the way. This place was nothing like Lily's little butcher shop. Dozens of people labored over limbs, torsos, and heads, stitching the dead together and sending them down the line. Further down, he could see someone shaving the dead and putting the hair into a barrel. Andrew stepped aside and pressed into the wall as he was passed by a man with a wheelbarrow full of heads. He kept going, hurrying down until he reached the end of the chamber. He pushed through the door and into the corridor beyond, drawing in a deep breath. The air was not so humid here, not so crawling with rot-hungry flies.

In another stroke of luck, there were signs here. One pointed to "Mass Reanimation" and the other to "Necromancers". Andrew didn't think they'd dump a prized body like the one he had read about into one of those charnel pits. He didn't really know much about the Necromancers—

only that they reanimated the dead. No matter how mangled the body, pieces would find themselves sewn together and revived.

If the champion's body was anywhere, it'd probably be with them. Andrew only hoped that they weren't there right now.

He followed the signs down the maze of corridors, cutting past another hall. The corpse-factory was quiet here, the thrum of machines subdued behind heavy concrete. There were no grubs or mold on the floor or walls. He continued, quieting the voice in his head that screamed at him to get out.

The door at the end was open and after peering in through the crack, Andrew entered. The air was cool here, almost chilling him through the thick coveralls. Somewhere nearby, someone was whistling.

Andrew froze and pressed himself against the wall. Down the hall, one of the doors began to open and a man in a heavy coat walked out. He was whistling, walking in the other direction before disappearing behind the bend. He had left the door open and Andrew took the chance to slip inside.

Sterile white tiles and gleaming metal basked in a cold light on the other side of the door. Only a few corpses were in the room, each one placed on its own table with great care. They were old and withered, except for one. It was the corpse of a large man, perhaps the same age as him, with a heavy, athletic build. It was the champion's body he had been looking for. Andrew almost shouted, trembling as he ran over to the table.

Even in death, he was a fearsome specimen. Unlike the crude butcher cuts of the corpses outside, bloodless incisions splayed apart arms and legs, pinned aside with needles. Tubes went into the body and to buckets by the sides of the table. All blood had drained away, leaving it white as the tiles of the room.

Kerensky would pay a fortune for this. Andrew felt jubilation rise in his chest. He could still set things right. He could get things squared with the loan-shark and use the rest to make things up to Lily. To Joey. All he needed to do now was get out.

Andrew stared at the massive corpse. How in the hell was he going to get out?

Distant whistling started again, creeping closer. Andrew grabbed the tubes and yanked them from the body. He bent down, hoisted the dead man over his shoulder and heaved. His knees almost buckled under the weight. He groaned and staggered towards the door with his prize. It would only be a short time before the necromancers noticed that the body was missing. If he was still here by then, his chances of making it out again as anything other than a stiff looked grim. He hurried back out into the factory and sprinted down the corridor as fast as his burden allowed him. The corpse was heavy, and Andrew stumbled into the wall as he tried to turn. Unable to catch his balance, he crashed into the concrete floor, knocking the wind out of his lungs. He groaned and crawled away.

Lily said they liked a corpse they recognize. Andrew looked at the body. He remembered the headless corpse at her shop.

He shoved the head of the corpse in between some pipes near the floor, propping the body up against the wall. He took a deep breath, then stomped on the throat of the dead body. There was a crunch as his foot slammed the neck into the pipe and he stomped again. A few more times and he'd broken the bone, then kicked away the flesh and skin that tethered it. Andrew picked up the head and cradled it in his arms, then ran.

He only stopped after he'd put distance between himself and the body. He slowed to a jog, his lungs burning. His legs wobbled and almost gave. He needed to get out of here—and fast. The windows had looked very secure from the outside, but now they seemed like the only way out.

Andrew started to go along the wall from window to window. They were secured on a wooden frame, thick iron bars more suitable for a fortress. Andrew clutched the head to his chest as he kept searching. One of the windows had a frame where the wood had become wet and rotted, splitting in places.

He put down the head and jumped, grabbing the bars. They were high enough so that he dangled with his feet off the ground. With his remaining strength, he pulled himself up and put his feet on the wall. Step by step, he climbed further up until he was almost hunched over by the wall, then pushed with his legs. So close to the window, he could taste the cool air, free from industrial death. At first, nothing happened. He pushed again, straining until he thought his legs would give out. His foot was beginning to slip just as the wood gave and the bars came loose, the iron and Andrew both falling back down to the floor. He caught himself just enough for his head not to bounce off the concrete. The heavy iron bars clattered down just inches from him.

Andrew groaned and rolled over, right into the head. It rolled down to the far side of the wall, leaving a small, wet trail. Andrew crawled over to grab it and briefly considered tossing it through the window to keep his hands free for climbing but thought better of it. He opened his overall and jammed the head inside as best he could, half closing the zipper over it. It was now or never. Andrew rubbed his hands together and with a running start made for the narrow window. He jumped and grabbed the ledge, pulling himself out. It was a tight fit, the bulging clothes snagging in the wood. With one final push, he squeezed through.

Never had the grey and smog-choked city been such a welcomed sight. Below him, a river cut through the city landscape. Open pipes from the factory spewed garbage, blood, and mold into the waters. Even from here, it looked less like water now and more like a river of rot. A layer of grubby slime covered the surface, giving it a sickly grey color mixed with streaks of crimson. Andrew took a deep breath, clutching the head tightly under the coveralls, and jumped.

He plunged beneath the surface and the water tore him from his course. He tumbled, the rushing water pulling him down the stream. The water was thick with corpse-sludge and it clung to him. It was moving much faster than he had guessed from above and now he was spinning around under the water. Andrew couldn't see more than a few feet and without light he couldn't even tell which way was up. With one arm still holding the head under his coveralls tightly, he started to kick and swim. He struggled and fought, taking the breath from his lungs. They burned and it forced his mouth open, water rushing down his throat. Another riptide pulled him down and he felt himself rush down the stream faster.

Andrew broke the water as it spewed out past an edge and fell freely. The filthy waterfall roared down the slope and crashed into a stagnant pool below. It ripped at him with such force that the stolen uniform was beginning to come apart by the zipper. He sucked air in as best he could before he hit the water again and started to sink. Releasing the grip of his prize, Andrew swam towards the light with eyes closed. Pushing through the surface was like breaking a thick coat of slime and he gasped for air again. A few yards from him, the head of the champion bobbed gently on the water, torn from his grasp by the water. Then it started to sink.

Andrew dove back into the muck. It hadn't gone far, and his exit had made a hole in the grime for light to filter through into the water. He could see something drift downwards and kicked down, hands closing around something. He could feel a nose and ears, then pulled it towards him. The head clutched tightly to his chest, Andrew broke the surface again and lifted it. One of the ears had almost come off and cuts marred the preserved face, but it was the right one. Andrew gave a jubilant shout and turned to swim to the shore.

Something hit him, vomited out from the river above him. A mass of organs and entrails, wound together by rope, struck him like a hammer. Andrew sank again with the weight, then pushed away and came back up. By the time he had made it back to the garbage-strewn shore, the head was nowhere to be found, lost again beneath the water. He retched, clumps of coagulated rot and muddy water emptying out from his stomach.

*   *   *

In an all too familiar repeat of his childhood, Andrew waited for the old man to strike him. Kerensky was red and flustered, waving his arms as he spoke. The heavy hands on Andrew's shoulder kept him down on his knees in the middle of the broken glass and blood-soaked alcohol of his apartment. Outside, people had closed their doors and locked them.

Kerensky pointed an accusing finger at him and said something, but Andrew wasn't listening. His heart was beating in his chest; every ounce of power he had was spent. How had it come to this? He had been so close. The reason for his debt was a clump of meat, rotting against the wall. He felt no satisfaction from the way his father's reanimated corpse had come apart and watched the flies swarm over it.

I wonder what they did with Joey, Andrew thought. The image of the young man with his mop of blonde hair cut like a knife. He imagined the lad stretched out on one of Lily's tables, disassembled for spare parts. Or maybe drowning in the charnel pit under the morgue. He wondered if Lily would miss him. It didn't seem likely, and now he was a killer. A murderer. There was another lurching twist of his stomach and he almost threw up again, even with an empty stomach.

"Give me another chance." Andrew's voice was cracked and weak. He had pleaded until it gave out. "I tried. I was so close to getting you that stiff."

"A chance to do what, Andrew? Get more people killed? Get the entire city up in arms, looking for us?" Kerensky scowled at him. "For god's sake, why didn't you just do the job Lily gave you?"

Andrew opened his mouth, but his voice faltered. The last thought he had before the wire tightened around his throat from behind was of his father.

*   *   *

Lily had worked on corpses she recognized before. Accidents happened around the factory every day, sometimes with fatal results. Most had signed their bodies over to the factory on the event of their death and considered it a small price to pay for steady work, a vanishingly rare thing. But this was a first. Andrew had an ugly blue bruise around his neck and his bulging eyes were shot through with blood. She'd have to do something about the bruise. Cheap as life and death was, it wouldn't do to have the marks of a murder displayed on the stiff.

The movements were mechanical. Cut, open, and disembowel. It helped to put a cloth over his face so she didn't have to see it as she hollowed the corpse. Without a face, the body just became inert meat, like any other she had handled before this. She considered removing the head but knew that Kerensky would like to keep it — perhaps one of the few who would remember Andrew. Instead, she removed the bruised skin with a knife and flayed it from the throat. Once it was done, she stitched some treated cloth in its place. The stiff wouldn't mind either way.

Lily lifted the left arm and examined the hand. Two fingers were missing and would have to be replaced. The body had plenty of scrapes and bruises still fresh on the skin, but they were nothing she'd normally patch up. She'd been furious when she had returned and found that—once again—Andrew had broken his word. Again, he'd left her to pick up the pieces of whatever mess he had made, forcing her to explain why the help she had said they should hire had just vanished.

The last time she saw him was in the ring, the latest stiff to fight. Lily steadied her nerves with more drink than was good and watched the walking dead beat each other to a pulp. Andrew ended the night standing over the other stiff, smashing its face until it stopped moving.

Finally, a victor.

LOOKING FOR LIGHT

by Christopher Dravus

CHAPTER ONE

"It's the most beautiful thing under the sun, and the sun don't even know 'bout this."

Arnott Gard waves his lantern slowly, the light from its fire catching on walls of stone so smooth they look like black ice. Every square inch of the cavern is flecked with silver, gold, and blue from the minerals ground into the stone floor by long-vanished rivers.

His voice echoes differently from what he's heard for the last few hours now, too. It doesn't bounce off narrow tunnel walls and back into his ears, but instead fades into the dark at the edges of his lantern light. This chamber is bigger than any of the others so far— one so large that even Arnott's lantern can't spot the furthest edges.

Most of the others push past him, eager to stretch out and feel empty air after so many hours of craggy, claustrophobic tunnels. While everyone else hollers into the void with a sort of glee that's born from countless hours stuck beneath miles of earth, Kasper Penn saunters in last. Not a drop of yearning in him for anything except the tobacco he stuffs into his pipe and lights. "Real pretty poetry, Arnott. You keep blasting holes in the tunnels like you're doing, and one of us just might survive to put that shit on your headstone."

"Look." Arnott points to the strange device he dropped next to the chamber' entrance. The auger is cannon-shaped and covered in fragile hoses and glass tubes; it can barely be carried by one man, and only Arnott was built for that kind of weight. He might be a decade out of Ghal Pelor's city guard, but he's not soft yet. "That damn thing has one setting, and like everything else those Bird Folks build, it don't do subtle."

"Their junk has *two* settings. On and broken. Might be our saving grace that it's out of charges now." Carlo Bastel pulls himself away from his canteen just long enough to lampoon Arnott Gard's use of Tengu mining equipment for maybe the tenth time now.

"Oh, didn't know you weren't a fan. Should have said so before." Kasper's tone drips with exhausted sarcasm. "Anyway, what now?" he asks while checking the oil left in his lantern. He remembers Bastel talking about something real miners called The Dark.

The Dark has always been there, but it's on people's minds after what happened at a silver mine near High Point Township. News said three miners were lost, ran out of lantern oil, and that it took four days for rescuers to dig them out. When they did, only one of the team was still alive. He went mad in the dark. Beat his friends to death with the empty lantern and wore his fingers ragged on the stone trying to dig his way out. Kasper immediately fills his light's reserve back to full and pushes the grim thought to the back of his mind.

The smallest of their number scampers up to the top of a nearby boulder and takes out something that looks to the rest of them like a telescope. Kasper knows better, though. Flefneight has been leading digs for longer than any of them has been alive. Each of the little pockets, pouches, and bags he's carrying have been filled with gear made for exactly this environment. The old Gnome doesn't so much as flinch while the rest all take their break. His nostrils don't even curl when Bekkrad takes a pungent piss uncomfortably close by.

"Either we're going back by Welch and helping move rocks or...," Kasper gestures into the dark ahead and all around them.

Ianston Flefneight simply groans and slides off his perch. "Digging ourselves out works just fine. We can spend a few days at it, and by the time we see sunlight, some elf patrol will be waiting to welcome us with leg irons and a one-way trip to the dungeons in Melanthris. I only left those three idiots back there to dig because I didn't need any more of you naysayin' in my ear while I try to make us rich!" Flefneight's scarred cheeks and dead eye seem to make his argument all the sterner, and the plan of action all the more obvious to Kasper. He has no room to complain until the dig takes half his face, too.

"Great, sure. We're either making a profit, getting arrested or dying down here. And arrested is the least likely, right?"

Flefneight grumbles to himself and turns away to start plotting the course forward. Bekkrad fastens his breeches back up around his plump dwarven belly and slaps Kasper on the back. "Look, when you're cashing in at the counting house back in Frial, all this is just gonna be a distant memory, my friend. Besides, like Flefneight said, all these old cave systems have rules. If we can find whatever river carved this place out, then we should have us a way to the surface. So, let's go find a river."

Kasper sighs heavily and watches the rest of the miners start packing up. It sounded like a much simpler job when they all met at Dullivan's Drop back in Frial. He remembers thinking how these sort of clandestine jobs are usually discussed in some dark backstreet or in the shadows of some rarely visited tavern, but Dullivan's Drop was neither. It was a bright morning, and the immaculately kept inn was filled with eager breakfast seekers and the clatter of tableware on plates. He'd been involved in a lot of sordid activities since finally making a name for himself, but none had ever come together during a busy brunch in the most affluent section of a heavily patrolled city.

Bekkrad Skognel's uncle was the man behind the whole expedition. Bekkrad and old Kloglem were cut from the same mold, no mistaking it. But time had not been kind to the elder dwarf Where Bekkrad was a plump grape, the sort that's ripe and full of flavor, Kloglem is a shriveled raisin that lived and died on the vine. He told them about precious minerals and gold that ran deep beneath the highlands north of Melanthris, part of the aloof elves' kingdom but far from any prying eyes. A place called the Bitter Depths. So remote was this cave that calling it part of their border territory would be generous. Kloglem showed them maps, charts, old dwarven almanacs predicting the yields that could be lying in wait for them. Kasper only paid attention to how easy a mark it would be. He was no stranger to mines and navigating caves. It seemed like the sort of oversight that could make him richer than the merchant-barons back home in Ghal Pelor.

No part of his risk-reward calculus ever factored in the possibility of inexperienced labor hands or an accident with Tengu digging equipment—and certainly not the collapse of the cavern's entrance. Slowly dying in this cave with a menagerie of Frial's most-wanted was far from what Kasper expected to be doing with his week. In fact, the only thing that wasn't a surprise about this turn of events was that someone else's incompetence was the thing that would kill him.

CHAPTER TWO

Meanwhile, on the surface...

"Rocks ain't going anywhere, might as well tackle them with a full belly instead of an empty one."

"Hey, try telling Flefneight that's why we haven't dug them out yet. Sorry boss, had a craving for quail eggs and biscuits, figured you could wait," Jaxon Dempster shouts to the stout little man rummaging through provisions as he wiped sweat from his brow. Jaxon thought Harland Welch was a Halfling the first time they met back at Dullivan's, based on the heaping of hash browns and sausages on his plate and because of his size. The rotund little man barely hits Jaxon's waist. Despite all the evidence, though, Welch is human. The short, sweaty, and greasy-palmed sort, but human nonetheless.

Welch reluctantly leaves the sack with only a small chunk of cheese broken off the wheel they bought back in Frial. He shrugs and mumbles something about multitasking before popping the morsel in his mouth and continuing on with the debris pile.

The light from the midday sun shines into the cavern opening and down the few dozen meters to the collapse, where Berton Wylie is working frantically. The Tengu resonance drill lays heavy on the ground where he dropped it. Every so often, the canon-shaped device emits flickering green light or a low static buzz. Each stone Wylie pulls aside is followed by a silent prayer to any of the gods that survived the Silence. He prays that the next stone won't have a familiar face beneath it.

Welch joins him at the rubble pile and digs in without hesitation. "Wouldn't worry so much about it, lad. The gear that bird-folk make is fickle even under the best stars." Wylie remembers the breakfast at Dullivan's and how Welch said he needed to consult his fortuneteller before agreeing to anything.

Welch seemed pretty excited when he was told the stars were right for this type of job. Now, in the dark, that fortune weighs heavily on Wylie.

He tried to use the second Tengu Auger they brought to blow through the debris; it only seemed to make things worse. After the screech of the machine died down, all anyone heard was quaking and collapsing stone in its wake. Wylie's best of intentions might very well have cost Flefneight and his men their lives.

"Well, if it's all the same, maybe we can keep digging as fast as possible anyway? Maybe the boss will be feeling generous and give us a bonus." Wylie knows that's not true, but if it helps motivate Welch to dig a little quicker then it's a lie worth telling.

Jaxon takes his last breath of fresh air and joins the other two at the rubble pile. He plays along with their small talk well enough, yet can't help but to indulge his imagination in regards to a backup plan. If they do find the crew dead and clear the path, the wealth would be split just three ways... or maybe one.

CHAPTER THREE

Meanwhile... Below
Nothing. It's a strange sound to describe. The complete absence of any noise aside from their own boots on the cavern floor. The

silence between steps is a terrible, terrible thing and Kasper can't bear more than a moment of it. "Anything else yet?"

Flefneight said earlier to keep an eye out for corridors. They'd more likely than not have been caused by flowing water, and flowing water is the enemy of even the hardest stone.

"Maybe? Boss, what do you think?" Bastel's lantern beam flashes across a breech in the wall, jagged and rough, the floor of it covered by pebbles. Flefneight looks it over briefly before shaking his head no.

"Doesn't look like water carved that one. Could be a pressure break or a wound left by some old quake. Might be something, but more likely it just narrows more and more 'til no path's left. That's a bad place to be."

Kasper and Bekkrad exchange a worried glance at that last bit of dire wisdom. The same vision plagues their thoughts: a clog of bodies, panicked breaths, and frantic scrambling to turn about. This is the fourth passage they've had to abandon so far. Without the pocket watch dangling from Arnott's belt loop it would be impossible to know how much time has passed in this new cavern. "Bekkrad, Can't you... I don't know, sense anything? Where to go? If we're on the right track? Anything helpful?" Kasper says, breaking up the dreadful return of the quiet. "Oh, 'cause I'm a dwarf and we're all 'one with the stone' or something, huh?" Bekkrad bites back. "I grew up in the same neighborhood as you! Closest I've ever come to spending an hour underground is sneaking into your parent's wine cellar with your sister! Ah, good ole' days those were."

Kasper and Bekkrad came up on the streets of Terrace Row in Ghal Pelor together. Running rum for low-level hucksters to avoid the tariffs and taxes was a profitable venture for two kids from Doxley Street. That led to smuggling weapons, artifacts from before the Fae War, even moving manacite for the Black Thorn Society.

Their friendly rivalry turned into a certain kind of antagonistic friendship that both have come to appreciate over the years. And now, here in these caves, it offers a small bit of protection against the growing anxiety clawing at the edge of their every thought.

"Oh, hey! Everyone! Look at this" Arnott calls from up ahead. Kasper has always been thankful for people to distract him from the full extent of danger they're in. He didn't protest one bit as the big man wandered off. Figured he'd be noisy enough on the way down to the bottom of any deadfall that it would be a solid warning for everyone else.

They follow his waving lantern to find him at the lip of another tunnel, yet something stands out about this one. Even the most inexperienced among them can make out the little chisel marks and scratches. "This is different, yeah boss?"

Flefneight runs his boney fingers along one of the grooves and frowns. "This ain't water and this ain't an earth scar, either. This has been dug out." "That's great news, right?" Bastel's excitement peppers every hopeful word. "Whatever did this probably also dug tunnels out of this damn place? Or at least knows the way out. This is good!"

"It's an option, and it's information," Flefneight calmly says back. "Down here nothing is good news till ya see it with your own eyes." Bekkrad waves his heavy hand at Flefneight's pessimism. "We've been in this new cavern for over two hours now and still haven't even seen one of the side walls yet. Searching this place will take forever. Someone dug this hole and by the looks of it, it goes pretty far. Lot of effort to dig something like this, I'm guessing. That probably means this is either the way out or the way to something pretty precious. I like both right now."

"You're not wrong." Flefneight says. "Doesn't mean this won't get us just as killed as any other tunnel down here, but you're not wrong. Keep your eyes open, though! We ain't equipped to handle too much more going wrong."

Kasper volunteers Arnott to take the lead, which he's more than happy to do, joking blissfully about being able to get his hands on any treasures first. That's another thing Kasper appreciates in an idiot: consistency.

CHAPTER FOUR

Delving Deeper...

The pocket watch ticks on, minute after minute, eventually bleeding into a full hour. The crisscrossing scraps, gouges and scratches form an almost hypnotic pattern all around the men. Bastel mentioned seeing what he thought were repeating patterns in some of the markings, almost like writing hidden amongst the chaos. But none of them, especially Kasper, are eager to hear out his theories. There's too much uncertainty hanging heavy around them. It's not just one tunnel but a network of passages large and small that branch off this one, each of them seeming to spiral down or cascade further into the depths. Each was made by the same unknown tunnellers, and none offered any hints of wealth or escape.

Bekkrad chews on candied fruits he picked up from a waystation near the Rylan Woods, and even though he sounds like a grazing cow, the treats add a bit of sweetness to the dead air. "A bath!" He announces to no one in particular. "Been tossing back and forth between what would be the first thing I do when we hit sunlight. Hot meal or a bath. It's a bath for sure."

"If your kin back in the homeland could hear you now...," Arnott laughs. "Getting clean over getting a full belly."

"You know, you all need to really broaden your minds when it comes to sterotypin' a whole people. Some of us like being clean!"

"Hush, all of you! Look!" Flefneight cuts off their conversation and points with his lantern to a shimmering sparkle coming from the tunnel wall. It's small at first, only a few flecks of silver. Yet, the vein seems to grow wider and spiral about the tunnel for a few meters as if who, or whatever, uncovered it was only interested in exposing the corkscrew pattern rather than harvesting it fully. The group's lantern lights start spotlighting other patterns further down: more corkscrews and brilliant designs splayed across the rock. Even the glittering core exposed geodes and veins of banded agate and quartz crystal. The further the team delves, the more there is to see until finally, the passage leads them into another yawning chamber. Its reach overwhelms the mind. The only difference between this one and the one Arnott found earlier is the light. There's so much light.

Pale white-blue illumination radiates from fungal blooms high on the cavern ceiling and trail along distant walls. More light seems to come from tadpole-like beings that wriggle through slight streams in the stone floor. The waterways are no wider than a forearm but rage like a river to these tiny swimmers. Even the air is alive. Clouds of kaleidoscoping light twist and turn above, merging then breaking apart. They're made of countless fungal spores carried by the subterranean breeze and chased by strange fireflies that make a meal of them.

Even the cynical Kasper and pragmatic Flefneight can't help but stand in awe of this symphony of alien colors.

"I ain't never seen anything like this," Flefneight says while watching a jet of color swirl into some far-off corner of the cavern. "Not ever."

A sharp noise shakes them all from their fugue. It sounds like the melodious buzz-piping of an onion flute more than anything, but before the men can even begin to guess at the origin, an answer makes itself clear. A creature stumbles awkwardly past them with all the speed of an excited toddler. The creature, no taller than a small dog on its hind legs, gives up chasing the firefly it had been occupied with to stare at them. Flefneight's team sees something that can only be described as a mole and pangolin jumbled together, and blessed with an extra set of arms. Its tiny scales are the color of polished gold; its eyes are like milky pearls, same as the nub-like claws at the end of each wide palm. A small blue whip of a tongue flicks out from a narrow snout a few times toward the men before the creature cautiously, slowly, and methodically starts to waddle in their direction.

"Come on, then!" Arnott drops his lantern and pulls two sharp daggers instead.

"What is wrong with you?" Bastel sighs. "Does it look dangerous?"

"Um, does it?" Arnott asks back, very honestly uncertain.

"No," Flefneight says.

"Definitely not," Kasper and Bekkrad echo each other.

Arnott's commotion seems to wake two of the massive boulders nearby. They unfurrow and flex their plates, grumbling with every slow movement. They're adult versions of whatever this pup is that's now standing only a few feet from Arnott. The boulders are taller than an ogre, built like they could shrug the attacks of one, too. Their scaled armor is the color of slate. Their claws, three on each hand and long as short swords, twitch about slowly. They stare at the miners with eyes that glisten and sparkle like sunlight striking a rough diamond. Each of them honks and whistles with that same kazoo-like call the babe made, but deeper and with a rattle that vibrates in the ears of each of Flefneight 's men. The behemoths taste the air with their whipping tongues for several long minutes before deciding whatever they found doesn't seem to be a threat.

Bekkrad slowly gestures for Arnott to sheath his daggers and for everyone to look as harmless as possible despite the slowly encroaching shadows cast by the creatures. One creature stretches to full height and begins scanning the area, stabbing the air with its tongue. Bastel carefully gestures to a long scar on this one's belly. It's a serious wound that's long since healed over. Yet, it's a reminder to him that no matter how intimidating the mole creatures may be, there's always something worse lurking down here.

The other adult flops down and crawls over to Bekkrad. Even at this height it still looms larger than a horse and makes him seem even smaller by comparison. Everyone stands frozen, jaws slowly dropping, as the second creature's head bumps into the dwarf several times. Its tongue flutes out and slithers into Bekkrad's provision pouch then snaps back with several pieces of his dried fruit.

"Hey! Um, sure have some," Bekkrad looks to the rest of the team for comfort, but there's none to be had.

Pup and Scar Belly both stare on at their inquisitive friend as it slurps the fruits into its mouth and swallows them whole. Its eyes go wide as it looks over to the others and answers their silent curiosity with a long, loud honk.

Pup and Scar Belly scamper over, full of excitement, and begin digging into the pouch as well to slurp up fruits.

"I hope you brought more," Bastel whispers.

"I hope when you run out, they don't go after the pound of em' in your gut." Kasper's version of comforting his friend is less than welcome right now.

When the last of Bekkrad's fruits are gone, the first of the bold fruit thieves lets out a disappointed blart and begins to saunter off into the wilderness with Scar Belly and Pup close behind. Fruit Thief stops for a moment while Pup and Scar Belly continue on. Fruit Thief honks several times at the miners and gestures with its narrow snout in what looks like a request to follow.

They shrug and exchange worried or curious glances before coming to a silent consensus to tag along.

"Brilliant," Kasper sighs. "Hope they're not just leading us into a giant boiling pot of water."

"Hey!" Arnott grumbles. "These guys are all ok so far. You know, not everything is out to kill ya? Some folks mean well."

"If you say so," Kasper instinctively checks to make sure all his weapons are ready for the draw and follows on.

CHAPTER FIVE

Back at the Cavern Entrance...

"Clear!" Welch's shout echoes in the tunnel. "It looks clear!" He points to a gap in the rubble and the open tunnel behind it. His lantern lights up the darkness when he jams his arm through. It reveals a small clearing, maybe a half dozen meters of open space at best and then more fallen stones.

"Damn... must of collapsed in waves. No telling how many piles there are," Wylie says grimly.

Jaxon peeks through as well and spots something: a drop in the floor that he quickly directs their attention to. Something heavy must have dislodged from the tunnel ceiling and hit a fragile spot on the floor and crashed through. A rough, ragged hole takes up about half of the open space between stone piles.

It doesn't take much for the men to clear enough space to cautiously edge toward the drop and cast a beam of light inside.

Their lanterns find a large pile of shattered stone and dirt, as well as the remains of the boulder that must have fallen here.

"Um… so," Welch takes a long, deep breath, "that looks like a pretty big area down there." The others can tell he's working up to asking a tough question.

Wylie asks for him. "You thinking there's a good chance that tunnel connects with the one Flefneight and the boys went down? Might be a good way to catch up to them and get them outta here right quick, eh?"

"Yep, that's what I was thinking," Welch nods.

Jaxon starts anchoring rope to the heaviest rubble and gathering up extra gear that will allow him to get out of the hole if it ends up being a dead end. Wylie collects all the extra water he can carry and any medical supplies that will fit, too.

Welch watches the darkness in the drop while the others prepare their equipment. Shadows, debris, and dust work together to clog any clear view. Yet despite it all, he swears there's something down there. Something moving.

Jaxon is the first down. He stays in the comforting columns of lantern light from above and quickly draws his hatchet and readies his own light source. Rock particulate dances in the beams of light, making seeing anything more than a few dozen feet ahead difficult at best. What he does see isn't particularly interesting though — wide tunnels, fractured stone, adjoining passages, and dark grey surfaces. He waves the others down and waits for them to settle into the dark before pointing toward the path that should, in theory, lead in the direction of Flefneight.

"I'll take the front. Welch, you get the rear, and Wylie, stay in the middle and stay close. You have all food and first aid," Jaxon says with a rather grim authority that no one cares to question.

There's no appetite for conversation among any of them, only a need to get this over with as soon as possible. When Flefneight and the others originally took to the caves, the surface team breathed a silent sigh of relief. Better them than me, all of them thought. Now that they too are steeped in the narrow blackness, the only focus is being done with this, and quickly.

Except for Welch. Something else snags his attention for the briefest of moments. A slow, slick clicking noise from one of the side tunnels that rattles inside his ears.

And it's growing louder.

CHAPTER SIX

With the Miners Trapped Below...

If any of them bothered to look at Bastel's pocket watch, they'd have seen another hour go by since they began their walk with the mole creatures, but the idea never crosses their minds. Even the growing ache in their feet is pushed to the back of their thoughts in the face of such alien wonder all around them.

The deeper they go, the more there is to see. Veins of glittering minerals encased in ancient rock. Fungal clusters so alive and complex they almost seem to behave like animals. Arnott even swears he saw a walking mushroom among the blooms and that it winked at him. Even though the others wave it off as nonsense, he's happy enough to have seen it whether they believed him or not.

They even watch the way Pup stays close to Fruit Thief. It must be the child's mother, for only a mother would have the patience to endure it crawling all over her, nuzzling against her and riding on her back. There's a sweetness to how she coddles and coos for the little creature that transcends species. She's a mother and even in the Bitter Depths, there is love.

After a long while, Bekkrad is the first one to speak. Hearing anything other than the sounds of the caverns is momentarily jarring. He points at a large standing stone, similar to a crude pillar in shape, and waves them all over. It's wreathed in glowing fungus and covered in a chaotic jumble of scratches. Yet, there's more to it than just that. Amid the gouges and other markings, there are more intricate images drawn in stone by careful hands.

A soft piping from Scar Belly announces the remarkably quiet presence of these hulking creatures. They're watching the miners and tracing the height of the obelisk with their eyes.

"Watch out, watch out." Bekkrad urges the rest of his comrades out of the way as Fruit Thief picks herself up on two legs and plods over to the rock. She gently caresses the stone, running claws along the many carved symbols and scratches with a reverent touch.

Their kind made this, and it tells a story.

The men watch as claw, tongue, and arms all work together to explain the stone's tale in a language the men will never know. Fruit Thief taps on a cluster of marks near the bottom, at figures that could almost be her kind, simple as they may look. Her nails softly drag along other symbols further up. She paws at a series of scratches around something that looks like a city and a figure made of the worst parts of serpent, squid, and jellyfish. There's no telling what she's trying to say, but all of the men can tell by the way she holds out one open hand and quietly hoots that it's a warning of some kind.

Bastel takes out a journal and silverpoint to scribble down everything. "I don't know what she's saying but this is… This is amazing. We might be the first people to ever hear this—whatever it is."

"What's that gonna be worth?" Kasper leans in to quietly ask.

"To certain people, a great deal. But, to the right kind of people—like myself—priceless," Bastel answers with a sneer. "Some things are more important than gold, you know."

"Haven't seen those things yet, but I'll keep an eye out."

Fruit Thief's gestures continue higher up the stone. She taps once on another symbol of the city and then points at her face. She slowly closes her eyes to mimic sleeping. Further along the stone, there's more she has to say but none of it makes much sense to them. That is until Fruit Thief points out a trail of creatures drawn in stone that look very human, aside from the sharp little triangular pips where ears would be. The creatures follow a path toward the sleeping city.

"Elves you reckon? Elves made it this far down?" Arnott asks.

"Maybe? They are old and this is their territory," Flefneight says while pointing to the surface above.

"There were rumors of exiled houses. Traitors to the elven crown who fought with the fae. If those are elves, they may not have come by choice," Bastel informs everyone without even once looking up from his notes.

Fruit Thief's story becomes more frantic and Pup soon crawls over to bury his snout in his mother's fur. She shows them those pointy-eared figures with forked spears, things that look like nets and mole-creatures in crudely drawn piles.

Scar Belly breaks his silence to sigh heavily and rake at the cavern floor.

Fruit Thief's claws pass by symbols of her kind, far from the sleeping city and few in number. Across the stone now are more pictures of the pointy ears and their forks, followed by her dead kin.

"Hunted probably?" Kasper adds.

The final image at the top, haloed by the scratch-words of Fruit Thief's language, is the city again. She gestures to her eyes once more but shows them slowly open, then points to the small pointy-eared figures now with strange loops all around them. Her attention shifts back to the base of the stone, where Pup helps her dig something up from the rubble.

Chains.

Strange chains made of some black metal none of the men had ever seen before. She then points back to the loops again while rattling the chains.

"Whatever happened in that city," Flefneight says slowly while looking over his team, "seems like something woke up, and those hunters got what they deserved."

Scar Belly honks and uses his long head to suggest they carry on now. Pup climbs on his mother's back while Fruit Thief buries the chains again before following her mate. Fruit Thief stops only to flick her tongue at the men and silently ask that they continue to follow. It seems to be the only option they have. Bastel is the last to leave the stone, though. His mind is steeped in the idea that Tairos' history runs deeper than anyone could have imagined. While nations were clashing above to carve out the world that exists, an entire world was taking shape beneath their feet.

He claps his journal closed and wonders for a moment about that city and what mistakes its inhabitants must have made to awaken it. Would any nation above have done better?

What little he knows of history suggests the answer is no.

CHAPTER SEVEN

Elsewhere in the Bitter Depths...

"It was coming from here. Stop looking at me like I'm crazy, Jaxon!" Welch shouts while his partner circles the small chamber with sword drawn and eyes scouring every possible nook.

Jaxon shrugs. "Look, maybe you heard something, maybe you didn't, but nobody is here."

Wylie fans his lantern around, spotting the same empty channels that connect to the room Jaxon pointed out already.

Despite the clammy chill down here, Wylie sweats. The other two argue about what's here or not here, but Wylie can't tear his eyes away from the dark passages all around the men. He's only half-sure which one Welch led them down to get here, and that thought worries him far more than any phantom sounds.

"Maybe we should just get going?" Wylie says while hoping one of his companions will point the way back with certainty and put an end to his dreadful thoughts.

"We came down to find Flefneight and the others, right? If they ended up down here, then great, we're done all the sooner. We can't leave 'til we know one way or the other though," Wylie says.

"Flefneight!" Jaxon yells into one of the empty tunnels. "Arnott!" He shouts in another before moving to a third narrow opening and calling for Bekkrad with still no answer. "No one's here, kid. Whatever you heard, it's in your head. I'd be surprised if there's so much as a tunnel rat down here."

Jaxon shines his lantern down another corridor, ready to call for Kasper, but only a few loud syllables manage to tumble from his lips. Something stands only a few perilous steps ahead of Jaxon: a creature dressed in strange reflective black armor, armor that looks more like beetle chitin than metal. It's shaped like a man and stands just as tall as Jaxon, but it's impossible to know what's inside. The only clue is the bald, chalk-white scalp and veiny, jaundiced eyes that sit above a strange mask that covers the mouth. It looks equal parts machine and insect, this mask, and its many legs bite deep into the pale flesh around it, holding so tightly to his face that the device leaves tortured skin and old scars behind.

Wylie and Jaxon trace the height of the black staff the creature holds all the way to the zenith, to a sharp and serrated fork that lurks above.

"We... we're looking for friends. We don't... um, we're not here to hurt you." Jaxon stumbles over his words while positioning his sword between him and the creature in the tunnel. In the one short moment between moving his lantern and bringing his sword forward, the creature is upon him. Its yellow eyes swim through the shadows, and it's soon standing chest-to-chest with Jaxon. The creature's fork, once obscured, is now caught plainly in everyone's lantern light. Ragged bits of Jaxon's guts and spine drip to the floor, slippery and shiny in the dark tunnel. Whatever the blade is made of is anathema to flesh and bone; everything seems to slide from the weapon like cattle fat off a hot knife.

The creature steps past Jaxon and pulls its fork through the rest of the way. The other men hear a heavy weight slap the ground before smelling copper and fresh death. The creature's free hand points toward both of the trembling men; it speaks with a voice both cruel and metallic. Neither of the men understand a word of what's hissed. It all sounds harsh, gravelly, and grating without a hint of mercy.

Wylie drops his own lantern to the ground and rips his dagger from its sheath. "Stop! Just stop! Whatever we did, whatever you want… you can have it!"

"Come on! Come on, come on, come on!" Wylie grabs Welch's shoulder and starts dragging him toward the nearest tunnel, but that clicking noise quickly resurfaces before he can take more than a step. The path is blocked by another nightmare, this one not at all humanoid. It's more like a beetle the size of bear and held together by bony growth and alien horror. Four of its spindle limbs carry it across the cavern floor quickly. The two largest terminate in heavy, slashing hooks that bite into the rock. The creature peppers the air with screech-clicks that only grow louder until the men's ears ache under every oppressive decibel.

Jaxon's killer seems unphased as he signals for the monster to advance on them. The closer the thing gets, the more hideous details come into sight. Nestled within the bulk of its shell and safely behind the crushing scythes is a beak-like organ that chitters at breakneck speed while a cluster of red eyes drinks up the men's panicked screams.

"What do you want? What do you want! Please! Please!" Wylie swipes wildly at the beetle, but it feels more like striking an iron bar than flesh that can be injured. After a fourth failed effort, the beak shoots several feet forward and clamps down on the wrist of Wylie's sword arm before pulling back again into its setting. The pain is slow compared to the lightning-like alacrity of the creature's attack. Wylie hears his bent dagger hit the rock below, then looks at the tattered stump of an arm that's left behind. Only a few working fingers remain and the skin... what little is left is hot with blood and throbbing pain. The rest was degloved and disappeared into the dark with the beak that took it.

Wylie doubles back and mouths a whispered apology to Welch before vanishing down one of the tunnels. The lone miner stumbles a few steps backward and falls into the growing pool of Jaxon's blood. He drags himself backward through the still-warm mess before butting up against a wall. "Wh. Wha. What do you want? Plea...se," he pants out, barely able to string coherent words together.

The master holds one nailed finger up that stays the otherwise relentless advance. Soon, the beetle slinks back into the shadows that it crawled from, obeying some unseen command. Wylie watches as the master walks closer to him now. His feet don't make a single sound as they hit the stone floor. In fact, it is only when his feet step in the red puddle of blood that a small sound makes this ghost seem real. The master then sinks down like a perched shrike beside Wylie; a faint rasping sound comes from that mask that only now can Welch hear.

"What... What do you want?!"

The master cocks its head at the weakly uttered question before slowly reaching into some pouch at its back and pulling something forth: a severed and bloody hand unlike anything Wylie's seen before. Three long claws rise off the palm; the rest is coated in hard grey scales like some kind of armored mole.

The master drops the limb next to Wylie and looks him squarely in the eye for a long quiet moment before speaking a single word, one Wylie understands perfectly.

"Want."

CHAPTER EIGHT

While the Miners Are Making Camp...

Flefneight draws from his birchwood pipe and lets out a heavy cloud of ruddy red smoke. The Tassleweed vapors warm his lungs and calm his thoughts while he watches the rest of his people set up provisions and muster together anything comfortable enough to become a makeshift bedroll. Their feet ache and their stomachs demand some kind of proper meal.

Their guides seem to have understood as well and stopped to graze on some kind of rust-colored mushrooms growing alongside the nearby trickle of a stream. Bastel is doing his best to play the good ambassador and speak with them. He's showed them a map of Tairos' surface and made a staircase-like gesture leading to the surface several times now. And, they reply the same way each time. With a low honk and bleating noise followed by a nudge of the mushroom patch.

"I think they get it," Arnott says. "They're just hungry and tired, too."

"I really don't want to gamble on them understanding," Bastel answers back. "A solid confirmation that they're helping us get to the surface would be nice."

A loud fluting bellow startles everyone, including the mole creatures. Bekkrad is holding a rolled-up parchment to his lips like a horn and smiling. Their guides' eyes fix firmly on him while flicking their tongues in the air. "You're just asking them the wrong way, that's all." He laughs before blowing into the paper horn again.

"The odds are at least 50/50 that they're just marveling at how ridiculous he sounds," Kasper whispers to his friend.

Bekkrad blows again, and the mole creatures pull themselves away from their meal to nudge him with their snouts and flick their tongues in his face. He then moves to each of his friends and taps them on the shoulder before unrolling his paper and gesturing to them again, pointing to the underside of the paper. The creatures' shimmering eyes look toward all the miners then back to Bekkrad, who's now pushing his finger through the bottom of the parchment and out to the top.

"That's so simple, I'm sure they understood," Bekkrad says, beaming with pride.

Scar Belly and Fruit Thief honk several times rather melodiously before turning back to their meal.

"That's probably them laughing at you," Kasper teases.

Pup stays behind, though, and looks around 'til he spots what he's been searching for, a large flat rock next to Flefneight. Pup scampers over on all his limbs and plops down next to the rock. With one long finger claw, he effortlessly carves drawings of all five of the miners into the stone. Flefneight watches and marvels at the strength even this little one has. Pup draws a horizontal line above them all and then scratches out a quick rendition of himself and his two parents. Finally, he draws a quick scratch that leads from his parents to the topside of the line. He finishes with a high-pitched blart before heading back to the mushrooms.

"Um… I'd say they got," Arnott says, impressed by what even the baby is able to grasp. "They're probably pretty annoyed you keep asking them the same question," he says to Bastel.

"Well, they could have just led with that then!" He sighs, closes his journal, and sits down for a bite of jerky and biscuits. It doesn't take long, though, before he's back in his book scribbling down notes about the whole interaction.

With their bellies full and Bekkrad passing around his flask of Ackley Ale, the men are able to rest easyily beneath a sky of stone and a rainbow of living stars.

CHAPTER NINE

Meanwhile, Lost in The Dark...

His chest burns. Every beat of Welch's heart feels as if it rattles his whole body.

Fear.

Fear owns him now. It has a way of making the familiar seem foreign and every impending moment feel wrought with fatal missteps.

Welch is lost in the dark now, desperate for the surface, for even a familiar passage.

The man's lantern quivers in his grip and swings wildly in the dark. "Please, please, please," he begs softly. From somewhere behind him, Welch can hear a loud, anguished scream that echoes painfully long in these tunnels. It's Wylie.

"I'm so sorry."

Welch picks a tunnel with a large crack that runs its length, one he remembers from earlier. Or, he hopes he remembers. At first the only sound Welch hears is the rattle of his lantern, his boots, and his own panicked breathing.

Then, steps that don't belong to him. Raspy, even breaths. A satisfied murmur.

He looks over his shoulder; his shaking lantern light waves over something else. Black armor. The biting mask latched into pale flesh. The killer dashes across the gravel, its fork hung on his back and one arm slowly raising toward Welch. Something on the wrist, a knotted lump of shell, sprouts two spidery legs that click into place and resemble the arms of a bow. A shard of crystalized something screeches through the air and shatters Welch's lantern.

"No, no, no, no, no!" Welch runs his hands along the walls, too scared to stay still and too scared to run. There's nothing. His world is black now, and all choice is gone.

The steps that aren't his grow closer. The breaths that don't belong to him now hiss in his ear. Welch hears alien words that swim around him in a sinister cloud. Something sharp and cold runs across his face.

Another sound, a new one. Metal striking rock and something wet falling to the ground. Welch can feel the killer's fork puncturing his gut and pinning him to the cavern wall. If he screams, it doesn't register to him at all. Everything is lost to a new kind of darkness now.

The killer stands over the dead man, watching blood and stone mingle on the floor; its eyes are made for this lightless void. The crunching of his hunting hound interrupts this silent daydream. The insect rejoins his master with Wylie strapped to its back. Wylie is bloodied almost beyond recognition, but breathing. The master had so much to learn about the miners despite the few words the men could share: How many miners there were, what weapons they might have and how unaccustomed their bodies were to pain.

The master left his city of Sha'Hidun to hunt for Dutroti. Their filter glands would reap a fortune from the Inoculators. And with more claws, the master could have a truly remarkable set of armor made. Yet, this was unexpected. Humans in the Bitter Depths. One brought in alive to the Dactyi would bring influence among those decrepit nobles and fame with the commoners, his people, the Drekh.

Dark Mother, Scroll Keeper or one of the other dead gods must haunt his fortunes for they were kind enough to give him not one but three. One beating heart for the tables of the lords, two more for his trophy rack.

With an armored hand, the master caresses the still-wet face dangling from his belt and then the empty spot beside it that waits to be filled. The silence is broken once again by a new sound: tortured meat and a skinning blade.

CHAPTER TEN

At the Camp...

Flefneight awkwardly climbs to his feet. The combination of Thistleweed, a full belly and a few hours of sleep make his first few steps unsure. Fruit Thief and Arnott are in a contest for loudest snore, but somehow everyone else still manages to sleep through it.

Flefneight's tired eyes look for a quiet place to relieve himself and have another smoke before returning to sleep. He spots an ideal patch of rocks near an arm of the little stream the men have been chasing and decides that will do just fine. He presses a few lumps of weed into the pipe before starting off toward the rocks, but stops quickly to listen to the strange, distant screech in the air.

Flefneight's pipe tumbles to the stone floor. Then, his body follows. Little is left of his head now, just a red hole and one wide eye.

The rest of the miners scramble and scream. They grab at small knives, lanterns, and anything else while frantically scanning the dark.

The Dutroti are not nearly as lost. Their eyes fix on a distant shape, on sharp ears.

Pup hops to his feet and starts shoving the miners with his head, pushing them to flee. Arnott and Bekkrad are the first to arm themselves and find some measure of calm. Arnott tries to shield Bastel while he shoves his books and maps into his backpack.

"What's happening? Is Flefneight dead? Oh gods... is he dead? Someone check!" Bastel screams.

"Yeah, I'd say he's dead!" Kasper briefly shines his lantern toward the tattered, yawning wound where Flefneight's face once was before clamoring to safety behind Scar Belly.

The Drekh hunter stalks slowly from boulder to boulder, watching darkness and death consume the daylighters. He imagines a world above filled with such weakness, such fear, and wonders how it is they even exist. Do they have gods who are happy preserving such fragile-hearted children? Could their world be empty of danger, one where the meek have thrived? Whatever the case, he comes to one simple conclusion: Only one man needs to be brought back to the Dactyi. Better the lords and hunters believe daylighters to be more of a challenge rather than mewling pups. He begins loading another quarrel into the insect-like Khulthacha on his wrist and starts to decide which of the surface dwellers the hand bow creature will extinguish next.

Before the decision can be made, the rock he's re-arming behind trembles with force, and a broad, heavy paw swipes from above. Fruit Thief's burst of angry speed and vicious swing managed to surprise both the hunter and the miners. Only a fraction of Fruit Thief's attack actually connected with the glossy gauntlet of the hunter's armor, but that alone sends a painful force through the Drekh's arm, shoulder, and neck. The Khulthacha on his arm is killed by Fruit Thief's powerful paw, though; the insect weapon is blasted against its owner and across the cavern floor.

Kasper watches Fruit Thief loom over the rock, swinging her arms and hammering blows on whatever might be hidden behind it. Her small family could have scooped up Pup and used their speed to leave Kasper and his team behind, but Fruit Thief chooses this instead, to risk everything and attack. Kasper is baffled by the bizarre logic of it all.

"What do we do?" Bekkrad asks breathlessly. His head keeps swiveling back and forth looking for any other threats that might be slithering up on them.

"We help!" Arnott shouts. "Whatever it is killed Flefneight, and we're next. Come on!" He then dashes toward Fruit Thief and the rock she's laying siege to.

"Yeah, no thanks," Kasper says. He then starts backing further and further away from the struggle. He turns to begin a full sprint, but his lantern light casts against a shape a dozen or so yards ahead, something difficult for his mind to make sense of. A lump of something black and glossy, large as a draft horse, too. Claws. Spindly limbs. And there is Wylie, beaten, bound, and bleeding on top of the beetle-thing.

"What... what the...," Kasper manages to mutter before he watches the shell on the thing's back split as venous wings unfurl. It takes to the air for a brief, sanity-shattering few seconds. Clicking. Buzzing. Wreathed in Wylie's agonized screams. It lands only a few feet from Kasper and turns its hacking arms on Scar Belly.

Bastel can't take his eyes off Wylie. The man moans, reaching and begging for help. Yet, he cannot speak. Not clearly, not anymore. This close and under the glow of lantern light, it becomes clear that Wylie has no face. Only desperate eyes and a mask of raw muscle and exposed bone.

"No, no, no, no!" Bastel repeats over and over as he runs wide around the beetle.

Scar Belly towers over his attacker yet suffers a barrage of attacks that slice and crush. He has little care for his own safety but instead works to keep Pup out of reach, and to Kasper's surprise, Scar Belly is relentless in his effort to land a finishing blow on Wylie. Their kind seem to understand mercy, something Kasper has no interest in right now. He pushes past the swirl of claws, grabbing Bastel's supply bag from the ground and keeps running, following the little stream. The sound of the combat behind him grows softer, more distant. The last thing he hears before it all dies away into the distance is the crunch that finally silences Wylie's screams.

Kasper runs until the echoes of the fight are no more and his lungs struggle for breath. Until the light of his team's lanterns is swallowed by the dark. Until the fungal blooms fall into the background and he comes face to face with solid black stone walls where the tiny stream dips down.

He scrambles through the bag looking for candles or oil—anything at all that would help—but all he finds inside are Bastel's maps and notebook. Kasper holds back a furious scream, desperate to remain unseen.

He is alone. Out of options. And watching his lantern oil burning away by the minute.

The dark is on its way.

CHAPTER ELEVEN

Meanwhile, The Battle Rages On...

The blades of the fork make a sickening noise as they're wrenched from the back of Arnott's skull. His body lays twitching on the cavern floor, smoke and flame dancing off his arm and flank from the lantern his body fell upon. The Drekh hunter has no time to revel in the beauty of that clean kill; he must keep moving.

The claws and pounding fists of the female Dutroti are a constant danger that show no sign of stopping. Each blow is slow, easily avoided, but it would only take one solid strike to end his hunt forever. The daylighters, however, are a different matter. The big one he just killed had been a constant nuisance, slowing him down and making him an easier target for the Dutroti. He had to die and quickly, even if it meant ruining any chance of preserving the human's face for his collection.

In the distance, the hunter takes an account of how his Eket beetle is fairing. It and the male Dutroti are trading stone-shattering attacks against each other. With cracked carapace and gnashed-open flesh, both look to persist on adrenaline alone. The hunter can only hope that his creature's will to fight can last just a moment longer than the male Dutroti's. The idea of having to avoid four more limbs is not a comforting one.

The hunter spins his fork about and angles it to receive the charging female that's once again trying to trample him into the gravel. This time he's ready, though. He focuses entirely on the cluster of arteries that pump just beneath the surface of Fruit Thief's throat, where the collar and neck plates meet. A small target, but he's harpooned smaller before.

"No more!" A shout from the hunter's side catches him by surprise, followed by a sharp pain in his wrist. This man is different, it seems able to see well enough in the dark, something he didn't expect a daylighter to be capable of. The stout little thing brings his shovel up again and prepares to strike the hunter's arm a second time, but his target dances to the side and flourishes his fork in a hypnotic flurry. So dazzling is the display that Bekkrad doesn't immediately notice the tip of the hunter's weapon open a gash across his neck and shoulder. It is only when Bekkrad feels warmth spilling over his chest that he realizes he's been slashed. Bekkrad stumbles and falls to the stone, gripping the wound tightly.

The Drekh prepares to thrust his blades into the troublesome daylighter, but the vibrations in the ground tell him there is no time for this kill. No time to do anything but brace. He looks toward Fruit Thief with just enough time to scream a hateful curse at her before they collide.

Bekkrad leans back, his head swimming and vision growing blurry. He can still manage to see Scar Belly, who flips the beetle-thing over and cracks open its soft undershell with a final hammer strike of his claws. The beetle collapses on the stone beside Scar Belly, who is breathing heavy and slow. Bastel's body is there as well, crushed against the floor by one beetle's claws.

He doesn't see Kasper though, and that brings a smile to his now pale lips.

CHAPTER TWELVE

Somewhere...

Kasper remembers scrambling along for maybe hours. There's no telling. Everything that happened back at their camp is a distant horror compared to the one that unfolded before his eyes just now. The fuel gauge on his lantern is dwindling. Soon the lantern light flickers, dying in the dark for a few painfully long moments and then... nothing. The light is replaced by pure terror.

Kasper scrambled. He begged. He wept. And eventually, he fell through some fissure or sharp decline. Whatever it was, the fall was brief, and the impact took away all the fear.

Kasper drifted in and out. He felt sharp pains here and there. A floating feeling from time to time. Familiar noises, too.

While he drifts at the edge of consciousness, Kasper dreams. He sees the beetle-thing and its claws. Wylie's face and his panicked eyes. The mole creatures. The hunter and his terrible taloned fingers reaching for him. Kasper dreams of light, too. The sky. The idea of there being a tomorrow.

His eyes shoot open, and they can see. There's light, not much but enough. He can see a cavern tunnel that ends in clear sky and daylight no more than a dozen yards away. There's pain in his leg but not enough to stop him from quickly, agonizingly, readying himself. Then, he looks behind to see where he came from and how he got here.

Fruit Thief lies on the ground, her massive belly rising and sinking very slowly. One sparkling eye looks at Kasper, locked on him. Her body is a patchwork of cuts and stabs; blood seeps from a particularly large gash near her neck. Pup and Scar Belly are nowhere to be seen, and Kasper is not sure what that might mean.

Beside her is Bekkrad. He's still, pale, and long since dead. And then there's the hunter. He is slumped against the wall near Fruit Thief, his insectile breastplate crushed and his own brackish blood spattered everywhere. Whatever sits beneath the strange mask is a mystery Kasper has no care to solve.

Fruit Thief honks at him the same way she did back at the standing stone. Ages ago it feels like. Her heavy paw carves a line in the stone, struggling as she does. Then, with a final effort she carves a line from beneath the mark to the top.

To the surface.

In that moment, Kasper weeps. Fruit Thief made a promise and she followed through. She brought them out, protected them against the hunter, died to protect them from him.

He doesn't weep out of gratitude, but shame. There's no way she could have known that he didn't deserve it. That he wasn't worth her life. There wasn't anything about his life that should have been paid for with blood and sacrifice.

Kasper looks at the light then back at her. He takes more fruit from Bekkrad's pouches and sits beside her, feeding her, holding her.

Daylight fades to night, and eventually he's alone again.

THE FURIOUS VEXES

by Tepherial

Amidst the cosmopolitan city of Irisul, a significant protest rages within the Grand Plaza's square. The trouble consists of mostly middle-class citizens crowding the Grand Plaza, a masterpiece of architectural art that is an apt representation of the nobility in Irisul; prosperous, precise, and prideful. And to anyone not a noble, patronizing. The cornerstones are the eight marble columns that circularly and evenly dot the perimeter, as well as three white-stone water fountains in a triangular formation. The square is situated within the residential district of the upper-class, with many estates and luxurious townhouses enclosing it parallel to the straight, cobblestone streets. On the north side of the square, the exemplary Margrave Rosenclair's mansion is the main focus of yelling from the protest. The mass is not organized in the least. Even to those participating, the combined noise of several hundred people is too incoherent as it drowns out the true intent of their outcry. As for the nobles, intrigued they may be in the matter, observing from their second and third story windows like watching a farcical play, they do not willingly subject themselves to a commoner's riot. As for the impoverished, they have better things to do than bother making a trip outside their element.

Towards the southern side of the square, where the back of the crowd is somewhat thinner, a man in flashy clothes leans his back against one of the marble columns. His long-sleeved shirt is some amalgamation between a vest and a midriff that flaunts his torso. It and his silk trousers are a dull green color with dark grey and black embroidery, complemented by a pair of dark, tanned leather shoes. The overall style is certainly striking, giving off a feeling of self-confidence on an irritating level. Others around him can't help but think so, and would likely heckle his fashion sense if they weren't already distracted. As for the man himself, he possesses an appealing, sculpted face with elfin traces and fair skin. His almond eyes are also dark grey, and his short, unkempt hair is like burnished mahogany. The most distinguishing feature is his ears — not quite an elf's sharpness, but nonetheless keen.

He folds his arms and watches with slight amusement towards the closest water fountain, about ten feet away. The people around him consists of those appearing more from an interest in the event like he, and are less fervent in the protest. With an abundance of loiters present, street performers can sense the opportunity for an easy audience. On the fountain's basin wall, a lanky older man sits and plays a tune on his lute while a nearby woman dressed in the alternating red and black colors of a jester performs acrobatic stunts around the edge. The song is fast-paced and evokes a feeling of incitement, harmonizing with the protest happening behind them, while the jester's act is flowing but solid. The performances do not mesh well together but are individually well executed. As for the conspicuous man, he considers the entertainment better than nothing while he waits. The other onlookers are amused enough, stomping rhythmically and admiring the maneuvers. These performers would be awkwardly out of place towards the front of the protest, but here the scene could almost be mistaken for a street festival.

A few moments later, a slap to his shoulder calls his attention from the left, and a voice strains over the noise, "Oi! You said you'd be at the back of the plaza, not in the crowd!" The voice is recognized as belonging to Stan Mihle, a young man from a small baronet family who's more a friendly informant than a friend. The man indifferently turns to him with a slight tilt of the head, acting as though he didn't hear. "Hey! Did you hear me! Ceto!? I've been looking for you for twenty minutes!" Ceto smirks as he stands straight, beckoning him to follow with a casual wave. He walks further south, away from congregation and noise, and Stan follows with a frustrated huff.

When they're some distance away, about forty feet from where the people begin to amass, Ceto moves to a close-by bench and lazily sits. Stan opts to turn around and keep an eye on the crowd as he continues to speak, "Okay, so my uncle confirmed that he does actually know how to use coal to drive a carriage."

Ceto glances dubiously at Stan, "No horses, and without using the Divine Presence?" The voice is clear, light, and pleasant like silver, and the tone is as self-assured as his image.

Stan faces Ceto directly, and nods enthusiastically in response, "That's right! We don't need those church priests!"

"And did he elaborate how at all?"

"Ehh, he said something about water, I wasn't really paying attention. I was distracted by… uh, something else." Stan has commented on the attractiveness of the housemaids on more than one occasion.

Ceto clearly doesn't look satisfied by the poor clarification, and lets out a short sigh, "That isn't enough for me, Stan. I don't know your uncle so I can't just take his word for it. It certainly sounds great, if it can be done, but I'm not going to lend on just coal and water. Since you're not informed on the matter, then I'll have to meet your uncle and he can hopefully convince me."

Stan is disappointed in the reserved answer, but accepts it nonetheless, "He said he would prefer to meet you too." As he speaks, some harsher yelling can be heard from the depths of the protest.

"That's good. Then, I'll visit you later this evening. Go back and let him know." Ceto turns his attention to the howling, which is now a collective noise of several people. "What's going on over there?"

Stan glances towards it with some concern but is dismissive, "Maybe the Margrave got fed up and sicced his personal guards on them. I'm not involved, so I'll head out." He departs swiftly through a nearby side-alley further back to make sure it stays that way.

Ceto gets to his feet on the bench, standing and straining to get a clearer view. The yells and screams are becoming more numerous, and several people are seen fleeing from the square as others get closer with curiosity. The panic quickly spreads out, and Ceto sees that even on the other end of the crowd, the ones actively protesting are starting to notice the precarious situation as they're pushed from behind and people rush past. On his side, he calls out to those who flee in his direction for an explanation, but they all ignore him.

As the mob begins to thin out, he notices those running away are becoming increasingly haggard, with many having noticeable blood stains on their clothing. Those that do are each overcome with coughing fits of blood, collapsing to the ground before.

Looking beyond them towards the epicenter, he sees even more bodies strewn about and unmoving. This is all that is required for Ceto to confirm the graveness of the scene, and his prompt feeling to avoid it. His choosing of the Grand Plaza for meeting with Stan was simply due to his interest in what would come of the protest; he has no personal stake in it. But knowing Margrave Rosenclair, Ceto has a premonition that being implicated is an unfortunate inevitability. Still, he's not going to linger this close when he doesn't know the reason behind this incident. He steps down from the bench and, like Stan before him, quickly leaves. While he makes a run for the closest exiting avenue, he realizes the outcries from only moments ago have altogether died.

Following the streets through the nobility district, Ceto makes it as far as the front courtyard of his manor when two figures waiting for him by the front door signal him down, "Baron Sleir, I am Guard Captain Dinn. Margrave Rosenclair requires your immediate presence." Dinn is clad in the decorated plate armor outfit of a guard captain, while the one next to him looks to be an accompanying guard, also in plate armor.

Ceto looks at them with suspicion, "How'd you get here so quick? I only just left the plaza." If he had seen these two first, he would most certainly avoid them as best as possible, but Dinn is apparently aware of that and made sure they'd inform him of the order before he could shirk responsibility.

"Private Trian can receive Her Honour's Holy Words." As her name is mentioned, the guard next to the captain gives a slight bow to Ceto. It's not as respectful as one should show towards nobility, but he isn't in a position to criticize formalities. "She received the order, and we were the closest." Ceto shakes his head in exasperation as Dinn continues, "We'll escort you to the Margrave's mansion now." He turns to Trian. "Alright, I'll lead, you keep a close eye on him from behind."

She acknowledges with a sharp, "Sir!"

As the trio depart from his house, Ceto turns to the woman behind him with a smile that belies his irritation, "Why are you in a guard outfit if you're a part of the priest corp?"

Because he is being treated as a detainee, Trian considers ignoring the question, but figures that in spite of that, he's a noble and not officially under arrest. "Baron Sleir, I completed my training three days ago and have not yet been issued a chaplain's uniform." The answer is terse but the tone intense.

"Ah." He faces forward, inquiring the captain next, "Are you aware of what happened at the plaza?"

"No, Baron Sleir. As I mentioned, we were nearby when we received the order to bring you in." There's a hint of annoyance by the guard captain in being required to respond to Ceto's questioning.

"I suggest we do not take the straight path and avoid it. A protest in there from earlier was attacked by... something."

"If that's true, we will deal with it when we come to it. I will not delay Margrave Rosenclair any more than I need to."

Ceto sighs in response, knowing there's no convincing him. The next ten minutes are walked in silence as he mentally prepares himself to return to the Grand Plaza. When they turn the last street corner, they can see in the distance that several guards are blocking traffic into it. As the three get nearer, one of the guards breaks off, approaches and salutes, "Captain Dinn, under the orders of Captain Meraso, access to the Grand Plaza has been closed!"

"Private, I have orders from Margrave Rosenclair to escort Baron Sleir to him," he gestures towards the plaza behind the mass of guards and anxious citizens, "And that's the quickest way. Is there an immediate threat?"

"Not that I'm aware of, sir! There has been no attack since the incident, we were simply ordered to keep the plaza clear!"

"Alright, if there is no threat, then we will proceed to the margrave's mansion. Carry on."

The guard briefly hesitates but complies with another salute, "Sir!" He returns to his squad and has them temporarily part for the three.

Further in, several dozens of other guards surround the plaza, blocking any decent view to the source of the incident. Several bodies can be seen scattered around the edge of the plaza. The corpses are shriveled and in pools of their own blood, as though they were forcefully exsanguinated. The whole scene is quite grisly, and Private Trian has to exert effort to not retch. Ceto relaxes somewhat, seeing that with so many guards around, the panic-inducing danger he witnessed earlier must've passed. The guards eye the escort as they pass, but noticing the captain's uniform, leave them be.

It takes another few minutes to reach the margrave's mansion that's on the opposite end of the plaza. Squads of guards that have been recalled are congregating at the barracks next to the margrave's mansion for briefing, and military priests move between the bodies. They recite prayers of purification, creating white, holy flames that briefly engulf the remains, rendering them unto ash in moments.

*   *   *

Inside the mansion, the scene isn't nearly as hectic. Priests fulfill the role of information relay, and though there isn't enough enlisted to station one in every corner of Irisul, they undoubtedly prioritize the margrave's residence to relay his orders instantly to the appropriate officers in the city. Ceto is more comfortable being in here with the mild-mannered employees than around the hardened military guards.

Captain Dinn addresses the other two, "I will inform Margrave Rosenclair of our arrival. You wait here." He proceeds to walk through the commons to ascend the nearby flight of stairs. He advances out of sight as he rounds the first hallway corner.

Contrarily, Ceto moves to the nearest chair meant for guests and sits, and Private Trian waits diligently to the side. Ceto considers making more small talk with the guard, but no sooner he can decide on a topic, the metallic steps of the guard captain suppress the notion. The two silently observe him descend the stairs and near before he tells Ceto, "Margrave Rosenclair will see you now, follow me," with a gesture to Trian.

"You could've had another priest message her. Don't you guys prioritize efficiency?"

"The priest corp is hard at work and do not need to be bothered with a trivial matter, Baron Sleir."

The subtle jab at Ceto does not go unnoticed, but just like Trian's poor bow from earlier at his house, he rolls with it quietly. Pleased with himself, Captain Dinn ascends the stairs once more, with the other two following as usual.

Ceto finally concludes on an inquiry for Trian, "Just how long were you and the captain in my neighborhood before you received the order for my escort?"

Trian is taken aback by the seemingly random question, but as she begins to answer, the captain cuts her off, "No fraternizing, Private."

"Sir!"

The captain knew Ceto's intent in asking that question and didn't want to give him the satisfaction of knowing that Dinn had been staking out the baron's place for a suspicious amount of time. Ceto grunts in amusement and the last stretch of the escort ends with silence. Minutes later, the three reach the margrave's office in the back of the third floor, with two guards stationed outside the door. As those guards see the captain's return, one of them turns to knock on the door to announce their arrival prior to opening it and ushering them in.

The office is a large rectangular room with bookshelves lining the left with many books and furniture for relaxation against the right. A larger table stands in the middle covered in various maps and documents, and a personal desk in the rear center faces away from a large stained-glass window. The margrave in question sits behind his desk, a handsome middle-aged man with clean, angular features, and short, slicked-back blonde hair. He wears an exquisite dark blue uniform that's designed to accentuate his authority, and two ornate pins with a rose motif decorate the sides of the folded collar, the bright reds stark against the dark blue. He pores over an open book while referencing a stack of records beside it. His left-hand writes notes upon parchment on the other side of the book, while his right listlessly stirs a cup of tea. It gives an impression of naturally higher levels of intellect that Ceto finds rather obnoxious.

The captain and private each hold a sharp salute to announce their arrival, to which, after a few moments, the Margrave reacts by looking at them directly to acknowledge their presence. Dinn speaks, "Margrave Rosenclair, as commanded, I have brought Baron Sleir."

Seeing Ceto, Rosenclair smirks, "Captain Dinn, find Major Donatus in the plaza for your next assignment. Private Trian, wait outside."

Both answer "Sir!" in unison and do as ordered.

With just the two of them in the office, Ceto looks to move towards the sofa but Rosenclair interrupts him, "Don't sit down, this won't take long." Ceto clicks his tongue and remains standing. "Do you know about what happened in the Grand Plaza?"

Ceto shakes his head with a casual shrug, "I saw some bodies walking in, but I don't know what it's about."

"There was a protest by the commoners earlier over the Viscount Riveostinlu murders."

"What about it?"

"Don't interrupt me—it's immaterial anyway. During the protest, something occurred within the crowd that caused the people to die and end up as you saw them. The initial estimate is at least a hundred and fifty dead, perhaps more we haven't found yet. All questioning of witnesses so far has turned over no reliable information. Many ran away when panic set in, so we will begin canvassing the residential district for them within the hour. In the meantime, I need you to fulfill your obligation and work the case." Throughout the margrave's monologue, his right hand continues to stir the tea.

Recalling that he was himself a witness to the gruesome outbreak on the citizens and their horrible state of death, Ceto considers his options to avoid embroilment. He knows that Rosenclair is practically a wall in negotiations and would definitely disregard any attempt to deflect this burden, so the next best thing is to get as much as he can out of it, "Fine, but this counts double and I get to stop as soon as your subordinates give you information from the leftover witnesses."

Rosenclair scoffs. He brings out a new sheet of parchment and begins writing in it, no longer letting Ceto into his view. He replies to the demand with audible contempt, "Your pitiful attempt at dancing gives me stress, so I'll explain your options—this will count as one, as it should, and you will see it through to the end. Or, you can serve your previous sentence, your assets are confiscated for Her Honour's Holy Order, and you'll have a rough ten or so years left when you're released. After all, you were gifted with a long, nevertheless wasted, life. Not even that baronet family would associate with you if they were fortunate enough to be around. Ah, but I am in a giving mood, so I will amend your original sentence; for all that, you will still perform this task and suffer the imprisonment right after. I will assume by your silence in the next moments that you have chosen what benefits you the most, as usual. You are in no position to appeal, so it is too easy to predict what you will do with just a tiny push."

Ceto imagines giving the margrave a crisp backhand slap against his noble face while hurling profanities, but swallows his dignity so he doesn't give Rosenclair the excuse. He did state that Ceto's silence should be the answer, so he isn't going to risk it being literal.

Rosenclair remarks with disinterest, "As I thought." He finishes writing, waves the parchment to dry the ink, and folds it into thirds. He then holds it out to Ceto, "Give this to Private Trian, she will supervise you. Any information you find you will report directly to her. The guards will give you access to the plaza and won't bother your work."

Ceto walks over to receive it with a sigh.

"Incompetence won't be tolerated," he adds. The margrave no longer acknowledges Ceto's presence, returns to reading, and finally takes a drink of his tea.

Ceto removes himself from the room right away, closing the office door behind him. Outside, the protecting guards stay at attention while Trian a bit further away waits. Ceto approaches her and hands over the parchment, "From Margrave Rosenclair."

She accepts and unfolds it to read the contents. Ceto is unable to make out anything on it from his angle. Trian nods as though the note was the margrave himself, and refolds it. She looks up to Ceto, "Proceed as needed, Baron Sleir."

Ceto nods in turn with a sullen expression, strolling past her for the stairs down.

*   *   *

Returning to the Grand Plaza for the third time, Ceto leads Trian to the scene of the incident. As they move across the front street towards the throng of guards surrounding it, he gives serious contemplation to his predicament.

Over the course of the last three years, this will be Ceto's seventh obligation out of his sentence of fifty. At the rate of two a year, he'll be done in a little over twenty, which is significantly better than the original sentence of one-hundred-and-twenty-years imprisonment. His conviction was passed down under a different margrave, who gave him the controversial work-release option. That margrave retired within the year, replaced by Rosenclair. Rosenclair's dominating attitude towards him was readily apparent but was fine with upholding the judgment. He had even given some ground and counted Ceto's last obligation as two, hence Ceto's attempt to negotiate again. Rosenclair's sudden reversal is strange, but considering how he always treats Ceto, that he allowed it the first time is more astonishing. Ceto can't do anything about it, so he can only speculate why. The thing that immediately comes to mind is this obligation he's about to delve into. It's certainly the bloodiest one he's done yet, but speculating on the significance won't do him any good with only this perspective. He is the filter through which the details will drain, so he can only perform as he's required and form conclusions as the information presents itself.

Thinking unto here, Ceto is a few feet from the guards. The nearest one stands in the way with a hand out to signal him to halt, and addresses him, "The plaza is closed to civilians, please state your business."

"I am Baron Sleir, under commission by Margrave Rosenclair to investigate the incident. I must be as close to the epicenter as possible to work."

The guard gives a slight bow, "My apologies, Baron Sleir. Please wait here while I authenticate your claims."

Before he can leave to do so, Trian speaks up, "I can authenticate for him."

"You are?"

"Third Chaplain Trian."

The inconsistency surprises the guard, "Chaplain? Why are you in a guard's uniform?"

"I served as Private Trian until a few minutes ago, and have yet to receive a priest's uniform."

Having to deal with a rare logistical impasse, the guard scrutinizes Trian, and elects to respond with caution, "I understand, but I need to authenticate." He leaves to find his superior.

Ceto faces Trian and helplessly shrugs with a smirk.

It doesn't amuse her, "Baron Sleir, do you have anything on your person to prove your identity? I will inform the other chaplains of your investigation, but the guards will need proof to let you into restricted access areas. I would like to avoid wasting time to observe this authentication procedure every time."

"That won't be a problem when you get into the priest uniform."

She shifts her gaze as she ponders the statement, turning to just ask, "Why?"

"As you say, the guards will follow the priest's words that I am to be given access. This happened because you're still in your guard uniform. If you were a priest from the start, we would already be in there. Thus, the problem is not proving my identity, but proving yours."

Trian opens her mouth wanting to refute the claim, but closes it realizing that what Ceto says is true.

Ceto casually waves his hand to dismiss the matter, "It's a trivial thing. You have military soldier protocol on your mind, so you haven't gotten used to the idea that you have a higher range of influence as a priest."

Trian is not amused, "Please don't patronize me, Baron Sleir."

Ceto chuckles, "You learn quick. If you were still a guard, any other noble would have you disciplined for that impudence just now."

Trian exhales in frustration and ignores him.

The guard from earlier soon returns, bowing again as he gestures towards the plaza, "Sorry for the delay. You may continue, Baron Sleir and Chaplain Trian."

Ceto moves past him, followed by Trian.

The Grand Plaza is a vast area, consisting of four equal streets that border the plaza's cobblestone square. Within the square, eight marble pillars encircle around three large water fountains. The water fountains themselves are in a triangular formation, while in the very center between them is an immaculate sculpture dedicated to Chevalier—the Empress of the Holy Order of Knights, more widely referred to as the Her Honour. Ceto expects that the originating area would be near this sculpture, but to his surprise, it is actually further behind, closer to the third water fountain. He warily recalls how close he was to this fountain before he had left as he walks past the statue towards it.

The priests' pace of purification gradually closes inward, but they have yet to reach here, where the greatest number of victims can be seen. Ceto steps up onto the basin wall to look around, and he notices the bodies sprawl outward from the fountain in an almost deliberate way. He calls for Trian, "Stand up here, tell me what you see."

To sate her own curiosity, she does so. Her expression is equally shocked as she realizes the same thing, though her tone is unwavering, "It's as though a great gust of wind burst out to fell them."

"My thoughts as well, but it doesn't explain the state of the corpses being withered husks in pools of blood."

Trian repeats his last words to herself in deep thought, "Pools of blood..."

He faces her for a moment, "Are you able to handle looking at it? You can leave if you'd like."

She quickly recollects herself, "I can handle it just fine, Baron Sleir, I was thinking of something else, so do not mind me." She steps down from the fountain with a huff, "But I cannot let you out of my sight, so can you stop stalling? Margrave Rosenclair wants information as fast as possible."

"I'm not stalling, Chaplain Trian," Ceto pronounces her title to mock her soldierly inflection, "I gather the information and make the conclusions through my own process. I'm here, aren't I? I have already begun working." He also steps down, sweeps a glance over the area one more time, and turns back Trian with some deviousness, "Also, I have a favor to ask."

Trian is becoming continuously more irked by her charge, and it shows, "...What?"

"I now require a minimal amount of silence. Normally I'd use earplugs, but they're at my mansion. And since you are prioritizing speed, then I expect you do not want to take the time to retrieve them and come back. Furthermore, due to the nature of the effort, I am unable to use my own hands, so I must ask you to cover my ears until I'm done."

She eyes him with extreme doubt and doesn't move.

"I go into a trance to see what others would miss, but the other senses become painfully keen. For taste and smell, I'd like you to beseech Her Honour with an Orison of Cleanliness. And then for touch and sound, you'll also have to remove your gauntlets, as they will be too cold."

Trian tries her best to find an indication of sarcasm or a trace of lying within Ceto's expression, but can only conclude he's either deathly serious or has the Duplicitous One's blessing. She sighs, probably one of many she'll have the rest of the day. She begins to unfasten the hand armor, "Fine. I'm interested in what sort of special work you do that garnered the Margrave's recognition."

"Ah, so you don't know?"

"Of course I don't. I was only a private until a while ago, and privates don't need to know the details." She considers the attention he brought to a minor point, "Why? Is there something I should know?

Now Ceto thinks about how to answer. Regarding their brief interactions so far, she's already skeptical of him and she's clearly sensitive enough to notice the hint there might be something more than on just the surface level. He assumes she would've already known from the margrave's written order, but her choice of words, like "recognition", wouldn't accurately describe his situation. He doesn't know how long the investigation is going to last, and it's likely she will discover him being under work-release rather than the commission he had stated earlier. Reasoning up to this point, Ceto figures there's merit to telling the truth and show his sincerity first.

"I was convicted of grand larceny a few years ago. But due to my good behavior, good connections, and good looks, they gave me a sentence in which I must provide my services to the Holy Order whenever they require it, and in return, I avoid prison and keep my legally earned assets."

Trian silently absorbs the confession, but she carries a look of understanding, as the baron's odd treatment makes more sense knowing the reason. "Who did you steal from?" she asks before she makes a personal judgment.

"Ohh, a dozen barons, a handful of counts and viscounts, and, uh..." he pauses to scratch behind his ear with a measure of humility, "Margrave Pralmoy."

The priest in plate armor studies the thief closely, and merely responds with a simple, "Hmph," but her face remains emotionless, as though unimpressed. She finishes removing her gauntlets and sets them aside on the basin wall.

Ceto turns around to show her his back, "From behind, so you're not blocking my view."

Trian abides without further retort. As Ceto feels her hands cover the sides of his head, he takes a deep breath to steady himself. He closes his eyes and, within the mirror of the mind, imagines a small sterling disc within an eternally dark space—his divine focus. The process is but a moment, and when he reopens his eyes, wisps of silver gliding across like water over spheres. Through Ceto's perspective, as these wisps move over his vision, they reveal the environment so bright all color is greatly desaturated, the contours of the physical world covered in thin white strands that bend and flow like wheat in a storm. Behind him, he can hear Trian mutter words of prayer to her goddess, Chevalier. The vibrations of her voice travel through her limbs to his ears, as though she were yelling it. The taste of metal is heavy upon his tongue as he breathes through his mouth, the fabric of his silk clothes rough and the warm air stinging. But Trian soon completes her orison, and the metallic air gradually melts to fresh, no longer offensive to Ceto's tongue and nose. The orison isn't truly necessary for him to work, but that doesn't mean he'll willingly endure it if it can be helped. However, curbing his already acute hearing is essential.

With his ability invoked, Ceto patiently observes his surroundings. Within the environment of the silver wisps, the bodies of the victims can be seen laying on the cobblestone as they have been, but the figures of Ceto and Trian perform their actions as they had just moments ago, stepping up and down from the basin wall, but in reverse. They walk backward away from the fountain towards the mansion. Some minutes pass and a man in a chaplain uniform walks backward in front of him, coming from the south street and towards the mansion as well. After him, a squad of guards in blindingly shiny armor slowly step in reverse, circling the area and sometimes stopping to look down at a corpse. They, too, leave to rejoin other shining guards in the distance. After a while, the vast majority of the guards briskly march in reverse from the various street openings around the plaza, leaving only about a dozen left.

As all these figures come and go, the blood upon the ground slowly rises and becomes damper. Then, the corpse furthest from the fountain has a slight, visual twitch. Then a more prominent one and the blood around it rises, flowing up across the frame. The once withered body swells, regaining color and shape. Near it, the process begins with a few more. Then a dozen more. Gradually, the fresh blood replenishes the dead all around him. Newly arisen, the victims fearfully run in reverse away from the water fountain. Further away, the commoners who avoided their fate appear from around the street corners to similarly run back to their protest. While he witnesses the scene more intimately, he keeps a close watch for one specific thing, the first victim. Whoever died first would be the closest to the impetus, and he could start from there.

Each time Ceto turns his head, Trian subtly shifts her position to keep his ears blocked. She does not understand what exactly he's doing, but she is able to get a glimpse of his eyes when he turns his head enough to one side. Compared to when he had first started, the wisps of silver are revolving around them significantly faster. She can plainly tell something is happening, but she's never heard of a prayer with this kind of effect. It seems to have lasted for almost ten minutes already, and she wonders how much longer it will take.

With his free hands, Ceto performs the faint motions to enact his limited control on the ability. He can slow or speed up the process to a certain degree, but if a moment is missed, he cannot freely go back to it again. The closer the people recongregate, the more Ceto decelerates the flow to its slowest. Then, he notices something peculiar. Ceto establishes that, without fail, those that are close to the fountain have invariably succumbed, with the furthest ones having made it about a hundred feet away. He recalls that he did not see any bodies in the streets outside the plaza, nor any priests purifying remains there, meaning all victims were unable to make it out from the plaza before dying. And then those that are closer to the proper protest, roughly sixty feet away, escape seeing another day. There has not been any variance in these inferences out of the hundred or so commoners around him, but then he sees a figure from outside the plaza sprint rapidly towards the fountain. She gets closer, and he recognizes the lithe physique of the acrobatic jester. When she returns to her spot atop the basin wall, Ceto sees that there are only a handful of bodies that have yet to recover, and they're practically adjacent to her position. "Is it her?" he asks, but underneath the facepaint, her expression is definitely one of fear.

Ceto looks away, vigilant for the first one to die. Fortunately, the crowd gave space for the performers, which allows him to see several feet from the jester, and the first indication of something wrong is a fallen lute. An old man lays on the basin wall, collapsed on his side, and there is not nearly as much blood surrounding him. In fact, there doesn't seem to be any at all. Ceto steps closer for a better inspection. The lute shakes and falls up into the old man's hand, who grabs onto its neck. He slowly rises to his seated position, and the lute adjusts itself within his lap. The old man's fingers start to strum it in reverse. "Why are you first?" he asks, but the ghostly figure does not reply, but Ceto gazes into the man's face. As this senior musician slowly performs, the emotion in his face is undoubtedly one of rage.

*   *   *

Trian has been holding onto the sides of Ceto's head for almost three hours now, and her arms are already feeling the exhaustion of uninterrupted lifting in armor. The light of the sun has just begun to wane, signifying evening time. In her fatigue, she rhetorically asks him, "How much longer, Baron Sleir?" And to her surprise, it evokes a response.

Ceto hears Trian's question loud and clear. The resonance from her voice causes the white and silver space to roil, bringing him out of his investigative daze. He also feels exhausted, but of a different kind. The scene within his vision is of the snail-like protest, but he believes he's discovered a line to pursue. He quickly glances towards the nearby pillar, where he glimpses the figure of himself motionless against it. He closes his eyes and imagines his focus, the sterling disc, to be completely enveloped in the darkness, and ending the effect.

He raises his arms to stretch his back with a lethargic grunt, "Thank you for the assistance, Miss Trian."

Relieved, she removes her hands and lets them fall to her sides at rest, "I hope whatever you were doing was productive."

"I believe so. It gave me a couple of ideas, and a probable lead." Ceto slowly opens his eyes, letting his vision readjust to the infusion of color. He notices that the corpses that should have been in close proximity are missing.

Trian answers his confusion, "You took so long, the priests purified the rest of the remains an hour ago."

"Hmm, is that so..."

She ignores the rhetorical reply, "My chaplain uniform should be ready for. I request that Baron Sleir accompanies me while I retrieve it."

Ceto is leery, "And why is that? I have somewhere to be as well."

"That doesn't matter. You must remain where I can see you, and I am going to retrieve my uniform now."

Ceto's wariness doesn't subside, "The Margrave's orders on supervising me isn't to be taken so literally. Do you mean to watch me every waking moment?"

"If that's what's required."

"Are you going to watch me relieve myself too? Sleep in my bed?" Ceto can't help but show a sly smile at the idea.

Trian realizes the ridiculousness of her assertion and promptly corrects herself with a shred of desperation, "Of course not! But chaperoning you to the quartermaster is not a breach of privacy!"

"As you say, Miss Trian, but it goes to show that your interpretation earlier wasn't what he had in mind. It's not as though he wants us to live under the same roof."

"Oh, actually..." Trian fishes out the margrave's parchment in a defeated manner and hands it out to Ceto.

Distressed, Ceto snatches it and practically tears it open, reading the contents in his mind with Rosenclair's loathsome tone.

Third Chaplain Trian, I have authorized your transfer to the priest corp, you can receive your uniform from the chaplain quartermaster later this evening. Your first order is to supervise Baron Sleir as he performs his investigation into the Grand Plaza incident. I want no delay in receiving information, so anything he discovers he will relay with you, which you will immediately report to First Chaplain Jallen via Her Honour's Divine Words. To facilitate this, you are temporarily assigned to Baron Sleir's residence until his investigation is complete. The baron is prone to distraction, so if you feel he is preoccupied with anything other than his task, give him a severe reminder of his priorities. You have full authority to force him with whatever methods you deem necessary. Inform me of any trouble that you are unable to handle, and I will. For the Glory of Her Honour, Margrave Rosenclair of the Holy Order of Knights

Ceto crumples the parchment and throws it down, to then stomp on it as hard as he can while yelling expletives. He makes sure they're at least not blasphemous for Trian's sake. Trian silently watches with some bemusement. When he calms down with a deep breath, he speaks to her, "Okay. Let's get your chaplain uniform, then we'll go back to my manor."

Trian nods in approval, "And what of the incident? You mentioned ideas and a lead, is there anything I can share with the Margrave?"

"Hmm, not yet. I need to get my thoughts in order first. I think... once I've gotten settled and washed off today, I should have a clearer understanding."

"Very well." She turns and leads him to the chaplain's garrison to attain her uniform.

During the intermission, Ceto mulls over what he's learned. The critical figures are likely the two performers. The old man was the first to drop, but there was no loss of blood like all the others. Then there's his emotion, which Ceto confidently regards as seething anger. During any other performance, a street musician playing with that face would be off-putting, but for an angry protest, the audience would likely believe it to fit the mood.

Considering just that, a raging performance isn't so strange, but the fact that he was the first to fall can't be a coincidence.

Next is the jester girl. When she had realized what was happening—when the first few people had begun to bleed and collapse—she was the first to flee. The rest of the audience hadn't yet been fully aware of what was happening. As Ceto recalls, it was as though her leaving in a panic had woken them up to reality. With her acrobatic talent, it's no surprise she had easily passed through the crowd and disappeared into the back streets. It's possible that she's the only one who survived in spite of being so close. If that's the case, then Ceto knows that he needs to find her and figure out what makes her special in all of this. But if not, then his next step would be to figure out as much as he can about the old man. Like any small, relatable community, street performers tend to be conscious of each other, so hopefully one of them can fill in the details.

The other significant questions he has in the back of his head pertain to the time and location. Why the Grand Plaza, and why during the Riveostinlu protest? If he can answer these questions, it would directly lead to the motive, if there is one. He has suspicions, of course, but it's better to rely on evidence than speculation.

*   *   *

By the time they return to his manor, the light of the sun is already dimming halfway towards dusk. When they passed through the noble district, Ceto was tempted to stop by Stan's house as they had arranged earlier that day, but he figures it's for the best that Stan and Trian avoid meeting. Stan has a tendency to not keep himself in check around women. Trian would probably block Ceto from having the meeting anyways.

Though it is a manor, Ceto lives alone, evident by its emptiness. Ceto gives Trian a brief tour of the living room, kitchen, the guest room she'll be residing, and informing her where to find his own room and study. He does not employ any servants, so the rooms and furnishings are tidy, albeit dusty. While she gets settled, Ceto takes a quick bath to relax, and afterward, he enters his study, where a Trian in chaplain uniform is already waiting.

The room is small in size, but it evokes comfort. Bookshelves cover all available wall space from floor to ceiling, while a bay window interior protrudes from the back. Ignoring the floor, the bumped-out window seat of the bay window is the only area that allows them to sit.

The chaplain prefers standing at attention.

Ceto has the case on his mind, so avoids small talk and gets straight to the point, "Here's what we know... A little after midday, people in the protest near the square's back fountain started to rapidly bleed from their orifices. Those with weak constitutions shortly collapsed, while others who realized the situation fled in panic from the square in all directions from the focal point. According to what I saw, I believe that the focal point was a certain individual—an old man who performed the lute sitting on the fountain. I had hoped to analyze this person's corpse more closely, but a certain rookie let the priests purify the remains from right in front of me."

The priest narrows her eyes with condemnation.

"But that's not important. What is, though, is that we find the one person whom I believe survived. Aside from the lute player, there was another performer, an acrobatic woman in a jester's attire. Of all who were present when they began to perish, she was the only one who made it out of the plaza." He sifts through the various bookshelves looking for a particular book.

Trian considers Ceto's words with some thinking of her own. When he finishes, she gives a nod to indicate her following along, and she asks, "Okay, that's good to know if true, but... what happened?"

Ceto paces between the shelves in search of his book, "There's no evidence that solves that mystery yet. At best, I can form a few conjectures."

"I see. I had hoped you could give something more definitive. I don't think Margrave Rosenclair will be happy with just this."

"I agree."

Trian sighs. "Then give me your conjectures. The Margrave will decide whether to act on them or not."

"I can do that, but they may seem fanciful." He eventually finds the book, titled Aindra's Theory on the Arcane.

She shakes her head to dismiss Ceto's warning, "That doesn't concern me."

Ceto takes a seat at the bay window and opens the book, flipping through the pages whilst he speaks, "Fine. The range of the incident leads me to think of two scenarios. First, the rate at which our industries have developed has accelerated significantly since the disappearance of arcane magic. This naturally includes the alchemical field. Imagine a deranged alchemist with no talent and no empathy for his fellow man. We can no longer consider him based on his capabilities from six years ago. Amidst the advancements, he no longer needs the talent to be capable, as newly discovered tools substitute the requirement for mastery. With these tools, he can now concoct lethal admixtures that he could only dream of before. Then he decides he wants to test his new creations. As it turns out, when he decided this was today, and the greatest congregation of people available was the protest. Perfect! He tries it just to see what happens."

"For the second, imagine another person, but opposite from our deranged alchemist. This person is cold, calm, and fancies himself a step ahead of his enemies. Envision that, whatever his reason, he decides to worship the Insatiable One."

With the mention of the Insatiable One, Trian is immediately on her guard.

"That would make his enemies anyone and everyone. Ultimately, he finds himself here, in Irisul, where he desires to mar anything connected with the Victorious One. He goes to the Grand Plaza square, prays to his goddess for blood, and is bestowed much of it because there are a few hundred pints around him."

Before Ceto can continue, Trian interrupts him, "I know you're just explaining your thoughts, but do not utter Her Honour and that filth in the same breath again. Chaplains find it blasphemous."

"You condemn her and her followers like they don't exist, but our world is devised of many kinds. There is bound to be someone who thinks themselves worthy of her blessing. Or they dream up reasons why they must go against Her Honour. As I said, whatever the reason, it doesn't matter. With the fall of the arcane, the people find new things to rely on, whether it's the sciences or faith. The extremes of both culminate in the scenarios I outlined. They're rare, but it only takes one."

"I'm well aware, Baron Sleir. These scenarios of yours, how likely do you think they are?"

"Not very. Only... 'filth' would go against Her Honour so openly, the Duplicitous One wouldn't approve of something like this, nor is it the Calamitous One's style, she's showier. But then that would imply that a worshiper of filth had penetrated Irisul's gates, which is—"

"No, that wouldn't happen," Trian finishes for him.

"Right. A deranged alchemist is the more likely one, but my rudimentary understanding of alchemy tells me otherwise.

Alchemical weapons do not discriminate, which runs counter to the old man's condition and the jester's escape. And the way the bodies were laid out is way too deliberate."

Trian carefully considers Ceto's observations, "I am not learned in alchemy, so I'll take your word for it. But I am in the matters of faith. I agree, this incident is something filth would do, but they are unable to enter Irisul due to Her Honour's Blessing.

"Nevertheless, the signs indicate that it's magical in nature." Ceto closes his book and sets it aside.

"So?"

"Come on, Trian, you're still thinking like a soldier. What's the first requirement to invoke the magic of the divine?"

She closes her eyes and raises a hand to pinch the bridge of her nose, feeling the start of a headache. However, she quotes one of the teachings of her church, "'A faithful prayer to the living deity, by the faithful, for divine presence'..." With a sudden realization, her eyes jolt open. "If there was no priest, then no prayer. If there's no prayer, there's no divine presence." She turns to Ceto in confusion, "Where did the magic come from?"

Ceto's face brightens when she finally asks the important question, "That's what I want to know."

*   *   *

The next morning, Ceto and Trian stroll through Irisul's westerly districts in search of their mysterious jester girl. In his vision, he witnessed her running from the western direction, and Trian agrees with the assumption. Ceto believes that if they ask around with the truth that they're searching for a survivor of the Grand Plaza Massacre, it's being called, they may be given the run-around to protect the girl. Instead, they establish a cover story that, Ceto being an actual noble, he supports the performing arts and was fortunate to witness a previous performance by the girl, and so is looking for her for a prospective sponsorship. Artists and entertainers view sponsorships akin to being set for life, so it should help convince the wary that they would help to point her out. As for Trian, she's just a very religious handmaid who attends Ceto in his outings. By the time Ceto introduces her as such, it's too late for her to express dissent, lest she ruins their cover.

Over the course of a rough two hours, they eventually come across an open, moderately populated street known for its street performers. Ceto directs Trian towards a dramatic actor attracting laughter and strange glances, while he inquires with acrobats across the way.

Trian converges on the actor, who is dressed up in cheap clothing meant to mimic a gross exaggeration of a noble, his face covered in white makeup and wearing a ridiculous wig. There's no doubt in Trian's mind that Ceto purposefully chose this one for her. But, surely the man behaves normally outside his performance, so Trian advances to the front of the modest audience, waiting for a pause in the monologue to interject.

The actor stands straight, looking slightly up and over the people as though they aren't there, speaking to himself in a shrill voice, emphasizing specific words with rises in his tone, "I was looking through the letter, and he wrote *several* pages on fashion, and with interest to my manor's waterfall valance curtains, his advice was very peculiar indeed. He said, and I have this memorized for such a moment of offense, that its style *harmonizes* with my figure, and its color with my complexion. Hmph, the *nerve!* I am much paler than my curtains!" Those watching chuckle at the parody.

Trian takes the opportunity to speak up, "Excuse me, sorry to interrupt, but I—"

The actor shamelessly interrupts her instead, "Reginald! Reginaaald!? Why is this church-bell speaking to me? I demand an explanation for her presence, at once! Must I explain that I, Baron Von Pue, does *not* consort with the common street rabble? Assuredly not!"

"No, no, I'm looking for—"

"And you're not even asking how I am before introducing yourself! Did your parents not educate you on proper manners? Tell me your name so that I may know whom I look down upon! Reginald, write this down!"

She quickly answers, trying to get as much in as she can before he can cut her off again, "I'm a maid in the service of Baron Sleir. I'm looking for a girl who—"

"A mere *baron's* maid! What has the Holy Order come to, allowing—"

Becoming impatient with the farce, Trian takes her chance to interrupt him back, "Enough with the act! I'm looking for an acrobatic girl who likes to dress like a jester. Baron Sleir would like to offer her a sponsorship. Do you know where she is?"

Baron Von Pue dramatically places the back of a hand to his forehead, turning away and letting out a loud, absurd cry, "Ahh! How *ghastly!* I am absolutely overwhelmed with distraught! I cannot even *think* faced with such aggression!"

"Do you know where she is, or not!?" She can't help getting caught in the actor's pace.

Baron Von Pue glances at Trian from his side with a frown a second, clicks his tongue, and points up behind her, capitulating in his regular voice, "Yeah, she's up there."

She turns to follow the gesture, looking up to the roof of a two-story building across the street, and spots a figure in red and black clothing sitting upon the edge. The figure swings her legs energetically as she regards the scene below. Trian also notices Ceto is right behind her, who is similarly peering up. He doesn't bother to hide his smile, as he was clearly a member of the audience watching the comical dialogue.

Ceto waves at the girl on the roof, and she waves back but doesn't move. He gestures for her to come down, but the girl shakes her head and mimics the gesture, telling him to come up instead. Behind him, Baron Von Pue resumes his act, "Reginald, I feel a *draft* coming on! Reginald!?"

"How much experience have you acquired in scaling up buildings?" Ceto inquires Trian.

"None."

"Alright, guess I'll go." Ceto moves across the street to the other side, looking for the easiest way to climb up. He decides on a neighboring structure that possesses large windows and a low angled, conjoining roof. He determines doing it her way should make a good first impression on Cloro. He takes it slow, but steady. His natural, half-elven agility helps to not make a fool of himself, or break his neck. It takes but a couple of minutes, and Ceto makes it to the top. From there, he carefully strides over to the roof Cloro resides.

Cloro claps with enthusiasm when he's near, "You made it!"

Ceto perches nearby but does not risk sitting on the edge as she does. Here, he gets a good look at her. She appears to be twenty or twenty-one years of age, her golden-blonde hair is long and styled into two braids that reach down her back. Her child-like features indicate that she's human, but her green eyes seem to elicit a light-pinkish shine around them. Even for him, it's the first he's seen that kind of characteristic. As for her outfit, it's made from leather that perfectly fits her nimble form. He's yet to see her standing evenly next to him, but Ceto thinks she's probably taller than him.

"Yes, well... I needed to talk to you."

"Mhm! My friends told me you were looking for me. A sponsor! I must be really lucky; acrobats never get sponsors."

Cloro's lively attitude is odd to Ceto. This is definitely the one he saw before, but she doesn't seem to have the mood of someone who survived a massacre yesterday. "I'm happy for you. But Cloro, there's something I need to ask you before I can accept."

"Ohh, what's that? I'll answer as best I can!"

"Yesterday, you were performing in the Grand Plaza square, weren't you?"

Cloro becomes discouraged instantly, "Yeah, I was."

"Can you tell me about the old man who played the lute?"

"He... I don't want to talk about him, it makes me sad."

"Why would you be sad?"

"Because he was a friend, and he gave up."

"Gave up what?"

Cloro shows anger for the first time, "Oh! Why do you keep asking me questions about Cothoza? You said something, not four things!"

Ceto lets out a light chuckle, "You're right, I apologize. I'm asking about Cothoza because I think he had something to do with the people who died yesterday, and I think you do too."

Cloro pulls her legs up and hugs her knees wordlessly.

"To tell the truth, I've been tasked by Margrave Rosenclair to figure out what happened, so that he knows how to prevent people from dying like that again. If you answer my questions and help me to understand what happened, I promise to sponsor you. Or, if you don't want me, I can recommend you to Viscount I know."

Cloro gives him a sideways glance to study him, and after a few minutes of silence, responds, "He called it 'isiqalekiso'."

"What does that mean?"

"In our language, it means a curse."

Ceto is first perplexed by the idea that the word wasn't gibberish, but belonged to a wholly different language, and one unlike he's ever heard. But more importantly, the incident being a curse carries powerful implications, if true. "Cloro, how long have you known Cothoza?"

"We met seventy-three days ago."

"And what reason did he have to tell you about isiqa—isiqalekiso?"

"He said I had a spirit immune to the curse, and he said that I had great wisdom because there was no difference between my belief and my truth." As she speaks, Cloro rests her head on her knees as she stares out into Irisul's horizon.

"This is... all very interesting." Based on what she's said, that means the old man had been in Irisul for a little over two months. Did he bring this curse with him, or did he develop it here?

"Did he say how one creates isiqalekiso?"

"Not really. He mentioned that imizwa was the key."

"And what's imizwa?"

"Emotion."

"Ah, that makes sense." That would explain Cothoza's anger during his performance. "Okay, one last thing I need to know, what did you mean by, 'he gave up'?"

"He was planning the curse for a while. He said his fury was too great to die, and that he would share the truth of his belief. I told him that his curse would kill many innocent people, but he said their deaths would be the truth." Cloro buries her face in her legs, plainly tired of the conversation, "He was my friend, so I tried to convince him. He was my friend, so... I thought he listened."

"Sorry, one more question, Cloro. What was he angry at?"

Cloro's answer is low and muffled, so Ceto leans in, "Sorry, say it again."

She speaks up, "He called him the Great Deceiver."

Ceto quickly stands up at the unexpected answer. He waves his arms a bit as he almost loses his balance. Down in the street, he sees Trian gazing up at them. "Thank you, Cloro. I guarantee you'll receive a sponsorship soon."

"No, I don't want it anymore."

"I'm sorry to hear that. Well, if you ever change your mind, my manor is on Deliswall Path in the southern noble district, the one with the most trees in the courtyard." Cloro doesn't move or make any sound to respond, so Ceto makes his way back down the same way he went up.

Back on solid ground, Trian hurries to Ceto and inquires, "What did she say?"

Ceto skips straight to the important parts, "I was right, it was the old man. And it is magic without a divine presence, but... it's also not like the arcane magic we knew. Something different." Ceto walks at a brisk pace back towards the plaza.

"Quit being cryptic! Just say it!"

"A curse, created a very special way, using emotions, truth, and belief." He sighs, "But no details on the process. Be that as it may..." but then abruptly stops and turns to Trian, "You should warn the Margrave right now that the water fountain itself is probably cursed. I suppose he can test it on someone if he likes."

"Don't be rude towards Margrave Rosenclair, he wouldn't sacrifice a subordinate's life just to confirm this. But I'll tell him." Trian closes her eyes and begins to mutter an Orison of Divine Message.

"Also, tell him I recommend to not let anyone touch the marble column closest to the fountain. Oh, and tell him that since I've solved this investigation, you're free to return to your own home."

Trian slaps his shoulder with a hand and exclaims, "Quiet!"

*　　*　　*

In a darkly lit room, a large figure in blackened metal armor from head to foot stares out the window in front of him, the only window and source of light for the area. From his vantage on the third floor, it provides an excellent view of the Grand Plaza below for the figure. It watches with bemusement as military priests work to purify half a dozen bodies in guard uniforms—the latest victims of the curse.

Behind the figure, a man appears from the darkness into the light and stands at attention. This one is middle-aged and lean, with an angular face and slicked-back blonde hair. The shadows of the room dampen his dark blue uniform.

The one in the black armor conveys his directive, "Margrave Rosenclair, has the trail been set?" The voice carries two separate tones as it speaks, one pleasant and smooth like that of a young man, but a deep and demonic undertone cannot be mistaken as it echoes the words.

The margrave bows respectfully before answering, performing "Affirmative. I've just confirmed the Silent Knight has met with the Jester, and now proceeds down it. Knowing him, he will not be able to help but follow it through to the end to sate his own curiosity."

"Good. It is ironic that the Mastermind's success in restoring the Arcane has provided me the opportunity to ensure his fall. And helped by one of his own, no less." A guttural laugh escapes the black helmet, "His sentimentality has always been his failing! He should have left it alone, and let you all struggle, as is your mortal obligation. He always fails to see the bigger picture, which is why he is not fit to sit where he does..." The figure trails off, brooding in anger.

The margrave retains his bowed position through the monologue, responding, "His regret will be endless."

"Mm. Make sure the Silent Knight and the Jester have continuous contact. Her soul will be important later."

"As you command. And what of the chaplain?"

"Immaterial. But she helps you keep an eye on him, does she not? Reinforce her orders, so she understands her role. If you ever believe she is compromised, discharge her immediately."

"As you command," is mimicked in confirmation, understanding the implication of permanence.

"Dismissed," emanates from the figure, and the margrave rises from his bow, turns sharply and melds back into the darkness.

Rosenclair continues through the rest of the darkly lit manor. He passes no other individuals on the way; no soldiers or servants of any kind. Yet, he can feel a supernatural presence from the darkest shadows in the corners, always watching him. He checks for any signs of people and exits from a back-entrance into an alley, heading towards the main street to his left. But before he steps out to the light, he closes his eyes in concentration, muttering a few words under his breath. No more than five seconds pass and he reopens them, proceeding forward. On the cobblestone, he swings right again, bringing the Grand Plaza before him.

A guard on duty barring entrance to the public recognizes the margrave as he approaches, and without a word, salutes, and steps aside. Rosenclair affords him a slight nod and continues forward.

In the square, Rosenclair recognizes a shouting voice belonging to Trian, "—risk, then remove the guards and other chaplains from the area! I already confirmed this with the Margrave!" He sees she is arguing with one in a guard captain's uniform, and near her, Ceto watches with his usual smirk. Other guards and officials notice the margrave and promptly stand at attention, which garners the awareness of everybody else. Trian almost performs a guard's salute, but catches herself and casually changes it into a rub of her shoulder. *Barely been a day, and already shedding the old skin,* he considers to himself.

"Baron Sleir, Third Chaplain Trian, accompany me as I give you your next orders. The rest of you, by my authority as Margrave, I decree the square is now prohibited from entry indefinitely without my direct approval. Anyone who ignores this decree will be quarantined, and then detained for five years and fined one-thousand pieces of silver. As Third Chaplain Trian warned, do not come into contact with the fountain or the column for fear of death." He glances between the faces of the guards before him, ending with, "Well, get to it."

As the guard captain's move to enforce the decree, Ceto and Trian join Rosenclair. He acknowledges them a moment before turning to walk towards his manor, continuing to address them, "Do not get relaxed just yet, Baron Sleir, your job is not done. You will sustain your investigation into this matter. Any resources you require you may request through Chaplain Trian. I want you to find out as much as you can about the perpetrator; who he was, where he's from, what he was doing in Irisul, and the mechanisms of his methods."

Ceto sighs, responding mostly to himself than the margrave, "Why should've I exp—"

Rosenclair cuts him off, "Quiet. Don't befoul the air any more than it already is with your flippant remarks. Just say 'yes'."

Ceto swallows hard, "...Yes," he answers. Trian is shocked at how brutal the margrave acts towards the baron, but she acknowledges it isn't as though Ceto doesn't deserve it.

Rosenclair addresses Trian next, "Third Chaplain Trian, I am promoting you to Second Chaplain, and will continue to monitor Baron Sleir as previously directed. I will make sure personnel is properly informed, so you should not run into any authority issues again."

Instead of her habitual 'Sir!', she properly answers as a chaplain has been taught, "As you command, Margrave Rosenclair." The elation in her tone is hard to miss.

The rest of the trek is awkward, with only their footsteps upon the stone sounding from them. At his manor door, Rosenclair halts and turns to the two, eyeing them both individually before speaking, "I appreciate the company, but you should perform your orders now. Get me results as you have been, and I'll consider rewarding your efforts." Without waiting for any response, he cuts back to the door, opening, entering, and closing it behind him.

Ceto similarly turns around, looking to the south beyond the square, "Why was he coming from there?" he asks, curious.

Trian briefly follows his gaze, and replies, "I don't know. Riveostinlu Estate is over there, so probably consulting them about the protest yesterday. It's not important. Anyways, it seems you won't be rid of me so easy." She folds her arms and a rare smile appears on her face, amused by Ceto's dilemma.

He doesn't give her the satisfaction of a retort, but changes the subject, "Right, let's get to it then. The next course of action would be..." he trails off, contemplating. Some moments pass by, and he turns back to Trian, resuming, "We're going to Apherton. We need to speak with Her Honour in person."

THE RAINS

by Alan G. Provance

Rain lashed the small tea house where Aurinka and Wolf played armies. Monsoon season had arrived two weeks ago, drenching the coastal city of Balleron and punishing the hundreds of laborers who earned their living outside, yet the city had plenty of tea and alehouses to offer respite. A cheery fire crackled in the room's central brazier, and owing to their shared dwarven heritage, Aurinka and the tea-house proprietor took good care of one another. She tended the shrine where his ancestors received gifts and prayers, while he always gave her the best seats and took the time to brew her a pot of coffee despite specializing in tea. Aurinka's undyed woolen tunic had already dried, and the steam from her coffee wafted pleasantly around her. Pondering the setup of pieces before her, after a moment she slid her tower into position near Wolf's general. The tall elf across from her gave a predatory smile and moved his warmachine to take it, prompting Aurinka to move her own warmachine down to threaten a tower and a consul.

"You have a strong command of obfuscation and misdirection for a holy woman," Wolf said with a chuckle. "Tell me, how does one of your talents pass the time between our games? Surely tending your shrine can't bring you any excitement."

"You flatter yourself." After Wolf's mock indignation and the hasty retreat of his consul, Aurinka pressed her attack. "Though in seriousness, the quiet is precisely the reason I feel grateful for my calling. Our ancestors deserve reverence, and speak infrequently. I reserve all my talking and interaction for the infrequent petitioners and a crabby elf who plays armies."

"Crabby!?" Wolf split his face with a grin. "My dear, I am the epitome of convivial. I endure being hustled by this humble dwarven priestess day in and day out, and you have the temerity to accuse me of being 'crabby'. Honestly." Moving his piece in turn, Wolf leaned back and took a sip of his tea.

He would know about obfuscation, Aurinka thought. Tea house rumors persisted that Wolf, like most of the elves in the city, lived here as an assassin in the Night-Blooming Garden. So many people assumed assassins maintained a grim affect with scars and cold stares and utter antipathy toward life. Further defying the assassin stereotype, Wolf wore silk clothing cut in the contemporary style, favoring pink and bright orange in a way that somehow didn't clash. His sepia colored skin bore no marks or scars at all, and glowed such that Aurinka suspected he used the beauty products favored by human aristocrats in the city. A handful of gold piercings and shiny shaved pate completed the look of an elf who conjured images of minstrels, not hired killers, but Aurinka knew better than to trust appearances. She also knew from personal experience that stealthy killers were adept at blending into all walks of life, such as the clergy, and she had known her friend for decades. Nothing can stay hidden forever, and their mutual understanding formed the foundation of the only strong friendship either had. Wolf interrupted her reverie with a bold move toward one of her consuls, yanking her attention back to the game.

"Tell me Aurinka, does your order bleach their hair for religious reasons, or is that a personal affectation?" Wolf's eyes twinkled as he asked, and as with most of their conversations, Aurinka knew he asked about a lot more than just hair color. Wolf never asked simple questions.

"We're devoted to the sun, as you know. We use lemon juice and spend a lot of time outdoors, and most of us dwarves bronze beautifully in the light, I think you'll agree."

"You're so vain for a nun, yet you hide the physique of a huntress in plain nun's clothing. Tsk." Wolf moved another piece. "Getting back to your hair. It feels like rain has fallen upon this city for years. Centuries, even. How do you tolerate this weather?"

The Emperor is supposed to be human, but he's lived for over three centuries. Why is Wolf bringing this up with me now?

"Rain comes and goes, stopping on its own eventually. While I'm sure we could scrape together enough mages to stop it, why bother?" Aurinka slid one of her pieces into position. The game neared its end.

"The city can only withstand so much. Any more of this deluge and half the people here might be washed away." Wolf surprised Aurinka with a threat to her remaining consul.

"Do you mean to take that up with rain clouds themselves?" Wolf balked at how close Aurinka came to disrupting their double talk. She used the surprise to elude his trap, though she couldn't get into a superior position.

"A stalemate! Aurinka darling, you're easily the second-best armies player in the city. High praise indeed for a non-elf." Languidly rising from his seat, Wolf tossed a handful of silvers onto the table. "Please, let me pay for the tea and coffee. Consider it a donation to your order."

Aurinka smiled over her mug of coffee. "Much obliged, Wolf. Will I be seeing you tomorrow?"

"Wouldn't miss it. Take care of yourself, Aurinka."

*   *   *

Monsoon rains blocked the fading light of the setting sun, bringing night down upon Balleron early. Torrential downpour smothered the city; the sounds of chatter and haggling and rowdy children had all vanished, and would have been squelched by the relentless raindrops pounding every building here. The scents of the busy city, from forgotten waste to exotic spices and perfumes from the market and everything in between, couldn't penetrate the rain either. The whole city slept as Aurinka doffed her simple nun clothing for garb spun from black sheep's wool and specially woven silk over the torso. A form-fitting jacket topped loose trousers, and her dyed-blonde hair got swept up in a nondescript head scarf common among women in the city. She smeared soot over her sun-bronzed face, completing the uniform necessary for her task, and assembled the simple weapons cleverly hidden around the shrine. Taking up her paper umbrella—a modest defense against the storm—Aurinka stepped outside and made her way to the palace.

The Brass Emperor's palace squatted atop the second largest hill in the city, and the long walk uphill could normally take an hour. Though rain dimmed the streetlamps, Aurinka had no trouble making her way through the roads, and almost no one else ventured outside this evening. Within half an hour, the hulking figure of a Praetorian warmachine emerged in the gloom, dimly backlit by lamps in the palace courtyard. Though most people couldn't see twenty feet in front of them on a night like tonight, warmachines used sophisticated magic to keep their pilots aware of their surroundings. Warmachines had also been invented by dwarves, back when the world was young, and the ancient race maintained a subtle mastery even over the designs built by humans. Aurinka grasped a talisman she wore under her shirt, and walked around the massive machine and into the courtyard. Passing within a few feet of it, she couldn't help but clench slightly as she glanced at the formidable energy cannon on the warmachine's left arm, but the pilot took no notice of her.

Praetorian guards still patrolled within the palace, their stoic reputation intact even in this weather. Aurinka knew Wolf's pattern; unlike the other patrons of the tea house, his proclivities had been revealed to Aurinka decades ago. Elven assassins all had similar infiltration methods, and as Aurinka searched hurriedly in the dark, she found a praetorian lying unconscious in a dark corner, his gear removed. Scanning the rest of the courtyard or the walls was futile, though Aurinka doubted that Wolf would tarry outside any longer than he had to. Locating a servant entrance far from any lamps, she slipped inside the palatial house dominating the Imperial estate.

Entering the kitchen, Aurinka crept silently around to the back of a distracted slave, and jumping up she managed to position her palm in just the right place on his forehead while slamming her elbow into the back of his skull. He'd wake up in a couple of hours with a splitting headache, but none the worse for wear. Aurinka had always strived to minimize kills on her missions, and she harbored tremendous sympathy for the city's slaves. That Wolf seemed to feel the same way on both counts is part of why the two had become such good friends, though Aurinka started worrying that she didn't know her friend as well as she thought. Attempting to assassinate the Emperor carried a suicidal level of risk; though

Wolf could easily slip past the praetors, the Emperor himself began his career as a formidable warrior, and became perhaps the mightiest human warrior in the history of Kytheria. He claimed half a dozen elven assassins among his kills, and Aurinka couldn't suppress the anxiety she felt on Wolf's behalf.

Tracking Wolf through the palace proved difficult. The elven assassin had disguised himself and moved more or less freely, while no dwarves worked in the palace, leaving Aurinka at four and a half feet tall with no serviceable disguise options. Instead she moved from shadow to shadow, dodging guards as she could, and making a good show of her progress despite the hurdles. Wolf didn't head directly toward the Emperor's quarters, veering off to either set up for a distant attack through a window, or perhaps because he knew the Emperor would be somewhere else. Aurinka focused on following him so much that she almost missed a guard who spotted her; to his credit he tried slipping away silently to raise the alarm, then shouted as she swiftly approached him. Republic soldiers all wore standard helmets with a large 'T' in the face and strong cheek guards, but these extended to a perfect length for Aurinka's purposes as she deflected a spear thrust and delivered a powerful backhand to the soldier's face. Deftly applied force drove the edge of the man's helmet into a nerve curving around the lower jaw and sent him reeling to the floor. A sharp kick to the same place ensured that the soldier would remain unconscious for some time, though the alarm had been raised. Still, this worked somewhat to Aurinka's advantage; an alert palace would dissuade Wolf from trying to complete his mission. Aurinka slipped back into the shadows and disappeared before the other guards arrived, but shouts spread through the palace and the barracks would be emptied in short order as the praetorians saw to their duty. Wolf's trail led Aurinka on and down a flight of steps into a cellar, which struck her as unusual. In a small room with stacks of boxed vegetables and aging cheeses, the sopping wet cloak that had left Wolf's trail for Aurinka to follow had been doffed, along with the rest of the armor Wolf appropriated. He had abandoned his disguise and seemingly disappeared.

Closing her eyes, Aurinka reached out with her mind to feel the prana swirling invisibly around her. She'd been reluctant to reach out to the breath of the planet in the main palace, as everyone knew the Emperor had been a prolific magus before his ascension and the ancient order specialized in prana manipulation. Aurinka didn't know if he could sense its use in close proximity but decided not to take the chance until now; now, she needed to find Wolf. Prana flowed with the air itself, and Aurinka felt the rush coming down toward the cellar, where it pooled slightly here, and then where it continued. Walking slowly toward the outward flow, Aurinka bumped into a stack of crates which turned out to be a hidden door.

The passage beyond had no light, but Aurinka was a dwarf and had grown accustomed to the pitch darkness under the earth long ago. Scuffing her feet as she walked, the echoes of her exaggerated footsteps constructed an image of the tunnel in her mind, allowing her to walk confidently down. The tunnel continued for fifty feet before opening into a series of catacombs. These must be closed off from the rest, thought Aurinka. There's no way the Emperor would permit a security risk like this otherwise. She'd stopped focusing on ambient prana around her, but her echo ability alerted her when one of the corpses began to slowly climb out of its alcove.

Aurinka drew the pair of kamas she carried just as light erupted from a small gem in the figure's hands. Despite the dusty, brittle armor, Aurinka recognized Wolf beneath it in a fraction of a second and diverted her kama strike from a vital area. Wolf likely recognized her too, as the dagger in his hand feinted without going for her vitals in earnest. Unsure why the other was in the palace but unwilling to give an opening, the pair eyed each other warily for a heartbeat and then surged together to clash weapons and limbs. Aurinka had devoted a human lifetime to combat with simple or no weaponry, but Wolf had spent equal time mastering every weapon under the sun, and wove a dizzying pattern with his lone dagger. Kicks were blocked, weapon thrusts parried, and after a brief exchange Wolf dropped his light gem to grab Aurinka and draw her into a grapple. The two fell to the ground, rolling in the catacomb dust until Aurinka straddled Wolf with her arms crossed and paired kamas at his throat. Wolf blocked her arms with his own, dagger perilously close to Aurinka's throat, and his other arm wrapped around her to trap her in the position with him. A long pause filled with heavy breaths followed, until Wolf finally broke the silence.

"What the hell are you doing here, Aurinka?"

She relaxed her grip slowly, and Wolf did the same. Setting her kama back in her belt, Aurinka still straddled Wolf. "I thought you'd come to assassinate the Emperor, and I came to stop you. I have no idea why you came down here, though." Wolf chuckled slightly. "I didn't peg you for an Imperialist."

"Quite the opposite. I felt concern for a dear friend, and wanted to prevent you from doing something suicidal. Surely you know of the elven assassins the Emperor has felled."

A shadow passed over Wolf's face, and Aurinka rolled off to let him up. The assassin stood up and brushed the dust and detritus off his subdued outfit. "I know better than anyone alive how well the Emperor fights," he whispered. "Rest assured, I wouldn't be so foolish as to try taking him on directly by sneaking into the palace alone one night."

"So what the hell are you doing here, Wolf?" Aurinka also dusted herself off. The two friends stood staring at each other in the catacombs, alone among the dead.

"A prophetic dream. It's an elven thing. I think I'm here to retrieve something."

"Are you serious!? You risked your life coming here for some item you're not even fully aware of, and you teased that information to me at the tea house like you were going to kill the Emperor? Damn you, Wolf!"

"Aurinka, it's more involved than you're making it out to be." Flickering torchlight appeared at the top of the stairs whence the pair had come, and Aurinka felt an intensely unpleasant sensation, as though the prana around her had been consumed, or drawn toward some great void. Wolf grabbed her arm and started pulling her deeper into the catacombs. "I meant what I implied in the teahouse," he whispered. "The rain will end soon, but that's out of my hands for now. And what I seek down here is part of that, but I couldn't say how big a part. I just know that I need to find it, and right now I'm glad you're here to help."

The pair passed through several small, twisting rooms, heading deeper into the catacombs. There weren't many branches in their path though, making Aurinka doubt they'd give their pursuers the slip. "Don't thank me yet. I'm the reason the guard knows we're here."

"Don't sweat it. The Emperor knew I'd come before I even entered the palace; he and I go way back." Wolf paused in a somewhat large room, dominated by a sarcophagus standing in the center. "There's no sense trying to hide from him. He's coming for me, and this close he can smell me out. By happy coincidence, this will be a good place to make our stand." Wolf crossed the room to the sarcophagus as Aurinka stared at him. Closing his eyes in concentration, Wolf called upon the magic all elves could tap into, and sheathed his fist with crackling energy before smashing the sarcophagus before him. Nobody waited within, but a spear fell to the floor, its dull grey blade unmarred by rust or corrosion. The smooth ash haft looked freshly polished, and even the sprig of mistletoe tied to the base of the spearhead maintained a lustrous green vibrancy. As Wolf reverently picked up the spear, Aurinka felt a rush of power from and around him, as though the world had held its breath until this moment.

"What is that spear?" she whispered. Wolf stared at the weapon transfixed for a moment before turning to face her.

"My dream... it led me here, to this spear specifically. Surely you've heard stories of ancient weapons with long, bloody histories. Honestly I think the spear itself asked me to come, as if there are events in motion that call to it and it must have a hand to wield it."

Aurinka started to ask an additional question, but heavy booted footfalls interrupted her. Torchlight flooded the hallway beyond the room where she and Wolf stood, and seconds later, half a dozen elite praetorians emerged, with a looming figure sheathed entirely in arcane-looking brass and orichalcum: the Emperor himself. Aurinka heard Wolf growl in the back of his throat, and the Emperor's gaze lingered on the elf for a second before turning to Aurinko. An ornate brass face plate and helmet cast to resemble a young, beautiful god rested on his head, leaving only his eyes exposed and looking full of a wisdom no human should be able to possess, and a sadness no human should be able to endure. The rest of his armor looked like an ancient warmachine in miniature, with pieces here and there that had clearly been replaced recently, while older patches were worn smooth from polishing. Spines emerged from his shoulders and Aurinka could hear the humming from them, indicating a collection of prana, which she certainly felt. The long purple cloak at his back framed his massive body to intimidating effect, neatly eclipsing any incredulity an opponent might have at the Emperor's paltry armament, which consisted of plain white staff etched with three runes. The praetorians moving in behind him had far more armament, and looked ready to employ it. Each bore a round shield and short spear with a falcata and dwarven pistol tucked into their belts, complete with steel armor from head to toe. They'd made no move yet, waiting for the Emperor to give the command or for their opponents to strike first. Staring once again at Wolf, the Emperor broke the silence.

"Good to see you, old friend. It's been some time." The deep voice rolled from the Emperor and around the large room, filling the space. "You look good."

"Three centuries is plenty of time to heal, friend. Though not if one lives them as you have, I suppose." Wolf spoke evenly, but Aurinka could almost feel his tension, and noticed the iron grip he maintained on the spear. At a signal from the Emperor, the six praetorians spread out to surround Wolf and Aurinko. Four of them opted to discard their spears, drawing falcatas or pistols.

"I'm not sure why you waited this long to break in or what this spear can possibly do for you, Loki, but I'll give you one chance to drop it to the ground and leave here alive. Old age has given me patience, but my foolishness is spent, and I'll brook no deviation from my terms."

Several things happened suddenly at once, with Aurinka saved only by the grace of long training and honed instincts. Wolf moved in a blur to strike at the Emperor, while two praetorians fired their pistols and the other four moved in to swing at Aurinka. Almost as soon as the spear struck, blinding light erupted from the impact, coupling with the reverberated pistol reports to utterly daze all nine figures in the room. Aurinka dimly felt prana rushing back into the room, as though the vacuum draining it had been disrupted, and focusing herself she managed to stand and blink the spots out of her eyes in seconds. One of the bullets had struck her silk armor but hadn't penetrated, and the praetorians' helmets somewhat protected them from the flash and bang, but they were just coming around. The Emperor had fallen to his knees, panting heavily, but as Wolf moved to make a coup de grace, dark orange flames and oily black smoke spurted out from the Emperor's hand, forcing Wolf to spin away as the dark fire licked at his clothes. Aurinka set herself to the task of taking down the bodyguards, grasping the spear haft of one and levering him into another, knocking both askew. *We can't face him. Wolf, please don't try to finish this. We need to leave.* Already the Emperor had begun drawing ambient prana into himself, now with a hunger that hadn't been there before. Aurinka moved toward the exit, parrying a falcata with her kama and bringing a knee up underneath the armored skirt of her foe. The man doubled over in pain and offered no resistance to the knockout blow that followed, leaving only one man between Aurinka and freedom. Looking back briefly to check on Wolf, Aurinka could scarcely believe what she saw. Wolf danced through the room with such grace that he almost flowed, the spearhead licking out to cut and chip away at the three praetorians who tried to confront him. It took mere seconds for him to drop all three, and despite legends of elven grace, Aurinka didn't believe it possible for any mortal to move as swiftly as he did. Disarming the praetorian before her of his pistol, Aurinka delivered a sharp kick to the knee with a satisfying crack and wheeled around to slam the butt of her newly acquired pistol into the temple of the last guard as he collapsed. She turned just in time to see Wolf charging the Emperor, and she reflexively squeezed her eyes shut.

Another dazzling flash erupted, washing over Aurinka with the warmth of prana. She whirled around to see the Emperor standing his ground, not staggered as before, and gripping the spear near the blade. Wolf had been caught off guard, and now strained mightily against the Emperor's grip, trying to drive the spear home into the Emperor's throat. In the fading torchlight Aurinka could make out what looked like black lightning crackling between the spear and the Emperor's hands, as though he were draining it of its energies. Wolf had started perspiring, while the Emperor straightened his posture, now looming over the elven assassin. Almost without thinking, Aurinka rushed the Emperor, sliding on her knees to bring her kama right into the back of his leg. Roaring in pain, the Emperor swung around, but his concentration on the spear broke and Wolf yanked it from his grasp only to whirl the butt around and slam the Emperor in the face. Aurinka followed up by unloading her new pistol directly at the Emperor's mask; though she sincerely doubted such a weapon would do any lasting harm, the small explosion temporarily blinded and dazed the Emperor, forcing him to stagger backward. Wolf hesitated for a second and seemed to weigh a final attempt on the Emperor's life before thinking better of it and dashing to the hallway with Aurinka, as pillars of fire burst from the ground around the Emperor. Even blinded and down on one knee, the leader of the Republic could not be defeated, and his deep laughter chilled both of the figures who charged back through the catacombs to race up the stairs.

At the secret entrance the pair used, six more praetorians lay in wait, sending spears and bullets through the door as soon as they realized it was the intruders. Like Aurinka, Wolf had grabbed a dwarven pistol down below, and the elf stood shoulder to shoulder with the dwarf as their respective silk armors absorbed the bullets. A split second later the two parted to hurl the spears and their wielders down into the passage using their own momentum, and both emptied their firearms at the remaining guards. Aurinka's sensibilities about the preservation of life were a luxury she could ill afford against so many armed and trained opponents, while Wolf didn't have the same compunction. The spearmen sorted themselves out and tried to return up the stairs, but Wolf's new weapon shot out and parried the oncoming attacks while neatly slicing the throats of the last praetorians. One made a valiant effort to press the attack despite his imminent death, but a sharp kick from Aurinka to the breadbasket sent him staggering back, what little breath he had now expelled. Wolf hurled the remaining guards into the passage along with a couple of crates to slow down the Emperor, who surely pursued them, before ducking into another room nearby with Aurinka. The palace buzzed with activity as the Praetorian Guard swarmed the halls, with the entirety of the palace barracks turned out and on alert.

"Well, Loki, here we are. How did you think you'd be able to do this by yourself? I'm not even sure if we'll be able to get out working together. It only takes one praetorian getting lucky to end a career tonight."

Wolf shook his head. "I haven't been 'Loki' in a long time. As for getting out of here, I've got an idea, but it will *not* be discreet." Waiting for the nearest guards to pass by, Wolf slunk out of the room, with Aurinka close behind. The two moved as quickly and silently as they could, darting from shadow to shadow, though the sheer number of guards made this difficult. Aurinka felt the prana around her shifting and rolling away, meaning the Emperor approached. Rolling out from her hiding place she buried the points of her two kama in praetorian necks, while Wolf took her cue and sent his spear through the neck of a third. The rest of the squad, five guards, stared at the two dumbfounded while Wolf and Aurinka each dropped another guard. Finally the three remaining praetorians regained their wits and began yelling out as they bore down on Wolf and Aurinka with their swords. Aurinka peeled one shield away with her kama and slashed her opponent's sword arm, barely dodging the attack from another praetorian. Wolf feinted with his spear and tossed a handful of fine sand directly into his opponent's eyes, sending her staggering. Reversing his spear he swept the legs out from the last guard as Aurinka nimbly evaded a shield bash to plant her foot and throw her bleeding foe to the ground. The Emperor's vacuous presence drew closer, and that coupled with the rattling armor of approaching guards sent Wolf and Aurinka running to the exit without finishing off their opponents.

Outside, the continuous rain had intensified, making the guards' work harder. Wolf and Aurinka ducked into a small alley between two outbuildings and surveyed the grounds, both noting that four warmachines now prowled the area, actively searching for intruders. All four were of the same type, a ponderous machine resembling a mobile fortress more than an agile fighter on a grand scale. The torsos looked like fancy conical helms on a pair of legs, with arms weighed down by lightning emitters. Aurinka hadn't looked too closely on her way in, but now as she waited for Wolf to unveil his plan, she took the time to appreciate these human manufactured devices. For a short-lived race they turned out some truly impressive feats of magical engineering and sophistication.

"They're not as pretty as elven machines" Wolf yelled, as if reading her thoughts. The rain drowned out so much sound the two could have shouted at each other all night without drawing attention. "You can become invisible to their sensors, right?"

Aurinka grasped the talisman under her thoroughly soaked shirt. "I can indeed. How'd you know?"

Wolf grinned. "It's my business to know things like that. Here." Pressing a small disc into her hand, Wolf readied his spear. "I need you to run over to one of those machines and climb up top. Once there, I'll join you."

Aurinka stared at him. "You want me to attack the largest warmachine humans make by myself, on foot? Look, I know this isn't the time, but you owe me explanations for all the shit that's happened tonight."

Wolf nodded. "Of course. And know that I really appreciate you being here, Aurinka, whatever happens. Now go get 'em."

Wrapping her talisman around her hand and gripping her kama, Aurinka waited until one of the massive machines got within fifty feet and dashed out from cover, running full tilt. Trusting its sensors, the warmachine had no light source and the patrols of guards carried only dim lamps, making her run surprisingly anticlimactic. Reaching the warmachine Aurinka leapt toward the knee and buried her kama into the joint, pulling herself up and repositioning before the next step trapped her weapons. The edges were dull, but the metal and points reinforced specifically for climbing, and even in the pouring rain Aurinka mounted the thirty-foot-tall machine in seconds. Sinking a kama into a seam in the metal, Aurinka grasped the disc Wolf had given her and he appeared beside her in a small flash of light. Though she was somewhat surprised, Aurinka maintained her grip and extended a hand to Wolf, who grasped her forearm and with all the strength and leverage he could muster drove his new spear straight down through the metal into the cockpit. The spearhead parted the steel carapace of the machine as though it were butter, and the metal titan lurched and stumbled, indicating that the spear had found its mark. In the blink of an eye Wolf had pulled out his spear and slid down to grab the hatch release and open up the machine. The pilot's body hung limply in its harness, unarmored with the runed sword the machine recognized as a key still in its slot. By the time Aurinka had slid down, Wolf had cut the body free and tossed it out of the machine before sitting in the slightly bloody cockpit.

"Nice ride you've got yourself. How the hell am I supposed to get out of here?" Aurinka yelled. Wolf gestured to the machine's right shoulder.

"Just hang on, my friend. I've piloted several of these in my life; we'll be out of here before you know it." Closing the cockpit before Aurinka could vent any of her mounting frustration, Wolf turned the machine and started lumbering toward the palace wall.

Aurinka had just settled into position when Wolf smashed through the brick and mortar barricade, taking off down the hill via the main thoroughfare. *He's pretty damned good,* Aurinka thought to herself. *Piloting one of these as it runs downhill in the rain is no mean feat.* Despite knowing that Wolf was the better choice for piloting, as the rain pelted Aurinka all the harder for the speed at which she moved, she still felt growing anger about the entire situation.

Wolf guided the warmachine down the main thoroughfare unmolested until the two approached the river at the bottom. Two smaller warmachines had been alerted to the intruders' scheme and converged to meet them before they could escape in the water, and the two were smaller scout builds, which made outrunning them impossible. Aurinka hooked her kama around a sturdy protrusion in the back and lowered herself down to hang against the machine's back, and just in time, as projectiles slammed into the machine Wolf piloted. The main road ran right down to the river docks, but this area of the city at the base of the hills held tightly packed shanties and warrens as the expanding populace built shelter wherever they could. The smaller scout warmachines approached from within this maze, a luxury the larger warmachine could not afford, and started battering Wolf from two sides. Wolf fired back, leveling both lightning emitters on his machine at the scout on the left and sending it reeling back into a building. Static electricity crackled around the machine despite the rain, and Aurinka felt it tingling throughout her body. As another volley of projectiles slammed into Wolf and he prepared another salvo, Aurinka tucked her legs and pushed off from the warmachine, flipping back to land on a tiled roof near Wolf's machine. Scrambling to find her footing on the slick tile, Aurinka only managed to slow her fall, gouging the roof with her kama and barely managing a graceful landing after falling fifteen feet. Her shoulder ached from exertion, and the constant activity of the evening started taking its toll. Above her, Wolf withstood still more of the metal slugs the scout warmachines hurled, staggering back slightly as he answered with more and more lightning. Aurinka rolled backward to avoid being stepped on and ducked into one of the numerous alleys. After getting her bearings, she started working her way through the maze of the slums, leaving Wolf to his own devices.

Aurinka's path lay along the river, running by one of the scouts. As she moved swiftly through the downpour a massive crash sent her staggering to her knees, and the shriek of rending metal cut through the deafening patter of raindrops. Concerned for a second that Wolf had been bested, Aurinka felt relief when bolts of lightning flashed across her vision, and she thought she heard the boom boom boom of the scout's projectile weapon fading into the distance. The sound of a massive splash reached her ears, and feeling that Wolf had succeeded in his escape, she turned her attention to melting into the shadows and swiftly making her way back to the temple she called home, any real fear of being followed having dissolved in the rainy night's embrace.

Muted sunlight filtered into Aurinka's window, gently pulling her from sleep. She sat up and vaguely wondered if the previous night had been a vivid dream, but the aches over most of her body quickly disabused her of that notion. A set of black garb sat in the corner of her room, still damp despite lying near the embers of Aurinka's small fire. Exhausted and hungry, Aurinka gingerly got up and performed her morning rituals. Making a note to stretch a bit more often, she entertained petitioners to the shrine for the morning before making her way to the tea house she patronized every day at this point.

The proprietor gave her an unusually dour look, and when Aurinka sat at her usual table and started setting up armies, he solemnly handed her a sealed letter with dwarven letters drawn using exquisite calligraphy. It said only 'my dream'. Aurinka broke the wax seal and unfolded the paper, reading it carefully as a smile slowly inched across her face. "Bjorn, when did Wolf leave you this letter?" she asked.

"He gave it to me yesterday afternoon. What's up with him? Did I just lose a customer?"

Aurinka shook her head. "He'll be gone for a while, but this isn't the end of anything. It's a beginning."

*   *   *

"Princeps." The man known as the Brass Emperor stirred, his reverie broken by the timid page calling out his formal title. He hadn't slept since the intrusion the night prior, and as the sun rose to battle its way through the omnipresent cloud cover, the damage to the city down in the river district could be seen even from the palace.

"Yes? What is it?" Slowly turning his massive frame, the Emperor regarded the young woman standing at the door. Senators typically assigned second or third sons and daughters to the Praetorian Guard or some other prestigious posting, and 'page' served as the first rank for new applicants. The Emperor wondered how someone so nervous now would be able to assume the mantle of warrior, but reminded himself that most pages were, in his presence. He'd had that effect on others for a long time. "The Senate has convened and humbly requests your presence, Princeps. Senator Timean in particular expressed concern for your wellbeing after the attack last night."

That sniveling worm, the Emperor thought. Useful all the same, but still. "Please tell them I'll join them shortly."

"Yes, Princeps." Rendering a crisp Republic salute, she spun on her heel and hurried down the hallway. The Emperor noticed she wasted no time, and had arrived still damp enough from the rain that she must not have tried to make herself more presentable first. The Emperor valued such commitment to one's duty over vanity, and mused that she might indeed be an excellent addition to the praetorians, once she had a few more years under her belt.

He hated skipping portions of his morning routine, but extenuating circumstances justified it. A swift polishing job on his armor and a calibration of the various devices fitted into it were all the Emperor took the time for, resolving to walk in his garden later. His shamed bodyguards from the previous evening all reported to escort him to the Senate building, as they served more of an honorary function for the Emperor despite being puissant warriors. Each of the six felt the Emperor's silence reflecting a brooding disquiet, but the man they called Princeps used words sparingly, and in fact still mulled over the events of the night before. He'd been vaguely aware of the link to the catacombs below the palace and had ordered them sealed off out of security concerns, but hadn't taken the time to thoroughly explore them in the centuries he'd occupied the place above it. Managing a republic didn't leave him much time for spelunking, but he still resolved to finish exploring below, lest he unknowingly guarded anything else. The Senate met a mere three hundred yards from the Emperor's palace (and the Senate building had a slightly lower elevation), and the rainwater on the Emperor's armor slid off almost instantly, leaving only his cloak weighed down by the rain. Two hundred senators filled the chamber, falling silent when the Emperor, Princeps, First Among Equals, Major Consul and Pontifex strode into the grand hall. Though the senate seats moved up in steps like an amphitheater, placing every senator above the Emperor, he still filled the room with his presence and commanded their attention. Some senators sought to align themselves with him for their own gain and others despised him, while most fell somewhere in between, jockeying for what political advantage they could while being forced to acknowledge their circumstances. The Emperor actually appreciated assassination attempts; one occurred every few years, and served as a bleak reminder of how ineffective they were.

"We are relieved to see you well, Princeps." The man saying this stood near the top of the steps, a porcine figure named Gorgias. His words dripped with sarcasm, but the Emperor paid him little heed. If he'd actually done more than eat confections and watch his men train while he commanded the Seventh Legion, his soft physique didn't show it, and his fortunes could only hire a small handful of assassins before he became bankrupt. Permitting these tiny rebellions released pressure that might build up into a larger one.

"Thank you, senator. Your page stated you all wished to speak with me. So please speak." Younger senators furtively looked at each other with perplexed expressions, while the older senators had long grown accustomed to the Emperor's brevity.

A woman from the middle terraces of the room spoke up. "Princeps, while matters of security and the Praetorian Guard are of course your sole purview, considerable damage was inflicted on multiple neighborhoods last night."

"In addition to Senator Lucretia's point, many citizens think it's time to deal with the elven assassin guild all but operating openly in the city," Gorgias interjected. "Surely your mighty guards could flush them out easily enough. We certainly don't blame the brave men and women defending you, Princeps, but the damage caused did kill several citizens, and has made three neighborhoods nearly impassible."

"No." The Emperor's voice had a way of filling the room without him needing to yell. "Seek damages in court if they have wronged your family, Gorgias. That is the law. As for the neighborhoods, I grieve for our lost citizens, but the influx of people have willfully defied city zoning and planning laws set forth years ago. This is an opportunity to open more thoroughfares and relocate anyone still living in those areas."

Murmurs rose in the chamber. Before any could snowball into a proper argument, a younger senator turned to address the Emperor. "Princeps, forgive me if I'm being impertinent, but what was the goal of the assassins? Rumors insist they had little interest in killing you. Is this true?"

Rumors indeed. Did the palace staff dream up these things, or the newer praetorians? "You are correct. The assassin did not act like someone intent on killing me."

"I thought there was more than one? And will you tell us what their goal was?"

"No." The Emperor's tone brooked no arguing and the senator, a young man named Anton, looked crestfallen. "Princeps, we senators are concerned for your safety. Will you not help us help you?" Gorgias effected his most unctuous tone, and the Emperor idly wondered what he could hope to be getting out of this.

"Hire a geomancer to oversee demolition in the damaged areas of the city. I will release money from my own coffers to relocate the citizens living there. Additionally, have someone dredge the mouth of the river; I doubt the assassin would keep the warmachine he stole. Lastly, send word to those commanding our legions and have them remain vigilant. Expansion of the Republic will halt for the time being." More murmurs erupted, as even the older senators were caught off guard. The Emperor turned and strode from the chamber, thinking to get back to his garden as swiftly as possible. He hadn't even exited the building when Gorgias caught up with him, huffing and wheezing from the exertion of moving so quickly.

"Princeps," he panted, "you must... do something... about the elves. Many nobles are calling for bl—" The Emperor stopped him mid-sentence by lifting him with one arm and slamming him against the wall. Pressed against the stone, Gorgias' face flushed as his breathing became even more labored.

"I already told you once, Gorgias, and I dislike interruption. The elves are of no concern to me. If you are too poor to hire as many as you need, or fear that another has made a contract on your life, I don't care." Leaning in close so that only Gorgias, whose face had started turning purple, could hear, the Emperor continued. "The Senate offers you vermin an illusion of control, and I abide the chaos of that chamber to stave off the greater insurrection I might incur by executing all of you. I suffer you to live, Gorgias, and do not ever think that I would be concerned about someone removing that burden from me. Interrupt me again for your solipsistic nonsense and I'll remove this burden myself."

The Emperor dropped Gorgias to the floor as the latter sucked in a huge gulp of air, trying desperately to catch his breath and stop the shaking that had overcome his body. Republic law only permitted the family of a murder victim to prosecute a case against an alleged murderer, and the Emperor had specifically stopped measures to change this to a state issue. He had also been granted immunity from court prosecutions due to his position, meaning that Gorgias knew full well that the Emperor had not made an idle threat.

Leaving the gasping man behind him, the Emperor retired to his garden at long last, to meditate among the green life around him; the elf last night had been Loki, his old master turned nemesis, of that he was certain. The second assassin had missed it, but the Emperor saw Loki mouth the word Pan, a name the Emperor had not heard in three centuries. He also had a vague understanding of the spear's import, despite never having seen it before, and subconsciously he knew that Loki risking the palace to retrieve it meant that something had started, something that could bring the Republic to its knees. Though he carefully monitored his time in the garden lest he drain too much prana for his plants to thrive, Emperor Pan mulled over the meaning of the previous night long after the garden and into the night. Events were now in motion that he didn't fully understand, a completely alien and disconcerting sensation for the man who had firmly ruled this city and its lands for so many decades. Regardless of his uncertainty, he would not be caught unprepared.

*   *   *

"It's about time you arrived." The elven woman addressing Wolf had snow white hair held back from her face by an iron crown, ancient but curiously free of rust. Her horse matched her hair color, and a powerful recurve bow left no doubt that she hailed from one of the rare nomadic elven tribes from the eastern portion of the Great Continent. Two other elves had watched Wolf pull up to the small island where they stood, the latter having discarded his warmachine for the discreet dinghy he'd hidden at Balleron's docks. One elf had bright red hair and pale skin covered in places by elaborate blue-green tattoos, and he bore a distinctly un-elven-like two-handed sword with a worn pommel and gleaming steel visible from the half sheath at his back. The last elf wore her raven-black hair cropped short, and carried a brass-bound drinking horn made from a beast that no longer existed. The brass, like every other artifact here, showed no sign of its age. The four elves and the horses three of them had brought with them had the island to themselves. The woman with white hair, referred to as Snow by most, continued. "Then the dreams truly are prophetic."

The red-haired man, known as Luat, drew his blade with surprising grace for its massive size. "Indeed they are. I stood upon the stone and Fragarach answered."

The last elf, the woman named Hekal, remained silent but raised her cup in a salute. The four stood silently together for a long while, taking in the significance of the moment, and the task before them. As the sun began to set behind the clouds, Luat began building a fire and Hekal produced a wine skin. Snow provided two freshly slain hares, and the four sat down for a meal as the rain slowed to a light drizzle. Wolf's chuckling finally prompted Hekal to speak.

"What tickles you, then? I didn't think the gravity of our mission would encourage such titillation."

"It's not the mission. Just... prophecy," Wolf answered with a smile.

THE REALM OF MOMENTS PASSED

by Larnce Hicks

THE VALUE OF MEMORY

The people who surrounded me told me it was going to rain again. I supposed it must have rained a lot in this land that I apparently grew up in.

The woman who sat to my left said her name was Eliza. I was told she was my wife; however, each time I looked at her, all I saw before me was a stranger. Beautiful though she was, I couldn't help but feel dissatisfied that she is the one I chose to marry. A few days prior, she showed me portraits of me and my family. I felt guilty as I watched her hold back her tears when I dispassionately looked at them as if they were casual pieces of artwork. The guilt truly set in when I walked right past a little girl that was supposed to be my daughter when she stood at the door to greet me. I thought she must have been another servant.

In the very few days that I can remember clearly, we wore lavish clothing and spent our leisure time in exquisite silks. We would stroll through a garden filled with foreign fauna. I must have been a fairly wealthy man to afford such things. My name and seal were clearly presented on the deed to the manor we slept in, but it did not feel like my home. Everywhere I went, I felt lost. Nothing felt familiar. Nothing felt truly safe. I was forced to trust that what people told me about myself was true, but I had no way of verifying anything that I heard. A constant state of paranoia flooded my every thought. I was certain those feelings continued for too much longer, I would go mad.

Our carriage came to a stop at the top of a hill deep in the woods.

"Where are we?" I asked Eliza.

She placed her hand on my knee causing me to reflexively flinch. The flinch frightened her, and I could see she was hurt by my response.

"We are south of Riverhill, deep within the woods," she said as her voice cracked. "This is where we will find the seer the alchemist told us about."

"The one who will cure my mind?" I asked.

"Hopefully, Love."

The carriage driver tied down the horses and opened the carriage door. I couldn't help but notice how strong he was as he helped my wife down from the high mounted door.

"I apologize for the mud, my lady," he said. "I tried to find dry ground, but the spring rains have made that impossible."

"It's alright, Allister," Eliza said kindly. "I'll manage."

Up along this flat stone path was a dark hut made of mud bricks covered with a tall thatch roof. A strange blue smoke billowed from the peak of the roof and trickled from the windows like a fog. Emerging from the tarped entrance was an old she-orc leaning on a cane.

The she-orc shuffled down the stone path carefully watching her steps to avoid losing her balance between each stone.

"Good afternoon, Sir Henry." Her voice was old and rough. "My name is Katya Nebavakich. I've been expecting you." I tried to ask her how she knew my name, but she interrupted. "And before you ask, no. We have never been acquainted."

"How do you know my name if you do not know me?" I asked.

"I know many things, my lord. It is my gift and curse to know things," she said as we finally stand face to face on the stone path. "Come inside. I've already prepared the ritual." Though she possessed a kyphotic hunchback, she still stood as tall as me. Orcs are truly a large species. I wondered if I knew any others.

Both Eliza and Allister followed close as the she-orc led us up the path into her hut. A horrifically strong odor penetrated my nostrils. The closer we got, the stronger the stench became. She pulled back the curtain that acted as her front door letting out a large waft of smell straight into my face.

My left eye was beginning to burn with dryness as it had been as long as I could remember which wasn't very long at all. This was a sign that I would soon be visited by another dreadful migraine. As I began to rub my eye with my gloved hand, Allister pulled a handkerchief from his belt and whetted it with his water skin. He cupped my head in his hand and dabbed my eye gently. Surprisingly, I did not flinch in the slightest. A cold relief averted the burning, but I knew a migraine was soon to come either way.

The inside of the hut was about what I imagined it would be. In the center was a large cauldron boiling some kind of blue liquid. That must've been where the blue smoke was coming from. There were three skinned woodland creatures hanging from the roof above it; no doubt the source of the dreadful smell. On the right, a large ritualistic circle was drawn on the floor with incense burning at each of its vertices. On the left was a table with a crystal ball sitting on top. Katya motioned for us to have a seat around it. Allister did so without hesitation, but Eliza struggled as she tried in vain to find a clean place to sit. Katya placed herself at one end with her cane at her side.

"I know why you have come." Katya's gaze never left me. "The alchemist told you I may be able to restore Henry's memory."

"That's right, Ms. Nebavakich," Eliza mutters. "How did you..."

"I told you, child. I know many things," she interrupted again.

"The alchemist said he pieced Henry's brain together perfectly after the duel and that he should make a full recovery with the occasional migraine. However, he had no way of restoring the memory Henry lost, and told us our only hope was you," Eliza said.

"The damage done goes far deeper than any dagger could pierce, and from the looks of it, even my conventional methods would not be enough to help your dear husband," Katya said.

Allister leaned over the table and took hold of Katya's hands. "Please, Ms. Nebavakich, I'm begging you. Is there nothing that can be done to help my lord regain his memory?" He sure was a passionate servant. I could see why we kept him close.

"I can help Henry to help himself," Katya stated ominously. "Henry's memory loss was not only caused by his physical injury, but also by damage to his very soul. It can be healed, but Henry must be willing to venture into dangerous territory."

"I will go in his stead," Allister passionately exclaimed. "Tell me where I must go!"

"I'm afraid this venture must be Henry's and Henry's alone," Katya said, shaking her head.

Allister retracted with a confused expression.

"Allow me to explain." She leaned over the table and put her hands on her crystal ball. As we all gazed deep into its mirrored center, images began to appear within.

"I intend to send Henry to a dimension known as the Realm of Moments Passed. It is a place where every single second that has passed goes to die. Destiny is created in the Halls of Time in the form of infinitely many potential futures that have yet to happen. As these infinite rivers of time flow through our material world from their origin, only one river exits becoming what we understand as history. These past moments manifest themselves as a series of universes that exist merely as a shadow that follows the present universe as it continues along its destiny."

I could barely believe what that woman was saying. At this point did it even matter if she is lying?

"These shadow universes look exactly like ours did in a past moment in time. Even living beings cast a shadow of their own called umbramorphs. These shadow beings feed off the experiences of the soul they are attached to and perfectly reenact the events that transpired in that specific moment. They see themselves and the world around them as the present and have no idea that they truly live in the past."

I looked towards my shadow as it was cast upon the wall by the cauldron's fire light. I moved my hand and watched as the shadow mimicked my movements. It's almost overwhelming to imagine our entire universe casting a shadow of its own.

"Using my gift, I can send Henry's soul on a journey through these shadow universes. By witnessing the events of your upbringing firsthand, the damage done to your soul will mend and your memories will quickly return to you."

Judging by her somber tone, I could tell it wouldn't be as simple as it sounded.

"Will I be in any danger?" I asked

Katya closed her eyes and took a breath. "I will not lie to you, my lord. This ritual is not without its risks, for the Realm of Moments Passed is not only inhabited by umbramorphs." She looked behind herself as if something were there listening, but there was nothing there. She turned back with wide eyes and a faster breath. "As I said before, this realm is where past moments go to die. Older moments are devoured by god-like beings known as time-eaters."

Eliza leaned forward. "That must be a metaphor, right?"

Katya shook her head. "Time-eaters are true to their name. They literally devour everything in their path until there is nothing that remains of that moment in history. They take no prisoners. They show no mercy. They exist outside the bounds of time and can pursue you anywhere within the realm. You must avoid them at all costs."

"How am I to avoid a god-like being?" I asked.

"Most time-eaters prefer the taste of older moments in history. Most of them will flock to the oldest moments they can find and devour that universe entirely before moving up the time-line. The further back into your past you go. The more time-eaters you risk running into. I would suggest you do not wander farther than ten years in the past."

I nodded. "Understood. How do we begin?"

Eliza grabbed hold of my arm causing me to flinch once more. "Wait, my love, perhaps we should reconsider. This sounds far too dangerous."

"I would rather be eaten alive than continue living a life that does not feel like my own with people I feel no emotional connection with." I turned my gaze to the she-orc. "Ms. Katya I will do whatever it takes."

The seer smiled. "I knew that's what you would say. The ritual is already prepared. First thing you need to do is lie in the center of the circle I've drawn for you there."

Eliza yanked me into her embrace and squeezed me tight. "I cannot stop you if you truly wish to do this. Please return to us. You have a family waiting for you at home..." She held me sobbing into my coat. I felt nothing but annoyed that my coat was being stained by her make-up and guilty for being annoyed.

Before I could head to the ground, Allister embraced me himself, but unlike Eliza, I surprisingly found myself embracing him back.

"Be careful, my lord..." he whispered in my ear.

I struggled to find the words I wished to say and said only the first thing that came to mind. "I will, Allister. I have no intention of dying here today." I patted him on the back and exited his embrace. I removed my coat and laid myself on the ground in the center of the circle.

Katya poured a bowl of the blue concoction she was brewing in the center of the room and blew on it to cool. "Drink this, Sir Henry. The whole thing."

I did as she said. The concoction was revolting. I could feel small chunks of under-cooked meat slither down my throat as I struggled to keep it down. I dared not spit it out for I did not wish for that liquid torment to stain my palate any longer than it needed to. I felt like letting out a massive exhale in relief, but nothing was coming out. I saw the back of my own head for a brief moment before my vision grew blurry. A lingering sense of déjà vu flowed over me and did not seem to leave.

I felt paralyzed on the floor as my vision blackened. Katya stood over me as she recited some form of prayer in a Borivajian dialect. After she finished, she leaned over my body and spoke, "I must warn you, my lord. You will not experience time the same way ever again. You will always feel like a spectator of your own life even when you return to the present." I could already see what she meant. I felt like I was floating behind myself with not real control of where I was going. I could only helplessly ride along as my soul drove me forward. I could not respond.

"Remember this. From your perspective, the events you are about to see have already happened, but from the perspectives of the umbramorphs that inhabit that shadow universe, they are living in the present. They have no way of knowing that they are living in a past moment doomed to be devoured by the time-eaters. Do not interfere with their dealings and they won't even know you are there. Any disruptions to their paths will send ripples throughout the realm and draw the time-eaters."

Katya caressed my forehead as my vision faded to black. I could hear only her voice whispering in my ear. "I will send you to the moment that led to your near demise first. Your memories will begin to return to you from there as you observe allowing you to navigate your past as you see fit. You will figure out how to do so quickly."

I could hear Eliza try to say something to me, but her voice muffled more and more. The terror of what I was about to go through hit me all at once as I prepared to plunge headfirst into another dimension. There was no going back... or perhaps back was the only way to go.

RECENT MEMORIES ~ HENRY'S DEATH

I awakened to find myself standing in the center of a list field where knightly duels were settled. The world looked... off. Everything seemed to be two shades too dark and there wasn't so much as a gentle breeze. The stillness was unnerving for it felt like the world beneath my feet had stopped turning. I felt like I was in a nightmare able to see the world around me but only able to see what was right in front of me with any form of clarity. It felt like I was trapped in a thick fog with no sense of direction.

I could hear solid voices coming from the stands unhindered by the atmosphere, so I followed their sound and approached. I walked up a flight of wooden stairs into what looked like the observation stands where people would sit to watch trials by combat.

In the stands I saw crowds of darkly shaded people that matched their darkly shaded world. These must have been the umbramorphs Katya was talking about. These shadows looked similar to normal people, but their emotions seemed exaggerated as if they were amateur actors in a play about themselves. Their smoky bodies shifted drastically to portray specific reactions and emotions. They jerked about maniacally when they laughed or expressed excitement, but would sit almost perfectly still when conversing with one another. Anytime I honed in on one of their conversations, their voices boomed in my ears with heavy distortion, so I did my best to keep my distance and keep my focus on the matter at hand.

I took a seat in a clear spot among the stands and focused my attention towards the center of the list field as a bard stepped forth to introduce the men who would be fighting there.

"Greetings one and all! I welcome thee to witness a duel between two well-known knights of our kingdom as they stand before Xobris, the god of justice, and lay their lives on the line so that He may choose who earns his favor."

The crowd of umbramorphs spasm and contort as they cheer.

"Today we have a unique pairing of enemies! A father defends his honor against his own son. Standing to the west, is the mighty Sir Cavil Wallace, the Butcher of the Green Vale!"

A chill ran down my spine at the mention of this knight. My first true memory in days finally races through my mind and all I can feel is rage, sadness, and most of all, dread. I knew this knight well. An image of his face appeared in my mind's eye. This man was my father.

"Standing to the east, is his heir and oldest son, Sir Henry Wallace!"

My gaze quickly darted to the other end of the list field. There I stood as clear as day dressed head to toe in steel plate armor. There was no doubt that this was the umbramorph that was feeding off my experiences in this moment in history. He looked exactly like me in every way except his color was darker than mine as was the environment around him.

"Sir Henry Wallace stands in defense of his claim to his family name. His father came before the court demanding his son be stripped of his title and his inheritance removed. Since Sir Henry refused to settle this matter in a court of law, Sir Cavil Wallace is forced to take his matter before our god. As Xobris demands, the two will settle this matter in a trial by combat! Though the victor has already been chosen by the all-knowing Qitos, it is through the throes of battle that Xobris will reveal the gods' judgement! May his will flow through the victor as blood is spilled upon this field today!"

The crowd cheered in a spasmic frenzy from the stands. Their loud booming voices shook my very core nauseating me. I tried my best to turn my focus towards my umbramorph below, but the crowd's noise was too much to ignore. After what felt like ages of horrific applause, the bard settles the crowd to a murmur.

The combatants took their positions, and the umbramorphs following them handed them their halberds. It was hard for me to see much from where I was sitting, but as the events continued to unfold, chunks of memories that led up to this battle flooded my mind in the form of visions.

The first vision was of my father. We were both in the great hall of my manor. He stepped forth and handed me a document. Though I could not read it, I could remember what it contained. He wished for me to sign it so that he may officially and legally remove me from the Wallace family for good and forfeit my inheritance to his newly born son. My half-brother, Jonas. Judging by my demeanor and feelings of anger, I must have refused. If my father couldn't convince me to leave my inheritance behind, it seemed like he was willing to fight me in a trial by combat to force me to abdicate. It appears I accepted his challenge.

Standing behind him was his wife holding their young son. Could that have been *my* mother? There was simply no way. She didn't look a day older than me. If she was my young stepmother, then what happened to my birth mother? What kind of woman was she? As I continued to ponder, more memories of her began to surface.

I couldn't recall growing up with my birth mother. I obviously had to have one at some point in my life, but she must have died when I was young. My recovered memories felt more like scattered recollections in a blinding dust storm making it difficult to piece together any clear story surrounding her. From what I could gather, she was a shelter from my father. A lighthouse during a storm. A scene flashes forth of my mother teaching me to read. I seemed to love reading stories of epic heroes and terrifying monsters. I gathered all the information I could about my birth mother from the collection of memories I had recovered though I hungered for more.

The vision ended sending me back to my seat at the trial. I sat watching the fighters take a few practice swings as the bard grabbed the ceremonial staff and raised it overhead.

"Combatants! Salute the crown of which you serve!" The combatants bow to the duke who sat upon a shaded throne on the other side of the list field. "Salute the one whose favor you hold!" The combatants approached different umbramorphs who stood daintily on the edge of the arena and kissed their hands. Those must have been Eliza's and my stepmother's umbramorphs.

A vision of Eliza shot through my mind. I could see her begging me not to do this, but I had no reason to think I would lose. My fencing instructors always told me how excellent my skills were in combat. They always boasted how their other students stood undefeated among their peers and how I was to be no different. My father was in his forties and I was relatively young, so I was in far better shape. I could remember stepping into the list field with the utmost confidence that I would easily beat my father into submission.

As the memory ended, the bard lifted the ceremonial staff high into the air. "Combatants at the ready? Lay on!!"

As soon as the bard stepped back, I could practically feel myself standing in my umbramorph's shoes as if I were reliving the fight. Even in armor, my father was as swift as a buck. I blinked only once and as my eyes opened, his halberd broke my guard and struck me so hard on the side of my helmet I nearly fell over from the force. Adrenaline filled rage flooded my every move as he followed through with one strike after another. I tried my best to execute the counter maneuvers taught to me by my fencing instructors, but none of them had any effect on a real opponent! I felt small and helpless next to this towering beast of a man as he grabbed hold of my pauldrons and threw me to the ground. The impact of the ground blasted the air from my lunges. I flailed about in a panic with tears rolling down my eyes as I pitifully tried to shove my father off of me. He kneeled over my helpless body with a heavy armored foot on my chest and drew his rondel dagger from his belt.

He bent down and whispered something to me. No one in the crowd could hear it, but I vividly remember what he said to me that day.

"I should have done this long ago, you filthy abomination."

I let out a scream of terror as I tried one last time to beg my father for mercy. "No! wait, Father! Plea—"

Before I could finish, my father plunges his dagger deep into my left eye. The last thing I could hear was Eliza wailing and the front of my skull cracking as the blade penetrated my brain. My father stood up and left his dagger plunged into my skull. My body laid there spasming giving off a loud horrifying low pitched moan with every breath. It was the only sign that I somehow still lived. Eliza's umbramorph rushed to my body and held it in her arms as the bard declared my father the victor.

I sat in the stands petrified by what I just witnessed. How could it have come to this? What could I have done to deserve being murdered by my own father? I had to know more.

Suddenly I realized that I was floating above my seat. The foggy world around me grew further and further away as I floated upwards. I concentrated my hardest on stopping and I did just that. Next thing I knew I found myself flying through a grey vortex filled with windows that led to different points in my life. I'm not sure how I knew where it was taking me, but after reliving a near death experience, this strange self-abduction felt tame.

I felt lost as I flew through the vortex that connected all of recent history, but at the same time, it felt like my soul knew exactly where I needed to go in order to restore my memory.

I rifled through my own mind looking through all the memories that had just returned to me. I could recall most of the major events up to my daughter's birth four years ago but there were still gaps that were left blank. It appeared that I lived such a bland life up to that point. My duel with Father was likely the most noteworthy thing to happen to me in my adult life.

As I looked back at the window I flew through, I pondered what the rest of my life could have been like. That was a horrific experience to live through, but surely the worst was behind me.

COMING OF AGE

The grey vortex felt overwhelming. It was a constant spinning thunderstorm filled with these circular windows depicting different moments in history. There were literally hundreds of them appearing before me at once that I could've flown including events that happened only seconds before the event I had already just experienced. I wondered if there could be infinitely many of these portals leading to past moments, and if so, how would I ever find the ones I needed? Just as I floated there sorting through the dozens of moments, I felt a tug in the back of mind. I felt drawn deeper into the vortex as if a gentle mentor were nudging me along from the back.

Flying gently through the vortex, I could see its hue growing darker the deeper I went. Suddenly I heard a blood curdling scream come from behind me and felt a wet drop splatter upon my cheek. I quickly turned to see what made that sound, but there was nothing there. The scream flew by me so fast, that it was gone just as fast as it appeared. I wiped away the wet spot on my cheek and saw that it was a splatter of fresh glistening blood. Unlike everything else around me, the blood was not a dark tint. It was quite red and normal colored. I cannot imagine why, but this sensation flooding my body is almost too uncomfortable to endure. I turn my gaze forward and re-center myself. I must press on.

I flew through the grey vortex for a few minutes peeking through each window that I flew past, but none seemed to catch my eye until I saw one from my pubescent years that shook me to my very core.

There I was. A young Henry no older than fourteen winters being choked by my father. My body and soul felt drawn to this window in history much to my disdain. This must be another major moment in my life that will bring a flood of memories back to me just as the last one did. With no other options presenting themselves, I reluctantly flew through the window.

I was surprised to find myself in a barn rather than a manor. My teenage umbramorph sat upon a cow milking stool and appeared to be well groomed as if he were about to attend the king's ball.

Memories of this experience once again filled me as they did earlier. I could recall feeling anxious. My palms practically dripped with sweat. Insecurity plagued me as I constantly checked the shape of my hair and wondered if it was more proper of me to have my coat on rather than off. My eyes darted to check the barn door every few seconds as I paced back and forth across the animal pens.

It became clear to me that I was expecting to meet someone here. Perhaps this was where I met Eliza for our first secret rendezvous.

I could remember waiting in that barn for the longest half hour I had ever experienced. Even my present self was beginning to wonder if anything would happen in this past moment when the barn door finally opened. I focused my vision on the face of the person entering the barn, but to my surprise, it wasn't Eliza. In fact it wasn't a woman at all.

Approaching my pubescent umbramorph was what appeared to be a young man. As he came closer and closer, his form became far more clear and less foggy. His humble attire suggested he was of the common folk and the tools at his side indicated he must be a craftsman's apprentice. He carried a strong stature with broad shoulders, yet a kind face that felt welcoming like a soft feathered pillow after a long day in court. Why was I thinking such things of a man?

My umbramorph stood with his fists closed in nervousness. I could recall fear, but of a much kinder nature. The boy's approach accelerated as he grabbed me by the waist and pulled me close. To my surprise, my umbramorph embraced him back and gently grasped the back of his neck. Our lips met in a fiery spectacle of light that illuminated the barn. I could remember a feeling of warmth unlike anything I had felt in my life.

Roland. I could remember his name now. This was my young flame, Roland. I had thought that my physical aversion from Eliza was only a result of my lost memory and paranoia, but now it all began to make sense. The way Allister would look at me and tend to my every minor need since my injury was not because he was just my head servant. It was because.... he was my lover.

Tears flooded my eyes and my knees felt weak. It was everything I could do not to collapse in pure happiness. Blank spots in my memory began to return to me of Allister and I sharing tender moments in secret. Our occasional strolls through my gardens. Sharing a horse as we rode through the woods to our secret grove. A slew of memories like this appeared one by one as I sat watching my younger self express his true self for the first time.

My blissful state was suddenly met with a look of terror as the memory of this first sensual encounter began to play out in front of me. I heard a thundering voice echo through my entire body inspiring a feeling of absolute dread. A harrowing umbramorph of my father blasted through the door with several of his knights to his back. He extended his solid arm and ordered his men to seize my companion.

"Get that corrupting incubus away from my son!" he screamed in a foaming rage that nearly shattered my ears.

The guards grabbed Roland and slammed him into the ground.

"What are we to do with him, Lord Wallace?" the guard asked.

"Flog this abomination until nothing remains and then throw him among the pigs where disgusting sodomizers like him belong," he said foaming at the mouth with rage.

They dragged Roland across the ground behind the barn. My younger self attempted to stop them only to be grabbed by my father.

"That boy has spoiled your mind and filled you with improper desires," he said as the guards dragged my companion out of the barn. My younger self was a scrawny weak child compared to my broad monstrous father. He took a few swings at my father's face. The towering umbramorph jittered violently expressing its rage as it slammed my younger umbramorph into the dirt with a single mighty blow. Flashbacks of our deadly duel kept flashing before my eyes as I watched hopelessly.

"Please, Father! Spare him! He came here only because I summoned him!" my umbramorph yelled with a squeaking voice.

The towering shadow that was my father lifted my umbramorph from the ground and pulled him close as he screamed into his face with the voice of a thousand trumpets.

"I warned you what would happen. You are my sole heir. You are responsible for inheriting the Wallace estate and passing it on to a dynasty that is to last thousands of years. I will not let you put an end to our immortal name just so you can run off and become a sodomizing monster!"

His thundering voice was too much to bear, but it paled in comparison to the screams coming from outside the barn. Roland would let out a blood curdling screech with every swing of the rod the guards beat him with.

I lost control of myself. Between the overwhelming noise of my father screaming at my umbramorph and my anger towards the guards that would dare harm my Roland, all I could see was a dark shade of red. I ran out the back of the barn grabbing a pitchfork on my way out. Grasping it tight in both hands, I aggressively approached the guard holding the rod. Just as Katya said, the umbramorph of that guard didn't even see me approach until I was right in his face. By then it was far too late as I rammed that pitchfork straight through his throat and pinned his disgraceful face into the dirt behind him.

The umbramorphs of both the other guard and of Roland turned to notice me with confused statures. The shadow under my boot contorted and twisted as it lay there reeling in a bewildered agony. It was a horrifying sight to look upon. The umbramorphs of my father and younger self slowly exited the barn to witness what had just happened as if they were not just screaming at each other. I took a few steps back grasping the pitchfork tightly. For the first time since I arrived, the umbramorphs noticed my presence.

They stopped walking as people do and began to slowly float towards me as their forms faded to pure black smoke. I thrusted the pitchfork at them trying to create space. They would jerk back to avoid my attacks but would seize every opportunity to close the distance between us. An anxious panic took over my body as I ran away. I dared not look back because I could hear the squealing of the umbramorphs close behind me. I tried to fly away as I did before, but my feet would not leave the ground. I pushed my legs with all my might to run as fast as I could away from my pursuers. Up ahead I saw the farmhouse with an open door. I ran inside and slammed the door behind me. The umbramorphs that chased me slammed into the door and battered it with their smoky fists. I knew I could not hold them back for long.

Inside the house, another umbramorph rose from behind the hearth. It skittered and spasmed as its form became shadow. I could do nothing to stop it as it slowly floated in front of me and extended its hand towards me. A streak of white light began to pull from my chest. It felt like he was ripping my heart from my ribs. I screamed in pain as I continued to push my enemies back. I felt my vision getting blurry as the umbramorph before me radiated from the white light flowing from my sternum. This was going to be the moment I died.

Suddenly from out of nowhere, a rumbling sound startled the umbramorph in the house. It stopped its life sucking magic and reared up in fear looking towards the windows. The shadows from outside stopped pushing and their screeching uproar was silenced. I heard an unorthodox growl that I could only describe as a large collection of stones grinding and rubbing together. A blasting roar that sounded like an extremely low-pitched horn bellowed through the area. The umbramorph in front of me swiftly flew through the window in fear. The others outside sounded like they were being thrown about. The grinding stone sound accelerated as the umbramorphs screeched in agony. It sounded like a tornado of stone was ripping them and the entire patio to pieces.

I maniacally crawled to the corner of the room opposite of the carnage outside and curled into a ball. I waited in terror for the sounds to stop. In a matter of seconds all I could hear was the sound of a breeze coming from outside as if I were sitting in a cave with a draft. Slowly, I creep up from my ball and shakily peak my head out of the window. Outside, I could see entire rows of the ground that simply looked erased.

I scanned the area to see if the beast that caused the umbramorphs to flee had gone. All I could see was the destruction it lay in its wake. I cautiously stepped outside through the battered door. Much of the patio was destroyed, but it seemed as if it was completely erased from existence for there was no trace of splintered wood or bricks anywhere. I walked to the edge of the carved ground where the beast must have come from and looked down. My mind could barely comprehend what I was looking at. It felt like I was looking at the infinite expanse of space as if I were staring into the night sky. I dropped a rock down the hole hoping to hear a thump. I waited for minutes without a single sound.

Waiting for the sound of the stone, I was startled by a crashing sound coming from back at the barn. I quietly returned to investigate. I peeked inside only for a brief moment, for what I saw inside nearly paralyzed me with fear. I saw a massive beast that had to be larger than an entire carriage. It looked to be made of rough crystals of many colors with smaller crystals that orbited around it. The beast slowly moved through the barn grinding everything in its path including the barn itself, the animals, and even the very earth beneath it. I couldn't tell too much from the glimpse I caught of the beast, but I knew I had to escape before it destroyed me as well.

I carefully made my way into the maize fields in the distance before taking off into a sprint. I ran until my legs could no longer move and collapsed among the crop. I listened intently for the grinding sound of the beast or its low-pitched call but heard no such indication of its pursuit. I had escaped for now.

That beast must have been a time-eater. Katya warned me that if I interfered in the past events that it could attract them. Though this moment in history had already come to pass, it felt too real for me not to interfere when I could. I loved Roland dearly and it killed me to hear him being whipped senseless again. I lived through it once as a powerless young man. I wouldn't allow myself to do so again.

With a moment to breathe, I could finally sort out the memories granted to me by this past moment. I could remember the few tender moments I shared with Roland when I paid a visit to his master's shoe shop. This moment in the barn was to be our first romantic encounter, but instead it acted as the catalyst that would forever spin my life into a living hell. Memories of abuse from my father flooded my mind. I could remember him forcing me to kill animals to prove my manhood, sending guards with me on every excursion from the manor, and even demanding to witness my wedding night with Eliza to assure I would produce an heir for him.

So far, every memory I have recovered has been nothing but a recollection of suffering. Why did my soul strive for me to see this? Had my life before my injury been nothing but escalating abuse from my bigoted father? Perhaps I would have been better off without my memory. I may have lived in anxiety and paranoia before, but now I was doomed to return to the present only to live a life of continued abuse from my father and deep depression. Without a single happy memory to escape to, was it even a life worth returning to? What was the point of living if I was only a collection of horrid memories?

Out of all the memories I recovered the only time I could remember being truly happy was when I was learning to read with my birth mother, but the memory was so weak that I almost felt as if I had made it up. When I focused on that memory, I noticed my feet lifting off the ground. It seemed like I had finally regained the ability to traverse the realm. Though Katya warned me not to go back in time too far, I knew that I had to. Even if it meant dying in the process, I could not bear to return home without at least some joyful memories to cling on to, for only through those memories will I find the will to carry on.

I flew into the air and re-entered the grey vortex as I did before. My soul guided me further and further back in time. The further I flew, the darker the vortex hued until eventually it reached absolute darkness. Up ahead, I saw a window to the past with me and Mother reading a book of epic poems. My soul craved this window, for it knew that only by venturing into the abyss would I find my memories of happiness once again.

CHILDHOOD

As soon as I entered the moment, I appeared in the middle of the courtyard of the manor I grew up in, but it looked as if I had stepped into a nightmare. It was just before sundown. Entire swaths of the stars above the night sky were completely gone and replaced with a purely black void similar to the hole the time eater climbed out of. Half of the architecture of the keep was missing. No doubt it was eaten by time eaters. I could hear the grinding of their crystalline teeth in the distance and could see them flying overhead devouring the very sky itself. I knew I had to be quick.

A tiny candlelight barely shimmered in a window up on the second floor. That had to be my destination.

Surprisingly, there were still many umbramorphs roaming the castle grounds. These must be the shadows of the servants and the Wallace family guard. I carefully and quietly made my way through the courtyard keeping my distance from any roaming shadows. I knew that a single collision that knocked them off their course would send an army of time eaters my way. I sidled along the outermost walls to try and give all the umbramorphs a wide berth. They paid me no mind as they continued to live out their false lives. I arrived at the entrance to the keep safely and reached for the door. Just as I leaned my weight into it, an umbramorph comes barreling through. It just barely missed bumping into me. It stops for a moment after its stumble and turns around. My heart stopped as I waited for it to turn into its shadow form and attack. Instead it speaks.

"Come now! We can't be here anymore!" said the umbramorph.

A second one follows behind struggling to put on its boots.

"I know that! I'm hurrying!" the second replied.

I squeezed myself tightly into the wall behind the door as I watched them leave the keep. I peeked through the door to assure no others were coming and made my way inside.

Even with a gaping hole going through it, the great hall was a marvelous sight. A large hearth sat in the middle with burning coals just about ready to fizzle out. My family must have been quite wealthy to afford such exquisite rooms. The room was clear of umbramorphs since the staff would be going to bed for the night at this hour. I listened as I walked through the keep trying my best to avoid the paths of any shadow people I may run into.

Finally arriving at the source of the candlelight, I slowly squeeze my way through the door. The sight before my eyes instantly brought me to tears as I slid down the wall at the back of the room.

I saw myself as a child within the warm embrace of my beautiful mother. She held a book in her hands titled *The Slaying of Kanraag, the Rise of Leon the Conqueror.*

"Leon was... a... strong... man, but..." my younger self struggled to read.

"Kanraag. It's alright, that word is hard," my mother said as she brushed my hair with her hand.

"Leon was a strong man, but Kanraag was a strong monster," I read with a smile.

"Very good, Henry!" She kissed me on the forehead.

This was it. This was the moment that would give me back all the happy memories that were missing.

I could remember meeting Eliza. Though our marriage was strictly strategic for both our families, we would eventually become the best of friends. I could remember her finding out about my affair with Allister. She was not angry, nor did she resent us. Instead she helped me keep it secret as long as she could while I let her pursue the man she truly loved. I believe his name was Trevor.

At last I could remember my daughter, Penelope, being born. No… it was only Eliza's daughter. She had a child with Trevor, but we needed to keep appearances, so I pretended to be her father. I could remember playing with her in her crib and rocking her to sleep during the late hours of the night. I would insist on doing it myself even though our nanny was more than happy to oblige. We would let Trevor see her in secret so that she may one day see him as a father.

All this time I imagined my marriage with Eliza must have been one dreadful moment after another, but in truth, she was… no… she is my best friend. I love her.

I lost track of how long I sat and watched my mother and my childhood umbramorph read the poems of Leon the Conqueror. I didn't want this shower of all my happiest memories to end.

Suddenly, a towering beast comes bellowing through the door. My blasted father.

"Put that boy to sleep. He and I are to go hunting tomorrow," my father said belligerently. He was clearly drunk.

"Go away, Cavil. Henry and I are reading," my mother said with perfect regality. She did not fear him.

"There you go again pretending to be the head of this house… You don't give ME orders!" he throws his glass of wine onto the ground.

My mother gently closes the book and tucks me into my bed. I was clearly terrified.

"I'm sorry, Henry. I will be back shortly," she said.

My father stumbled out the door and my mother followed slamming it behind her.

This was as far as my memory could recall.

This was also the last time I saw my mother.

I had what I came for. I could even feel my feet being able to leave the ground and return from whence I came. There was nothing stopping me from escaping this nightmare world with my memory intact. But this would be the only chance I would have to witness what happened to my mother before this moment in history was lost to the time eaters forever.

With a heavy heart, I dashed through the hallways in flight until I found my parents in the great hall below. My father had grabbed my mother and shoved her against the wall. She didn't even show an ounce of fear. "You have three seconds to let go of me, Cavil. If you harm me or Henry again, I will go to my father and he will strip you and your family of their titles."

"You always have to say that don't you? You have to remind me how the Wallace family are slaves to the Masons. You think your position makes you better than me?" he strikes her across the face. "Could your father stop that?!" he continues to beat her. She drops to the ground as he lets her go, blood dripping from her nose and lips.

"That's it, Cavil. You've sealed your fate!"

"You're wrong, bitch. I received word that your father's illness is taking a turn for the worse. I'll be inheriting his estate soon. I don't need you anymore." He grabs the searing poker from the hearth.

I was told mother was killed in the night by assassins hired by enemies of the Mason family. I was about to witness her true murder.

My mother fled up the stairs of the keep. My father slowly followed her with the poker in hand. It took everything in my power not to shove that treacherous bastard down the stairs, but I knew interfering in this moment would bring the time eaters. I could have just left, but a part of me needed to see this through to the end. Even my soul beckoned me to watch.

I flew past my father and found my mother trying to barricade herself within the library. I so badly wished to comfort her and tell her it was going to be alright. I expected my father to come through the door at any moment. My mother reached for a book off the shelf titled *The Justice of Xobris* and began writing along its margins. I could not see what she was writing for I did not wish to risk interfering. She frantically ran to the desk where letters from our family were written and she began burning wax into the page. She slammed the book with the seal on her ring and placed it in a hidden compartment in a chest.

I recognized this chest. When I moved to the country with Eliza, she took this chest with us...

She backed away from the chest and braced herself for my father as he finally broke his way through the door.

"Listen to me, Cavil. You don't need to do this!"

"I've wanted to do this for a long time," he screamed with a distorted umbramorph screech as he charged her.

He plunged the poker deep into her gut. She fell to her knees clutching her stomach trying to keep her insides from falling from the hole as she tried to crawl away.

At this point, all logic left me. This bastard just killed my mother.

I ripped a wooden leg off of a chair and approached my father from behind. He had no idea I was there. I clumsily swung the club as hard as I could right into the back of his head. The club split in two over his skull and cracked it. He spun around and grabbed his wound as blood flooded from under his hand. With a hefty kick, he went flying backwards onto the floor as his form began to spasm into its shadowy state. His limbs and body began to twist and melt into pure smoky darkness as the moment began to unravel. Before his shadow form could reach his face, I stomped my boot onto his chest and felt the ribs crack beneath my heel. With the broken club in hand, I gave my terrified father one last look before I plunged the splintered club into his eye. I felt the bone beneath his eyeball crack as I leaned my body weight into the club and shoved the stake into his brain. His shadow began to dissipate as he lay there motionless.

I quickly ran to my mother who was still crawling on the floor, but dared not approach. She began to take on her shadow form as well despite bleeding all over the floor. It was clear she meant to attack me. I had to keep reminding myself that this was not my real mother. My mother died here in this library. This was just her shadow.

Thundering bellows echoed in the distance like wolves howling. The time-eaters could sense the disruption to the passed moment and would be upon me soon. I so desperately wanted to read what my mother wrote in the margins of that book, but I could hear the monsters' low trumpeting approaching faster than a diving hawk. I have the chest she placed it in at my manor. I must return alive to read it.

I glided through the halls of the keep as fast as I could back to the great hall and flew straight up through the hole in the roof to try and find the entrance to the grey vortex. As my head peaked through the top, a time eater zoomed past nearly scalping me in the process. Its crystalline teeth circled around its tubular mouth grinding everything it came across to mulch. It tore through the tower next to me with ease. Before I could try to hide, another time eater spotted me and let out its uproar. Its arms grinded together with its body with every movement letting out an agonizing, teeth-gritting sound. Their bodies would shift between all colors of the rainbow at random and unlike everything else in the environment, they radiated a bright display of light like the sun beaming through a stained-glass window.

With all the speed my astral projection could muster, I flew away. The window to the grey vortex opened before me and I flew through without hesitation. The vortex grew from a dark black to a dark grey as I moved myself further and further through the timeline. I listened in terror as I heard the grinding of the time eaters pursuing me even through the grey vortex. They could fly faster than me, for their noises grew louder and louder no matter how fast I flew.

Up ahead at the end of the vortex was a white light that must have been the way out. Just as I was about to fly my way through, I felt the claw of one of the time eaters swipe me in the leg. Its attack knocked me into a spiral through the vortex sending me flying through another window.

Spinning through the air, I crashed down in the center of my trial by combat. Looking down towards my leg, I could see that the time-eater had only grazed me, but they were far from through with me. In the sky above, I could see them diving towards me. One slammed in the ground above my father crushing him to pieces in one brutal impact. The other trailed behind waiting for me to fly away again. The crashing time-eater struggled to regain its composure after its crash and shake off the blasted remains of my father's corpse and armor from its vision. I quickly grabbed the halberd my father dropped and lunged at my pursuer. I swung the axe head with all my might at the creature's arms, but it felt as if I was striking solid stone. The creature swung at me blindly with its claw and I just narrowly dodged. If I had been just an inch too slow, that blow would have split my spine in two. Grasping the halberd closer to its head, I stabbed forth towards the beast's bright exposed eye crystal with the spear end of the halberd. The eye crystal cracked a bit sending the beast reeling backwards. I took this opportunity to flee as the second beast had decided to dive after me.

The umbramorphs in the stands scattered into the skies like a swarm of locusts as the illusion of their present moment had shattered the moment I came crashing in, the flying time eater began to chase after them as its teeth began to blend through dozens of shadows at a time. A combination of blood and shadow came raining from the skies as the second time eater blazed through the fleeing umbramorphs. I ran beneath the stands hoping the beast behind me was too big to fit between the planks. With my spear in hand I laid in wait for the beast to approach. The second his face became visible to me I stabbed forth once again with all my might aiming for his eyes. My attack landed true, sending the beast back once again, but it refused to flee. It bared its crystal teeth as the massive mouth in the center of its body opened wide and began to spin like a hurricane. I tried to stab inside its mouth, but the halberd was quickly shattered and disintegrated into nothing. The beast slowly glided forward as the planks of the stands became mulch in its mouth. With nowhere left to run, I climbed and glided my way through the stands as fast as I could. The time eater followed me relentlessly keeping right on my heels since I needed to dodge planks and it only needed to move forward. The stands began the creak and crack as the supports beneath them were destroyed. I dived straight outward in an attempt to escape the impending doom as the stands came crashing down around the beast forcing its mouth closed and trapping it beneath the immense weight of the wood. With the other beast still occupied with the swarm of umbramorphs in the sky, I flew away as fast as I could through the vortex and didn't look back.

Right up ahead, I saw the white light. My soul practically screamed at me to fly forward and escape this realm. It did not need to tell me twice.

THE RETURN HOME

I slowly awoke in dripping sweat.

My heart was racing though I did not have the energy to panic. I could hear voices calling to me and hands on my cheeks, but my ears were ringing so badly that I could not make out the words.

As my vision returned to me, I could see Allister kneeling next to Eliza who was holding my head in her lap. With every ounce of energy I could muster, I sat up and wrapped my arms around Allister's broad shoulders. We kissed with a fiery passion as tears began to form in both our eyes.

"Henry! You remember!" I heard Eliza cry.

Allister helped me up and kept me standing with an arm over his shoulder.

"I remember everything, Eliza," I said with a smile.

She hugged me tight. I did not flinch at all. "Thank the gods," she said with tears flowing down her face.

Katya had a rough smirk on her face. At least I thought she did. It was difficult to tell when orcs were smiling.

"You have done well, Lord Henry. It seems your journey through the Realm of Moments Passed was a difficult one, yet you made it back in one piece," she said. Though it seemed as if she was looking behind me though there was nothing there.

"Lady Katya, I cannot begin to thank you for this. The silver you requested does not seem enough. Ask anything of my family and I will do everything in my power to see it done."

She beckoned me to lean in as if she wished to whisper something in my ear. "Keep your gaze to the future. It's much less painful that way," she somberly whispered as her gaze continued to look at my shadow cast upon the ground. "Now I foresee that you and your family have much work to do and so do I. I'll take my payment for now, Lord Henry. That is all I require," she said out loud. "Go in peace."

Before we leave, Eliza gives Katya one last hug and we begin walking down the stone path to our carriage. She stood just outside her curtain to see us off, but she had a focused stern look in her eyes. I was too exhausted to pay much mind to her strange looks.

As I slowly walked in Allister's arms, I began to sort through my memories. Though the majority of what I had lived through had been torment at the hands of my father, I was grateful to have my memories back. Life is pain. It is only through this pain that we know that we exist as real people and not mere shadows of ourselves. Each and every trauma and blessing I went through made me who I am today. This was the person Allister fell in love with and the person I intended to be for the rest of my life.

With bliss and relief coursing through my body and soul I reach for Allister's head intent on celebrating my newfound joy with a kiss.

Suddenly from the sky, I heard a low-pitched trumpet bellow down upon us. Before I could even scream, a time-eater crashed down onto Allister and split his body in two before me with its massive claws. His arm and half his torso fell on me as I fell to the floor. Unable to move, all I could do was helplessly watch as the time eater stood up tall before me. It reared its chest back and opened its massive gaping mouth in the center of its body.

I screamed so loud that it felt as if my mouth would split open. I looked around frantically for Eliza, but she was nowhere to be found.

"How is this possible?! How can you be here?!" I scream.

I try everything in my power to crawl away, but my body is too weak from my journey to get far. The beast grabs hold of my leg and begins scooping me feet first into its blending teeth. My legs are ground into a bloody heap of splintered bones and ripped muscles as I reel in agony. I punch at the beasts embrace around my chest weakly to no effect. The pain was indescribable.

Up ahead I see Katya staring directly at me. Another time-eater floats behind her and takes a massive bite out of her arm. She stands motionless as if it had no effect. With two fingers extended on her remaining arm, she points to both her eyes and then points forward, the beast still blending her body to pieces without a reaction.

I look in the direction she pointed, and visions began to crowd my eyes. Up ahead I see Allister, Eliza, and I getting into the carriage and driving away. I see my daughter Penelope running to welcome us home as I meet her in a warm hug. Further forward, I see myself in my own library, digging through my mother's old crate and finding the book she wrote in just before her death. Inside was a note telling others that it was my father who murdered her, with her seal to authenticate it. I see my father standing trial for her murder and being hung as my uncle seizes control of the estate. I see me and Allister being married in a secret location with Eliza and Trevor giving us away. Penelope looks so beautiful in her dress and Allister so handsome in his suit.

It is then that I realize what I am. I am not Henry Wallace. I am his shadow. I am the umbramorph feeding off his life as he lives it. Going on this journey has made me aware of what I am. Now it is time to accept my fate. As my vision grows dim, I feel no pain as I keep my gaze forward and take my last fill of Henry's beautiful future.

HUNTING MISFORTUNE

by J.L. Allred

Gentle red light spilled out of the open pouch sitting on the bar. The light of firestones. They belonged to Rowan of House Stoutfire. Ten stones were in the pouch. *That should be enough to get through this hunt,* he thought. He turned his attention to the bounty card that sat next to it. *Reward. Larval Bane Creeper. Disturbance High.* The words were large to grab the attention of Banehunters, like himself.

Rowan twisted a red stone between his fingers as he read, the only one not in his pouch. He felt a connection to it as if a thin thread ran from it to somewhere near his heart. He picked up the bounty card and scanned the rest of it intently.

Eventide Mine Closed. A larval bane creeper has halted the mining operation after killing twelve and wounding four. A bounty has been issued for the removal of the threat of the lesser

*bane and restoration of a safe environment for the Earthstone mine
to return to full operation. Please see Mayor Winehearth with the
jaw of the creature for payment.
Class Bounty - 50 Silver chips
Disturbance Bounty - 5,000 Silver chips*

Rowan slammed the paper down on the bar. Burning fools. He
wished the ones who founded this settlement were in front of him
so he could ask them a couple of questions before he knocked them
around a bit. Namely, what idiots put a settlement in the shadow
of a mountain range? Out of reach of the Pillar's light. *Hidden from
our only defense*, he thought. *Well, not our only defense.* That's why he
was here.

Normally if some creature like a creeper was threatening a town
it would be because it had simply become corrupted by darkness.
Once corrupted it was known as a bane, a creature that hungered
to spread its corruption. But in this case the town was threatened
because it had actually been set directly in the shadow of a
mountain, making threats by corrupted creatures a regular
occurrence. His right hand gripped the firestone tightly, it pulsed
warmth as if in answer to his anger.

"Are you going to solve our bane problem?" A tall and yet still
plump man said to him from the other side of the bar. He was the
innkeeper.

"What gave you that idea?" Rowan asked.

The innkeeper nodded to the bounty card in Rowan's hand.

"I'm afraid your bane problem will be ongoing innkeeper. But
this one I will handle," He replied.

The innkeeper leaned in discreetly and spoke in a hush.

"My cousin went on a banehunt once. He says when one's in a
room the lights go dim. Like the light is being sucked out of the
room. Doesn't matter if it's torchlight or stonelight neither. It's not

natural. Not natural at all." His hand trembled slightly as he poured in some more of the clear amber liquid Rowan had been sipping. Rowan nodded his thanks. He picked up the glass, swirled the drink around and set it back down.

"Someone once told me light and dark are ancient enemies. In every room a silent battle rages between the two. The light from a stone and the shadow on the wall are battle movements in this long war. A bane is darkness given flesh and when one encounters light the battle rages. Greater darkness will beat weaker light. Greater light" he nodded past the walls of the inn towards the Pillar of Light that stood just south of the mountains that shadowed this settlement "will always beat weaker darkness." He took a large gulp of the drink before him.

The innkeeper glanced to the side at the earthstone lantern hanging on the wall. Its light flooded the room. But there were shadows too. Behind the bar, under tables, Rowan's own glass cast a shadow. Rowan watched him see it with fresh eyes.

"Aren't bane all that's left out there? Out in the dark beyond the Pillar's reach?" He asked Rowan as if he expected firsthand knowledge on the subject.

"I don't know. I guess that's most of what's out there, that's all that comes across the border anyway." Rowan had heard rumors of people living outside the border but that couldn't be true so he didn't bother bringing it up.

"Maybe we're like ghosts then. Holding onto another's world," the innkeeper said thoughtfully.

"You are quite the philosopher innkeeper, aren't you?" Rowan asked with a chuckle. This snapped the man out of his thoughtful stupor, and he laughed deeply.

"The only kind of philosopher you can trust!" He laughed "And what house are you from again?" Rowan saw his eyes run over the sigil on his leather breastplate. It was a shield with flames licking up the sides.

"House Stoutfire," He replied. The man returned his answer with a blank expression. Rowan shifted on his stool. He never got used to the uncomfortable silence and awkward expressions he received when he answered that question.

"We're a new noble house. A house of banehunters."

The man nodded vaguely.

"Are you very good? At hunting bane, I mean?" he asked, running his eyes across the many facial scars Rowan wore. One in particular seemed to have caught the innkeeper by the throat and he was unable to speak or look away. This would have been the scar running the length of the side of Rowan's head. He often found that people were distracted by his scars. He didn't mind the attention. He had his hair pulled back in a braid and the sides of his head shaved to give this one the prominence it deserved.

"This one was from the time I fought three lesser bane creepers," he said, gesturing to the scar.

"Ah creepers, those have a hundred legs, don't they?" the barman asked. Rowan nodded.

"That's right and each is as sharp as a blade. One caught me as I was trying to duck it. I got him but it nearly cost me my life. My father had to cauterize the wound to stop the bleeding."

The innkeeper winced. "That must have been unpleasant."

"I remember screaming but I don't remember the pain thankfully."

The innkeeper's eyes stopped on another scar near his collarbone. Only the very edge of this one was visible as it was mostly obscured by his leather armor. There was a bad burn and a sunken gap in his collarbone. It was the only scar of which he was ashamed. The only scar that represented failure on him. A failure that had cost his father's life. He still had guilt to this day over it.

The innkeeper seemed to sense his discomfort as his eyes rested on the scar and he spoke. "Do most banehunters have a lot of scars?" Rowan bristled slightly, he heard doubt in the question.

"Most have some scars, though many take more pains to hide them. I see them as marks of success. Every scar shows my service to the kingdom and that I survived the encounter with darkness."

"The other hunter didn't have any scars."

"What other hunter?" Rowan asked, suddenly alert.

"Another hunter was here earlier before going up the mountain."

"How do you know he was a hunter?"

"He had the same bounty card as you. Wore a greycloak."

Rowan dropped his stone, it hit the wood with a thunk and stayed. Greycloak? The elite guard of the Wildwood wore greycloaks. What would one be doing so far from their border?

"Was he from the Wildwood?"

He scratched his chin. "Now you mention it he did feel like a foreigner. Had a funny accent."

"How long ago was he here?" Rowan asked.

"Couldn't have been more than three hours ago."

Rowan stood up quickly and reached into his pack. He pulled out a handful of coins and tossed far more than were necessary down on the bar and grabbed his crossbow and spear. He was in the doorway of the tavern when he felt the thread pull taut. He had almost broken the invisible connection between him and his firestone. He turned around and could see it across the room lying on the bar softly pulsing. Internally he pulled the thread and it flew across the room and into his hand.

"Hey Banehunter!" A voice called from back inside the tavern. He turned on his heel to face the innkeeper.

"Yes innkeep?"

"A lone hellcat was spotted near the mountains this morning after the dimming ended. Be careful."

"He probably sensed the bane up in the mountains," Rowan said. If he could find the hellcat, it could lead him right to his target. He turned and walked out.

Rowan climbed a well-worn path that acted as a natural staircase on the side of the mountain. His eyes followed the path to a pass that he expected would lead to one of the mine entrances where his hunt could begin. This side of the mountain was a curious sight. Though the dimming wouldn't happen for many hours this side of the mountain range was always dim. Direct light from The Pillar would never touch it. But the southern side of the range would be fully lit all day until The Pillar dimmed in the evening.

On the light side of the mountain the vegetation consisted of plants that enjoyed the heat and needed very little water. This side was a completely different habitat. Rowan was surrounded by trees with massive trunks to support their climb towards heaven. They were bare of much vegetation for hundreds of feet, saving it all for the tops where they could drink enough of the precious light that slipped through the gaps between the peaks and the clouds. Smaller plants that could survive on the low ambient light alone covered the ground as well.

One of those plants caught Rowan's eye. It had no flower and its leaves unrolled in thin spirals. Its fronds were green, but the tips were red. *Feverfern*, he thought as he pulled a knife from a sheath on his chest. He cut a frond in half and separated the leaves from the stem. He had seen feverfern work before when one of his friends had been bitten by a small baneling rat. The corruption was not severe, but it had gotten into the boy's blood and once that happened it was beyond being burned out by a firestone. Since no earthstone users were nearby their small town to draw out the corruption, feverfern in the right dose was the only option. He could still remember the heat that came off him and the seizures that racked his body for what seemed like hours. It was horrible, but it had saved the boy's life. Rowan hoped he didn't need it but now he had the option.

While he finished gathering the herbs a dark figure moved in his peripheral. A wave of adrenaline hit him, telling him to act quickly. His pouch of essence stones hung off his belt just below his hand and he felt the thread connecting him to his firestone. In an instant it could be in his hand and he could be weaving an attack. But he didn't know what it was. If it was a larger predator like a hellcat or the very creature he hunted, he did not want to frighten it into attacking. Instead, he reached slowly into the pouch, gripped the stone and turned his head. Nothing was there. No, something *had* been there and now it was gone. While scanning the area, he took the stone in his left hand and guided it into its slot in his steel vambrace. He no longer felt the thread. The firestone was now part of him just like his limbs or an organ. And if it were damaged, he would feel it until the all-too-painful severing of the connection between him and the stone. He reached into the pouch at his side and pulled out another firestone that was only partially charged. It glowed softer than the one in his right vambrace. He dropped it into its slot and listened for a moment. There were no other sounds or signs of anything to fear. He slung his pack back over his shoulders and picked up his spear.

It wasn't long before the ground in front of him became level. He had reached the pass. Periodic gusts of wind were guided through the mountain pass by the surrounding slopes. One hit him with some force knocking him back a step. He bent his knees and leaned forward slightly into the wind. After a moment the gale subsided, and he nearly fell forward. A few yards in front of him in the side of the mountain was a large opening. There were pickaxes strewn about and a couple carts as well. *This must be the mine entrance,* he thought. Just then another strong wind blew in from the west and turned him sideways. He could see two other mine entrances on the opposite side of the pass with similar signs of being active mining sites. Now which one to enter first.

He remembered what the innkeeper had said about another banehunter. If Rowan could identify which entrance the other hunter had gone in, he could gain some ground on him. He looked for some sign of tracks, but the rocky ground guaranteed there would be little in the way of tracks for him to identify.

Clack clack clack. The sound of rocks being disturbed and bouncing down the side of the rock face echoed in the highlands. Rowan looked up and around for the source of the sound. The wind howled above him. Maybe that's all it was, the wind disturbing some rocks. The sound of something sliding towards him shattered that thought. He turned just in time to see its black body leaping down. He rolled to the side, pulled his crossbow, and stood back up all in one fluid motion. The creature was in his sights, but it was walking away from him. It sniffed some of the digging equipment and Rowan got a look at its massive frame supported by four muscular limbs. It didn't have fur so much as coin-sized plates that interlocked like a suit of armor. The plates were dark yet glassy like obsidian. It turned its head to the side taking note of Rowan but otherwise unconcerned at the weapon of death pointing at it. Rowan saw its glowing coals for eyes. His finger twitched slightly on the trigger. The Hellcat turned around and walked away towards the other entrances sniffing as it went. Rowan lowered the crossbow. He didn't understand the creatures, but he knew when they were on the scent of a bane: they found it and took down anything that stood in their way. That thrill of the hunt, Rowan *did* understand.

The first entrance he had seen looked to be the largest and have the most signs of activity around it. This must have been the main entrance. It was as good a place as any to start. He started into the mine and then the Hellcat entered his peripheral again. To his left about twenty yards away there was a shadowy corner. It looked like a dark corner of the mountain and nothing more. But then the hellcat's entire body disappeared into the shadow. Rowan waited for a moment and it didn't reappear. He walked over towards the shadow and as he reached the corner, he could see a small gap in the mountain. He ducked the low entrance and squeezed himself between the sharp edges of the rock and once he came through the secret pass, he reached out in front into the sea of darkness and felt the sides of a tunnel that he could follow.

The firestones on his arms glowed faintly. More light would be nice, he thought.Seemingly in response to this realization they began to pulse brighter. That was better but he still needed more. He traced a circle in the air with his right finger and a ball of flame filled the exact tracing of his finger. He held his hand out, palm up and it hovered above. Further down the passage he saw the burning coal eyes turn and look at him again. He wouldn't get in its way. He would follow it up to the moment it found the giant earth-eating bane and then, he would strike.

Their smaller tunnel connected with a larger one. Rowan kept back while he watched the creature turn left into the larger tunnel. He followed on after it. He had followed like this for at least an hour, keeping a good twenty yards between him and the hellcat. Rowan didn't have any delusions that the creature didn't know he was following it as it periodically turned and looked to see if he was still following. He knew it was silly, but he couldn't shake the feeling that it was making sure he was still following it. He had followed for another mile or so when he saw light down the passage.

Earthstones, he thought, *a lot of them.*

Earthstones, like fire, wind, or water glowed with energy. However, earthstones were white and the light they emitted was brighter than the others. There were also stones that were forbidden to use. Corrupted stones. Darkstones. The more corrupt the darker they became until they turned solid black. A known corrupt stone user was branded "darkstone" and wanted throughout the land. Not only that; there was a catch to using a darkstone. Your ability to use pure stones was tainted forever as their power came from another source. The same source that spread and turned creatures to bane.

Before they could reach the earthstone deposit the hellcat turned down a dark side tunnel. Perhaps it wanted to stay out of the light since it was hunting. He turned into the tunnel as well. A moment later he heard a loud metal clang ring out and the hellcat let out a yelp of pain. Down the tunnel a fire came alive. As he neared it, he could see the hellcat struggling to free it's leg from something. It was caught in some type of metal trap and trying to burn itself free, but the metal wasn't melting. The heat was intense, and Rowan couldn't get any closer to help. He looked up. His ball of fire still hovered in the air above him. He reached up and pulled at the edges with both hands widening it out in front of him. The glow from it softened as Rowan drew heat back into the stones at his wrists. What he had in front of him now was a net that could absorb the heat and reflect it back so that Rowan could get close enough to see the device that had trapped the Hellcat and, if possible, free it.

He held his hand out in front of him, holding the shield with an invisible grip. The heat from the hellcat surrounded Rowan but suddenly curled back and was sucked into the shield. Rowan pushed forward towards the creature. The heat was growing less intense; it was giving up. Rowan came up next to it and looked at the steel jaws that had it in its grip. The metal glowed but, amazingly, it was still intact. He could see the release pin underneath; he just needed the creature to be still. He looked at his free hand and wisps of heat reached out of the stone and enveloped his hand. Similar to the shield he held, this heat glove would take and absorb additional heat. He reached up and stroked the thrashing creature. There was a look of recognition on its face. Maybe something that could withstand its intensity could be trusted. It stopped thrashing and let its fire burn to a smolder. Rowan moved back to the creature's leg and found the pin. He pulled it and the trap released the tension. The hellcat's leg came free and it sprang down the tunnel and around a corner.

"And here I thought we were forming a friendship," Rowan said to himself as he let go of the heat shield and organized it back into a ball of fire. It hovered above him lighting the scene. He looked at the trap and felt anger surge inside of him. He was going to make sure this trap couldn't be used again. He put the pin on the ground and motioned the ball of fire down towards it. The fire crashed down onto the pin with force and held there until it was nothing but a few beads of molten metal.

"That should do it," he said.

The trap could just as easily have caught him. Instead it scared off the creature that should have led him right to the bane.

When I find that other banehunter, he thought then paused. Or what if he's found me?

He looked up and around half-expecting a man in a greycloak to be staring down at him. The tunnel was empty. He relaxed. But as if in response to his relief he heard light footsteps around the corner. Rowan quickly released the fire weave hovering above him, and it dissipated into the air. As the light quickly faded, he caught sight of an alcove on the opposite wall of the tunnel from the trap. He moved to the alcove, removed the fire stones from his wrists and slipped them into the pouch at his side. He still felt the strong tie to his favored stone. It pulsed in the bag urging to be used. *Not now!* he said internally. Light from the bag reflected on the ceiling of the alcove and Rowan quickly pulled the strings tightening the bag closed.

Another light shone down the tunnel. This one wasn't steady like the light from essence stones. A large, cloaked figure holding a short spear in one hand and a torch with flickering flame in the other walked by the alcove.

A torch? he thought. *Why wouldn't he use an earthstone for light?*

The light inside an earthstone was bright enough even without using it and it didn't give off the same heat a fire weave did. This made it ideal as a light source. The benefit of using a fireweave for light to Rowan was having something he could already use without having to build a new weave. The figure that walked by was hooded and wore a mask over the bottom half of his face. Rowan watched him and the color of the cloak as the light fell on it. It was grey. He was definitely the other banehunter. Suddenly, the figure turned his head and shined the torch into the alcove where Rowan hid. Rowan flattened himself to one side of the entrance. The light shined in, but the other hunter didn't step in and look around. Instead he turned, knelt down, and looked at the trap. Rowan caught a glimpse of the unmistakable green glow of a windstone in the man's wrist. No doubt he was noticing the missing pin. He looked down and touched the now dry metal beads on the tunnel floor. While he was distracted Rowan slung his crossbow off his shoulder and soundlessly crept behind the man. He was right behind him when the man spoke.

"Are you the one who sabotaged my trap and set my bait free?" Rowan froze. Somehow the man knew he was there without looking at him.

"Of course you are, you were waiting in that alcove for me to come back and check my trap." The man sighed when he finished the sentence. His accent was definitely foreign. It didn't even resemble the dialect of the Wildwood tribesmen that lived near the border of their two countries. On top of that, his condescending tone and slightly nasal voice gave Rowan all the more reason to dislike him.

"You could have just as easily caught me in that trap, and I would be feeling a lot less friendly right now. Instead you injured and scared off the hellcat before it could mark the bane for me," he said, his crossbow aimed in the hunter's direction. He'd better not move. Rowan wasn't a murderer, but the other hunter walked a thin line between enemy and obstacle. And Rowan didn't have much use for enemies.

"If you were caught in that trap you would be down a leg so that is fortunate for you. *I* am the one who should be angry here. This will take a lot longer and be a lot more dangerous without bait and that is your fault."

"I'll be sure to tell the Bards of Brithomere to get started writing a dirge for you. Right now I've got a bane to hunt and I don't need you in my way." He took a step towards the man. "And just so we're clear: killing, injuring, or maiming the hellcat in any way will count as getting in my way." The Greycloak drew up to him and Rowan was reminded of his shorter than average size to most people he squared up against. He stood his ground anyway.

"What you need to understand, tinderbox, is that I have been given a mission and Greycloaks do not fail. We overcome or *cut down* obstacles that get in our way, but the *mission* will always come first."

"I'm Rowan of House Stoutfire. We don't back down from any hunt. For anyone." Rowan felt the color climb up into his cheeks, but he didn't say anymore. He turned down the tunnel and started in the direction the hellcat had run. After only a few steps he heard footsteps behind him. The Greycloak was walking in the same direction.

"Are you following me?" Rowan asked, incredulous.

"Of course not! I'm following the hellcat, like you."

"Oh, now you adopt that technique after maiming it first. Smart."

"I wouldn't have had to adopt that technique if *someone* hadn't released it!" Rowan was successfully getting under the man's skin. A thought came to his mind and he grinned.

"You know I saw the hellcat get a scent off the trap before it ran off. I'm not sure it'll be too forgiving when it smells you near it again." No answer came from behind him. He turned his head and saw the Greycloak walking silently. Yet in the dim light of his torch Rowan saw the very pale outline of the man's face beneath his hood. He smiled. He hadn't really seen the hellcat get a scent before it ran away but for all he knew it did.

After a bit more walking they came to a fork in the tunnel they had been following. Rowan noticed a small pool of blood at the fork.

"Which way did it go?" the Greycloak asked.

"Not sure," Rowan said simply while crouching down and looking closer at the blood.

"What are you doing?"

"Tracking." Rowan reached into his pouch and pulled out the bonded firestone. He closed his eyes and dipped a finger in the blood. He could feel the trail vaguely stretching down the tunnel.

Though every drop was not physically connected, the essence of fire was in every bead as something like the magic contained in Rowan's firestone ran through the hellcat's veins in liquid form. He could sense it. He could touch it. He could channel into it. Lights flickered to life down the tunnel one by one in broken asymmetrical lines. Rowan stood up satisfied. He glanced to the side and saw the Greycloak staring down the tunnel with his mouth slightly agape.

"Did that weave...track the hellcat *for* you?" he asked Rowan.

"Not exactly. I detected the fire essence in the blood and was able to sense the trail through the tunnel. Once I had it the weave lit the trail," he explained.

"I've always known the reputation of Ciallmhar is wisdom and innovation. I guess it's true what they say about your countrymen," the Greycloak said.

"I guess so. So, do you have a name you can give me so I don't have to make one up?" Rowan asked.

"My name is privileged information. This mission is privileged information for that matter," the man said reverting to his serious demeanor.

"Okay. Priv it is," Rowan said with a smirk.

"Priv?"

"Yeah short for privileged information."

"That's not what I me—"

"I know, Priv, I know," Rowan said as he started down the tunnel towards the burning trail.

They had covered a hundred yards or so when the fires ceased. The trail had literally gone cold. Priv looked behind them and cocked his head. Rowan turned as well to see what he was looking at. One by one the small flames were doused starting farther away until the last trail fire ceased at their feet.

"The fires only stay lit for a short amount of time. It's a built-in protection for the hunter using the spell," Rowan explained again.

"How does it protect you?" Priv asked.

"Because if what you are hunting circles back around those fires become a trail to you."

Priv nodded in understanding and they both turned around. The trail may have gone cold but not before leading them into a large room of dark rough stone floor with smooth reflective stone running up the walls. Earthstones lit the expansive room. On the first floor they filled up carts and littered the stone floor. On the second and third levels they reflected off the slate rock wall in which they were set, as yet unmined. There were carts and pickaxes like at the mine entrance but many of the carts were turned over and many of the pickaxes were damaged.

"The trail is gone. Any more hunter tricks up your vambrace?" Priv asked.

"The trail isn't gone, it's just changed. Now the trail becomes more subtle. Look for a footprint in debris, fire burnt material, anything to give a clue," he finished, uncertain if they would be able to find the next clue that would put them back on the hellcat's trail. Rowan hoped he hadn't seen the last of it. He was growing fond of it and the last thing he wanted was for it to face the bane alone.

Priv went to one side of the cavern and Rowan went to the other. There was a minecart smashed to splinters and its white gemstones piled against the wall where it had impacted. In fact the more Rowan looked around the more he noticed damage all throughout the room. Split hafts of pickaxes and more carts of earthstones smashed against the wall. It was as if something had scattered them away from itself. Rowan had an idea of what might want to knock away caches of earthstones. He came across a pile of earthstones and at the foot of the pile something caked onto the floor illuminated. It was hard to make out on the dark floor, so he crouched down and ran his finger along it. Blood. Dried blood. He looked up and around. Now he could see the dark opaque stains all along the ground and walls. It had the look of a crime scene. There were no bodies, but Rowan hadn't expected to find many. The bane creeper was killing for food which meant these bloody stains were all that would be left behind.

Rowan looked up towards the other levels. A system of ropes and pulleys served the lift system as there were three levels in this room. On the second level tucked into the side of the stone there was a wooden room. Likely where the foreman observed the operation of the mine. Something told him to go up there. He followed the wall to a set of stairs roughly cut into the rock. They were uneven in spots and slick in others, more caked blood causing him to lose traction.

As he neared the second level a foul smell filled his nostrils. At the top of the stairs and just around the corner he found his first corpse. A red-haired man slumped against a wall. He couldn't have been there for more than three days as the body had not begun to bloat. His brown eyes were open but distant, head down chin touching his chest. He was missing a large piece in his side and here is where he succumbed to his injuries. Rowan noticed he held a keyring in one of his hands. He pried the fingers open and took the keys. They would most likely open the foreman's office up ahead. While he moved the man's hand to get the keys, he noticed a faint glow of something hanging from his belt. Rowan unclasped it. From the shape of the scabbard it looked to be a dagger. Light escaped from inside the leather. Rowan unsheathed it and its light blinded him momentarily. His eyes adjusted but it was still difficult to look at it directly. The color and glow were unmistakably earth essence which meant the blade itself was an earthstone.

Essence stone weapons were difficult to make. Cutting them into such a thin shape was rarely done well resulting in blades that could crack easily. This one was the finest attempt at one he had ever seen. He clasped it to his belt, closed the unseeing eyes of the man and nodded his thanks before heading towards the door of the foreman's office. The wooden structure was still intact except the window facing out towards the room looked broken. He leaned his spear next to the door and took the first key and stuck it in the lock and tried to turn. Not that one. He went to the next one. Not that one either. He was at the last key on the ring. He put it in the lock and turned.

A steady sound started from behind the door. Like someone sawing at wood very loudly. It had the sound of something large producing friction. Why did it sound so familiar? He quickly slotted in two firestones then grabbed his spear. He bent his knees holding it with both hands and eased open the door with the tip. Behind the door, was a tangle of scales, slime, and black eyes inside a flat shovel shaped head. There was a sheen on its skin that reflected the light of earthstones shining in through the broken window and open door. It writhed back and forth, scales scraping against each other in long continuous strokes warning Rowan not to come closer. It was coiled and ready to explode towards him.

A sudden gust of wind hit Rowan, knocking him sideways. The roof of the foreman's office blew off as well and the larval bane creeper was pinned to the wall. The earthstones in the wall and ceiling nearest the bane instantly dimmed slightly. Rowan glanced over his shoulder to see Priv standing below in the middle of the room. Arm outstretched and hand cupped towards the creature. It flailed against the wall but remained pinned by the wind. Several earthstones in the wall right next to the creature were completely suppressed.

Rowan steadied himself and walked towards the pinned creature. He had killed bane creepers before but never seen their larval form. If they were anything like their adult form, he just needed one good lateral slice with his spear to separate the head from the body. The wind increased and Rowan lost his balance sliding against the wall. That was a little overkill. The creature was already pinned, yet Priv was increasing the gust. With this wind it would be difficult to form a fire weave as it would almost immediately be blown out. The wind died suddenly as Priv yelled out. Below Rowan saw a large cat covered in black plates squaring up towards Priv. The Hellcat had found him.

The ridge of plates on its back stood up and it burst into flame. Rowan quickly turned back to the bane. It was starting to regain its wits. He charged it, throwing his weight behind the spear and into the creature. Its head pushed to the side but instead of digging in the blade's tip slid off barely making a scratch. He raised an eyebrow before the creeper's head lunged right for him. He rolled to the side and made a downward vertical slice. Again the blade slid down but didn't penetrate.

Eternal flame! What is going on? he cursed.

He threw a bright spray of sparks from one hand, blinding the creature, and spun to the side of its wild attack. He reached for the earthstone dagger he had pulled off the corpse. The light from it was suppressed being this close to the bane but it was still an earthstone and he had to try something different. While the creature was momentarily blinded, he buried it in its side. It didn't go in deep, but it did penetrate the initial layer of scales. The creature writhed and the dagger ripped out of Rowan's hand. While it thrashed about, he ran and dove for cover behind an overturned cart nearby.

He wouldn't survive long if his attacks remained ineffective. He needed to get it downstairs to give it more than one threat to deal with. Rowan peered around the cart and saw one of the lifts hanging away from the ledge above the first level. That would be one way to get down quickly. He had to distract it somehow so he could make it to the suspended wooden platform. His usual distraction technique was to light something on fire. A flaming wooden cart might do the trick. He stayed low but put a few steps between him and the cart. Then he hit it hard with a blast of flame that simultaneously ignited it and knocked it into the air. It hit the scaly bane in the face. While it rounded on the cart he ran.

The edge of the second level was fast approaching. He pushed hard off the ledge launching toward the rope-suspended lift and caught the edge. The rope holding it snapped and down the lift went and him with it. He let go of it and his momentum carried him just feet from where it landed. He hit the ground and rolled to absorb some of the force of the fall. When he stood a moment later, he was looking right at Priv whose greycloak had a tear in it though, inexplicably, he had managed to keep his hood up. He turned around. The hellcat was circling them both now but looked less certain with Rowan standing between them.

"Did you kill it yet?" Priv asked as they continued to match step for step with the hellcat.

"About that, my spear isn't hurting it," Rowan said.

"That is discouraging, Rowan," Priv said.

"Imagine how I feel."

"Where is it?" Priv asked.

At that very moment it jumped or did the closest thing to jumping as a leg-less bane could. Soaring above them was the entire hulking body of a larval bane creeper. Priv dove to one side, Rowan and the hellcat dashed to the other. Instinctively Rowan sparked a fire-weave to life. In a few heartbeats it had grown to a blaze. A second later the bane impacted shaking the ground violently, several large pieces of the ceiling split and fell. Rowan leveled the wall of fire at the creature pouring everything from the firestone in his left vambrace into it. As he sent his attack, a twin stream of fire came from somewhere else. Both hit the creature at the same time. He glanced to the side to see the hellcat fully lit unleashing a blaze of its own. In spite of this Rowan could see the bane moving towards both of them.

How is this possible? he wondered.

Suddenly it was struck in the side of the head by two large boulders that Priv had apparently been keeping from crushing them both. It was knocked to the side for a moment. Rowan's left vambrace was empty, the hellcat now barely smoldered as it was drained too. Rowan looked back at the bane. It was shaking it off. Not just the blows from the rocks but the burnt skin from their attacks was peeling away too. They had hardly damaged it. Rowan glanced at Priv who looked grave. His eyes met the black eyes in that abnormal shovel head, and it charged him mouth open, teeth bared. He lowered his spear toward the bane and braced. It slammed into him and pushed him across the floor. He hit the wall hard and something snapped. The creature let out a roar and jerked backwards. Rowan faintly saw the haft of the spear lying on the ground, the head had broken off, buried somewhere inside the creature.

"Did I get it?" he heard himself asking as he dropped to the floor.

Stars wheeled above. No not stars, earthstones. His vision was becoming clearer. He sat up. He was in the large room with the mining carts and—the bane! What had happened to it? The last thing he remembered he slammed into something hard and his spear head snapped off. He looked at the haft lying next to him. Burn it all, he'd liked that spear. Rowan noticed a large dark lump laying a few yards from him. It was the hellcat; its plates were folded against its bulky frame. Its chest rose and fell indicating it was just sleeping.

"It passed out the same moment you did." Priv walked around in front of Rowan as he spoke. He was rubbing the forearm that had the windstone in it.

"Strange connection you two have," he said.

"Connection? What are you implying, Greycloak?" Rowan asked.

"It happens on occasion with elemental creatures under the right conditions. The Griffin riders in my country all have to form a bond with their Griffins as the final part of their training. If they can't form the bond, they can't be Griffin riders."

"I don't have a bond with this hellcat, Priv." He wasn't sure why he was being so defensive. Maybe it was because he always saw himself as a lone hunter. Similar, in a way, to hellcats who almost always lived solitary lives. Others couldn't get hurt that way.

"You may not have one yet, but you're forming one. You touched it with fire essence from a bonded stone when you rescued it from my trap didn't you?" Priv asked.

"Yeah, so?"

"And then you channeled into its blood."

"Right, still—"

"And then your magic touched again when you attacked the bane together."

He had thought it odd how coordinated the hellcat's attack seemed to be with his. Could the Greycloak be right?

"What happened to the monster?" Rowan asked, eager to change the subject.

"It fled after eating the head of your spear. I do not think it enjoyed the flavor."

Rowan thought back to the encounter. The bane had scales, no legs, and a flat broad head. It didn't have mandibles but a ring of teeth on the inside of its mouth. The bounty card said it was a creeper larva, but he had never seen a creeper that looked like this one.

"Did that look like a creeper to you?" he asked Priv.

"Not like any creeper I've seen in the Wildwood. Perhaps that is what creepers are like in Ciallmhar?"

Rowan shook his head. "I've never seen a creeper without legs, even in their nymph form they have at least twelve legs."

"Scales on creeper bane in Ciallmhar?" Priv asked.

"Not that I've seen. They have chitin. Tough chitin but nothing compared to those scales."

"Seems like this bane was misidentified," Priv said.

"Misidentified and misclassified. There's no way that was a lesser bane."

"Perhaps it was a lesser bane when it drove the workers out of the mine. Something is changing it, making it grow. Making it more resistant to attacks, more than usual for a bane."

"I think you're right. But that still doesn't explain what it is. If I don't know what I'm up against, how am I supposed to kill it?" he asked, exasperated. This was why he hunted alone. He got himself in over his head and others got hurt trying to help him. He shouldn't care much for this winder, but now he was in over his head again and he knew if something happened to the man, he would carry the guilt like he did for his father.

The dark lump near him shifted. He looked over and saw the hellcat stirring. It stretched its hind parts up into the air and yawned showing it's huge razor like teeth. Its glowing eyes opened and instantly locked with his. It slowly walked towards him sticking its snout up into the air smelling something. It was a few feet from him when he heard it make a sound. Was it purring? It rubbed its head against his arm. Thankfully its plates were lying flat at the moment and it was a plus that it wasn't on fire. It continued to purr and rub its head against him. Then it moved around his back and he winced as it rubbed against his shoulder blade. It wasn't broken. He would've been in a lot more agony if it was. But it must've been severely bruised which was plenty painful.

"I see the bonding is going well," Priv said, noticing the activity. The hellcat began a low growl at the sound of Priv's voice. His eyes widened and Rowan grinned.

"It really is amazing how it knows exactly what I think of you," he said. It snarled and bared its teeth at Priv.

"Rowan, call it off!" Priv said, backing away slowly. The hellcat advanced.

"Hey you," Rowan said.

Amazingly, the hellcat turned its head and looked at him.

"We need his help. Don't eat him yet, please," Rowan said, standing up and starting towards the staircase in the corner of the room. It seemed to grunt in disappointment and turned and followed Rowan towards the stairs.

"Where are you going?" Priv asked.

"Back to the foreman's office where this started to look for some clue about the bane."

Rowan winced going up the stairs as his shoulder twinged with pain. Hopefully that would heal quickly. With some effort he made it to the top. He approached the office and among the debris that had fallen from the ceiling something bright caught his eye. He walked over and knelt keeping his back straight. It was the earthstone dagger. No doubt its effectiveness was suppressed by the bane's own dark essence, but it didn't have a mark on it and had done actual damage to the bane. He picked it up and slid it back into the scabbard clasped to his belt.

Before he stood up, he heard a short burst of smaller roars come from behind him. The hellcat was marking something. It growled and whined a bit wanting him to come over. He stood up gingerly and slowly walked closer to the office missing the roof. The bane they had just fought was definitely not inside, so he cautiously made his way inside the wooden structure. To his left when he entered the room against the wall was a somewhat large cage. Inside was a scaly worm a little less than two feet tall coiled around an earthstone. The sound of scales on scales met his ears again as he saw the worm writhe in such a way as a warning.

"Could it be?" He heard Priv's astonished voice behind him. Apparently, he had decided to join Rowan upstairs as well. "They were the same species."

"Not possible. You saw how big that thing was. These don't get any bigger than a dog."

"What is the little devil?" Priv asked, crouching down level with the creature.

"These are worms they use to locate earthstone deposits. They make nests beside them, it makes their skin tough as nails...and resistant to fire as well."

Rowan thought back to the encounter in the foreman's office. Its skin had a strange sheen to it. Then when he and the hellcat used their attacks some of its skin peeled away.

"Maybe it was looking for a safe place to molt," Rowan said, everything clicking into place. "And why wouldn't it feel safe in the room where it molted in the past with others of its kind?"

"Others of its kind?" Priv clearly wasn't following Rowan's thought process.

"Yeah the other scale worm in the cage."

"I thought you said it is not possible they are the same species?"

"It's the only thing that makes sense. It explains the resistance to fire and our weapons. Somehow the corruption is causing it to grow to a massive size," he said.

"This is why it was identified as lesser bane. It was lesser bane at the time before it grew again," Priv said, catching on. "So what do we do now?" he asked.

"What we should do is leave right now."

Priv looked at him confused.

He continued, "This is a full bane. If it molts again who knows what class it will be. This is not a two-man job. But by the time we come back with a team this thing could have molted three or four more times. It could be twice the size it is now. Who knows what damage it could do and how many it could kill when it starts looking for more food? We have to end it here and now. But how?"

Silence for a few moments. The scale worm in the cage had stopped it's threatening writhing and was very still. After a moment it began flexing and inching out of its skin. It was molting. It looked like an exhausting process.

"You said it was looking for a place to molt," Priv said. "Why don't we let it?"

"I just told you Priv—because when it's done it'll be even bigger and stronger. Are all Greycloaks this slow?"

Priv waved the insult away. "But while it's molting, it'll be like this little devil. Weak and slow. It will be vulnerable."

Rowan nodded thinking. He had a point. He continued watching the smaller worm in thought. It was almost halfway out of its skin. Didn't molting take a lot longer than a few minutes? A minute later the worm had finished. It began eating the skin slowly. It turned Rowan's stomach. Priv made a face. The earthstone in the cage with the scale worm looked much dimmer than it had when he first saw the creature. Had it instinctively channeled the essence from the stone to speed up the process?

"You have a good plan, but it can't be that simple. They molt quickly. This one because of the earthstone, our bane worm may draw on the dark power of its corruption to speed up the process."

"What do you propose, tinderbox?" Priv asked.

Rowan raised an eyebrow. "I propose we put a firestone in it, overload the stone and then,"

Rowan put his hands together in a circle and then spread them apart. "Boom."

The plan was in place. Rowan gave Priv the earthstone dagger to be sure he could cut in deep while the bane molted. Priv had acted strange when Rowan gave him the dagger. Handling it delicately, he hadn't even taken it out of the scabbard to inspect the work of art Rowan had told him it was. It leaned beside the opening to the main tunnel as he and Rowan examined a map they had found while going through the foreman's office.

The top of the map said, "Mine Progress" and had X's over the tunnels closest to where they were indicating which had been cleaned out of earthstones. Since it seemed sensitive to the earthstone dagger they both agreed it was likely to choose a spot that had already been heavily mined of earthstones. The first two tunnels marked with an X branched almost immediately off the main tunnel. The first branch went to the left and the next went to the right. The left branch dead-ended and then had another side tunnel off of it to the left and an exit to the right that led out to the Pillar of Light. The only use for the exit would be a rudimentary garbage shoot as the environment this close to the Pillar was too inhospitable to use it for anything else. This had Rowan thinking it unlikely the bane would go that way as it would have to pass too close to the Pillar before turning to the left down the side tunnel. They settled on taking the tunnel that branched right off the main tunnel.

Priv walked slightly in front of Rowan and the hellcat. His hood was still up and his mask covered his mouth.

"So, Priv, is it a crime punishable by death to let your hood and mask down in the Greycloaks or just a personal preference?" Rowan asked.

"My identity is privileged, remember? That includes facial features," Priv answered gruffly.

"Wow that is some serious control. Are you able to have any life outside of the next mission Priv?" Rowan asked, genuinely curious.

"Not for a long time." His posture didn't change but his cadence sounded forlorn to Rowan.

"Ever wish you had chosen to do something else with your life?" Rowan pushed a little further.

"I did not choose this," Priv said forcefully. "I mean, you cannot choose your calling. It chooses you."

Rowan didn't think that is what he meant but he decided not to push any further. He didn't want to fluster him before what he hoped would be the end of their hunt. The branch to the left came and went. The right branch would only be a little further. A growling sound drew Rowan's attention. He turned to see the hellcat behind them sitting by the entrance to the tunnel entrance they just passed. Priv turned around too.

"What is it doing, Rowan?" Priv asked.

"I don't know, why are you asking me?"

"Oh I forgot, you are in denial about your bond." Priv chuckled. Rowan ignored Priv and gestured for the hellcat to follow him. The hellcat gestured with its head towards the tunnel entrance it sat beside.

"No, it wouldn't go that way. Come on!" Rowan said

The hellcat just grunted again and started down the left tunnel that Rowan thought they needn't visit. Priv began to follow it.

"Priv what are you doing?" Rowan asked.

"I thought I would follow the hellcat, a hunter once told me they were great at marking bane." Rowan noted Priv's nasal-ness came out stronger when he was being sarcastic.

"Priv, I'm the one who told you that," he said annoyed.

"I know, tinderbox," Priv said with another chuckle. When did he get so cheeky? Stupid winder, stupid hellcat, and stupid bane if it did go that direction. He followed them both. He was being stupid himself continuing to hunt this eratic bane; but he might as well not be stupid enough to look for it alone.

After a minute or two more of walking Priv slowed down to walk beside him.

"So explain to me again how this overloading technique will work?" he asked.

Rowan sighed. "I have a strong connection with the stone in my right vambrace. It's bonded to me. I have a fully charged firestone in my pouch that is not bonded. This firestone," he said, pointing at his vambrace, "can recognize my other stone. If I channel fire energy into the fully charged stone from my bonded stone it will overload and—"

"Boom," Priv cut in.

"Yes. Boom. In fact," he reached into his pouch, "I can just give you the stone right now so you have it." Priv took the stone in a gloved hand and it lit up part of his arm that was unarmored. It was wrapped and faintly he could see blood seeping through.

"Why didn't you mention you got injured during the fight with the bane, Priv?" Rowan asked.

Priv quickly stowed the stone in a pouch of his own and his arm disappeared under his cloak.

"It is nothing to be concerned about. Just some blistering when the hellcat got too close." He seemed to wince remembering. The hellcat hissed at him after he said that.

"Hey, what did I say before? We need his help!" Rowan raised his voice slightly. The hellcat scarcely seemed to notice but it did leave Priv alone. As they walked the hellcat suddenly turned into another tunnel that hadn't been on the map. It looked like it had been recently dug. Rowan read the map using the stone in his vambrace for light.

"I guess digging its own tunnel is one way to avoid the Pillar. This tunnel should avoid the dead end by the Pillar entirely and cut straight across," Rowan said.

They followed the hellcat in silence the rest of the way. Rowan could feel the adrenaline start to pump into his veins as every step brought them closer to a monster unlike anything he had faced before. The end of this tunnel was approaching. They began to hear cries from what Rowan assumed was the creature molting. He imagined it was a painful process. Stretching, changing, leaving behind a part of yourself. It was a process the creature itself probably didn't understand. But, like an animal that's gone rabid, it needed to be put down.

They came to the opening and could see the large, lengthy body of the bane. It was dimly lit by the few earthstones that had been left in the rock above due to some unknown impurity or defect. The room itself was mostly open. A naturally formed column stood to one side created when a stalagmite and stalactite met and connected ground and ceiling. Rowan gestured to them to follow him as they moved low to a closer stalagmite that was large enough to provide them all with cover. From here Rowan could see most of the giant worm's head had pushed out of the skin. Good, it wasn't molting as fast as the worm in the cage. Its muscles slowly convulsed where the body pushed its way out of the skin otherwise it seemed completely still.

"All right, Priv, you're up," Rowan said, turning to him.

"Do not look so concerned, tinderbox," Priv said annoyed, probably because he was the one that got to sneak up to the bane while it molted then stab it and shove something inside of it.

"I would use an air weave to insert the stone Priv, who knows what this thing's blood will do to your skin if you try to do it by hand. And be quick about it, we don't know what it will do once we've interrupted its molt. It may be paralyzed until the process is done, or it may just get really really angry at us."

"I will be sure to move like I am stabbing a big angry monster with a little splinter."

Priv moved low out from the cover of the stalagmite. He reached the natural column near the end of the creature's body. Rowan lost sight of him behind the body of the large worm as he walked the length of it. The firestone in his vambrace brightened expectantly as if it knew he would call on it soon. Rowan never knew if this was something he did subconsciously or if the stone really was doing it independently. Suddenly, a bright light appeared near the creature's head. It let out a terrible cry as, no doubt, Priv had cut into it with the dagger. The hellcat paced anxiously behind the stalagmite. Rowan waited for the signal the firestone was placed. None came. The creature began convulsing and thrashing wildly. Where was Priv?

"Come on, we're not waiting anymore," Rowan said to the hellcat. It looked pleased. They both dashed towards the column to get closer to the creature. When they got to the column Priv was running towards them.

"Did you get it in Priv?" Rowan asked urgently.

He shook his head.

The creature roared as its old skin ripped from its body. A long barb stuck out from the end of its tail and a horn protruded from its head. More mutations brought on by the corruption. It whipped its length around looking for them. Suddenly to Rowan's horror he saw the hellcat standing out in the middle of the cavern. Rowan felt it's fire coming to life. It darted out of the way of a downward blow from the barbed tail and roared, launching several fire balls at the worm that detonated on impact. They didn't seem to faze it. A swing of the tail was its answer and the hellcat rolled low avoiding it.

There was a dark cloud of some kind that seemed to be building around the bane's horn. Suddenly a beam of shadow fired from the horn at the hellcat. It was caught off guard and knocked to the ground. The tail came down to strike again but buried itself in the rocky ground as the hellcat rolled out of the way again. Despite being wounded the hellcat's fire seemed to burn more fiercely and it roared, sending its own beam of bright flame at the creature. The clouds around the bane's head thundered and it countered the hellcat with another beam of shadow from its forehead.

The beam of light and dark collided in a shower of sparks. The dark beam was quickly overpowering the hellcat's attack. Rowan had to do something. He could feel the fire essence living in the hellcat just as he had felt the essence in its blood while tracking it. It had a firestone inside it, but its power level was dropping. His own stone pulsed urging him to use it. He instinctively channeled along the bond from his firestone into the hellcat's stone. The already bright flame of the hellcat turned an even brighter blue and pushed back. The beam of shadow stopped advancing. Both creatures roared and Rowan was barely aware that he was now standing out from behind cover, arm outstretched, letting out his own yell of defiance.

The blue beam sheared through the horn on the bane's head. It fell to the ground with a crash. Rowan dropped to one knee in a daze. Burn it, that had taken a lot out of him. He lifted his head and saw the hellcat looked woozy as well.

"Priv, we have to finish it. While it's down," he said through labored breathing.

Priv walked by Rowan toward the bane passing by something leaning against the column. *The dagger, he thought.* He could see it still leaning against the column.

"The dagger Priv! Get the dagger!" Priv didn't seem to hear him. He stopped in the middle of the room and lifted his left hand. The cloak fell back revealing a vambrace with a stone in it. A dark stone. Priv's feet were planted apart, bracing. A cold wind blew in and swept his hood back, but he kept his footing. The darkstone began to radiate something. Not light but anti-light. It was pushing away the light from around it. As it did, Rowan saw the bane stir and rise.

No, he thought, then the bane's horn repaired.

"No!" he yelled as Priv led it over to the smoldering hellcat. The anti-light fell across his face and made him look inhuman. It revealed dark veins running up his neck and behind his head.

"I am sorry for my betrayal, Rowan. As I said, my path was chosen for me. The Blackstones have taken an interest in this bane and I have someone whose life depends on me. I cannot fail them. I will spare your life, but I cannot have the hellcat follow me and the bane has just molted. It has to feed."

"I am sorry," he said again, a tear rolling down his cheek. Burn his tears, burn his regret!

"NO!" Rowan said, rising to his feet. All the firestones in his pouch pulsed in unison. He felt the threads on all of them humming with energy. Mentally he pulled the thread on every single one. All at once they leapt from his pouch and found their places in the armor of his arms, legs, and chest. They pulsed. No, *he* pulsed. He couldn't feel where the fire essence stopped, and he began.

Glowing like a human flame, he faced Priv and clapped his arms together. It pealed like thunder and a storm of fire and lightning erupted from his hands and screamed towards Priv and the bane. It hit the bane and knocked it back into the wall of the cavern. Priv summoned a dark wall from his stone that absorbed the inferno that was hurled against it but then it faltered and Rowan heard the unmistakable sound of a crack. Its anti-light failed, and it fell from the slot in his wrist in two pieces.

Behind him a thunderous roar shook the ground as the bane recovered from Rowan's attack. It rushed at Rowan, knocking Priv aside. He wove a heat shield just before the creature slammed into him with its tail. The shield barely blunted the blow and he was knocked into the stalagmite column. Something definitely felt broken in his shoulder now. The giant worm leapt and a shovel shaped head full of teeth came down on top of him.

Rowan blinked. Just above him the creature struggled, suspended in mid-air. Priv stepped forward, a new dark stone in his wrist. The anti-light ball he stood inside grew larger with the strain of lifting the mammoth bane and nearly pushed all light out of the room. Rowan heard a loud grunt from Priv as he hurled it into the narrow tunnel it had dug as a shortcut into the room. Then he pulled down the ceiling on top of it. The anti-light from his wrist faded and he rushed over to Rowan's side.

"Come on. This stone will fail if I try to use it to control the creature again which means we are out of options," he said.

"Oh, you think we are on speaking terms just because you saved my life after nearly getting me killed?" Rowan spouted as Priv helped him up.

"I think your shoulder is broken and I do not want you to die here because of me."

"And what about her? Are you okay with her dying because of you?" Priv looked at Rowan confused.

"What? I know the hellcat is a she. It's the bond thing you were so sure about," Rowan said.

"I am Misfortune, Rowan. That is my name. I bring calamity down on all who know me." He looked away as he spoke as if remembering something. Rowan just stared.

"You always were dramatic. Come on let's get her up and get out of here," he said.

Rowan kneeled down. He pulled out some feverfern and held it under her nose. She stirred and slowly stood up. Rowan closed his eyes and let the power from one of his stones empty into her stone. Her smoulder rose to flames. Priv helped Rowan stand back up again and they started down the tunnel leading away from the shortcut. The ground started to shake.

"Of course that didn't kill it," Rowan said.

"The mutations caused by the corruption are very unique. It only gets stronger the more damage it takes."

"What?" Rowan didn't know how to stop it; but they couldn't allow a bane this dangerous to survive.

Could it grow into something that would end the entire Kingdom?

"We have to kill it," he said.

"We cannot kill it. We can only survive," Priv said. The tunnel reverberated with cries from the creature. It was coming for them. Rowan sensed the hellcat behind them holding it off. *Don't die on me, girl,* he thought. The impression came back that she had heard him. They approached where the tunnel could continue straight or turn. There was a faint light at the bottom of the tunnel that went straight. It was the garbage chute that sloped down and led out to the side of the mountain exposed to the Pillar of Light. If they could get it out into the Pillar's light it would be greater light versus lesser darkness.

"We're going straight down the slope and out into the light," he said to Priv, but somehow he knew the hellcat heard him.

"It won't follow," Priv said, matter of fact. Rowan heard the dogged efforts of the bane trying to get to them. If not for the hellcat, it would have them already.

"Oh I think it will. Though it might need a last nudge out the door," he said.

Rowan had eight remaining fire stones with charge not including the one bonded to him strongest. As they moved down the slope, he consolidated their energy into four fully charged stones. They were passing scraps of wood, metal, animal bones. They were nearing the end of the slope where all the garbage had piled up.

"Priv—when we get out of the tunnel—I need you to collapse it behind the bane," he said between breaths with the occasional wince of pain.

"What will—you do?" Priv asked, breathing heavy as well.

"Kick it out the door," Rowan said, a smile curling his lips.

Their eyes had no time to adjust to the blinding light flooding into the tunnel's entrance. They ran straight through it. Rowan had never been this close to the Pillar before. It towered above them climbing ever higher until it disappeared from sight. It was oppressively hot.

Rowan shook his mind from the heat and mentally called the hellcat. She was at his side in a moment. She took something from him and ran near the entrance. The bane shrieked as it neared the tunnel entrance and felt the heat. Before it could retreat farther back into the tunnel Priv collapsed it as planned but the creature still was not out in the light and the immediate sounds of scales slamming on rock were heard as it desperately tried to get back inside the mountain. It could tunnel, they had to hurry.

The hellcat bolted in and came back out. Rowan felt the threads of the stones and sent everything he had from his last stone down the threads. He felt the thread of the bonded firestone fade to nothing as the last essence of fire left it. At once explosions blew rock, garbage, and the bane out into the white heat of the Pillar. It writhed and screamed in pain.

Rowan watched the battle between light and dark. The bane didn't stand a chance against the column of light that stretched from ground to sky and was wide as a mountain. With a few final slams of its ugly shovel head into the sand the creature went still. Flakes of skin began to blow off it as the entire creature broke down in a mere minute. All that was left were two darkstones. One the size of a melon was oblong and uncut. The other was much smaller and would fit in the slot of a vambrace; Priv's vambrace.

Rowan looked around and saw Priv walking toward a gap in the mountains where there was some shade. He wasn't getting away that easily. He hurried to catch up to him.

"Hey! Where do you think you're going?" he asked.

"To find some shade."

"And then what? Back to serve the Blackstones?"

"I told you I do not have a choice. Someone is depending on me," he said while holding the bandaged arm seeping blood.

"Are you okay? What really happened to that arm?" Rowan asked.

"There are consequences when a darkstone user channels through a pure essence stone."

"You keep saying someone is depending on you. Are they really worth all this?" he asked, gesturing to Priv's general sorry state. One arm was wrapped from blisters and still seeping blood and the other had jagged dark veins running up it. His face had paled quickly in the light of the Pillar. The dark veins around his neck seemed to have mostly receded.

"It is my sister, she is my only family. It has been like this since the beginning. If I do not continue to do their will, they will hurt her," he said.

"I don't get it. You seem pretty capable. Just grab her in the middle of the night and go!" Rowan said.

"It is not that simple," Priv replied solemnly.

"Nothing ever is, Priv. Priv? Should I still call you that? What's your real name?"

"I like Priv," he said.

Rowan paced trying to think of what to do. If he brought him in to be arrested, chances are he would be in prison for a long time. Who knows what would happen to his sister. But he couldn't just let him go. He looked out of the gap in the mountain and began to speak. He didn't see Priv back into a particularly dark shadow in the gap or see the glow from the darkstone pulse as he disappeared inside the shadow.

"You must know I can't let you go back to the Blackstones. I'm honor-bound to bring you in but maybe I can—" As he spoke, he turned around. No one was there. He looked out of the gap on both sides. There was no sign of him out on the flat lands next to the mountain side. He stepped back into the gap and saw something leaning against a dark corner in the rock. It was the scabbard holding the earthstone dagger. Next to it was a firestone. The one he had given Priv. There was a drop of blood on the ground. Rowan knelt down and picked up the firestone. He touched the drop and closed his eyes. "Got you."

SANCTUM OF SNOW AND BLOOD

by C.R. Christiansen

The yells of the people sound like a thousand bees buzzing around me. I flail through the crowd. Hands shoot forward from every angle, fingers snake around my arms and legs. Someone has grabbed a hold of my ankle. I kick, maybe they will let go? My heartbeat hammers, almost as if my heart is about to abandon me, spring from my chest and flee down a nearby alley. I can't breathe, I can't. It feels like swimming, but the water is not clear. It's like swimming in ink at the dead of night, and I'm drowning.

Someone pulls at my clothes, the ground gets nearer and then I'm laying down, a stone lodges itself into my side. It digs into a rib, tears at my skin. I raise my head, but only slightly. It's heavy, like lifting a sack of bricks. I crack an eye open, only just a sliver. The light dims as people gather around me. The voices sliver their way in and out of my ears, tangling and interchanging. Only fragments slip through. A sharp pain blooms in my stomach, my sight flickers, and coughs ripple through me as I hunch in on myself. One of the villagers is laughing, a rumble from deep within his chest. It sounds like a threat.

"Kick her! —must be punished —an abomination —traitor —spy from Ildres!"

I fight to keep my head up, to keep my eyes open. Another kick hits my stomach and a cry rips itself from my throat. This time the crowd cheers him on. Luka. Bile rises in my throat, I try to swallow, to force it back down, but it's already a lost fight. They all know now. They know and now they will not rest before my head is on a spike on the town walls, for all to see. Jumbled, panicked thoughts fly through my mind; I retch up my breakfast on the dirt-road beneath. The smell hits my nose as a disgusted mumble swerves through the crowd. My throat burns as I gasp for air. Cracking my eyes open is a challenge and when I force them open, dots dance all around me. His eyes meet mine, the brown no longer looks warm to me as it used to. *Danger* echoes through my thoughts. Stones dig into the palms of my hands, I claw at them, but I don't get anywhere. He shoots me a wicked grin as his boot makes contact with my jaw. A loud crack rings through the air, my entire head throbs. I might just throw up again.

I put my hand on the ground in front of me, the green of my skin stands out amongst the fair-skinned villagers. Blotches of light skin litter my complexion, it switches back and forth crashing against each other like waves. Almost as if it has its own life. I prop myself up on the other elbow. Maybe I can get away. The world tilts as I raise myself up, little by little.

A scream tears out of me; my back burns as a kick sends me tumbling down, my hands slip and the world slows as I head for the ground, face first. It's a challenge to even breathe. The small puffs of air I do manage to get out blows up the dust from the road and my ribs throb. I can't help but cough. Dry hands grab my aching jaw and yank my head to the side. Then another hand meets my cheek and the slap echoes between the small houses. Tears spill over my cheeks and I suck in a breath of air. Adrenaline rushes through my veins and I open my eyes. A sneer greets me.

"You'll get what you deserve, you half-breed scum" Luka spits out the sentence like it is poison on his lips. The words nearly sting more than the pulsing pain in my jaw. Heat rises within me; my hands shake from the anger and embarrassment. I bare my fangs at him, and he stumbles back slightly, his expression falters. Some of the fire dims in his eyes and he looks shaken, but the wicked smile grows back on his face in record time. His eyes flicker from my face and to something behind me, then I feel a sharp pain on my skull. The villagers roar as I head for the ground once again. Luka's face blurs; his mouth is moving. My brows furrow slightly. Why is there not any sound? My face hit the gravel before my eyes shut completely.

*   *   *

A sudden breath tears into my lungs. I gasp as I shoot up from where I'm lying, eyes flying wide open. Flashes of angry screaming humans pop through my mind. It's quiet, and I can hardly see. I squeeze my eyes shut and rub them one after the other with the back of my hand. My head is pounding.

This time, the room I'm in doesn't appear blurry. It's cramped, and it smells like a wet cellar. There's a heavy dark oak door in front of me. I'm on a hard, wooden bench. It's placed against one of the stone walls. The only source of light is a couple of sunrays shining in through a tiny, bar-covered window to my left.

Where am I?

My head goes woozy as I push myself up. My entire body aches and I groan as the pain hits me with full force. Black spots dance in front of me as I try and make sense of everything. I clear my throat; it's sore and dry as I try to swallow. It feels like I've munched down the entirety of the southern desert. Perhaps gurgled with a bit of vomit as well.

It looks like a cell and that's exactly the one thing which would make sense. My heart is racing, *I don't recall how I even got here.* I must have fainted. But how long have I been out for? Faint red lines show on my ankle, I'm bleeding. I reach out to press my fingers against it. Still wet. Maybe I'd been out for a couple of minutes, maybe even close to an hour.

"H— Hello?" I call out, my voice cracks and bounces off the walls in the small room. Nothing seems to be happening on the other side of the wooden door. The noise of turmoil can be heard outside the window though, it's getting louder. No one answers me.

One foot after the other, I place a hand to support myself. My knees buckle and I react without thinking; my hand shoots out to grab onto a protruding stone from the wall and I stay upright by clinging onto it. I grunt with every step I take towards the window. There's grass and gravel outside; and a lot of feet. Yelling. Someone is yelling.

"Why don't we just kill her now, eh? I reckon I can finish her right here." A heavy-set man is shouting and grunting while some guards cling on to him. Three men are struggling, one on each arm and one around his stomach. He can't reach all the way around though. "Why are you letting that thing rest!"

"I promise you all, she's one of them damn spies from Ildres!" He raises his voice and whips his head around to look at some of the onlookers that have gathered. "I bet she's sent back information about all of you lot to the Iwachi, none of you's safe, you hear me!"

A crowd has gathered by now, they're all staring wide-eyed at the crazed man. He twists and turns in the guard's hold, trying to snake his way out of their tight grip. I hold on to one of the bars to support myself. Green and clawed and very much not human. I draw back my hand, almost as if I've been burned. A woman looks me in the eyes as I tear my gaze from my hand. Her eyes are wide, and her face is frozen, her eyebrows drawn down. But she doesn't look angry. No, she looks scared.

A loud bang echoes through the cell, I flinch and throw myself down with my arms caged over my head for protection. Footsteps. Boots scuffle along the worn stone floor; it's only one person. I peek out from behind my arms, expecting a guard but—

"Come on Amelia," her voice is hushed and hurried, she grabs my wrist and pulls. "Get up!"

Her eyes are wild and when she pulls me up from the floor, I let myself be pulled along behind the tiny, young woman. Dana Famir, the younger sister of Luka Famir. They're both from the same neighborhood as me. She drags me through the door and out into the cramped and dark hallway. My eyes go wide as I realize that we're in the basement of the town-jail.

"Where are you— Where are we going?" I whisper, but she only shushes me as she quickens her pace. She's determined to hold onto my wrist, her curly black hair whips around her as she looks over her shoulder and then into the hall on the right-hand side. I stumble along and we reach the stairs.

"Hurry, would you?" she almost sneers at me, but she doesn't look at me while tossing the command my way. We reach the ground floor, but no one is here. There's usually a handful of guards but for some reason, it's empty. We step around the nearby desk and only then does she let go of my arm. There's a handprint on it from her holding on so tight. I rub my aching wrist and turn to walk after her when something catches my eye. It's a guard. He's passed out on the floor behind the desk, next to him is what seems to be—or—no, yeah it is—it's the pieces of a chair. I whip my head to look at Dana, but she's already off and heading straight for the back door, she doesn't even glance in the guard's direction. Did she assault the jail-guard with a chair?

"Look we don't have much time" Dana starts, "the other guards are out holding back old man D'Lachen."

The commotion is still happening in the front, I can faintly hear D'Lachen's yells. Dana drags me out into the alley, then along another road. It's all back roads and alleys, all quiet at this time of day. She stops abruptly a few minutes after, I stumble and almost smack into her back.

"I don't mean to be rude, but could you maybe get a hold of…" Dana looks at me, an eyebrow raised as she waves her hands up and down in the air in front of me. "… that?"

Oh yeah, I'm still green. She looks at me as if she expects something, her brown eyes have an intense shine to them. Her chest is rising and falling quickly, and she has a faint blush on her cheeks from all the power-walking we've just done, though it's hardly showing on her darker complexion. She raises an eyebrow at me— Oh, I'm staring. I shake my head as I try to focus enough to get some words out.

"I— It's hard to control when I'm emotional?"

I trail off, I'm not sure what to say. She sighs and pinches the bridge of her nose and then she throws a glance over her shoulder. The alley behind her is dirty and narrow, litter is spread around the edges in piles resembling those snow make when the howling winter wind forces it into every nook and cranny. The buildings look worn, vines crawl up and down the walls, weaving between each other and over bare spots and cracks in the paint. There's laundry hanging on several wires that are suspended between the windows on each side. A mischievous grin blooms on Dana's face as she eyes the fabrics and then me, she clicks her tongue loudly.

"What?" I ask, my eyes are wide as I say the word carefully.

"Grab that, will you?" Dana points at what's seemingly a tablecloth. *What does she need that for?*

"Look, getting a tall Iwachi-looking girl out of Kellan in broad daylight is nearly impossible."

Out of Kellan? I shake my head and look at her.

"Stop furrowing your brows at me, do you want to die or what?" With her arms crossed and an eyebrow raised, she shoots me a look that tells me she *knows* she's right. I shake my head again. It would definitely be in my best interest to not die.

"Great!" she exclaims as she throws her hands up in the air.

"Then be a darling and grab the bloody piece of fabric, will you?" She says, pointing a finger at the tablecloth.

We drape it over me as if it were a cape and somehow make it to the outskirts of town. I limp most of the way, trying to hold back groans and whimpers as I accidentally brush against my full-blooming bruises. Dana isn't saying much, only the occasional direction, some muttering, or a sigh here and there.

Some people stare; my heartbeat quickens whenever someone glances in our direction for more than a second. We do look strange though, I'll give them that. We must be a peculiar sight. A tall person with a ratty old piece of cloth thrown over their head; no arms insight and ripped, bloody clothes. As well as a small southern looking girl—which is rare enough in itself in Kellan—but the way she's muttering under her breath would throw anyone off.

A woman glares at Dana and mutters something before scattering off as fast as her feet can take her. I only catch one word though: curse. For some reason, there are still some northern people who believe that the shrines in the south still work. Some theorize that the leaders of Wodila'hei send up magic-users to take over

Edrea. That's just ridiculous though; the world hasn't seen a single magic-user in over a hundred years.

Dana doesn't notice the weird elderly lady; she's walking a few steps ahead of me, pushing herself up on her tippy toes to look over the heads of the few people in front of us. I want to ask her what's going on, but I think it's better to stay silent. I do my best to stay close behind her as she zigzags her way through the streets and the people. She leads us to a deserted road and a farm on the outskirts of town.

"Wait here, don't draw attention alright?" Dana turns towards the farm. I grab her arm, her eyes shoot to meet mine, they're wide and awaiting. My arm is still green. I draw my hand back under the tablecloth.

"Sorry," I say, "I just—where are you going?"

"We need food and water if we want to survive a long trip."

I linger as she walks off in the direction of the main house, she sets running the last part of the way there. Her statement plays through my mind, "we" replays the most though. No one else is on the gravel road. A small bit of the tension trapped in my shoulders bleeds out, finally, I can take off the tablecloth and stretch my arms. But if someone comes, I shouldn't be standing here.

There's a small area of trees on the other side of the road. It's quite overgrown, there are bushes and low hanging trees. Tall grass. I stumble towards it, it's ideal for hiding. Shallow breaths puff out of me as I crouch behind a bush. The world tilts slightly as I stumble and land on my hip and I flinch. At least I'm out of sight.

Birds fly by, they're chirping. Small sounds come from all around me. My hands shake as I reach for a strand of grass, my claws are still there. They won't go away unless I calm down. My heart still pumps, and I fiddle with my claws. My arms are wrapped around my legs in an attempt to look smaller, just in case.

"Amelia?!"

Dana's shout tears my eyes off the grass in my hands. She has her arms full of bread and what looks to be a water skin. Her eyes dash around, and her voice jumps as she shouts my name again.

"Over here!"

She twirls around and her gaze turns sour as she spots my hand waving in the air.

"Are you trying to give me a heart attack?" She mutters as she takes a few steps towards my hide-out bush. "Get up, we're going now, no time to waste."

Before I'm on my feet, she's already walked off in the opposite direction of the town. Pain shoots through my legs as I run slightly to catch up, gripping onto my disguise as the wind nearly blows the ratty fabric off my head.

"About that—uhm—where are we going?" I pant out as I slow down beside her. Without looking at me, she smacks some bread against my stomach, I fumble as I try not to drop it. "And why are you coming?"

"I'm coming because I just helped an actual half-breed escape its cell" Dana sneers, I flinch. "And I don't know if you recall, but that was right after I had assaulted a prison guard."

I mutter a low okay as she slows down a bit, I copy her pace. I'm not sure where we're going, and the road doesn't look familiar at all. We must be on the road which heads north, but I could be wrong. I've only ever taken the east road out of Kellan, that's the one that takes you to the capital city of Edrea.

"I don't understand why you would risk everything to save me," I turn my head right and look at her, she makes a point of not looking back at me though. Her eyes are transfixed on something ahead of her. The only thing there is the road and some trees though.

"Trust me, I don't understand it either" she mutters as she glances at me. Her eyebrows are knitted close together and she's frowning, but she looks away again, her head hanging slightly. I let the conversation die out, she's not giving me any answers.

We walk in silence for what feels like hours, the sun is closing in on the horizon and the skies are painted in a pleasant array of hues. Orange, pink, and purple gradients adorn the sky, the clouds almost look black in contrast. Dana is walking ahead of me by a few meters as if she doesn't want to be seen with me, but by now we've been in the forest for hours, there's no one else here.

The forest is thick and dark, the trees here have low hanging leaves. Shadow crawls along the grass, warping and ever-changing as the sunlight disappears behind the treetops. Threatening figures jump at me from all angles, it almost feels like the trees are watching us. Or maybe something else is. Leaves crunch under my feet as I speed up, looking over my shoulder every few seconds just to be sure that we're alone. Dana is too far away for my comfort; she shoots me a look when I appear beside her.

"I think someone might be watching us," I explain. She lets out a huff as she rolls her eyes, muttering something along the lines of me being a *scaredy cat* and *paranoid*.

"I'm not paranoid!" I insist. The hairs on my neck stand up and I look behind me again, but there's nothing there.

"What? Did you see something?" Dana asks as she pushes aside a branch that's in our way. The path here is narrow and I pull back to let her pass first.

"No, I haven't seen anything but—"

Dana let's go of the branch and it whammies me right in the stomach. I let out a small oof, Dana looks back at me and snorts lightly under her breath when she sees me toppled over. I push back the branch and set after her, sighing and shaking my head.

"Heard something?"

"No, but—"

"So what seems to be the problem then?"

"I haven't actually seen or heard anything—" I duck to avoid other low hanging branches as I follow Dana, "but my gut is telling me that something's wrong."

I let go of the branch that attacked my stomach; the leaves rustle as a slight breeze blows its way past us. "Right now, I'd listen to that gut-feeling. I always detect more when I'm—you know—like this"

"What? When you're big, green and have yellow eyes?" Dana says. Her tone is off. She doesn't sound hostile, it's hard to pinpoint but she sounds guarded.

"Yes, exactly," I mutter.

The atmosphere between us has taken a turn for the worse and my mind clouds with worry and doubt. The mention of my whole situation seemed to unnerve her, which doesn't make sense. At least it doesn't make sense after she risked her neck to break me out of jail. It wasn't just from any jail either because she helped me escape from the one her parents and brother help run. I don't say anything else, and neither does she.

My fingers tap against my right arm as we continue to walk, ducking under and jumping over various obstacles. Big mossy stones start appearing more. They're slippery and all-around a health-hazard, at least that's what I jokingly say to Dana after I manage to down myself after stepping on one. She doesn't laugh though, only nods and continues walking, leaving me to sit on the cold, damp ground.

The back of my pant legs are littered with small pieces of grass and bugs, but Dana is already disappearing between the trees. I give chase, panting as I run after her. It hurts to heave in the air as I do right now, even my ribs are sore after the day I've had.

"We should probably find a place to sleep." The words stumble out of me almost as I breathe in shallow breaths and my face scrunches up, it takes longer to catch my breath than I would like.

"I know. There's a small clearing up ahead." Dana points directly in front of us, I crane my neck, but I can't see it. If anything, the trees are more crowded. I turn to Dana, but right before I'm about to speak I clamp my mouth shut. She's intimidating and though I'm a head taller than her, it feels like she's towering over me. But she's right, we make it to a clearing right as the sun sets.

We scramble to find some branches. I pull out the string that holds the top of my blouse together and we make a tiny tent from that and the tablecloth I stole.

We both fit in there, though everything below my knees sticks out from the tent. Dana's back is pressed lightly against mine; she shuffles around quite a bit. A low rumble rips through the silence, my heart thumbs as I push myself up. But then the sound stops, Dana starts mumbling and sighing. Oh. That was a snore. Dana was just snoring. I thump back down on the cold and hard ground, but even as I let sleep overtake me, the hairs on my neck still stand and the feeling of being watched hasn't left me

*   *   *

Birdsong weaves its way through the lively forest, I crack my eyes open. I groan in pain as I try and stifle a yawn. I almost forgot everything about yesterday, but the sharp pain from my jaw reminds me. It hurts when I ghost my fingers over it as lightly as I can; it sparks a reaction from my tear ducts, and I wipe at my face before the tears get a chance to run down my cheeks. I try and sit up, but something pins me down by my stomach, it's heavy and warm. A sleeping Dana.

A blush creeps up my neck and my cheeks burn. She's laying with her arms over me, using both her hands and my stomach as a pillow. I manage to move her away, cradling her head as I lower her to the ground. It's hard to crawl out from the tiny tent without waking her up. I hold back a groan; I can feel some of my wounds tear as I maneuver out.

Dana talks to me more while we walk. She even cracks a joke, but something still feels off. My entire body aches with every step I take, but I power through it. We gather some wood throughout the day as we move further into the forest. Much of it is damp, so we leave it in the scorching sunlight to dry. When the sun sets, we've already set up our improvised tent, made a small fire to bring us warmth and then we go to sleep. Throughout the day, I haven't been able to stop looking over my shoulder. Maybe I am just paranoid; at least that's what I hope.

*   *   *

I wake up to Dana shaking my shoulder repeatedly. I groan and roll over on my stomach. The tent is small, so I end up with half of my body weight on top of Dana's legs. It's barely light outside, the birds are chirping their wakeup songs and I rub my eyes.

"Amelia, we need to move," Dana says. Her voice is low and steady, and her worry is painted on her face. "I think you might've been onto something—you can hit me with the *told you so*—My neck has been prickling, we're definitely being watched."

My eyes widen as I look at her. When I take a closer look, she has dark circles under her eyes and her hair is a mess. I probably look just as ruffed up though. Dana leans in close and drops her voice down to a low whisper.

"We should get a move on," she says, eyeing over her shoulder discreetly. I look around as well, my stomach churns and I suddenly feel more uneasy than I have the last couple of days. I squint at the trees, but I can't really make much out.

"Don't look around like that!" Dana hisses, her tone is anything but calm, but her body language is the opposite. She's smiling at me; a big and brilliant smile, which is utterly unsettling. "Act like nothing is wrong, someone might be watching."

"Also, you're back to human-looking—or well, mostly."

Dana crawls out and takes down our makeshift tent, humming a bit to herself as she goes along. My entire body feels like it's humming with adrenaline when I try and eye my arm in a non-incriminating manner, almost as if I'm just examining the dirt on there. I suck in a breath of air; pale skin peeks out from under the dirt and dried blood splotches. My nails are still thick and sharp, but otherwise, I look human. My body aches as I push myself up from the hard ground and I go to work. I end up packing our limited food supply and the water skin.

We trek through the forest, whispering to each other in hushed voices as we go along. The noises from the forest bring paranoia and panic with every snap of a twig and every rustle of leaves. We walk as fast as we can, over and under and through everything that's in our path. We even wade through a stream, and though my feet are drenching wet, it's nice to cool off a bit. Dana fills the water skin with the fast running water from the stream, claiming that it's relatively safe to drink. At least it's better than no water.

"So, um... could you tell me where we're headed?" I whisper in her direction, breaking the silence between us. I'm panting rather hard, but she doesn't pay it any attention. My side is aching from all the fast-paced walking. I try to mask my shortness of breath, though Dana seems to have no trouble, and my ears burn from the rallying sound that escapes me.

"Ever heard of Halivaara?" she whispers back.

"The frozen wasteland to the north?" I question. The disbelief and confusion I'm feeling shine through in the way I whisper-shout it.

"Yes exactly," she answers. "My parents told me it has some sort of sanctuary in one of its towns."

I furrow my brows. I've never heard of this so-called sanctuary before. As far as I know, the only ones who live there are the Iwachi outcasts who aren't even welcome in Ildres.

My legs were longer yesterday, and though I'm still slightly taller than Dana, I'm having a hard time keeping up. Dana suddenly stops and I stumble and almost fall over her leg. Before us are a lot of fallen trees all laying over each other, creating a complicated barrier. I groan at the sight of it. Dana is already scouting the area to check if we can take another route nearby. But she comes back with her head down, sighing loudly and shaking her head as she looks at me.

"Bloody perfect," she mutters, "we have to pass over here, seems to be the easiest way."

I turn my head and look at the giant wall-like mess of trees, widening my eyes. I look back and forth from her and the trees a couple of times. She catches my insinuation, huffs, and stalks over to the base of the mess. The tree trunks are mossy and muddy, as well as overgrown. Some of the trees have kept growing even after falling and it has created a strange look of tree crowns facing the right way, even though the tree trunk is parallel with the ground.

"If anyone of us is going to have a problem with this obstacle," Dana says, as she swings a leg over the first trunk and hitches herself up skillfully, "it's not going to be me."

I set after her, she's already meters above the ground. My foot slips as I step down on a thick trunk. Dana swears at me as I tumble down. A branch saves me as I grip onto it and avoid the muddy ground below me. A twig snaps somewhere close, but Dana is going as steady as ever, no broken branches in sight. Then a sharp intake of air sounds behind me. With a pounding heart and a dry mouth, I whip my head around. *Please let it be nothing.* But around 20 meters away is a broad-shouldered man in full leather with a crossbow in his hands pointed straight at us; his eyes narrow as he cocks the arrow in place.

"Dana get down!" I scream as he fires the arrow, it swerves through the air and it graces the skin on my forearm as I throw myself out of its path. I cradle it as I do something utterly reckless; I run straight at him. He scrambles back and tries to get another arrow ready, but he's fumbling too much. My heart and head pounds and I head for him, red etch my vision and a deep burning overtakes my skin. It bleeds over with green, taking over my arms and hands. I don't even acknowledge it, I don't care. Red etches my vision as my upper lip curls back in a vicious snarl. He finally gets the arrow knocked in place and he takes aim. Dana yells behind me, it steals his attention for only a millisecond.

I surge forward and hammer my fist straight into his windpipe. He chokes and I grab his crossbow and I yank it out from his grasp, tossing it behind me forcefully. It lands with a hard thump. I raise my fist again, but he's faster. My ears ring as the backside of his hand smacks me in the temple. He's bigger than me, even in my Iwachi form. Dana shouts profanities as I go down, she sounds frantic. I make out a smirk on my attacker's scarred face, my head is spinning. He leans over me; his eyes are icy blue and so cold.

"Ready to meet your end?" he cackles, his eyes look crazed and I shake as I try and claw my way back. He brings something shiny out from behind him. I squint to try and focus. It's a knife. Dana is yelling louder now, but he doesn't pay attention to her anymore.

"This really was easy money," he says as he leans down over me. With a raised head I try to look brave, but I know he can hear my breath hitch and see the frantic rising and falling off my chest. He leans in close. The cold, sharp metal of the blade rests on my throat.

"Pleasure doing business with you."

My chest tightens and I squeeze my eyes shut as the cold metal is pressed harder against my skin. The blade pierces, it burns and throbs all at the same time. Warm tears trickle down and I fight the need to breathe. But even though I worry about me, I worry about Dana more. He's chuckling above me but then a whistle sounds and he slumps over me, an elbow in my stomach and warm liquid dripping on my face.

When I crack an eye open, I'm face to face with the pale skin of his neck. It's dripping dark crimson blood from where an arrow has pierced through his windpipe; he splutters as he takes in rallying breaths of air. Bile rises in my throat at the sight and I throw him off me as I turn my head to puke. The crossbow tumbles onto the grass and Dana's breath shudders and jumps. She looks at her shaking hands in horror, eyes wide and tears swelling. She falls to her knees and squeezes her eyes shut; one single tear trickles down her cheek.

"Thanks."

I choke on the word as it tumbles out. I try to catch my breath, to get my breathing under control, but I shudder and shake. I look down at the assailant. The sound of his rallying breath has stopped, his eyes almost look like they're staring off into another realm. He's completely still. I get up as fast as I dare, black spots dance around me but I don't care right now. I cradle Dana's sobbing frame tightly against me, patting her back.

"It's okay, we're okay" I murmur, my mouth pressed up against her hair. I try to calm her down with more reassuring words and soon she stops sobbing loudly. My fingers paint patterns on her back and I whisper in her ear and cradle her head against my neck. Her sobs ebb out and she is reduced to silent tears. I draw back but I keep my hold on her shoulder and her face. Her eyes are red and puffy, and her cheeks are stained in tear-trails. She ducks out of my hold and her head drops; a hand wipes the snot from her nose.

"We should keep moving." She stutters a bit as she forces the words out, she wipes the tear stains away as well and tries to put on a brave face. I furrow my brows. We've just had a near-death experience, resting would be better.

"We have to," she reasons, almost as if she'd heard my thoughts. "There could be someone else out there, what if he wasn't alone?"

"You're right," I admit, her shoulders unclench and the tenseness bleeds away from her frame. "We should see if he has anything useful."

I let Dana sit on the ground as I move towards his body. His blonde hair is splayed on the dirt around him, tangled in the grass and twigs. He's as pale as snow now. His neck is craned in an unnatural angle and the arrow is still protruding from it; its tip is buried in the ground. Most of his clothes are bloodied, but his cloak and his boots were mostly spared. I gag as I pull the shoes off him. They look to be my size, they're a well-needed step up from the old and ratty ones I'm wearing right now. I tug the cloak out from beneath his legs and untie the stained top from around his neck and tear it off with fumbling hands.

"Those boots are for riding," Dana says. I look at her in confusion and she sighs. "He must've ridden a horse here; we could use that."

I feel dumb when she points out the obvious. We're quite far away from any town and he found us without knowing exactly where we were. Of course, he had a horse. I shuffle through his pockets, taking the few marks of copper he has on him. My fingers grace over what feels like a piece of crumpled paper. I pull it out. It's laced with red, but I can make out a couple of letters.

"Uh... where do you suppose it is then?" I ask her as I start unfolding the note as best as I can. I smooth it on the surface of my leg, something is drawn on the other side. I freeze up as I turn it over.

"My best guess would be..." She shifts and points with a limp arm to the trees behind me, the direction he came from. "Over there somewhere."

I nod at Dana, but I don't even look at where she's pointing. My eyes are locked on the crude drawing on the paper. It's a figure with big fangs, lines down her face over each eye and pointy ears. It's a wanted poster. They've offered 500 gold to anyone who could bring my head back.

"What's that?" Dana is looking at me, she almost looks concerned when I finally tear my eyes away from the damaged paper in my hands. I offer it to her. She scans the page over quickly, then her eyes zero in and her face slackens when she realizes. The paper is torn from my grip, her face is almost pressed against the yellowed piece of paper as she reads the faded text.

"Did you—" Dana swallows hard and tries again. "Did you read what it said?"

"Just the bounty," I mutter. I look up at her face and her expression is odd, alarming even.

"Why?" I ask, "does it say something else as well?"

Dana looks at me, her head is hanging low. Her eyebrows are tilted, and she looks like she might cry again. But then she squares her shoulders, takes a deep breath and her mask is back on.

"Yeah, it says that you—um" She trails off, I raise my eyebrows and nod, encouraging her to continue.

"It says you kidnapped me out of revenge?"

It sounds more like a question than the statement we both know it is. Dana's voice jumps an octave during the sentence, and she looks guilty. She sighs at the paper, not meeting my eyes again.

"Does it say why?" I ask. It doesn't make sense. How would I get revenge by kidnapping a girl who lives near me? For all they know, we don't even know each other except for a few exchanges of pleasantries on the street—which is the truth. Dana opens her mouth to answer, but she falters slightly. The hesitation in her body language only worries me more. They could've written all sorts of horror stories about the "evil half-breed."

"No," she answers, my head jerks up at the revelation. "It doesn't say anything else."

I'm about to ask her if she's certain, but the words get stuck in my throat. She doesn't say anything else and the entire atmosphere almost feels like we're mourning the find of the poster. She stuffs the paper in her pant pocket.

"We should really get going now though," she says. I just nod.

I change into the boots as quickly as I can, but Dana ends up having to lace them for me; my claws haven't gone away. I insist she takes the cloak. She's been shivering since she killed him, and even though it might be because of the shock and not the cold, I still make sure she's draped in the navy fabric before we take off. We take his arrows and quivers as well as his crossbow before we leave. I chose to carry it for a while, I don't want to force Dana to even look at it.

We make it to a tiny clearing. He wasn't very careful with moving around and the path he'd taken stands out clearly. Scuff marks from his boots litter the ground and there's an irregular abundance of broken twigs and branches are strewn all over; some are still dangling from where he's snapped them. Just as Dana predicted, there's a horse there. A beautiful white horse with a leather saddle and a tightly braided mane.

I end up sitting firmly in the saddle with Dana seated in front of me. I blush slightly from the closeness. Unfortunately, the blonde man didn't have a double saddle. That would've been handy right around now though. Dana holds the reins, and I lock my arms around her stomach as we ride off.

*　　*　　*

Dana and I realize rather fast that it's quite hard to ride a horse the way we're doing it. I must do the leg part and she has to manage the reins. We have to do it all in sync, so it matches, and the horse won't just throw us off. We find a path around the wall of fallen trees after almost an hour, and then we ride straight in the direction of Hinall, the northernmost town in Edrea. From there, we plan on crossing into Halivaara. Dana tells me that the town we're heading for is called Arcmore, and it accepts refugees from all over Morlea; human, half-breed and Iwachi alike.

After hours of riding through the forest, we stop. My backside aches even more than it did yesterday, I'm not used to riding anymore and that can be felt clearly when I dismount the horse. I'm out of practice with everything about it, and I stumble down. Unlike Dana, who dismounted with so much grace that I couldn't even hear her feet touch the ground. Dana doesn't laugh at me when I almost go face-first into the ground, she's already begun setting up camp. I tie the horse to a nearby tree, to make sure it won't run away during the night.

"If we get up at first light tomorrow, we'll be able to reach Hinall before the shops close," Dana says, not looking up from her handiwork. It's colder today than the other nights. I nod at Dana's statement, but she doesn't look at me, so I end up saying "great" as well.

"Maybe we should try to make a small fire?" I ask as I head over to pick up some sticks and other flammable things.

"Sure, we could use the heat," Dana says. Her voice is as cold as the starry night and when I turn to look at her, she's frozen in place and staring into the air. Tears sparkle on her cheeks, but she wipes at them aggressively, shakes her head and goes back to tying up the stained tablecloth. I linger back, hesitating and debating whether I should say something. Then she looks stern and I decide to just leave her. She needs time to process and being pestered by me won't help.

It takes longer to light the fire tonight; Dana ends up falling asleep in the tent before it's even lit. When I come in, she's shivering and mumbling in her sleep. Her hair is all over the place and her face is scrunched up in dismay. The cape is fastened around her neck but it's laying away from her. I lay down next to her, and after debating whether I should do it or not, I reach over her and grab the cape. It's soft and heavy and she stops whimpering when I drape it over her. Tonight, I'll be fine. I lay my head on a tiny bit of the cape and close my eyes, praying that I'll fall asleep fast.

*   *   *

The next day ends up being uneventful in contrast to the journey we've had so far. I wake up at the crack of dawn, disoriented and confused until I look at Dana. She's whimpering like she did last night, and she's writhing and twisting in her sleep. I sigh and try to rub the sleep out of my eyes. My neck aches and it feels like someone chose to punch me square in the face with a brick.

"Dana, it's just a nightmare," I whisper. Poking her does the trick; her eyes split open rapidly, they're wide and panicked. Before I can say anything, she slams her arm into my throat and topples me over. My world tilts and turns and my head and the ground collide, sending shockwaves through my tired mind. An *eep* escapes me, and I scream from the shock. When Dana finally realizes what's going on, she backs away. We're both hyperventilating. The look she sends me is nothing short of seething.

"Why would you do that?" She says, taking a deep breath. The pressure of her arm leaves my windpipe and I take a big gulp of air, I cough violently as I push myself up.

"Sorry," I mutter, "I thought you were having a nightmare."

I massage my violated and abused windpipe; it aches and only adds to the thudding pain I feel all over my body. I'm littered in bruises and scratches by now, this one will be a nice addition to my growing collection.

"I wasn't," Dana answers. We both know she's lying, but I keep my mouth shut.

We pack up our humble camp in a few minutes. I end up wearing the tablecloth as a cape, so I don't have to carry it. We eat the last of our bread for breakfast. After double-checking that we have everything, we leave on the back of our stolen-goods horse, setting course for Hinall.

We ride until the first signs of civilization pops up, it turns out we weren't that far away from the town. Three hours on horseback is more than enough though, and when we finally reach the outskirts of the tiny oasis, my bum is sore and aching. The town is colorful and lively, there are people everywhere tending to their own business. The houses are small and nestled together, they're all built of wood. Not odd when you consider that Hinall is a lumber-town.

I drag my feet along the cobblestones of the main road, Dana is walking behind me with the horse on his leash. The street is narrow, not compared to the other streets here, but compared to those in Kellan. It snakes its way between the wooden houses, twisting and turning the further it gets. Flags are hanging from multiple windows; the iconic red Edrean flag with lion print. Potted plants adorn all the entrances, there are even a couple of hanging ferns over some of the doors. I'm so preoccupied with staring that I don't even notice all the heads turning when we walk by, at least not until Dana points it out.

There's a market square, in the middle of the town; colorful booths have been set up in the shadows where the vendors are lounging, hoping for customers to come by. Dana ends up walking off and leaving me with the horse, whom I've ended up naming Fay. Dana thought it was stupid—she even shook her head at me—but it only seemed right to give him a name.

We decide to rent a room from a woman named Ms. Gerali. She has the fiercest red hair I've ever seen, and she looks otherworldly in her big green dress and the flowers that are weaved in her braids. Dana jokingly asks me if we're related while tugging at my hair. I point out that mine is more orange, but she won't listen.

Ms. Gerali shows us the room, which is in her own home in the middle of the town. It's in the attic with one big bed, although quite old and tattered. But we don't complain, the rent for one night is less than the price of 5 loaves of bread.

We go to bed at the end of the day, well-fed and newly washed. My hair hasn't been this clean for days. Dana is sitting on the edge of the bed, combing her hair. I'm already lying under the thin blanket Ms. Gerali provided us.

"Um... Dana, I just wanted to ask about the place we're going," I begin, but I trail off unsure of how to ask properly.

"Arcmore, you mean?" Dana asks. She looks at me over her shoulder while pulling forcefully on the comb, but it's stuck in her dark curls. I nod, peeking up at her.

"It's cold there, but quite nice for anyone on the run," she grunts out while working on the back part of her hair. I listen intensely as Dana continues.

"It's controlled by some Iwachi who were thrown out of Ildres," she says, "My parents complain that some of the half-breeds they tried to catch fled there."

"Are you staying as well then?" I ask. The question I've wanted to ask the entire time.

"I'm not sure," she says. Her gaze drops away from my face, and silence grows between us. My heart drops. I hadn't expected anything else—except for a no—but it still wasn't the answer I hoped for.

"Sleep well," I say, curling closer in on myself under the blanket. Dana blows out the candle and we're plunged into darkness. The mattress bounces as she settles in. We lay back to back and I can't see anything now. I sigh and snuggle into my arms; I use them as a pillow since the bed has none.

"Goodnight" Dana whispers back. A smile creeps onto my face as I close my eyes.

*   *   *

We depart Hinall in the early morning hours and say our farewells to Ms. Gerali, who sends us off with a small bag of food, a prayer, a blanket each and an overenthusiastic wave. Fog drapes over the town like a thick, white blanket, lit up by the sun peeking over the roofs. The rhythmic clacking of Fay's hooves against the cobblestones echoes through the empty streets, breaking the silence of the sleeping village.

The trip to Arcmore should take two days, but we'll only make it in time if we ride the entirety of the hours with daylight. We can't afford to stay in the cold for too long, but it's impossible to reach the town in one day. There's no way Fay has enough energy for that.

The first hours of riding go by smoothly, as we work together better than yesterday. I cling onto Dana's torso as best I can; the terrain is rocky and it's challenging to hang on without the reins. The further we get, the more the temperature drops and soon I can see my own breath hovering in the air in front of me as I shiver in the worn leather saddle. Dana is shaking as well, though she has the thick cape wrapped around her. I don't have that luxury. I'm wearing the tablecloth as a cape, but it's tattered from our journey and the fabric is so thin that I almost forget it's even there. I've also volunteered to have crossbow duty for today.

I grow more awkward for every minute we ride in silence. I readjust every few minutes, trying to get comfortable but I just want to stretch my legs and walk around. Not that that's necessarily possible right now. I strain to focus on anything else—anything!— but even mere minutes without stretching and flexing my leg muscles feels like holding my breath for hours and the restlessness only haunts me more.

"Amelia, I'm really not trying to be rude here," Dana starts. My head snaps up from where I'm intensely staring at my right leg as if sending it the death glare would make it stop twitching. "But to put it lightly, you're bloody annoying right around now."

"I'm sorry it's just—just my legs," I stutter, not entirely ready for Dana's brash comment. She hums in agreement.

"Yes, I noticed it was your legs." She doesn't look back at me, but I can almost hear her eyes roll.

"Should we stop for a minute?" she asks, her tone softens as she tugs at the reins. "There's a stream up ahead, I'm sure the horse needs water."

"Thanks, that would be nice," I mumble.

I try to keep my legs still but to no avail, but Dana doesn't comment any further. We stop not long after near a freshwater spring. The slow trickle of the stream and the rustling of the leaves make for very calming background noise. When I finally get to hop down from the saddle and stretch my legs, I let out a slow groan. I stroll around in circles for a bit. Dana leads Fay to the stream and though she hasn't mentioned it, I can see that she's walking rather stiff, she's in pain as well.

I lock my eyes on my feet, I'm placing them heel to toe as I walk; it's oddly calming. The grass is yellow and dry, there are multiple bald spots with nothing but mud. The Laicha mountains peek up over the treetops. The weather is clear today, and I can see the snow on the top. It looks just as cold up there as it feels down here. I hum a slow tune as I keep wandering about until something crumbles under my foot and I stop dead in my tracks.

It's a piece of paper, or rather, the bloodied piece of paper. Dana must've dropped it. it has a crooked fold from where I stepped on it and a muddy bootprint as well. I nearly call out to Dana to ask her if she wants it back when something catches my eyes.

There's quite a bit of text under the drawing, more than just the information about the kidnapping. My eyes trail over the words, I reread them. But it doesn't change what it says.

> *Wanted: Dead or Alive. Amelia Ovidssen. Half-breed, red hair, pale skin. Armed and dangerous. Kidnapped the hero Dana Famir as revenge for being reported to the authorities by her.*

My eyes lock in on the last sentence. I'm hyperventilating, frantically searching for any other text, anything but it says nothing else. I look up at her, she's laughing at Fay, he's splashing water everywhere.

Dana laughs louder. I'm frozen in place, my eyes strain from staring at her so hard and my hands are shaking, rattling the paper back and forth. She did this to me. What did I ever do to her? Dana's laugh rings through the entire forest, then she calls my name. I don't answer her, I'm not sure what sound would come out if I did. My entire body hums with anger and the need to scream wells up within me, I bite my lip hard to keep it in. When she doesn't receive an answer, Dana throws a glance over her shoulder. Her bright smile slides off her face when her eyes flicker to where I'm clenching the paper tightly in my hands. Her posture turns rigid and her face dark.

"Amelia, it's not what you think!" She calls out frantically. She sets running towards me, stumbling over stones, twigs and her own feet. The rage swells within me and I try to control my breathing. My skin stings and ripples as green overtakes it. The taste of iron flows through my mouth as my fangs pierce my lip. The sound of ripping paper tears through the air and when I look down, my claws have shredded the corner of the wanted poster. Dana's footsteps falter as my upper lip pulls back in a sneer.

"How could you," I scream out. My voice wobbles and jumps like a rabbit on the run. "How could you!"

"I— It— Please just let me explain!" Dana pleads with me, she halts a few meters away from me, her warm eyes are filled with despair and grief and her shoulders hunch in on themselves.

"Explain what?" The volume of my voice is so loud that Dana flinches as I yell at her. I tower over her as I take a step forward. "What do you want to explain, huh? That I'm a monster, a good for nothing half-breed?"

"No!" she exclaims, she steps closer and reaches out to hold my hand.

"Do not touch me," I sneer, "don't you dare!"

"Please listen, it was a mistake, Amelia!" Tears are trickling down her cheeks now, but I feel nothing but fury as they fall to the ground. She doesn't even have anything to cry for. "I am so sorry."

"My brother— He— He forced me, please Amelia." She's sobbing now. "He overheard me, threatened to tell my father if I didn't. He— He said he'd have me charged for aiding a traitor!"

"I know I shouldn't have said anything, I do and I'm sorry!" Her cries fall on deaf ears. Emptiness overtakes me as I stare off into the trees, her words dance around me in a hurried and jumbled mess that I almost don't register.

"I don't think half-breeds are monsters, least of all you!" she says, her lower lip wobbles. I want to comfort her, but I don't. She doesn't deserve it.

"Good," I say, my voice is cold and devoid of any emotion as I glare at her. "Because I think we can agree that you're the only monster here."

I walk straight past her and I almost knock her over when I bump my shoulder into hers. She yells my name over and over, but I don't look back. I grab Fay by the reigns and haul myself up, shooting Dana a last glance.

"Go back to the humans, they'll hail you as the hero you are." I spit the words at her then I let out a sharp, humorless laugh. "You could even say you took down the horribly dangerous half-breed."

Dana runs after me as I set off, but I gallop at full speed, I don't give her a chance to catch up. The carefully constructed wall I've built to keep the emotions in cracks and only now do I let the tears flow freely. Sobs rip through my body like riptides and when I've put some distance between us, I slow down and stop completely. I curl myself against Fay's neck, nuzzling my face into his mane. It's not particularly soft, but his warmth comforts me as I slide my hands through his hair, undoing the messy braids.

I shake as I try to hold the cries in, but it feels like I have no control over my tear ducts, and I give in as I slide off his back and throw myself onto the grass. It's entirely too cold to be lying on the ground and the crossbow digs into my back, but I pay it no mind. I almost choke on my own saliva as I scream at the sky, scream at myself and most of all scream at Dana. I know I'm stupid for already missing her, and I feel bad for yelling at her. She deserved it and would have deserved more than that, but I still regret it even after repeating it out loud to myself over and over until I simply can't anymore. At one point, I'm no longer capable of crying, as if I've run out of tears and my eyes are as dry as the desert Dana's family used to call home.

I just lay in silence now; Fay is munching on some grass beside me. Well, at least I'm silent, but the bustling of the forest around me almost feels mocking. It just reminds me why I'm not saying anything, and it reminds me that I'm not currently bickering entertainingly with a person I thought was becoming my friend. I snort and let out a sharp cackle of a laugh, slamming my arms against the ground. How pathetic and naïve can one person possibly be?

Thoughts flash through my mind; I fly up from where I'm laying. Pain shoots through my aching body but I ignore it and get up on my feet; I'll never reach Arcmore if I spend all my time wallowing around in self-pity.

I clap Fay on the side of the neck and pull myself up and swing my leg over. It must be around midday, the sun is high in the sky, which means I've wasted valuable time crying and feeling sorry for myself. I ride off at a low pace, I don't want to push Fay further after I made him gallop. I don't make it far before I hear something that chills me to the bones.

The unmistakable sound of a wolf howl tears through the silence and with it follows answers from all around me. My heart picks up its speed as I realize. The northern white-wolf. It only howls when it's in danger or—I take a big gulp of air—when it's found prey that needs to be killed. I whip my head around, expecting to be jumped at any time, but there's nothing there. When a familiar scream rips through the silence I finally realize. I'm not on the menu tonight, Dana is. And no matter how much I wish to never see her face again, I know I can't possibly ride off knowing I let her meet her end like that, without even trying to help.

I turn Fay around and for the second time set into a full gallop. My heart hammers as fast as his hooves hit the ground and it feels like we're flying. The forest is nothing but a blur of greens, browns and yellows as I call her name with everything I have. My voice cracks and my throat aches. The wolves howl over and over, drowning out any other noise. Then Dana screams out my name and it sounds like she's close.

I falter when I see her, she's clinging onto a thick branch with both of her arms and under her is a fury of white fur and teeth snapping at her feet. They're wild and ravenous and one of them latches onto her cape, pulling it downwards with all of its strength. I reach for the crossbow and an arrow and struggle to knock it in place, and I can barely aim. I'm shaking like a leaf. I take a deep breath and pull the trigger; the arrow burrows itself deep into the flesh of the wolf's shoulder.

At once, the wolf-pack freezes, then they snap their heads to me and they advance, their heavy paws thunder against the ground. Fay sets off, a panicked neigh escapes him, and I cling on for dear life as he jumps and tramples through the pack. But instead of running to safety, he goes in circles. A wolf leaps at us and buries its teeth deep within Fay's flank. Black spots flicker before me as Fay throws me off and I hit the ground hard, the world spins and bile rises in my throat as I fight to get up. Dana screams as she falls and I tear my eyes away from where the wolves have thrown themselves onto Fay, tears well up as he goes down. I shake my head, he's already gone.

I stumble towards Dana, running as fast as I can. It spins and turns and twists, stones seem to move just to trip me, but I finally latch onto Dana's arm and I pull her with me as I run. My feet won't move properly, I try my best to focus. It feels like we're running in water. We're not putting enough distance between us and the beasts, but we keep stumbling. Dana let's out a scream as she trips and we both go down, tumbling on the ground. I cling to her, curling myself around her as I hear a couple of wolves come at us. This is it. This is where my journey ends. I can feel something breathe on my leg and then a blinding white pain shoots through my calf as a wolf chomps down on it, I cry out in pain and try to kick it off.

A loud growl echoes through the forest and then the wolf let's go of my leg with a whimper. Blood trickles down my skin and drip into the grass and I wail as the pain engulfs me and burns through my body. Dana shakes me and points in front of us and I almost snap at her until I see it; the wolves run off with their tails between their legs. A shaky breath tears through me, and I look at her with wide eyes. She looks just as baffled. I shake and whimper as I push myself up. Dana surges forward to examine the wound, it's gushing blood at an alarming rate and my head is spinning.

"Are you okay?" Her hands flutter all around the bitemark and she tears a piece of her cape off and wraps it around my leg tightly. "I'm sorry that's a dumb question I know, I'm really sor—"

She cuts herself off mid-sentence. Her hand shoots out and she latches onto my shoulder with a tight grip. Then she points a shaky finger upwards. Something has cast a shadow over us; a creature's fur is blocking the view of the sky, but it is way too big to be a wolf. When it lowers its head, I realize I'm wrong; it is a wolf and it's the largest wolf I've ever seen in my life. It towers above the trees and its fur glows like a thousand bright blue stars. It nudges me with its damp snout and my eyes roll back in my head and I collide with the hard ground.

*   *   *

Next thing I feel is harsh wind swirling around me and cold air biting at my nose. Something warm and soft is under me, and as I crack an eye open, I'm met with the wondrous sight of gleaming blue fur. The forest flies by as I'm rocked up and down repetitively, a rhythmic thumping fills the air as the glowing wolf dashes through the forest. I bury my face in the soft coat. It smells like morning dew and autumn air.

*　　*　　*

I'm roused from the darkness of my slumber when my shoulder is shook forcefully.

"Wake up," A whispering voice breaks through and I shoot up, knocking my head into something, hard. Two wide, emerald eyes peek down at me, it's a young woman. Her skin is deep green and she has light marking down her cheeks and short and ragged black hair. An Iwachi. Her marks resemble my own.

"It's okay, you're safe," she says. Her voice is warm and comforting and I close my eyes again and slump back down on the mattress I've been sleeping on.

"What happened, where am I?" I mutter out, my eyes flicker over her face. "Who are you?"

"So many questions," the woman chuckles slightly, "My name is Yael and you're in my home. I found you outside in the cold not long ago."

"As for what happened, I was hoping you could tell me that," she says, smiling slightly. "When you arrived you were mumbling about something blue."

I shoot up again, heart hammering and hands sweaty. Memories come flooding back. Wolves—Dana—Blood and... a giant wolf.

"I— I think—" I sit up and rub my eyes as I try to understand the pictures flashing through my head. "This might sound ridiculous..."

"Try me," Yael smiles at me with a knowing look in her eyes. When I take a closer look, the whites of her eyes aren't white. They're yellow.

"I think I was on the back of a," I let out a sharp laugh as I pinch my nose, "Giant, glowing wolf."

My cheeks burn from embarrassment as I peek up to look at her.

"That's not the first time I've heard that story, the myth of the Cadekiero is common around these parts" Yael smiles with a smile that makes me think she knows more than what she tells me. A comforting hand rests on my shoulder and she squeezes it reassuringly.

"The Cadekiero?" The words stumble over my lips, the pronunciation feels odd and foreign.

"We call her the guardian of the north" she answers, but I'm almost more confused than before. "Your companion mentioned the creature as well."

I almost shoot up from the bed at the mention of Dana, but Yael's warm hand and steady gaze keep me grounded on the mattress. Yael must've noticed my reaction though, a warm and bright smile paints itself over her features.

"Would you like to see her?" she asks me, "She's in the next room over, she woke up not long ago."

My throat is dry, and I just nod. She pushes me back down and tells me to rest and my eyes slide shut. My leg is throbbing, and my head feels like it's just seconds from splitting in half. A flurry of curly hair and short limbs launch at me suddenly and then I have my arms full. Dana hugs me tight and I hug back, snaking my arms around her waist. I bury my nose in her hair and it smells like absolute garbage. I pull back and cough, my ribs hurt from the effort, but I manage to shake out a laugh.

"What?" Dana says, eyes crinkling as she smiles.

"You reek of death and destruction," my tone is teasing, and she just shakes her head at me, shooting me a warm smile. Then I look around and I realize that something is off. The room is filled with furs and there's a fire nearby with a pot roasting over it. Yael is tending to it. Nothing looks vaguely familiar, not even the architecture. It's dark outside, I can make out a golden gate and thick snow on the bushes right outside the small glass window.

"Dana, where are we?" I ask.

She takes my hands in hers and she trails her fingertips over my skin as she looks deep into my eyes.

"We're in Arcmore."

The meaning behind her words doesn't hit me right away. My mind works it over for seconds before it dawns on me and when it does, I surge forward to capture her in an even tighter hug than before. I don't even care about the way my leg aches as I pull her closer or how dry my throat is when I let out the most genuine laughter, I've ever heard myself produce.

We made it.

FULCRUM

by Travakh

Meetings at Headquarters were drab affairs. The facade of the Mercenary's Guildhall was a granite stoneworks meant to resemble an old castle, tall and imposing, a monolith to impress upon the casual bystander the might and gravity of their duties. The result was the building was poorly lit, even in the middle of the day. A bright and sunny day in the Etoile Capital City, and Vance Randell found himself sitting in a dim conference room, squinting at a piece of parchment. He held it to the light.

"Aren't there other candidates for the cartography jobs?" He tossed the contract back onto the table. "I thought promotion to the first rank meant no more babysitting."

The older man across the room chuckled. "It usually means more." Siegfried of Archos was an imposing battlefield figure in his fitted heavy plate and a warhammer on his back, but in his city garb he gave the impression of being a kindly grandfather. "In any case, this contract's got a lot of money behind it. Funds allocated for the full season duration, private chartered Power-sail, and a Principality Master Trader on board. We, or you in this case, would be providing security."

Vance leaned forward. "A trade mission's more than a simple mapping, then. Why are the Cartographers hiring mercs instead of requesting an escort?"

Siegfried shook his head. "Some of the people out there past the frontier don't take kindly to seeing Principality soldiers. My guess is they want to play friendly." The old warrior pointed to the map on the wall. "There's an islander society a few days past Erimia Tradepost, and word from the District Commander there is that they have a new leader who wants to have closer trade ties with us."

"This sounds political. Now I'm really wondering why the Principality doesn't handle this themselves." Vance leaned back again. The chair he was sitting on made a strange cracking noise before buckling; the hunter quickly stood with a grimace. "Ugh. Or why they'd need our help, since we can't keep our furniture from collapsing."

"There's groundwork to be laid first." Siegfried stood up. "Constantine can't send formal delegations to every random group of frontier villagers who suddenly decide they want to become Etoilean."

"Hah, right, the 'majesty and grandeur' of the Principality has to be maintained." Vance kicked the broken chair away. "Fine. What's our payout?"

"Twenty-six thousand florins plus expenses covered by the Principality during the deployment, within reason."

Vance whistled. "Now I'm interested. How'd we get that much for this kind of work?"

"The Cartographers said they wanted the best, so I made sure to milk them. Make sure you get this done right." Siegfried walked over and clapped the hunter hard on the shoulder; Vance winced. "It's a simple escort and security job from our perspective. Try not to think too hard about the rest of it, it's outside our paygrade."

"Just make menacing faces, got it." Vance dipped his thumb into the inkwell on the table and thumbed his print onto the contract. "Let's begin."

Siegfried eyed him. "Go get a fresh chair out of storage first, you broke the one here."

"It was *already* broken!"

*   *   *

Normally, Vance would have taken the tram over the two miles to the Cartographer's Lodge, but Siegfried had decided that official business merited official transport. The spare power-wagon in the back of the Guild's coachhouse looked like it had seen better days, but its doors had the Mercenary's emblem painted on, and that was good enough. The streets were packed, of course. The Capital was infamous for the sheer number of power-wagons on the street. A harried-looking guardsman signaled, and the power-wagon rattled its way forward over the cobblestones.

"Damn it." Siegfried cursed and pulled a lever; the wagons ahead were at a stop. A power-wagon had hit a pole and broken it, and a maintenance team was hastily trying to make repairs; power was out to the block. One of the rod pieces the pole was supporting was hanging loose in the air, twisting back and forth, still trying to deliver power through its broken linkage. Vance watched as one of the men gingerly extracted the crashed wagon's flywheel from the wreckage.

"More accidents recently." Vance shifted his weight. This power-wagon was an older model and was a bit cramped for passengers, and the slow going was magnifying every bump. "It's getting to the point where it'd be faster to walk."

An irritated grunt in reply. "That's why the licensing restriction rumor's going around. A test before you can operate a wagon."

"No way the Princeps would approve that. There'd be riots."

"That might be preferable to this mess. Finally!" A gap between two wagons had opened up in the intersection ahead. Siegfried yanked a lever back, and they lurched forward out of the commercial district. The streets leading to the academic ward were lined with robed researchers and students, who gave the wagon a wide berth. With a grinding noise, the wagon came to a stop.

The Cartographer's Lodge was a less imposing building than the Mercenary's Guildhall, a simple and charming estate with a small circular courtyard. In the center was a bronze relief of the continent of Saibh, positioned at precisely the worst possible angle to reflect sunlight directly into Vance's eyes. He held his hand over his face as he stepped off the wagon, following Siegfried past the relief into the building.

"Ah, the mercenaries have arrived." There were two women in the foyer of the building, relaxing on the overstuffed lounge chairs. The closer one stood up, holding out a hand. "Siegfried, it's good to see you."

"And to you as well." The warrior took off his boater and shook hands. "I don't believe either of you have met Vance here, so I believe a formal introduction is in order. He'll be your escort into the frontier."

Vance stopped and reached into his vest pocket to pull out his insignia. A small sword, held in a reverse grip with a mailed fist, painted yellow, the emblem of the Mercenary on a small chain. He held the chain in his palm, arm outstretched, allowing the insignia to hang freely before him, and bowed. "Vance Randell, Mercenary of the First Rank, Spear and Bow. At your pleasure." The two women had stood up and drawn their own insignias.

"Rathnait of House Numio, Master Trader of Etoile. The pleasure is mine." The taller woman gave a bow, the bottom of her fitted silk overcoat brushing the ground. Her insignia was a scale, lacquered in black, blending with her black tresses. She stood up with a click of her boots.

"Iocathe Black, Prime Cartographer. And mine." The shorter woman bowed as well, the sleeves of her academician's frock hanging low and loose. Her insignia was a compass and sextant overlaid, silver and gold, respectively. She smiled brightly, brushing light curls out from her dark eyes. "It seems we've assembled a team of some merit."

"I would hope so." Rathnait pocketed her insignia. "It's essentially first contact. Korr has been closed to the Principality as far as anyone can remember, and we need to show them the best of us."

Vance raised a hand. "Pardon me for not knowing much about the frontier, but closed? I didn't know there were towns out there, and I was under the impression that the Principality had a policy of knocking by siege-sail."

Iocathe laughed. "That may have been the case during the era of the First Princeps, but we're in more modern times. And yes, there are a wealth of them." She gestured to the floor of the lobby, a massive painting of Saibh in meticulous detail. "There are at least fifteen towns outside the political control of the Principality scattered across the eastern expanse, and many smaller societies. And no," she paused, "we try not to start off by killing people."

Rathnait shook her head dismissively. "Bad for business. The tribes don't concern this venture, though. Only the larger towns hold trade potential."

"Not tribes, societies." Iocathe wagged a finger. "Remember what the Askri said about this."

"None of us here are Askri, are we?" The trader leaned against the wall. "If they haven't started farming and still hunt and gather, they're tribes."

Siegfried sighed. "Academic semantics. In any case, now that the meet and greet's done, I'm finished here. You got the rest, Rathnait?"

"Of course. Randell." Rathnait turned to Vance. "Our power-sail is being spun up on the eastern side of the Canal, Pier Sixteen. We'll see you there in the morning?"

"Got it." Vance touched a finger to his forehead by reflex. "Anything I need to know or do right now?"

"Just be packed with all the non-consumable supplies you need. Equipment's going to be hard to come by out there. I'm assuming you have armor, it wouldn't do for you to wander the frontier wearing a waistcoat." Rathnait paused. "Also, now that you're officially on this, could you stop by Central Post? Pick up whatever's bound for Erimia. Selunn will kill me if she misses her mail."

*   *   *

The seas were fairly rough, and the Meridian's crew was uninspired company, so the sight of a dock gave Vance some cheer. Two weeks of roiling ocean on the direct route had turned his legs to rubber, and Iocathe had the surprising trait of being a cartographer with seasickness. The endless blue expanse had lost its novelty, and games of Fortuna had become quite stale once everyone memorized the scoresheet.

"So that's Erimia? Very frontier-sy." Rathnait stood, stretching her legs. The Principality outpost looked like a ramshackle collection of wooden buildings clustered around the harbor, with wild jungle in the backdrop. Nobody was visible from offshore. "Is there even power here?"

The captain spat over the side. "That's the only reason to sail to this place. It's a slow wheel, it'll be some hours for a full recharge." The power-sail pulled in smoothly along the pier, and the captain pointed. "Or longer. Looks like their hookup is broken." The power clutch plate alongside the pier was visibly disconnected and rotating freely in the wind.

"Ugh." Iocathe stepped onto the deck. "No offense, Captain Kardu, but the longer we stay on land, the better." A sailor shoved the landing ramp onto the dock.

"Spoken like a true city girl." The captain gave a short bark of laughter. Vance sighed and picked up his pack. Rathnait was already off the ship, talking to one of the porters hauling down cargo.

"Where are we headed?" Vance looked around. Not a soul was to be seen from the dock, and the tradepost seemed oddly quiet, with only the sound of waves. "Something feels wrong here."

Rathnait seemed unconcerned, focused on checking a crate of goods. "Well, that's your job, right? The lodge should be at the center of town next to the District Headquarters. Go have a look, we'll meet you in fifteen." She waved him away.

Walking past the dockside warehouses, Vance turned a corner. A number of buildings faced a central square, but the most obviously important one was the white marble facade of Headquarters, the radiating sun emblem of the Principality front and center above the doorway. The coachhouse next to it had a power-wagon that looked like it hadn't been touched in seasons. Across the square was a lodge, the largest wooden building on the square, with a placard nailed next to the door, 'The World's End'. A guard leaning against the side of the lodge waved Vance down.

"You just get in? Sorry about the reception, everyone's at the fighting pit." The guard frowned. "That means we need to get the dock power link fixed."

Fighting pit? Vance relaxed the hand he had on his dagger-hilt. "I've just come from the Capital. We're on a Cartography mission into the frontier and need to resupply."

"Lady Eudelind will be happy to hear that. She's been going a little stir crazy." The guard gestured with his thumb. "You'll find her at the pit, let her know you're here and she'll get your affairs handled."

"My thanks." The arrangement seemed a bit informal to Vance, but perhaps he had spent too much time in the Capital. The hunter walked down the indicated pathway to the rear of the inn, quickening his pace at the sound of strikes and impacts.

The fighting pit behind the lodge was a roughly ten-foot circle dug two feet deep, where a young woman was beating her opponent into the dust while roughly thirty spectators cheered. There was an obvious mismatch in skill, as the man she was fighting was too slow to block any of the incoming elbow and knee strikes, and any return strikes were easily parried.

"Yield!" The man threw up his hands after being thrown to the ground. The woman grabbed his hand and pulled him to his feet. "You need to go easier on us, Lady Eudelind."

"Why?" The woman smiled widely. "All you have to do is get better." The crowd laughed, and the man gave an embarrassed grin as he climbed up out of the pit. "Any other challengers today? I'm not done training. You!" She spotted Vance. "A new face, and with a spear at your back. Come down and let's have a fight."

"Not in the business for fighting without pay, and I'm on paid duties." Vance folded his arms. "You're Eudelind, then?"

"I'm the District Commander of Erimia, and if I have to, I'll order you to get down here. Bring your spear." She gestured to the crowd, whom upon closer inspection had a motley collection of half-healed bruises and scrapes. "The longshoremen are good sport but none are trained fighters, and you have the look of one."

Vance sighed and dropped his pack. He'd have to fight in his traveling leathers. "A warning. I'm quite good." He jumped into the pit, spear overhead.

"Ooh, boastful." Eudelind had strapped on a pair of fighter's gauntlets and shinguards, leather with riveted steel plates, but was otherwise unarmored, in only a tunic and breeches. She taunted with her left hand. "Visitor gets the first shot."

Vance didn't take the bait and kept his spearhead low to the ground, circling Eudelind. He was significantly taller and had a longer reach than she did, but her specific style of unarmed combat was unfamiliar to him. He dropped low and attempted a sweep; she checked the strike immediately, his spear ringing off her shinguard. Vance rolled to the side; she had followed up her check with a spinning kick which grazed the top of his head.

"Interesting style. Your own?" Vance found himself retreating as Eudelind pressed the attack, parrying the jabs but unable to make room. She was *fast,* much faster than he anticipated, and he couldn't get his spear readied for a thrust.

"No. This is Freeport style Pugilism." She aimed a knee at the gut and Vance brought his spear to contact, with a sharp scraping noise as the spearhead gouged into her shinguard. Vance used the opportunity to lunge forward into a shoulder check; Eudelind rolled with the hit and stepped backwards into a three-point stance. "You're the first real fight I've had since I've arrived here." She grinned and knocked her knuckles together, the steel plates echoing in the arena.

"Good to know." Vance planted his spearhead into the dirt and leaned forward.

"Tired already?" The woman feinted to the left on the approach. Vance yanked the spear out of the ground, flinging a spray of debris onto Eudelind's face. She ducked underneath and threw a low wheel kick, but Vance had already sidestepped to her blind side. He extended a quick thrust at her exposed neck. Eudelind twisted and slammed her fists together to catch the spear between her gauntlets, inches from her throat. Vance pressed forward, forcing the woman into the ground.

"Nice try, but your eyes betray your footwork." He shifted his rear hand to the butt of his spear, ready to drive it home. "Do I hear a yield?"

"You can get into a lot of trouble for killing a Commander of the Principality, you know." Eudelind's gaze was locked on the tip of the spear in front of her. "Yield."

Vance pulled his spear back and with a practiced motion looped it onto his back harness. He clasped his hands together and gave a quick, mocking bow. "A pleasant fight, Commander Eudelind." He offered a hand.

The woman snorted, pulling herself up and tossing her gauntlets aside with a grimace, but there was a twinkle in her eye. "I'll win the next bout. In any case, allow me to wash up and meet me at headquarters. We can get your paid duties handled there, and I would learn your name."

*   *   *

Headquarters Erimia was little more than a single office with a single oak desk, overflowing with paperwork. The three travelers sat on small rattan chairs positioned haphazardly around the room, interspersed between discarded books, packed boxes, and general clutter. Vance had the nagging urge to lean back, but these were the kind of chairs that would probably disintegrate if you looked at them funny.

The door banged open, and the fist-fighter from the pit stepped into the room, now wearing her official garb as an officer of the Principality, red waistcoat over black leggings, a belt slung over the shoulder and looped around the waist, brown braid topped with a pointed cap, inscribed with the Etoilean sun. She looked significantly more regal than she did in the arena; Vance stood by reflex, and Iocathe came to attention as well. Rathnait simply put a hand on her chin.

"Welcome to Erimia, travelers." She presented her insignia, the radiant golden sun of Etoile, but did not bow. "I am Selunn Eudelind, District Commander, and the voice of the Princeps."

"Vance Randell, Mercenary."

"Iocathe Black, Prime Cartographer."

Rathnait smiled. "You know who I am, Selunn."

With that, Eudelind pocketed her insignia and immediately grabbed Rathnait in a bear hug. She was smaller and shorter than Rathnait, but stronger, so Vance watched the trader get squeezed like a melon as Eudelind lifted her off the ground. "Ah, it's been soooo long! How *are* you doing, Rathnait?" She sounded like an excited schoolgirl.

"I'd be better if you weren't trying to force my breakfast out." The trader had a pained expression; Eudelind let go, and Rathnait patted her on the head. "How are you doing, kitten?"

"Kitten?" Iocathe cocked her head.

"We grew up as neighbors." Eudelind circled the desk and sat down, and motioned for the others to do the same. "Two little girls with dreams of the world, and now look at us," she grinned, "at the world's end!"

"That explains the name of the lodge." Vance relaxed a bit. Eudelind was a far cry from the stuffy bureaucrat he was expecting. "So how did you end up out here on the frontier?"

"You first." Eudelind leaned back into her chair, an ornate piece made with hardwood and velvet. "Our resupply power-sail only comes by three times a season, and you're off schedule. What are you doing here, other than delivering my mail? Much appreciated, I must note."

Iocathe frowned. "This is a Cartography expedition? We were told that Korr had reached out to you to open trade relations and establish formal first contact. We're the initial contact team." She blinked. "Didn't you request this?"

"No, nothing of the sort." Eudelind shuffled some of her paperwork. "This may be a bit embarrassing, but the last letter I sent to the Capital was a modification of my journal subscriptions some weeks ago. And the Korr?" She muttered. "They're the last group of frontier folk who would want to establish contact."

"Why is that?" Rathnait leaned forward. "We've done them no harm."

"We, the Principality of Etoile, representing the Princeps, haven't. But according to the archives here, they were victimized by pirates some time ago," she said, "Pirates that sailed in power-sails, who apparently claimed to be Principality representatives before looting one of their temples of its gold and jade." Eudelind sighed. "Word of that tale has spread among the other local villages, and it explains why this tradepost is so barren of activity. The men have little to do, the market is empty, and I've been reading the archive here, bored out of my wits. The situation isn't ideal."

"Pretending to represent Etoile is a remarkably dangerous game." Vance sat up, thoughtful. "The last thing any pirate should want to do is get marked for a punitive expedition."

Eudelind rested her head on her hands. "The other potentiality is that it was the Etoilean Navy itself."

"Unthinkable!" Rathnait had a taut expression. "That would be treason against the Princeps!"

"Only if anyone found any proof." Vance flexed his right hand. It felt a bit sore from the sparring earlier. "But who sent that message to the Capital, if it wasn't you? The locals?" He paused. "And you didn't tell us how you ended up out here."

Eudelind tossed her hat onto the desk. "Long story short? Rathnait, you remember that fool captain's son from the gala two years ago?" A nod. "He somehow lost most of his teeth after somehow finding himself doing something he shouldn't have been doing." Eudelind flicked her quill across her desk and scowled. "Of course, big scandal if that got out, since our families are such 'exemplars' of Etoilean nobility, so I got a nice promotion to District Commander. And wouldn't you know, I'm assigned somewhere where I can't make trouble, at least for a year or two."

"Exile, then."

She clicked her tongue. "Principality politics as usual, and to be honest some time out of the City is good for the constitution. As for your travels, the power linkage to the dock will be repaired by nightfall, and the supplies here are at your disposal. Rooms at the lodge will be allocated to you and your sail crew. Korr is a few days north of here along the eastern trim, and you'll likely find answers there, one way or another." Her expression lightened briefly. "This is so dramatic, isn't it! A team of adventurers sailing for secrets in dangerous waters. I wish I could come along!"

Rathnait laughed. "Hopefully we won't need two sets of hands to cave skulls in, Selunn. We're not here to pick a fight, just to take a look around."

"I know, I know, you can't solve everything with a fist. A pity. Vance." Eudelind gave him a stern look. "Keep these girls safe, will you? I don't like how this all feels."

"They hired the best. You've verified that yourself." Vance tried his best to give off an air of easy confidence. "There should be no threat out here in the frontier that the Mercenaries can't handle."

"Other than the Navy." Iocathe had a troubled look. "I'm not sure how to handle making first contact if the people in question don't want to be contacted. This is a novel situation."

Rathnait stood. "In the worst case, we pay tribute, get home safely, and report our findings. We have the full backing of the Principality, and the locals will be accommodating one way or the other."

"'One way or the other'? What do you mean by that, Rathnait?" Iocathe raised her voice. "Surely we're not already at the point of threats?"

"Stop." Vance held his hands out. "Do you two mind if we actually visit the place before we decide anything?"

*   *   *

Korr was a small coastal village and the moored power-sail was easily visible on the horizon, so there was a group assembled on the rocky shoreline waiting to greet the landing launch. Their island was one of the larger in this part of the archipelago, according to Iocathe, so she suggested landing on the other side and travelling on foot to try to be less conspicuous. Rathnait had vetoed that idea, as it would have meant slogging through miles of open beach or crossing a significantly sized mountain and its surrounding tropical forest.

"That's quite a crowd. I count at least fifteen." Rathnait handed her spyglass to Iocathe. "Anything out of the ordinary here?"

"Everything lines up with what we already know. Their dress is fascinating!" The men on the shore were wearing robes covered in ornate curving styles in vibrant primary colors, while the women's robes had cross hatch patterning. "Especially strange given the humid climate."

"I don't see any weapons." Vance squinted, hand blocking the sun. "They look friendly enough." One of the men on the beach waved as the launch got closer, and Vance waved back, causing the boat to rock a bit. Iocathe turned her head sharply and grabbed his arm.

"Don't do *anything* unless we know exactly what it means. For all we know, waving might be a sign of hostility!" The cartographer's brow was furrowed to a degree where Vance feared it was permanent. "Let me take lead on this. We have to tread lightly."

"They're people, Iocathe. Not some strange race of monsters." Rathnait waved as well. "Captain Kardu, how long will we have here?"

The captain stopped rowing for a moment and frowned. "We'll be moored offshore for eight days. Flag us for pickup anytime from now till then and we'll return to Erimia to recharge the flywheel." He gave a dubious look at the shore. "If things go poorly, what's the course of action?"

Rathnait reached into the pocket of her coat. "If we're not on the shore for a pickup in eight days, return to the Capital and file this with the cartographers." The trader handed the Captain a folded note. "Everything that the Principality needs to know is here."

"Understood. Good luck, then." Captain Kardu pulled the oars with a last great heave, and the bottom of the launch scraped against the loose pebbles. Vance climbed out of the boat to give it a push onto the shore, and the launch shuddered to a halt on the rocky beach. Iocathe and Rathnait stepped off the boat to greet the approaching locals, while Vance and Kardu moved their bags off the launch.

Two of the Korr stepped forward. The larger of the two was an imposing man with a full and shaggy beard that made him look somewhat bestial. The other was a woman, of height with the man but younger and rail thin, as though she would fall in a breeze. One of her eyes was a pale milky white; she was blind in the left.

Iocathe bowed deeply. "Greetings to you from Etoile. Aho. K'ian. Talissm. Oriadle." Vance recognized the second as a greeting in Old Askri, but the other words remained foreign. Not receiving a response, the cartographer continued. "Illadh. Deemis alar. Rassafil rrhakirre." Rathnait raised an eyebrow.

"Hold. I and others speak some Etoilean, though your language ability is...good? No, impressive." His accent was thick, and his sentences ran together. He raised a hand, palm outward. "A greetings, woman of Etoile, I am Urrthus, a fisherman of Korr, and this is my wife, Sphira." He clasped his hands behind his back and nodded. "We would like to welcome you to our small village, but what is your reason for being here?"

Iocathe bowed again, deeper than before, her curls touching the rocks. "Thank you for receiving us, Lord Urrthus. I am Iocathe Black, a Cartographer of Etoile, and these are my companions. The Principality had received a message stating that Korr wished to open trade relations. We hope to learn more about each other and establish a trade to our mutual benefit." Vance watched Urrthus intently, but he betrayed no emotion. "Before we continue, however, we would like to know if that message truly represents the intent of your people. If Korr remains closed to us, we will leave at once."

The villagers behind Urrthus exchanged whispers. Their leader scratched his beard, but Sphira spoke up in a thin, lilting voice. "Your arrival makes a.....problem, for us, as we cannot give an answer and know that it is the will of all of our people." Urrthus nodded, and turned to the other Korr as she continued. "Yet we will open Korr to you and yours and share our food and hearth, as honored guests, while we explain this...issue further. Agreed?" The villagers murmured their assent.

"The honor is ours, Lady Sphira." Iocathe smiled.

"Sphira, if you would. We do not use your titles." She turned to Vance. "A question. Is it custom that the men of Etoile are always so well armed? Your warbow is no hunting tool, and you wear heavy armor for this heat."

Vance shook his head. "I'm a hired guard, bonded by contract. If necessary, I will disarm myself." He unbuckled his harness and handed his weapon belt to Kardu.

Urrthus turned back and nodded. "You may keep the sheath knives under your vest, but it would be best if you did not bear weapons openly during your visit. Now, if you would follow, I would bring you to Korr. You must have had a long journey from your great Cities."

Rathnait gave a slight smile. "It has been some distance, Urrthus. Captain, go ahead, we'll see you in eight days."

*   *   *

Within the borders of the Principality, Korr would have been little more than a quaint seaside village, with its shell-studded walls and lines of drying fish swaying in the breeze. The people were far louder though, and the children were everywhere—packs of them running back and forth, screaming and yelling and getting underfoot of the procession in their excitement. Iocathe had her eyes wide open and was frantically scribbling notes as she walked.

"Is it like this every day?" Rathnait reached into the pocket of her coat and held out some candies. The children snatched at them greedily before sprinting away. She watched them warmly as they chased each other.

"We told them to stay inside the gates after sighting your ship, otherwise they would be in the fields or woods playing. But as long as you are here, they will beg you for more sweets." Urrthus led the train past a row of small homes made of kiln-fired clay and into a small market area. Most of the local adults looked friendly enough, but a few turned away when Vance made eye contact. A group of women were in a circle around a fruit stall, feeling them with their hands while talking. Urrthus approached one of the women, exchanged some words, and grabbed a number of bluish fruit, the size of a common peach.

"We get...harvest these from an island just north of here, they do not grow in other places. Dimisteen, in our tongue, this is roughly 'blue gem' in your language. Have a taste." Urrthus offered one to Vance. A warm, sharp citrus flavor, coupled with a cloying, sweet aftertaste.

Rathnait chewed with a thoughtful expression. "There are similar fruits to be found at some of the outer tradeposts, but these are significantly larger." She brushed her mouth with her kerchief and reached for her trader's bag. "What do these cost in your market?"

"We do not use money as you do." Sphira was walking ahead. "Ours is simply the trade of goods in kind, and all such exchanges are made equal over time."

The trader blinked. "No currency of any sort? Your ledgers must be quite something indeed, to maintain those records."

Urrthus laughed. "We get along. Myself, I think that no money means we are free from money. Our traders do not agree, but this is how we have lived for many seasons, and we have come to no harm." The procession had arrived at a wooden greathall, a two-story building larger than any other in the village Vance had seen.

Above its gate, a massive leather tapestry was pinned to the rafter, an intricate series of scuffed leather hides stitched together, each painted with a different design—a two headed boar, two fish circling, four hooks intertwined.

Urrthus paused at the gate and glanced up. "Ours is a town of families, and each family bears a mark. Should the last of a family leave us, their mark is added here, so we may remember our roots. Does a likewise custom exist in Etoile?"

Iocathe shook her head. "Our houses of nobility bear a similar symbology, but we don't have a specific equivalent. This is beautiful!" She was rapidly sketching some of the designs.

"There will be some time for you to explore the town to your desire. Please, enter the hall." Urrthus pushed the gate open and stepped inside. The inside of the hall was bathed in the afternoon light, with a series of wood benches arranged around a central cooking pit. Some villagers were already present, and they stood as the entrants filed in.

"Urrthus. Sphira. So the meeting went well." The woman speaking was wearing an unpatterned robe in pure white. She put a hand to her chest. "Welcome to Korr, strangers." Her Etoilean was accented but precise.

"An honor." Iocathe sat on a bench in the center of the room, taking notes as quickly as she could. Rathnait and Vance sat next to her.

"We are all here? Assembled? Let us begin." Urrthus clapped his hands, and a number of people left the room, leaving only the three travelers, Urrthus, Sphira, and three women in white robes sitting around the cookpot. Sphira reached for the cookpot and spooned out eight bowls of a brown broth, passing them around the benches. Vance stirred his bowl. It was a hearty brown beef stew, with floating carrot chunks and sprinkled with cilantro. He ate a mouthful.

"Saumann spices? This is delicious!" Vance dug in with gusto. The spice of the broth was tempered by the thick meaty flavor from the beef, which had been softened to the point where it disintegrated in the mouth.

Rathnait put her bowl down. "Not Saumann spices, they cut the tongue deeper, but likely related. Don't look like a pig, Randell, we're supposed to be dignified." She sat ramrod straight on the bench. "Thank you for sharing your food with us."

"Under one roof and from one pot we share life with each other." Urrthus finished his bowl solemnly and stood. "Now that we have had a meal, I would greet you with respect, I am Urrthus, chosen to be the leader of my people. My wife, who cooked this meal, Sphira." She gave a bow. "Moira, our spirit guide, twenty and six in that lineage." The tallest of the three women in white nodded. "Rivan, her student." Rivan looked up but refused to make eye contact. "And Lodia, an acolyte." The hooded girl made no move.

Urrthus continued. "Decisions in our village are made by the shared voices of all, and I can no more order anyone here than they could order me. Yet, ours are the voices many listen to, and we with respect welcome you to our community. If we could get your names?"

The three stood at once and pulled out their insignia in unison, bowing.

"Iocathe Black, Prime Cartographer of the Etoilean Cartographer's Guild."

"Rathnait of the noble House Numio, Master Trader and Officer of the Principality of Etoile."

"Vance Randell, Mercenary Guildmember of the first rank."

"A mercenary?" Sphira cocked her head. "So you are only here then for the promise of coin?"

"A simplification, but yes. We sell our martial talents in service to those willing to pay." Vance felt strange explaining the purpose of his Guild. "Our contracts are vetted and approved by the Principality."

"Barbarous." Moira murmured. "This may sound of offense, but such an idea is evil. To kill out of lust for gold. What prevents you from being bought again, to slay your master for additional coin?"

Vance spoke carefully. "Contracts that demand crimes are themselves crimes and invalid. We're not simple murderers or robbers, we usually protect from such. Mostly our contracts are guardwork or hunting down bandits."

"Still, you would not be here if it were not for the money. Am I correct?" Moira had a sharp gleam in her eyes. "If these two women did not have the means to pay you, they would have arrived here without a defender."

"Hopefully there's nothing here that requires them to be defended, is there? Skill at arms is a skill of value, and it rightly commands a price from those who require service." Vance matched Moira's gaze.

Sphira nodded. "Enough. We are not here to talk about the good or evil of money." She turned to Iocathe. "We are here because someone sent a message to your Etoile saying that we were now open to trade. Now that you have arrived, we must figure out who sent that message, and what we can do to fix this problem."

"Easy to answer. It was me." Urrthus had a tired expression, while the other three Korr spun to him.

Moira leapt to her feet. "Why would you contact them? Our affairs are our own! What would we possibly have to gain, compared to what we would lose?"

"Calm yourself, Moira. I am sure Urrthus can explain." Sphira turned to her husband. "Am I correct?"

Urrthus leaned back on the bench, arms folded and eyes closed. "Moira, the loss of the Temple of Mezic was how long ago?"

"Sixty-eight seasons ago." Seventeen years. "I remember it as though it were last season, and I would be shocked if you did not."

"I do." He scratched his beard. "Yet it is time we move past it. The Etoileans will come again, sooner rather than later, and I would much rather work with the ones that speak with word and coin than the ones that speak by sword and arrow. The world is changing, we must change with it."

Iocathe frowned. "The record keeper for this area informed us that you were victim of a pirate attack. If so, on behalf of Etoile I would like to apologize."

"Not pirates." Rivan spoke for the first time. "I have visited some of your trade posts. Those ships were your military vessels, the ones with the rotating towers."

A siege-sail with launcher turret. "So it was the Navy." Rathnait muttered. "But why? Why would the Principality attack you here?"

"I would answer that as well. One of your ships wrecked not too far away around that time. The ship's plate said 'Windhaven'." Urrthus gestured vaguely westward. "A large ship, carrying many people and cargo. We found bodies on the beach and some of the cargo, but when the Etoileans came they believed we had hidden some of it away, even after we returned what we found. They sacked our temple at that time and looted our relics when their search found nothing."

Rathnait had a dark expression. "With proof, this is treason. Political actions are under the sole purview of the Princeps, and attacking a non-Principality people and land is inherently political."

Iocathe shook her head. "Unless they were fool enough to leave obvious evidence behind, it would be our word against that of the Navy. We're not in a position to threaten the military, especially not on behalf of a foreign society." She looked troubled. "Needless to say, Urrthus, I and my cohort had no idea of this history and would like to extend our deepest apologies."

"Save those apologies, Etoilean." Moira stood. "There are sixteen emblems on our tapestry that were added after those events. I made them myself, and I will remember them until my own passing. Urrthus, we will discuss this later." She left the room with long strides, the other two white robes on her heels, though the hooded one tilted her head at Urrthus before departing.

Vance flexed his right hand. "Now I see why the situation's complex. Still, this is more than a simple request to trade, isn't it?" He glanced around the now-empty hall. "If trade in technology was your goal, you could have started trading at Erimia or the other outposts. Instead you extended your invitation directly to the capital. Why?"

Sphira spoke quietly. "We need your help."

Urrthus sighed. "My own apology for not being wholly truthful, but I had to speak without Moira or the others. I did send that message, and I wish to open trade, but you are here to stop a threat to our village." He paused, before speaking with a low voice. "Did you look at that third girl, Lodia?"

Rathnait narrowed her eyes. "I did. She does not resemble the rest of you."

Sphira nodded. "We found one alive from the Windhaven. A girl still swaddled, her mother drowned to keep her daughter above water. Now our own adopted daughter, though she is not aware." She exchanged a sad look with Urrthus. "And now, a faithful acolyte of Recol'taya, the spirit of prophecy."

Iocathe looked stunned. "You refused to give her up to the Navy, so they sacked your temple in response?"

Urrthus gave her a hard look. "We would have returned her to her parents, had they survived, but the Etoileans that did appear were angry....no, violent, and not open to conversation. Keeping her was no mistake."

Vance spoke with unease. "I doubt the Navy was aware of her existence. Everyone else was dead, why wouldn't the baby have been drowned or eaten by a Nautilus? My guess is it was pretext—the attack on the temple was likely inevitable once some greedy whoreson of a Captain saw the gold."

"Hold on a second." Rathnait cocked her head. "How is she not aware of her heritage? Surely she has realized she looks different from everyone here. Forgive me for saying this, but your face marks you as from the frontier as easily as my face marks me as Etoilean."

"She has never seen an Etoilean, before the three of you." Urrthus stared at his hands. "She must have doubt now, but that was my intent. Her presence, now that she has come of age, is a major problem for us, as she can no longer simply be hidden away." He looked up. "At some time, an Etoilean would have arrived, and as soon as she was seen, questions would arise, yes?" He spread his hands outward. "Why a young, blind woman of your Principality was seen amongst the savages of a small island village."

Iocathe shook her head violently. "It is not our custom to consider any of you savage. The First Princeps decreed that no one was above any other in any imagined hierarchy."

"Ah, of course, which is why your First Princeps ate in the common halls with your laborers and beggars." Urrthus gave a sad smile. "We know of the news in the 'frontier', and we know that your Principality has been growing ever further, moving from island to island, taking villages and their peoples, bringing your laws and soldiers to bear."

"I've heard nothing of this." Rathnait crossed her arms. "Even if that were the case, what would you have to lose? Power makes life easier, and our science cures diseases previously thought mortal. The Principality has no interest in destroying local traditions."

Sphira raised a sleeve of her patterned robe. "Our clothing is an example. The clothing you wear is made with machines, correct? I have been told this by visitors from other villages." She swept her arm forward, casting the cloth of the sleeve over her knee. "In our custom, the parents of each person weave their clothes for them by hand until their passing, and we weave for our children in turn, mending and repairing. A slow process that fills the days, but each of our robes tells a story passed through the families and ages, written with the hopes of our people." She clasped her hands forward. "Now, the day comes and your machine clothing arrives. Would any young man or woman of the village mend the robes of their forebears?"

She looked at Rathnait, her right eye clear. "Moira wishes combat... to fight. She wishes to protect our custom no matter the cost, but she and her followers do not understand the strength of your Principality. My husband and I know that we cannot stop you. We wish to merely protect some aspect of Korr, so that we can survive once more of you come."

The group fell silent for a moment. The cooking fire had gone out, and the stew in the cookpot was forming a surface sheen. Vance looked up sharply. "You mentioned blind. She didn't seem blind to me as she was walking out."

Urrthus looked at his feet. "Our daughter is an acolyte of Recol'taya, and upon the next brightmoon she will gain her true vision." He closed his eyes. "It is our belief that when Recol'taya sees a woman give up her eyes, she will embrace the sacrifice, and share her sight. Through those visions we will see the future." He opened his eyes again. "My own wife was an acolyte until her ceremony failed."

Vance flexed his hand again. "You don't believe in it."

"No." Sphira turned her good eye to him. "It is an old custom and no more than that."

Rathnait had a grim expression. "I can see the rags back home. 'Etoilean girl maimed by frontier tribe'. The journals do enjoy their scandals." She held her palm out. "So, we're here. You've called us. I'm more than happy to discuss trade to our mutual benefit, and far be it for me to be the one to trample your ways, but this problem seems out of our ability to handle. We cannot stop others of the Principality from deciding to pay a visit, nor would we be able to successfully petition the Princeps."

"Yes." Urrthus paused, looking at the rafters. "There is only one thing you can do. Take Lodia away from here, before the ceremony, with her eyes whole. And as far away as possible. Her being here is cause for Principality takeover, and she will not be safe here."

"No," Iocathe snapped instantly. "The first thing Etoile does here cannot be a kidnapping!"

Vance spoke slowly. "It's a straightforward solution that eliminates the immediate danger. A simple plan, if she's agreeable."

Iocathe turned to Vance with a snarl. "You're talking about taking a family's *daughter* away from them! A community's religious symbol. And presumably against her will and that of their religion. What would you know of this, mercenary?" She dropped her voice. "In the Principality, this would be an enormous crime. We will not simply do as we please because we are on the frontier. Our law underpins our civilization."

"It is no small thing for us to ask, as our daughter is not willing, most like." Sphira went to her feet. "There is a bunk house on the edge of town where travelers may stay the night. Tell none of the other villagers of this, if you would be kind, and let us talk again in a day or two once you have had time to think."

*   *   *

The next day was a gloomy one. Iocathe had gone to map and draw the village, and Rathnait went to talk to the villagers about spice and trade, leaving Vance alone with his thoughts. The locals gave him a wide berth as he ambled around the perimeter of the village.

The cartographer was correct in many ways. There was no reason that they wouldn't still be bound by the law of the Principality, and they had no obligation to act in any interest other than that of Etoile. It wasn't their responsibility if the Korr decided to take up arms, and it especially wasn't his responsibility, as he was only here to provide security, no more than that. Moreover, even if events did occur the way Urrthus feared, why would they need to take action? Surely Urrthus could have simply spirited the girl out of the village at some point. Vance walked past a collection of barrels, filled to the brim with dried fish and harvested seaweed. That was the question at hand. There was still a missing piece — something that had kept the girl's parents from taking action themselves. There was something that required Etoileans, in specific, to save the village.

"Mercenary." Vance looked up. Moira was sitting on a chair against the wall of a small crafter's hut, threading together a shoe. She stood, leaving the needlework on her seat. "Randell, I mean. Apologies for my curtness." She bowed her head slightly.

Vance nodded. "Did you have business with me?"

The woman looked stung by his cool tone. "As I mentioned yesterday, I did not mean to give offense." Her expression softened. "I fear I may have been a bit hostile, but rest assured that I bear neither you or your companions ill will."

"No offense was taken." Vance considered his words for a moment. "Urrthus told us a little of your goddess, Recol'taya, but I was wondering if you could explain her further."

"Not a goddess, a spirit, and easily the most important of them. No doubt Urrthus tried to explain her as best he could. Walk with me." Moira picked up her needlework and started for the village gate, with Vance in tow behind her white robes. "What do you believe about the nature of your life? Or, rather, most Etoileans? The question of where we came from, why we're here, what happens after we pass?"

"So uh, personally, I don't really think about it, but it's hard for me to speak for the entirety of my people." Vance scratched his chin. "The question of the origin of people is being researched, but there are many who keep the ways of their forebears. Myths such as the Separation, or the Shrinekeepers and the Gods they allude to. Nothing I personally believe in. My best answer for what happens after we die is that I have no idea, and it won't concern me as I'll be dead."

"Not an unexpected answer." They passed through the northern gate, on a well-trodden path leading into the rainforest. "It is sad to me. If the entirety of the world can be explained through study, and you simply ignore what cannot be explained, then there appears to be no room for wonder."

"You sound like the Grand Philosopher we have back at the Etoilean Academy. He goes on at length on these topics. Me, I'm just a hired spear, so I don't think too much about this sort of thing." The trail meandered through the forest floor next to a stream, with the pathway showing signs of being regularly cleared. "Where are we going?"

"The Shrine of Recol'taya. I believe it would be better to discuss her there." Moira stepped over a creeping vine. "The faith of Korr does not claim to provide the answers to my earlier questions, but it does try to maintain the wondrous nature of what we see around us. It is our belief that accepting the vastness of existence will humble even the proudest man."

"That's a pretty strange belief system, if it also has a spirit of prophecy." The hunter ducked a low branch. "Wouldn't the unknown of the future present the most wonder, under your rules?" He could hear a muffled voice through the trees, singing.

"It continues to do so. Prophecy is imprecise by its nature, and all of the spirits of the world revel in being fickle." The path they were on opened into a clearing. A small waterfall burbled across the way, with its waters encircling a patch of ground covered in white and yellow flowers. The flowing water lent its backdrop to the song.

Ard nummien crratubria terbi
ispir allt carrtikio
sllemp fliu srens emptorrhis
illyam o'sn negait

A stonework altar was placed in the middle of the flower field, simple and unadorned, surrounded by flat rock seats, under a woven net of vines. The vines overhead had been tied and pinned together to form a near solid canopy over the clearing, casting the altar in shade. A girl in white robes was singing in front of the altar; she turned at the voices. She was blindfolded.

"Lodia. How goes the preparation?" Moira cupped the girl's face, picking dirt off of the blindfold. "Cho'rrian akthei."

"Menos rhrila." The girl turned her head. "Is one of the Etoileans here?" Her Etoilean had the barest hint of a trader's accent.

"Yes. He wished to learn more about Recol'taya, so I thought it best he converse with her acolyte." Moira took a seat. "Ask what you wish to know, Randell."

Even knowing that Lodia was Etoilean, Vance was unprepared at how little she resembled the others of Korr. All of the locals he had seen were light of complexion and hair. This girl had the olive tones and sharp face of an Etoilean of the Capital. "Good afternoon, Acolyte Lodia. Who is Recol'taya?"

The girl nodded. "She is the spirit of prophecy, the queen of the natural spirits, and she who tends the gardens of the future."

"Natural spirits?" Vance flexed his hand again. "What do you mean by that?"

The girl gestured to the rainforest. "All of the world is imbued with the spirit of that which composes their essence. The jungle, the spirit of unending growth, life, sustenance." A finger upward. "The sky, the spirit of the wind and the change it brings, and the bringer of pure water." A finger down. "The earth, the spirit that resists change, life's cradle, and to which life returns." She pointed at Vance. "You and I are spirits as well, the spirit of thought, of creation and destruction, merely present in human form for the short period of our lives before we return to the earth. And above it all is the spirit of the future, fate woven and ordained, she who we name Recol'taya in our arrogance."

"Iocathe would have a field day with this," Vance muttered. "Urrthus told me a bit of the ceremony. Why would Recol'taya demand your eyes?"

Moira sighed. "Urrthus is a good man, but at heart he is a simple fisherman and no great thinker. You have arrived in our village seeking trade, correct? Everything works in the same way."

"All spirits demand exchange." Lodia placed her fingers on her blindfold, above her eyes. "The spirit of the jungle demands earth and water for life. Life exchanges air and water, and creates thought and idea. The thought and idea is sustenance for the spirit of the future."

"Okay. I'm not quite following. If the spirit of the future needs thoughts to create that future, why does she then need eyes?" said Vance.

"The thoughts form the future, but it remains veiled until it washes over us as the tides. But foresight can be had early, with a trade." Lodia bowed her head. "In times of need, the faithful of Korr will volunteer their sight, to bear vision onto a true prophecy and foretell the future as Recol'taya would speak." She tilted her head up; despite the blindfold she seemed to be looking directly at Vance. "Did you know that your arrival was foretold?"

"No," Vance said. "Although, was this before or after Urrthus sent his message?"

The girl smiled at that. "Three seasons ago, prior to the passing of the old acolyte. A man and two women, arriving on our shores, with packs glittering with wealth but behind them the bright sun of Etoile, in front of a red sword of conquest. That is what she saw in her vision, and it requires little interpretation." She turned back to the altar. "I know that you bear us no ill-will, but your arrival signals our end. Our faith will fall as the old Temple did, and your cold and unfeeling machines will take its place. Only the next prophecy that I will read can tell us how to achieve victory in the face of this fate."

A true believer, then. Vance spoke quietly. "Lodia. Are you aware that you are an Etoilean?"

Moira cut in sharply and stood. "She is no such thing!"

"I'm not a fool, Vance Randell." She turned and untied her blindfold. Green eyes. Capital nobility most likely, contrasting with the greys and blues of the Korr. She gave him a penetrating stare. "I knew as soon as I saw you enter the great hall. Still, Moira is correct. It is my faith and my choice that makes me what I am, not some simple accident of birth, so my eyes and my face ultimately mean little and less."

Moira grabbed Vance by the arm, leading him forcefully out of the clearing as Lodia tied her blindfold back on. "The acolyte must have time to prepare for the ritual. You have learned what you wanted, and it is time for you to finish whatever business you think you have in Korr."

*   *   *

Vance sat cross-legged on the earth floor of the bunkhouse. It was midnight, or near enough, and none of them could sleep. The hunter had no mirth left. "Who was on the Windhaven?"

"We'd have to go back to the Capital to find the records. A power-sail, lost deep in East Saibh, seventeen years ago." Rathnait frowned as she leaned against a beam. "You are absolutely sure she had green eyes?"

"I've seen enough nobles," said Vance quietly, "and even though not every noble I've seen has green eyes, everyone with green eyes I've ever seen was a noble. No question about it."

"What difference does it make?" Iocathe sat against the side of her bunk. "Why should her nobility change anything? That's an awful sentiment."

"It matters because it ups the stakes, if she's a noble of one of the Foremost families." Rathnait crossed her arms. "There's no way she can stay. If news gets back to the Principality that a daughter of one of the Foremost had taken up with frontier savages? Do you realize the amount of wealth she would command? And how many idiot treasure-hunters or deluded patriots would try to steal her away, if for no reason than greed?"

"That must have been why the Navy attacked. They knew who was on that siege-sail and Captain Moron thought he had a golden ticket. If she were the last survivor of her House, as her 'rescuer', he could make a claim for guardianship." The trader exhaled sharply. "Our journey here was on public record. Anyone who knew of the circumstance those years ago will wonder why the Principality has now suddenly taken an interest in a closed off society. The

Principality itself would be forced to act if the news became public, that 'frontier savages' blinded a stolen noble child to try to hide her green eyes. And the Korr are not likely to react peaceably given the last time Etoileans showed up."

Iocathe pulled her knees to her chest and spoke slowly. "I hate this. This was supposed to be a mission of journey and discovery, and now we're caught up in conspiracies." She rested her chin on her knees. "You make good points, but again, who are we to determine this girl's fate? We cannot kidnap her. We can't know if our actions wouldn't simply make things worse."

Vance put a hand to his forehead, exasperated. "Have either of you killed anyone?"

The cartographer shot him a look. "No, of course not, but we're not killing anyone here."

"No." Vance flexed his hand. "Let me tell you a story of my early days as a mercenary. I was of the third rank at the time, hired muscle on a job looking for a bandit group that had attacked caravans. We found them, flushed them out, their leader had dragged a woman out and was holding her hostage, threatening to kill her if he didn't get a horse to escape on. I had a shot lined up from his blind side. You've seen my warbow. One hundred thirty-pound pull, enough to punch through a skull. I was the only one with a clear shot, since he held her as a human shield."

"I hesitated. I never killed anyone before. He cut the woman's throat, and I put my arrow through his neck, right under the skull. But when the time came, I did not act decisively, and a woman died without reason. Suffice to say that I don't believe that inaction is the wise choice in most circumstances." He made a sweeping gesture. "People here will die fighting Etoile if we don't act."

Iocathe had a silent tear running down her left cheek, and her voice cracked. "We should never have come. Korr is doomed whatever we do." She blinked and wiped her face.

"Not necessarily." Rathnait ticked off her fingers. "We can take command of this fiasco. One, return the girl to the capital, explain her story, find her origins. Two, find the people who attacked this town and bring the justice of the Principality on them. Three, negotiate a trade deal that allows those here to maintain their ways as best they can. Improve the lives of the people here. The people here will be better off thanks to Etoilean trade."

The cartographer buried her head in her arms. "It's all lists and numbers to you, isn't it, Master Trader? What absolute arrogance. How sure we are that we can always make things better. As though we of Etoile stride the world and rain down our benevolence as gods." Iocathe looked at Vance. "What will you do, Randell? This discussion is academic unless you choose to act."

"I'm a simple mercenary, working your security. What I do is going to be your call." The hunter gave a tired smile in the moonlight. "Siegfried told me before we set out. 'Try not to think, it's outside our paygrade.' But I've just realized something, Iocathe. All three of us are high standing members of our guilds, correct?"

"What of it?" Iocathe tossed her insignia on the floor. "What good does it do?"

"Urrthus knew, or at least he was able to guess that she was someone of special import in the Principality. That's why he needed a diplomatic mission to do what he couldn't—return Lodia to Etoile. He knows little of Etoilean politics and knew that he would be unable to keep her from being used as a pawn, but that we could navigate the waters." Vance stood. "That's my hunch, at least."

The trader picked up Iocathe's insignia. "The danger to Korr will pass once we establish at the Capital that Lodia is who we think she is. She'll be able to return here as a Principality noblewoman in her own capacity and advocate for her interests, and I'm sure Eudelind would keep an eye on her." She held the chain out. "I believe with the three of us we can minimize the harm to Korr and establish a trade relationship on good terms. Anyone trying to steal her away or violate the terms of any agreement with Korr after the fact would be committing treason against the Princeps."

The cartographer took her insignia and rose to her feet. "This cold-blooded course of ours. I do not like it, but if you need me to voice agreement..." She turned to her bunk and sat with her back to the others. "As you will."

Rathnait gave Vance a look. "Do what needs to be done."

*   *   *

The village was small enough that all Vance had to do was look for the white robes pinned to drying lines. The task was simple. Rathnait kept a bottle of ether handy, and Vance had a length of rope in his pack. The wooden window cover was easy to pry open with a sheath knife, and he slipped into the small one-room house silently. It was for naught; there was a candle lit, and two women were watching him bemusedly.

He awkwardly got to his feet. "Rivan. Lodia. This, uh, isn't what it seems."

"Is this a courtship ritual of Etoile, where the man breaks into the home of the woman and steals them away?" Rivan shook her head. "Get going, Lodia." It was only then that Vance noticed that Lodia was dressed and packed to travel, wearing a striped shawl over a leather overcoat, with a woven shoulder bag. "Vance Randell. Moira told us this would happen after your conversation at the shrine. She told me to sound an alarm as soon as you showed yourself." She sighed. "Lodia would have none of it. I will say this. If you allow any harm to befall Lodia, I swear upon the spirits of my ancestors and the earth that I will hunt you down to the end of your days. Not just on behalf of myself, but all of us in Korr." She choked up. "Keep her safe. We will sing for her return."

Vance turned to Lodia. She gave him an irritated look. "Are we going, Etoilean, or did you want to tie me up anyway?"

"What about your ritual?" Vance frowned. "Earlier today you were discussing the importance of prophecy, yet now you're willing to discard it?"

She pointed to her left eye. "There is something important about the way I look, correct? Something that shocked you to your bones, and made you resolve to steal into my home and take me away." She spoke without hesitation. "I know of the discussions. I have overheard Sphira and Moira debating deep into the night, moving my future as though I was simply a stone to be placed here or there. As soon as whatever mystery surrounding my birth is solved, I will return, having learned more of your Etoile, the better to defend Korr from it."

"You know that's impossible," Vance said. "Moira wouldn't accept you simply returning to the life of an acolyte. And the Principality would arrive as well. This village will change."

"Then I will be the master of that change, mercenary." Lodia regarded him coolly. "I love my family and all of Korr, but they are driven by fear, in the end. My father fears an attack. My mother fears for my life. Moira fears for our tradition. I fear for nothing." She opened the door of the house. "Let us go discover whatever is in store for my people."

*   *   *

The docks at the Capital were always busy, so the Meridian had to wait an hour before being directed towards the farthest pier on the western side of the Grand Canal. Rathnait had her spyglass out as the power-sail pulled in to make charging contact. "Trouble. Got some people coming."

Three cloaked and hooded figures were walking up the pier. Vance kept a hand on his dagger's hilt. "Stay behind me. Attacking a Guild Mercenary in the Capital is a fool's move even in the best circumstances."

The power-sail latched onto the dockside clutch with a click, and a longshoreman laid a ramp to the deck. Vance stepped onto the pier in front of the first hooded figure and spoke with a sharp tone. "State your business with the Mercenary's Guild."

"This is the Meridian out of Erimia?" The shorter man gave a glance at the ship's plate.

"I would know why you have an interest, friend." The two flanking figures were tall and bulky, their cloaks were hiding armor and arms. Vance tensed his grip on his dagger.

"All of Etoile is my interest." The man lifted his hood and held out an insignia, the radiant sun of Etoile, in pure white. Constantine didn't look much like his portrait on the florin note, with his pinched nose and a scarred cheek. He grabbed Vance's shoulder. "No bowing or going to the knees. Not here."

"Princeps." Vance glanced around. Rathnait and Iocathe had overheard and remained standing. "An honor that you would grace us with your presence."

"Save it for a moment. You were part of the mission to Korr." A statement, not a question. "Those girls on the Meridian's deck as well. Cloaks on, hoods up, follow me to the street. We can discuss in detail once we're at your guildhall." He turned and strode away.

The four travelers tailed the Princeps as he marched down the dock and past the main dockside warehouses. Vance noticed that other hooded figures were falling in step behind them as they walked. The harbor street was crowded with power-wagons, but a particularly large one was marked with the emblem of Etoile on its doors, and the guardsmen around it ensured that the surrounding space was empty. They climbed in.

"This is powered by the same mechanism as your ships, correct?" Lodia was looking all around the cabin of the power-wagon as it smoothly rolled down the street.

"It is." Constantine kept a neutral expression. "Not from around here, are you?"

"Merely visiting." Lodia gawked out the window. "There's so many people here. I never could have dreamed of this many."

"This is the Capital. Follow closely." The power-wagon slowed to a stop; the Mercenary's Guild was only a few minutes away from the harbor. Guardsmen wearing the Etoilean sun were already posted at the doors, rendering salutes as the Princeps strode through the entry hall and into a conference room.

The dimly lit room seemed ill-suited to host the most powerful person in the world, but that didn't stop the Princeps from pulling up a chair and sitting at the common table as though he were anyone else. The four travelers sat, facing him, while his guards stood watch. Constantine eased into a practiced slouch, the pose of one used to the exercise of power.

"Apologies for the cloak and dagger methods, but some events have transpired in Etoile while this mission was away, and I dislike unnecessary risks. A group of Navy men tried to steal a power-sail. Under questioning, they admitted they were bound for Korr, but they claimed that they acted on their own initiative." Constantine had his fingers on the table, tapping a staccato. "Tell me what occurred at Korr."

Rathnait straightened. "Princeps, our arrival at Korr was met by the locals. We entered discussions about potential trade negotiations, and promised to return at a future date."

"...And?" Constantine folded his hands. "Speak. I must know what you have discovered."

Iocathe looked away. "We believe we've uncovered evidence of a crime. A Principality Navy Captain sacked and plundered one of the Korr temples seventeen years ago."

"Hrm." The Princeps seemed unsurprised. "I had archivists pore over everything we've ever done in that area of Saibh. In our records, it was a search and recovery operation prompted by the loss of the Windhaven, for any survivors of the House of L'Asair. The captain in charge recovered some cargo but no survivors."

Vance sighed. "So it was one of the Foremost. Princeps, there was a survivor. This is Lodia." He gestured to the acolyte.

The Princeps gave her a glance. "Lodia of L'Asair. Welcome back to Etoile. Can you verify that this search operation was in fact an attack on your community?"

"Yes." Lodia didn't seem at all intimidated. "The remains of the temple are still there, as well as the word of all of my people who bore witness to the events that day."

"No need." Constantine was casually dismissive. "I have the evidence I require. Seventeen years ago, questions were raised as to the sudden newfound wealth of Lord Numidine, and as to why the House of L'Asair in its entirety was on a single power-sail deep in the frontier. Circumstantial evidence it all is, but fortunately I am Princeps, and not a Magistrate. The man was a fool to draw my attention and will learn the consequences of his skullduggery shortly." Iocathe sucked in her breath at the implication. "Vance Randell." He turned his gaze. "The Principality of Etoile requires your service."

*   *   *

It was night in the Etoile Capital City, and two men were standing on the roof of a building. One was holding a warbow and an arrow with a strange, bulbous head. The warbow had a contraption attached onto it with a lens and weighted swing. The other man was holding an arrow, wrapped in rags, and a small hand lantern.

"You can go downstairs if you want, Alistair." Vance raised his warbow. "I can handle this myself."

Alistair glanced around the rooftops, the light of his lantern dancing against the rotation of the rooftop power-shafts. "No doubt, but that's my long-range bowsight you're using. Last thing I want is for this to somehow come back to me."

"It won't." Vance drew; the sight's counterweight swung freely in the air, and Vance lined the lens up with his target. "Two hundred thirty feet to the estate, yes?"

"That's correct." Alistair closed his eyes. With a muffled whistle, Vance fired the arrow deep into the night sky. There was a crash; the fuel arrow had landed and scattered its load. Alistair lit his arrow before handing it to Vance. The hunter loosed the fire arrow. It traced a luminous arc in the night before landing, and a roar echoed as the flame made contact with the fuel. This was a special alchemic formulation meant to ignite and spread quickly, and the two men watched the column of black smoke rise against the flames. Panicked screaming echoed in the distance.

Vance lowered his bow and drew a note from his vest. "Lord-Captain Troyes Numidine, you have been chosen to die for the crime of conspiracy against House L'Asair and the Princeps of Etoile." He crumpled the note and patted Alistair on the shoulder. "Come on, we need to tell the girls that this is dealt with. Lodia wanted to visit her old estate tomorrow morning, but before that I wanted to try out that new restaurant near the Chanticler's for breakfast."

UPWARDS, or THE GREAT FALL

by Garrett S. Lewis

The pain in the man's broken body was almost forgotten, whisked away in this strange, nonsensical sensation. In the dark, dry red stone lined cave he had stumbled—and his shelter had swallowed him whole as he fell into some unseen crevasse. The odd sensation of falling *upwards* enveloped him. It wasn't as if he had never felt the unseen force pulling him towards the ground— certainly, as any citizen of Lliaq ought to, he was very familiar with it. Whatever it was, it felt as if it had released its unseen grip on him. As if he was plummeting towards the sky, covered by the darkened body of rock above him. At any moment he was certain that he would find himself dashed against that rough cave ceiling. Yet its image never moved closer, neither did it move farther. He closed his eyes and waited for his death to come.

Perhaps this was for the best, what good would a man with a broken leg be to his community? In his complacency, he had made a fatal mistake along the seemingly endless, glistening white expanse of the Tchoul Salt Flats while harvesting. Foolish was he, thinking a single step on the brittle crystalline sea without the proper weight-distributing footwear—which kept the wise from breaking its surface and falling into the mud beneath—would be harmless. If his comrades had attempted to save him, they too would endanger their lives as their footwear could not support the weight of two men. No, like proper Lliaqeu men, they left him to his fate. He had long been taught that this was the right way to live—yet it pained him, somewhere deep inside. A deep, stabbing pain—the pain of *betrayal*. He crushed the thought as best he could, steeling himself. He must pull his own weight now. That's why he had crawled for what felt like an eternity across the rough, salted surface, towards the orange-red mesa in the distance.

He opened his eyes, finding himself in a deeper cavern. The brown-red stone beneath him dimly lit by the vestiges of light from above. He had, in fact, fallen down—yet he couldn't shake the thought of the odd feeling from his descent. Stranger still—he found himself without further injury. Placing a hand on the rough stone beside him in order to bring himself back up, he found it somewhat *spongy*. The ground gave slightly as he placed his weight on it, as though the trickling rays of sunlight from above had somehow weakened its structure. He winced as some remaining salt particles found their way into the scraped surface of his palm. He paused for a moment, then placed his other bloodied palm on the ground below him, finally, managing to sit upright with much effort. He took a deep breath and waited a moment more, wondering to himself just how he would attempt standing.

As he moved his good leg, he felt something move with it. Squinting in the dim light—as if trying to channel as much of it that remained into his field of vision—he could just barely make out the dim outline of a worn wooden beam. Luck was with him, it would seem. In the flats he had torn the beam from the wooden sled used to collect salt crystals, using it to carry his weight in place of his broken leg. He kicked the beam towards him with his heel a number of times, eventually getting it close enough to grasp. Inspecting the beam, he found it to be in fair shape; same as himself, it had somehow avoided damage in the fall. As he grasped it in his right hand, a sliver of fractured wood splintered off its worn, salty surface and fell to the ground. As he lifted himself up, he accidentally placed weight on his injured leg—just about crying out in pain. Yet, remembering the tenets of any strong Lliaqeu, he attempted to suppress the cry—sharply exhaling in its place. He managed finally to get up, with a final push—placing weight yet again on his broken right leg. *Just this once...* he thought. He shifted his weight, and let out a guttural scream.

As he began to move, he noticed that the soft qualities of the ground beneath him were no more. Each step landed on solid stone, nothing gave way. Had he imagined it? Certainly, after such a trial that couldn't be out of the question. He didn't have long to ponder this, however, as his investigation into the matter was interrupted by a loud, reverberating cracking and crashing of stone followed by a sharp animalistic cry somewhere nearby.

He moved his head to the right, trying to follow the sound. The dim light surrounding him didn't reach whatever was emanating the sound. More grunts and what sounded like a struggle soon followed—if he had had any bearings on his surroundings he might have tried to escape. He glanced behind him, only to be met with a precipitous wall of red stone. *A few steps towards the wall for some semblance of safety couldn't hurt,* he thought to himself. Instead, he let out a surprised gasp as he tried to move backwards, pain shooting up his broken leg once more. In the distance he could hear scuttling, and a grinding of stone—as if whatever was lurking in the distance had been scared off by the sudden, unplanned sound. Still unable to see, the man remained motionless, listening for any more movement. He thought he could hear heavy, labored breathing, but there was no more audible struggling or movement. Just how long he stood there, he did not know, but eventually the just barely perceivable breathing, too, finally ceased.

The man would need fire to be able to see whatever was there in the distance, and if he was going to find any way out of the caverns whose hungering maw he had stumbled into. Yet, he did not have a torch with him. Slowly, he turned about and looked at all he was able to see in the dim light. A particularly smooth, beige colored stone along the edges of the light caught his eye. Slowly, quietly, he limped towards it. As he got closer, he could see that it was not, in fact, a stone at all—it was a sack. A sack, it seemed, containing *something* that may be of use. As far as the man could remember, he did not have such a bag with him when he fell, nor even before as he crawled through the flats. He attempted to lean over and grab it, but stopped realizing his broken leg was about to touch the ground once again. He stood there for a moment, lightly acting out different methods of leaning over before settling on throwing the bad leg backwards as he leaned onto the beam—this enabled him to just barely grasp at the edges of the sack and pick up. As he hesitantly lifted the concealing flap, he found it full of exactly what he required—torches. The strange fall, the ground seemingly padding his descent and protecting him from injury, and now this strange sack full of exactly what he needed; he felt as if he was playing directly into some unseen force's hands, and he very much did not like this thought.

Regardless of whether it was luck, or an outside force—he needed the aid desperately. The man pulled the torch from the sack, then slung the bag over his shoulder. He pondered just how he might be able to set the torch alight, and held it up before him to inspect its make. In a sudden flash, a pale green light emanated from the top of the torch—a soft, verdant flame which oddly seemed to spiral and curve downwards, rather than move as a flame should were it to operate under the natural laws of the world. Now bathed in this green light, he could see that the torch, too, was abnormal in make. The core of the object was made from a light material, with many holes throughout, seemingly like something had eaten away at all but the very strongest structure of it. He would say it was a light green, but given the color of the light around him, he could not be sure. Rather than a fabric wrapped around the top, there seemed to be another material hollowed out and placed over the core. The bulbous material was of a lighter color, and was full of somewhat hexagonal holes, leaving a light frame around the core of the torch. The flame illogically seemed to emanate from these hexagonal holes rather than the material of the frame itself. Just how exactly this operated—the man feared to guess. In this new light, he could see that the sack over his shoulder was also of a strange make—somehow it appeared to be woven of stone. The fibers themselves did not twist and bend as textiles should, instead staying stiff as they moved—yet there was enough space between them to allow the whole of the object to move as if it truly *were* made of some textile.

The hand that held the torch trembled, the man's instinct was to throw the strange object as far as he could—yet as he raised his arm to do just that, he was able to pull back the reins on his bewildered fear. *I need their aid—if they can do something as strange and terrible as change the very properties of the ground, what would happen if I were to decline their gifts?* He shuddered at the thought. There was no doubt in his mind now, something was pulling the strings, something was leading him somewhere—and he had no choice but to follow. His Lliaqeu pride stung with this acceptance of aid, but this—being forced to accept aid—felt somehow *freeing*. The man closed his eyes and took a deep breath, then began to move in the direction of the sounds he had heard earlier. As he encroached upon the location of the sound, he began to find himself more used to walking with the aid of the beam.

The unusual green glow of the torch illuminated stalagmites along the ground floor as he walked, eventually closing their tendrils of light over the smooth body of a deceased creature pierced through the heart by what appeared to be a fallen stalactite. Pale, oily skin covered a bipedal form with a short, stiff neck, and a short, flat tail. There were no arms to speak of on the creature, and its rounded head possessed no eyes—but in the center of its bulbous form was a strange, twisted horn. Along the bottom of this bulbous head was a wide mouth containing an array of serrated teeth—if he had to guess, this must have been a predator. He would have attributed this to another case of strange, uncanny luck—were it not for the strange scratches and injuries along the pale skin of the creature. It looked almost as if something had scraped a collection of nails across its surface, creating rough, bloody trails marked by many small holes along their widths. At the end of these bloody trails were holes where flesh had been torn out—as though something had fed on the beast. Inspecting the stalactite that pierced the creature's body, he thought he noticed similar markings along its edges.

Seeing no immediate danger, now he felt was the time to take advantage of his luck. Eventually, he would need food, and he had no idea just how large this cavern may be—for all he knew, there may not even be another exit. He tried not to think of this, however. He produced a small knife which had been tucked under his belt, placed the beam on the other side of the corpse, leaned over as best he could—and began to separate a leg from the beast's body. The skin of the creature was surprisingly resilient, whatever had trailed injuries across its body had to have been fairly sharp, like the head of a pick—he tried not to think further about it, lest fear well up within him once again. Finally, after some time—and a painful slip once again onto his injured leg—he freed the leg from the beast's torso. Taking note of its significant weight as opposed to the sack over his shoulder, he elected to fasten it to himself by strapping his belt over it. He did not trust the spiraling verdant flames he carried, while they certainly provided light, he was unsure whether or not food touched by its strange, curved arms could be safe for human consumption. In fact, he didn't even know if they even *were* flames. He thought for a moment about setting the rest of the corpse alight to see, but ultimately thought better of it—not knowing the size of these caverns, filling them with smoke could easily kill him. Perhaps he may have to settle for raw meat.

He just about fell over as he repositioned the beam in front of him, balancing on a single leg. He thought back, how had injuries such as his been treated in the past? Alchemists, typically, would offer some strange concoction to "promote faster healing"—not that it really helped. One would still find themselves bedridden or nigh useless for quite some time. He had heard before of—and even seen—the more extreme measures taken by desperate parties, and willing alchemists. It was frowned upon by his people, seen as admitting weakness in one's own body by supplementing it with another—mutation.

He once knew a woman named Cipa, back during his military training as a young man of seventeen. Cipa, like many other young Lliaqeu, was quite competitive—and held lofty goals, aiming to one day become a great general. This competitive personality led her to take risks, cut corners, and often end up with injuries. As she was young these often healed quickly, or were luckily of little to no consequence. Her luck, however, eventually ran out. While attempting to scale a cliff for a mock ambush exercise rather than take any one of the clearly defined paths, she found herself gripping a weak stone—and on the ground shortly thereafter. Something in her back had snapped, dislocated, or warped from the fall. She had to cease her training, but she was confident that she would be back in a mere few months—those months turned to years.

Her family grew tired of aiding her weakness, her inability to pull her own weight—they had decided to throw her to the streets if she could not heal. She did not want to become one of the many broken beggars along the city's streets—they were *weak* and she was *strong!* Surely, she was strong? There must have been a way! Cipa had once been an alchemist's apprentice—and had experimented in private with mutation on small animals. She thought—perhaps—infusing herself with the spine of another creature could heal her? No one would notice, and she could still say it was her own strength that overcame the injury. She made the unfortunate choice of a fish as her subject—repurposing the spine from a finished meal. Upon imbibing the concoction, her once orange-brown skin took on a slight bluish tint, and her spine twisted painfully sideways. Her back was healed—of this there was no doubt—but she was permanently marked, and while she could now lean side to side at inhuman angles—she could no longer bend forwards. Her family cast her out for giving in to her own weakness, and she resumed her military training—becoming a feared warrior who would die a heroic death.

The man chuckled to himself, it was a childish thought— alchemy requires skill, and specialized tools with which to brew. Neither of which was in his possession. No, he'd have to make it through this himself. Though, he wasn't exactly alone, he felt. In just what direction should he head? The strange, downwards-spiraling flame in his hand did not appear to flicker with any movement of the air around him, which to his own limited senses felt as still as the stone encapsulating it. He felt he could spend forever trying to come up with a reason to head any which direction—he decided to cut this short by simply beginning to walk forward.

*   *   *

The flame was beginning to fade, oddly not shrinking in size— only decreasing in opacity. Its reach lessened with this, and the man decided to finally replace it. Not knowing the effects of the torch, he elected to leave it on the ground rather than place the weakened flame in the sack. He tossed it somewhere ahead of him, and heard the unexpected sound of what seemed to him to be the torch hitting *water*. As quickly as he could in his injured state, he produced another torch from the sack, and began to move in the direction in which he had thrown the first. He hadn't thought of it until now— no, in truth it had been on his mind the entire time, he had simply been ignoring it—he was incredibly thirsty. Just how long had he wandered through the salt flats? How long had he been trapped in this vault of stone? As he approached the thrown torch, there appeared to be a small stream, and he was thankful to find that it was—at least in appearance—water.

His immediate impulse was to throw himself to the ground and begin drinking—but he stopped himself after beginning to outstretch his arms and feeling the beam in his right hand. In his excitement—he had almost forgotten his broken leg. Instead, he would have to drink from the stream on his back. Before doing this, he dropped the sack of torches onto the ground. Leaning back as best he could without falling over, he bent his good knee in order to get closer to the ground before releasing his grip on the beam and falling onto his back. This way, he suffered no further injuries. He miscalculated his height, and his face ended up directly in the cool water—though this was something he did not mind. Like a dehydrated dog, he thirstily lapped up all that he could.

After his thirst was sated, he stayed still, the cool water gently running against his face. Hobbling as he had been was incredibly exhausting, if something such as a stream could exist in these caverns, they may very well be deeper than he can traverse in his condition. Exhaustion may be his greatest enemy, not light, water, nor food. He did not know how long he stayed there, but eventually he found the strength within himself to grab the beam once more and prop himself back to his feet, or foot. As he began to hobble forward once more, towards the bag of torches, he heard a strange cracking sound somewhere above him. He looked up, noticing the light faintly illuminating a stalactite—a faintness which slowly crawled up the stone's length—as if it was growing rapidly from the cave ceiling above. It was falling. In this same brief moment, the man instinctively threw himself forward—dropping his torch in the process. Incredible pain shot through his leg as it collided with the hard stone ground. He looked behind him, and could see what appeared almost to be a stone moving towards him—but the coloration was slightly different than the stone around it, and the thing moved by dragging itself along the cave floor with short, pointed appendages lined with sharp claws on their undersides. He could hear a terrible grinding and cracking of stone as the creature's claws dug into it—slowly but surely making its way towards the bewildered man.

Surely, he thought, *this must have been what killed that other creature before*—and he did not wish to let the same happen to him. Painfully, he used both feet to stand again, in the interest of speed—though the pain made him take pause for a brief moment. His grip on the beam tightened, and he fearfully began to hobble as quickly as he could in the opposite direction of the strange creature. It may appear slow now, but for all he knew, it could have means with which to leap great distances, or simply be moving slowly to conserve energy when it could truly move faster than he could hobble. Into the darkness he descended, until soon the torch's dim light left his vision, and some time after that the grinding and cracking sounds faded away, too. He continued onward for another few moments, to ensure that he had lost the creature's pursuit.

He stopped for a moment to rest, carefully sitting down on the cold cave floor. It didn't take long, as the adrenaline wore off, for him to realize he was without light. A tightness gripped his chest as the reality settled into his addled mind. His breathing became more erratic even than as he fled, his head throbbed, and his ears rang in the vast quiet of the subterranean hell he found himself in — fear was taking hold. He tried to calm down, but it wasn't long until he could hear faint whispers — was he imagining it, in his fear? These whisperings were too quiet for him to make out any clear words, but as he sat still and silent, fear began to tighten its grip on his mind — and the volume of these whispers began to increase. Their language was none that he had known, it was harsh, and seemed as if it required a biology entirely unlike his own to produce. Despite this, he felt just as though he could understand their words.

"Shigal, n'oum shigal."

"Adapt, you must adapt."

"Nahggyz y'or nolghom, cu'ughm iyl t'kogg!"

"Become more than you are!"

He clasped his hands over his ears, like closing great doors, trying his best to drown out the words. The voices were almost alien, something about their qualities caused his very soul to vibrate within him. He looked up, and instead of being met with the endless black void he expected — he could actually make out the shape and form of the cavern around him. Yet it seemed incorrect, the way he had come was blocked by a wall of stone — and the more he looked the more it seemed as if the stone around him was warping and changing somehow. Almost like it was undulating water. Small holes begin to show uniformly across the stone, in strange geometric patterns that could not be created naturally. Slowly but surely these holes begin to expand, then contract again, repeating this cycle—as though the cavern around him was breathing through these orifices.

The man shut his eyes, warding off the strange sight. Not wanting to bear it any longer. Yet, again, instead of the darkness he expected—he appeared to see through the eyes of another. An older man, someone he did not know. His dark skin similar to his own, the older man's calloused hands were delicately operating an alchemy kit. Lighting the fire beneath the lyez clay retort—a special spouted container made of a special, distilled clay—meant to distill the properties of what lay inside its belly. Yet he did not possess this knowledge—he had never learned of this, the older man had. Despite this, he felt as if he had known it all along, and he understood the process as the older man's hands moved through the entire operation. Mixing the resulting distilled liquid with a dry wood dust, and placing it back into the retort to produce yet another, more pure, liquid—which he then brought to his lips. The older man's hands enlarged in size, and possessed a newfound inhuman strength which he tested by bending an old dagger into a circular shape.

"Ne'alizrog."

"*Power,*" the older man whispered to himself.

He opened his eyes, and could see Cipa—her body bent to the side at an impossible angle—smiling. He shut his eyes and shook his head, attempting to dispel the vision, opening them to find the undulating cavern was falling apart. Great cracks formed along the ceiling, walls, and floor—separating the whole into great pieces that began to drift from one another. In the spaces between was a polychromatic field of stars. Yellows, blues, greens, purples—every color imaginable, and even those unseen—speckled this void as they mixed and melted into one another. A crack began to form from the floor opposite him, snaking its way closer and closer, its thin head trailed by an ever-widening canyon. The man tried to stand and run—but fell back to the ground screaming as incredible pain shot up his leg. The crack trailed beneath him, and he tried to crawl as best he could from the widening hole—but he could not outrun it, and he fell into the varicolored sea of stars beneath.

Colored whispers flew past his ears, he could not understand this language as anything but formless audible colors. Blood reds around him faded from vision and became sound, changing to orange, yellow, and back to red—creating a strange smacking sound as they collided with the sounds of other colors and mixed into something new. He tried to scream but all that escaped his lips was purple. He could feel that strange, terribly unnerving sensation once again—that sensation of falling upwards. He tried to force his eyes shut but could only manage to blink—leaving him unable to look away as he fell towards some distant bubbling form of black.

As he came closer to this form, he could see that its surface rippled in many small expanding rings—as if assailed by cosmic raindrops. Its prodigious size became apparent as it soon dwarfed him, its massive dark bulk blotting out the polychromatic space behind it. Terrified, the man wondered if he was facing a deity he had disregarded as mere myth long ago. Its surface, save for the ripples, was uniform in color—and as such, he was unable to make out its true shape. From the ripples he could only guess that it was made of a collection of ridged round shapes, broken by jutting sharp, angular forms placed periodically along their surface. He couldn't discern his distance from the form, and he feared he'd be dashed against it—dying without a chance to move away. This thought frightened him deeply.

He did not know how long he had been falling, and soon enough, the great black form blotted out all else from his vision. *This must be the end!* The panicked thought repeated over and over within his head. After some time, he felt something beyond his experience as a creature of flesh and blood—something he felt no living being ought to be subject to—the feeling that he himself had been transposed into a being of *pure audio.* He felt himself vibrating, floating through nothingness. He could see nor hear anything beyond himself—not even time was perceptible. He had no idea whether or not he had been in this state for minutes or years, but he mercifully found himself solid once more. He fell onto a blackened stone floor on all fours, throwing up an unsavory lack of anything visual accompanied by a terrible grating sound that told him he was retching the sound of yellow onto the ground beneath him.

He wiped his mouth with the back of his left hand, despite there being nothing *to* wipe, and shuddered. He heard the sound of black fading to a dark grey and back. Something about its cadence seemed oddly intelligent to him, and he raised his head to look for its source. He was in an open, circular clearing in what appeared to be a great city. Tall, sharp twisted spires of what can only be described as metallic obsidian-like stone carved by giant hands—leaving uneven, jagged surfaces along the walls of the structures—rose around him to dizzying heights. These structures took on a slow gradient, with the grand majority being a deep black like that of the form he had fallen towards, and which he now assumed he was within. Towards their precipices, they faded in opacity, like clouded glass, with deep bands of solid black throughout. This glass would appear as either a pale grey, blue, or red—changing from structure to structure.

Lower towards the ground were many smaller black structures, appearing to be made of spheres made of many loops—leaving ridges periodically along their surfaces. In neither of these were there any windows, doors, or openings—how exactly the beings occupying the area were able to come and go he hadn't the slightest idea. These structures were sprinkled around a vast sea of terraces connected to each other not by roads—but by a tangled web of thin silver wires which were faintly visible as they floated between structures and attached short strands to their lower walls. He could see strange statues of forms he had never once imagined, and a number of what he could only assume were silvery plants were placed in what appeared to him random shapeless clumps of various sizes throughout the city. Their bulbous ends gently swayed back and forth in an unseen breeze.

Somewhere in the distance a great structure of prodigious magnitude loomed over the rest of the city. It appeared to be of a similar obsidian material as the rest, but it bore bright bands of fantastical colors, curving along its edges, and expelling any hints of darkness in its make. Thick bands of pink were bordered by blues which gave rise to yellows, darker reds, and oranges also showed throughout. There were no sharp edges to be seen along its surface, which appeared to have been painstakingly smoothed. Ridges rose and broke the surface throughout—but they, too, were smoothed. Upon the very top of the structure appeared to sit a great black orb on a thinned spire of the colorful obsidian material. Whatever light hung over the city caused the colorful surface of this great structure to scintillate—nearly blinding the man. Despite this, he could not stop himself from staring at its smoothed surface, which acted as a reprise for the eyes from the harsh jagged edges of the spires that would dominate the skyline were it not for this grandiose building. *Do I still reside in reality? Have I fallen between the cracks and arrived in a twisted realm not meant for creatures of normalcy?* He wondered as he stared across the alien city's skyline in bewildered awe.

As he stared, he heard the strange shades of black once again. He looked for their source—and found a strange being standing nearby, near the edge of the clearing. He tried to stand but found himself without the aid of the beam—and thus unable to get up. As he fell onto his side, he saw another being, and that strange audible blackness emanated from somewhere within it. Their bodies were both composed of what appeared to be a mix of many different parts atop a similar core. Each was made of a thick, luminous white cord which started from the ground and after a short while of shooting straight upwards—coiled into a loose spiral consisting of three loops each, before straightening out towards the sky once more. Within these coils floated a series of even brighter grey spheres of varied diameters, which each had the appearance of containing a greater depth within than their sizes would logically allow. At the top of the straightened cord rested a human-like head without the features any man should possess. Instead, wildly placed along their surfaces, were numerous small black gashes which opened and closed independent of one another periodically.

He could tell, at least, that was how they *should* appear—now seeing their altered forms beside the statues of their original shapes. Instead, these two each appeared differently—the first had seemingly replaced what the man could only describe as a leg with that of another being—some dark brown mottled shard of stone or metal was in place of a white cord. Several of their inner spheres were instead green, transparent glass pyramids, and another was a large orange shape he could not recognize. The second being possessed what appeared to the man as a goat's leg, along the side of its uppermost coil. In fact—it seemed as though the being had adorned the majority of this upper coil's length with an entire array of goat's legs. Their furs were all of different colors and patterns, and one in particular was oddly luminous. The being's face held a massive black void that appeared as if a great cylinder had been pressed and twisted into its skull—yet the void was of seemingly infinite blackness, and thus he assumed these beings were without skeletal structures. He shuddered, knowing not whether he did so in fear—or if he was still vibrating.

The first being, with the stone leg, made another series of black sounds—creating a sequence of differing shades. The man's shuddering stopped as he realized *these beings must speak in color...* and with this realization he could just barely understand what they were trying to communicate to him. In this great city—something grander than even the great city of Lliaq from which he hailed, something grander, he thought, than mankind could ever dream of creating—here were its creators, and they stood on their own, even as amalgams. They stood strong, and he thought he could just barely understand a tone of *pride* as they spoke in brighter shades, nigh white. They were trying to tell him that there was no shame in mutation. He had been weakened, wounded, left to *die* by his brethren—and he believed that he should accept this fate. It was tradition, after all. He closed his eyes and bowed his head to thank the two beings, and when he rose and opened his eyes—he found himself lying in a subterranean stream lit by a green flame.

He quickly rose, as best he could. He searched for the beam with his right hand along the cave floor and after a few silent moments of groping, his fingers brushed upon something odd. His fingers had felt what seemed to be a leather strap. If his memory still functioned properly, he did not possess such a thing—and yet here it was. He grabbed the strap, and pulled it closer towards him. There was an odd weight to it, and as it came closer, and he looked—he immediately recognized it as an alchemist's kit. He quickly opened it to find the ever essential lyez retort—a round, pear-shaped lidded pot with a spout pointed downwards sprouting from the side made from a special distilled clay— kindling, a mortar and pestle, flasks, a stirring rod—everything he needed was there. *Had I been carrying this all along?* He wondered. He could hear a strange sound from somewhere nearby — something that could only be described by him as the sound of black fading to grey.

As vague memories came to him, he almost immediately claimed an idea. He pulled away from the stream, onto drier stone. He found the beast's leg still attached to his belt, and quickly detached it. *Alchemy is the answer!* His hands moved almost on their own as he recalled the process for distilling a body part's essence, as if he had somehow had years of training and practice — yet he had never so much as visited an alchemist. He lit a fire beneath the lyez retort, leaving it to gain strength as he cut a sizable horizontal slice from the leg, breaking the bone with his hands when his serrated knife could not cut through. He took the lid off the retort, and dropped the slice inside. He quickly recalled that he needed a base — and turned to collect water from the stream within a clay flask, quickly lifting the retort's lid and pouring it inside. The water hissed and wisps of steam nearly burned his hand as it came into contact with the heated lyez clay.

With the flask placed under the retort's spout, he watched patiently as the first wave of distilled liquid dripped inside. After around an hour, a quarter of the flask was filled with a deep purple liquid, which he then poured back into the retort with the remaining chunks of flesh and bone within, and added more kindling to the fire. Over the next several hours the man repeated this process until the remains of the leg dissipated completely, and distilled the resulting liquid once more for good measure. Finally, the flask was filled with a deep purple liquid in which shimmering silver flecks floated throughout. The man looked at the purpled, swollen skin around the break on his shin. He would suffer it no longer, and smiled as he gleefully threw back his head and emptied the flask into himself. The taste was of strong iron, and some odd, sweet flavor he could not place.

What followed was pain beyond what he had felt within his short lifespan, something that could not keep him from howling like an animal and rolling along the cold stone floor. He pulled in his leg to his stomach and cradled it as he did so, able to feel the hairs on his legs falling off, the bones lengthening, twisting, and bending. Terrible, wet, grating sounds seemed to echo in his ears as his body changed. This wasn't what he wanted! He wanted to heal the leg of a man, and keep it as such. Yet he knew that he'd likely be left scarred and warped. Still, he couldn't help but hold on to some deep-seated pride in his humanity—which he now believed to be forever tainted. He screamed yet again as he felt his foot, too, rapidly changing.

*   *   *

Finally, mercifully, after some time—the changes stopped. Shivering, the man couldn't tell if he was covered in sweat, or water from the stream. He was afraid to look down at himself, to see what he had become. Yet he couldn't help but notice—the pain was gone. Not just the pain of the rapid mutation—but the pain brought by his broken leg. As he lay on the ground, he lifted and put down the leg, placing weight on it, testing. No pain. In fact—it felt *stronger* than ever. Cautiously, he attempted to stand up. To his surprise, there was no more pain there, either. He walked in a small circle for a few moments, making sure it wasn't just a brief lapse in pain. Nothing. Finally, he rose the leg and inspected it. In the dimming green light, he could see that his orange-brown skin had paled significantly in the leg—akin to the skin of the creature the leg had come from. His leg was now bent backwards, again, much like that of the creature he had procured the leg from—and his knee now operated in the opposite direction. His foot, it seemed, had also been warped—splitting halfway into two diagonal segments. Despite such drastic changes, he still stood at his normal height, and the newly formed leg did not give him a lopsided gait. However, hints of his original, human, form were still visible. His toes, for example, had only shrunk in length—they did not completely fade away to mimic the creature's exact form. The leg's mutated skin was not the same pale white as that of the creature, and it still was tinted with its original coloration—even fading into that familiar orange-brown tint as it met with his torso.

He placed the leg back on the ground, and let out a hearty laugh. *This is absolutely amazing!* He thought to himself. *What power! How had I gone so long being callously ignorant of alchemy?* He ran around in circles, getting used to his newfound leg, until he grew tired. It was then, in his joy, when his distress had been temporarily lifted—that he finally recalled his hunger. In the distance, he could hear a familiar scraping and grating along the stone ground. He smiled, this time, he would be the one to hunt. He elected to leave the alchemy kit sprawled out on the ground. This, he decided, would serve as his camp for now. In one hand he grabbed his knife, in the other, he wielded a newly lit torch—it's pulsating green flames no longer bothering him. They were almost reassuring, now, and he swore he could pick up the nigh imperceptible hint of a strange sound emanating from within their spirals.

As he approached the sound, the green light once again showed the mottled gray stone-colored skin of that creature dragging itself along the ground. It had already noticed the man—and was already pulling itself towards him. He hesitated and took a half-step back, as if already deciding to retreat. Yet he remained still afterwards, watching the creature dragging itself towards him at a pitiful speed. It was not as he had believed in his panic before, the creature seemed incapable of increased speed. This hunt would be easy.

Slowly, cautiously, he approached the creature, moving to its left side as he got closer. It attempted to face him once more, but was slow in doing so, enabling him to simply walk behind it.

As he stared down at the creature's feeble attempts at reaching him, he almost pitied it. It was only the size of a small pot, its four pointed appendages slowly but surely turning it around and dragging it along. He only stared for a brief moment before quickly running his knife through the center of its body. It gave a low screeching sound as its appendages lifted and curled upwards in an attempt to pry the foreign object from its most vital organs—but it was only a brief period of time before all four appendages fell lifelessly to the ground. He grabbed the knife and freed it from the back of the creature, not bothering to wipe the blood off its surface. He attempted to pick up the body from the stone floor—but found it surprisingly difficult. After pulling for a few more moments with increasing strength—he stopped. Pulling himself to the ground, he tilted his head to see what exactly kept the body stuck to the stone.

Claws. Rows and rows of pale tooth-like claws. The entire underside of this creature appeared to house numerous claws which pierced the stone beneath. How exactly, they were able to possess this power, he did not know. A smile formed across his lips as an idea came to him. *Why stop with just one leg?* He may not understand how exactly its claws were able to operate, but he would certainly be able to take advantage. Delicately, he used his knife to pry the creature's claws out of the stone, gently pulling their curved shapes out and upwards with light repeated taps— eventually allowing him to take hold of the appendage and pull it free. With enough time, he was eventually able to pull all four free and flip the body over to inspect the whole underside.

The underside of the creature, too, was of a mottled grey that mimicked the stone around it. Each appendage was lined with five rows of pale white claws, with the central row of each housing larger claws than the rest. In the very center of the creature's mass, lay a pale white beak that ended in a sharp point. This beak appeared to open into four separate pieces, which the man theorized would allow it to more easily rend flesh from its prey. Satisfied, he held it by the center, and walked back to camp. He didn't take time to rest, immediately beginning the task of prying free as many claws as he could from the creature's appendages. He found that each seemed to attach to a small muscle, which he need only sever to free the claw. However many hours this task took, he did not know. A torch dimmed as he pushed through the monotony, bloody fingers mindlessly made the motions as time lost meaning.

After he had finished wresting each and every claw from its seat within the creature's body, he collected them into the alchemy kit's mortar, and began grinding them down to dust with the aid of the pestle. Before he was through, he needed the use of yet another torch as the previous began to fade. As he finished, he placed the resulting powder into the retort—alongside a few of the severed muscles which gave them part of their strength. Water, too, for a base was always needed. The fire beneath was lit, and the distillation began. He repeated this process about three times before finding himself satisfied, and he threw back the resulting liquid without hesitation. It had the taste of dry grain, cooked meat, and again—that odd, sweet flavor from the leg's brew.

A numbness encroached upon his arms and legs, he could still maneuver the appendages—but they felt dull and lifeless. A tingling could be felt along their lengths, which was shortly followed by a sharp, shooting pain. He watched as he grimaced, turning the inside of his arm towards himself. Rows of bone-colored claws were sprouting from beneath his skin—piercing it, yet not producing blood. This created a simultaneously mesmerizing and horrifying visual of great lumps expanding in size, before being cut as if with knives, and the claws peering out from underneath before rising to their full heights. This continued for some time, moving in horizontal rows down the length of each appendage, before finally stopping. He wiped the sweat from his brow with the backside of his hand before rising and approaching a nearby wall of stone. He quietly placed the inside of his arm against it—and willed it to stick. The new muscles within listened to their master, and the claws sunk into the stone with a satisfying cracking sound. The man smiled.

He released himself from the wall and sat back at camp, grabbing a torch and testing it against the creature's body. Oddly— it seemed to not light on fire—yet it seemed to heat up as though it had been. Perhaps there was no danger in it after all? He could not wait any longer—his energies had been spent. He had to eat. He held the torch still as the smell of cooked meat slowly began to emanate from the corpse. He soon lost patience and began to devour as much as he could. It had the strangest taste of a grilled fish, and stone. It was the best thing he'd eaten in years.

*   *   *

He had no dreams as he finally slept afterwards, or only dreamed of a great form of black—he could not tell. Regardless, he felt refreshed, renewed—and reborn. He thought of how he should attempt to return home, now that he was healed. To his own surprise, he laughed at the thought, and said out loud.

"They'd call me weak! Yet I crawled my own way to survival— the cowards would never see me as an equal." He chuckled to himself once more before continuing. "No, indeed, there is no reason to return." He smiled softly as the realization dawned on him. Lit by that dancing verdant flame, he grabbed his knife and set out into the depths before him with renewed purpose.

ABOUT THE AUTHORS

As a shy, awkward kid, **M.K. Beutymhill** adored Victorian charm, fairy tales, and RPG gaming—none of which she ever outgrew. Over time, contact sports and work abroad balanced her out into a proper ladythug, and she now writes genre-blending fantasy about adventure, discovery, and other badassery.

#CharmCity tough and #SacramentoProud, she currently resides in California with the love of her life. She's passionate about historical costuming, sports, and forestry services.

Find M.K. as *mkbeutymhill* on World Anvil.

Nicklas Erik Larsson works as a game developer by day and might be a costumed crime-fighter by night. Dead Meat is his first published work, but you can find the rest of his stuff on his World Anvil page, where he spends too much time inventing particularly weird settings. Such worlds include light-hearted dystopias, fractured timestreams and the Necro-Industrial Complex featured in Dead Meat. One of these days, he will definitely write something much more cheerful. Maybe.

Find Nicklas as *Qurilion* on World Anvil.

Christopher Dravus has been a gamer, storyteller, and dungeon master for over twenty-five years, with experience in the Sci-fi, Fantasy, Steampunk and Horror genres. In 2018 he and two friends created Ironrise Games, a company focused on putting out the kind of gaming products that offered the playstyle and narrative they were always seeking out from other products. Their first game, the self-titled Ironrise, board game was released in 2019 with a second game slated for late 2020. Christopher is the head of Creative Development for the company and has a passion for developing stories, characters, and worlds with rich backgrounds ripe for exploration. He lives in Chicago with his wonderful dog Winston and is surrounded by supportive, creative friends who help make his work possible.

Find Christopher as *thechosenone* on World Anvil.

Tepherial is a fantasy and cosmic horror enthusiast just trying to get the stories out of his head.

Find Tepherial as *Blossora* on World Anvil.

Alan G. Provance grew up in southern New Hampshire, and has been reading fantasy and science fiction books from a young age. Also an avid tabletop gamer, he's been writing for campaigns and characters since his teen years, and developed a passion for reading and writing that lasted throughout his life. After a few years in the military, Alan finished school to become a history teacher. He still lives in southern New Hampshire with his family.

Find Al as *Somrael* on World Anvil.

Larnce Hicks is an aspirant fantasy writer who has been constructing epic stories for over eight years. As a well-practiced historical martial artist and medieval warfare enthusiast, Hicks is able to bring enough realism to fantasy warfare to truly immerse his audience in the action.

Find Larnce as *Theelix* on World Anvil.

J.L. Allred was born in Jonesboro, Arkansas in 1990. He met his wife Erin while living in Ormond Beach, Florida where he attended Daytona State College earning a Bachelor's Degree in Information Technology. He has been reading and writing science fiction and fantasy since he was in the 3rd grade.

Find J.L. as *Naur432* on World Anvil.

C.R. Christiansen is a young author based in Denmark, who makes her debut with the work *Sanctum of Snow and Blood* in the World Anvil Anthology. Christiansen has been storytelling for as long as she can remember, even before she learned how to write. She mainly writes speculative fiction and enjoys writing magical settings more than anything. However, her education in biotechnology and as well as her considerable interest in history and anthropology has certainly shaped many of the concepts found in her works.

Find C.R. as *ninne124* on World Anvil.

Travakh is a software engineer based out of California, pretending to be a writer. His hobbies include driving slow cars fast, eating fast food slow, and looking for the best of unintentional comedy.

Find *Travakh* on World Anvil.

Garrett S. Lewis has been writing horror since the age of 14 when they fell and hit their head on the pavement one chilly September morning. This only added to their ever-growing collection of artistic pursuits, which currently includes traditional illustration, digital illustration, pixel art, video editing, graphic design, tabletop game design, and coding. Each is often marinated in the odd and surreal. In their free time not spent on making things, they enjoy reading, playing games, talking with friends, engaging in creative communities, and occasionally releasing unspeakable horrors from their mountain abode to terrorize the local villagers.

Find Garrett as *Timepool* on World Anvil.

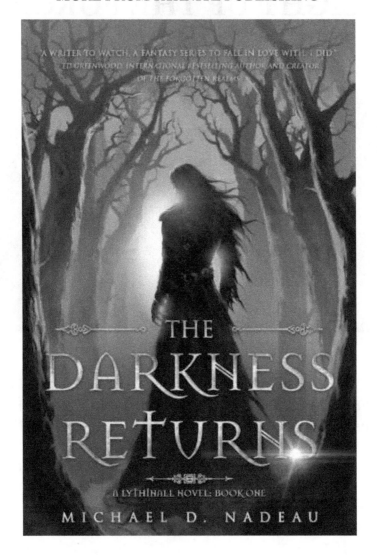

When an ancient evil is loosed upon the land of Lythinall, a young warrior is swept up in a perilous journey with the legendary bard Karsis and the Princess of Everknight to realms he never knew existed. They will be tested as hidden forces watch with bated breath, knowing this could be the end.

Glade Balladeer is a simple tavern bard who uses her skills in music and magic to entertain, and to work as a Warden, guarding the borders from the Wild beyond. When a powerful businessman discovers that she is also hiding that she is partly Wild herself, he blackmails her into taking a delicate case along with two other not-quite-legal Wardens. They discover more than just a missing girl and have to learn to work together to uncover a plot that might restart a centuries-old war with the Wild.

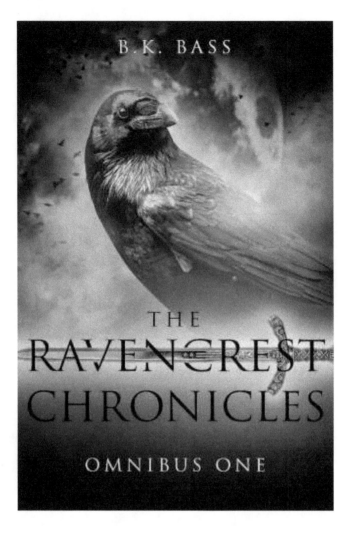

In the city of Seahaven, dark threats loom around every corner. In such a desperate place, it falls upon the shoulders of thieves, pirates, scoundrels, and even orphans to fight to protect the people from things lurking in the shadows.

The Ravencrest Chronicles Omnibus One includes the first four books of the series: *Seahaven, The Hunter's Apprentice, The Giant and the Fishes,* and *Tales From the Lusty Mermaid.*